THE ROAD
TO EHVENOR

JOEL ROSENBERG
THE ROAD
TO
EHVENOR

A Guardians of the Flame Novel

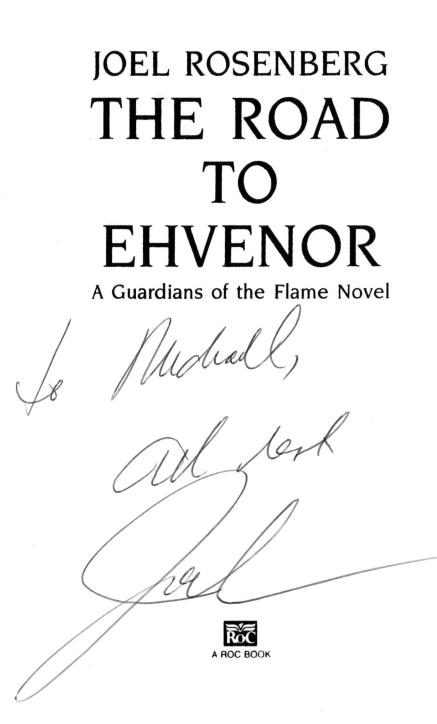

RoC
A ROC BOOK

ROC
Published by the Penguin Group
Penguin Books USA Inc., 375 Hudson Street,
New York, New York 10014, U.S.A.
Penguin Books Ltd, 27 Wrights Lane,
London W8 5TZ, England
Penguin Books Australia Ltd, Ringwood,
Victoria, Australia
Penguin Books Canada Ltd, 10 Alcorn Ave., Suite 300,
Toronto, Canada L3R 1B4
Penguin Books (N.Z.) Ltd, 182–190 Wairau Road,
Auckland 10, New Zealand

Penguin Books Ltd, Registered Offices:
Harmondsworth, Middlesex, England

First published by Roc, an imprint of New American Library,
a division of Penguin Books USA Inc.

First Printing, December, 1991
10 9 8 7 6 5 4 3 2 1

Roc is a trademark of New American Library,
a division of Penguin Books USA Inc.

PRINTED IN THE UNITED STATES OF AMERICA

This one is for
Mary Kittredge

Acknowledgments

I'm grateful for the help and advice I've gotten with this one from the others in the workshop: Bruce Bethke, Peg Kerr Ihinger, and Pat Wrede; David Dyer-Bennet; Harry F. Leonard; my copyeditor, Carol Kennedy; my agent, Eleanor Wood; my editor, John Silbersack; my wife, Felicia Herman; Diane Duane, for the hiccup cure; and, particularly, for some ongoing research assistance on the subject of fatherhood, my daughter, Judith Eleanor Rosenberg.

Prologue:

The Dream Is the Same

THE NIGHTMARE IS *always the same:*

We're trying to make our escape from Hell, a whole crowd of us running through the slimy corridors. Everybody I've ever loved is there, along with strange faces, some of which I know should be familiar.

Behind us, there's a screaming pack of demons, some in cartoony shapes, some that look like misshapen wolves, all of whom have me scared so bad I can hardly breathe the scalding, stinking air. The walls keep trying to close in on me, but I push the hot, slime-covered surface away.

The exit is up ahead, a gash in the wall, and the crowd starts to push through. I can't tell who's gone through, but I can only hope that my kids are among them. Please.

Some have made their escape, but there's no way for the rest of us: the demons are approaching too quickly, and they're going to catch us.

And then I see him: Karl Cullinane, Jason's father, stand-

1

ing tall, face beaming, his hands, chest, and beard streaked with blood and gore.

"We're going to have to hold the corridors," Karl says. "Who's with me?"

He smiles, as though he's been waiting his whole life for this, the fucking idiot. Figures push out of the crowd, all of them bloodied, some of them bent.

I guess I notice Kościuszko and Copernicus first, although both of them are shorter than I thought they'd be.

A buddha-faced Chinese steps forward, his face shiny with sweat that he doesn't seem to notice. "A boddhisattva," he says, "is one who pledges not to attain heaven until the rest of humanity does."

Another man stands tall, lean as a sword, not seeming to notice that the right side of his chest is cut open, slashed to the grayish liver. "Of course," he says, taking his place next to a slim, hawk-faced woman in what looks like a burial robe. Her robe is burning so hard I can hear her flesh crackle, and she winces in pain, but it doesn't stop her.

"Moi aussi," she says.

Two nondescript men push forward together. "Once more, Master Ridley," the first says, his accent clipped and British.

The other shakes his head and smiles wearily. "I'd thought—but no: once more, then."

A heavy-bearded, heavy-set man, still wearing his hangman's noose, his eyes wide in madness, pushes forward, shoulder to shoulder with Georgie Patton himself.

Humanity streams by us, and it's all I can do not to be swept along with it.

The corridor has always seemed tight, maybe twenty feet across, but the line of them—thousands of them, arms linked tightly—can't quite stretch across it.

They need one more to close the ranks, or it's all for nothing, and the demons are fast approaching.

One more. They always need one more.

Karl looks at me—they all look at me: Brown, Ridley, Joan, Ahira, Horatius, all of them—his bloody face puzzled. "Walter? What are you waiting for?"

Then I wake up.

2

PART ONE

HOMEWORK

CHAPTER ONE

In Which I Spend a Morning at Castle Cullinane

If you don't think that sex is violent, next time try thrashing around a bit.

—WILL SHETTERLY

MY NAME IS WALTER Slovotsky.

As near as I can figure, I should be turning forty-three in the next tenday or so, and maybe it's time I grew up. I've spent the past couple of decades as, variously, a hero, a trader, a farming consultant, a thief, and a Jeffersonian political fanatic. Oh. And a killer. Both retail and wholesale. I'm sort of a jack of all trades.

In addition, I've managed to father two daughters (that I know of; I, er, got about a bit), generate a few hundred interesting aphorisms, and sleep with an even more interesting variety of women than I did in college (see above), including my second-best-friend's wife-to-be (we weren't all that friendly at the time. When he found out about it he almost killed me, but we all ended up as friends) and, some years later, his adopted daughter (he never found out about it; I'm not sure how that turned out, not yet).

But here I am, getting on in years, about to make some

major changes in my life, and I thought I'd do it this way. May as well start with food.

Food's an important part of my life.

The early morning crowd, plus me, gathered for breakfast. Settling into a new castle makes for long hours and helty appetites. I've always had the latter, anyway, hangover or no. "Please past the bacon," I said. I don't miss the taste of nitrites; they do good things with smoking pig parts in Bieme. Just the thought of beans and hocks, Biemestren style, makes my mouth water.

"In a hurry?" Jason Cullinane gestured with an eating prong. "Father used to say that death is always willing to wait until after breakfast."

He looked disgustingly fresh for this pre-goddamn-dawn hour of the morning: face washed, dark brown hair damp and combed back, eyes bright. Hell, I wouldn't have been surprised if he sprouted a bushy tail.

My mouth tasted of bile and stale whiskey, and my head ached. I'd had a bit too much to drink the night before, but only a bit, I decided: my head was only thumping, not pounding.

It's a sin to let good food go to waste, and I like to pick my sins carefully—I chomped into a thick piece of ham, then washed it down with a swallow of milk from a glazed mug. The milk was fresh, but not nearly cold enough. Milk should be just this side of cold enough to make your teeth hurt.

"Kid," I said, "your father stole that line from me. Like most of his good ones."

I was rewarded with a flash of teeth, the sort of smile that his father used to have. Despite the tenday's growth of beard darkening his cheek and chin, it was hard to think of him as an adult. He looked so damn young.

His gaze went distant, as though he was thinking about something, and just for a moment a flash of the other side of his father crossed his face, and there was something distant and cold. But the moment passed, and he looked about fifteen again, even though he was a couple of years older. Good kid.

Jason Cullinane favored his mother, mainly. I could see Andrea's genes in his cheekbones and the widow's peak, and

6

in the warm dark eyes. But there was more than a little of Karl Cullinane visible—in the set of his chin and shoulders, mainly. I'd say that it frightened me, sometimes, but everybody knows that the great Walter Slovotsky doesn't frighten. Which only goes to show that everybody doesn't know a whole lot.

"The bacon?" I gestured at the platter.

Tennetty finally passed it. "What's the hurry this morning?"

"Who said there's a hurry? I'm hungry."

The first time I'd seen Tennetty, years ago, when Karl and I were running a team of Home raiders, she had just staggered out of a slave wagon, a plain skinny woman of the sort your eye tends to skip over. No character lines in her face, no interesting scars.

Even from such a start, Tennetty hadn't worn well as the years had gone by; her bony face sagged in the morning, and the patch fit loosely over her empty left eye socket. She rubbed at the scar that snaked around her good eye, then tossed her head to clear her bangs from her eyes—well, *eye*. Tennetty was getting sloppy, maybe; in the old days, she wouldn't have let her bangs grow that long.

The old days. The trouble with old people is that they always talk about the old days like they were the good days. I don't buy it. Maybe because my memory is good—there were too many days out on the road, sleeping on rocks, never sleeping fully, because there's always trouble ahead. Hell, we were looking for trouble, then. Part of the plan.

"So?" Jason said. "What are you up to this morning?"

"I've got a date with a bow and some rabbits, maybe a deer," I said. Or maybe not. More likely, my date was with the limb of an oak tree. No, not to hang from it—to put some arrows into it.

Tennetty nodded judiciously. "You and the dwarf?"

I snorted, but I shouldn't have been surprised. Even after twenty years, Tennetty still hadn't noticed that Ahira didn't like to go hunting. Not for food, unless absolutely necessary; not for sport, ever.

"Not his cup of tea. Ahira's still asleep." So was my family.

7

There had been many late hours of late, and the sun wasn't quite up. I didn't blame it. The time before dawn is when I like to start staggering toward a bed to sleep in, not staggering out of it. It was uncharacteristic of me to be awake at this hour, but one thing I learned a long time ago is to do things that are uncharacteristics—keeps you young, maybe, and alive, sometimes.

Or maybe I'm just kidding myself. I've never been good at consistency. Maybe I was up because of the damn dreams, and because of Kirah.

I poured myself another cup of tea. I don't know what U'len was putting in the mix, but it had a nice nutty smell that I had gotten very fond of. Not the sort of thing I'd dare have on the road—you can smell it in the sweat for a day or so; when you're on the road, you eat what the locals eat, or keep it bland—but very nice.

Jason eyed me quizzically over his mug. "Are you feeling okay?"

"Just fine," I said, easily. Lying always comes easy to me. I have been having a lot of trouble sleeping of late. Not the only kind of trouble. After several years of getting better, Kirah was getting worse. Some things even time doesn't cure. Some things just lie beneath the surface and fester.

Damn it all. It wasn't my fault.

Back before I met her, before Karl and I freed her, Kirah had been ill-used. One of her owners was worse than simply brutal, and while there were no scars on her body—believe me; in happier days, we explored that matter *very* thoroughly—the scars of her mind had festered over the years.

A miracle was needed, and I didn't have one handy.

We Other Siders have seemed to work wonders at times, but it's only a matter of seeming to—we've just used the skills we brought with us, or acquired in the transition. Of the original seven of us, I was an ag major; Karl a dilettante; James Michael Finnegan a computer science major; Andrea, English; Doria, home ec; Louis Riccetti, engineering; the late Jason Parker (R.I.P.; he didn't make it through even twenty-four hours on this side), history.

The real treatment for what was ailing Kirah wasn't available on This Side and whether it was available on the Other

Side was debatable, if you like debating useless questions. Pyschotherapy can help, but it can't work miracles.

The real treatment for what was ailing *me* could probably, as of last night, be found two rooms down from Kirah's and mine—in the bed of Jason's adopted sister, Aeia. Assuming, of course, that Aeia wanted to pick up where we left off. Alternately, it was time to go out on the road.

I didn't like either option much. Resuming my relationship with Aeia would be dangerous, and it made sense to stay put in Jason's new barony for the time being, keeping in shape, waiting to hear some word about Mikyn.

So I didn't like either choice, not at the moment. I also didn't like the idea of Bren, Baron Adahan being under the same roof, whether he really was there to help the family settle in or to pay court to Aeia. Most of all, I didn't like the fact that the universe doesn't appear to give a fuck what I do and don't like.

Jason speared the last piece of bacon and set it on my plate. "We could use some more food out here," he called out, not getting an immediate answer. Service was less than wonderful.

Tennetty shook her head. "Not like the old days at the castle. Used to be you could hear a servitor jump."

He made a be-still motion. Unsurprisingly, it worked, at least for now. After years as Karl's bodyguard (that's the nice word for it) Tennetty had fallen into the same pattern with Karl's son.

It was just the three of us alone around the small round table in what had been the old cook's nook in the castle, a small room between the kitchens and the formal dining room, its mottled glass windows covered with bars on both inside and outside.

The table and room could handle as many as eight or ten people, so Jason had coopted it as a breakfast room for the family three weeks—pardon me: two tendays—before, when we'd arrived to take over what had been Castle Furnael and now was Castle Cullinane.

Over the clatter of cups and saucers out in the kitchen, I could hear U'len berating one of the younger cooks, her voice rising in simulated anger, then falling into real, grumbled curses.

Pick your theory: if you assume that what you need in staff is experience with the people living there, I would have been tempted to do a complete staff switch with Thomen Furnael—excuse me, with the Emperor Thomen. Plan A: screw it—pay the two dollars. Plan B would be to keep almost everybody in place, under the theory that experience with the local facilities is the main issue. The baronial keep didn't need a quarter the staff that the castle did, after all.

Either way would have been reasonable, either way would have worked, but nobody was asking Walter Slovotsky's opinion. Ahira and I were teaching the boy about what we tend to call the family business, but running a castle has never really been part of that, and we'd kept our opinions largely to ourselves.

Unsurprisingly, really, that Jason had settled on an untheoretical compromise: bring in a few of his own people, keep on all but a few of the locals, and let them and them bump into each other all over the damn place.

Which is why the rolls were blackened on the bottom, my rooms hadn't been swept out in a week—although the flowers were changed daily—and hot baths were just plain not available without special arrangement and a lot of effort.

Tennetty gave a quick glance at Jason; he nodded, and she turned back to me. "Need some company?"

"Eh?"

"Need some company? Hunting?" She cocked her head to one side. "We were talking about hunting, no?"

"Yeah. And not really, no company needed," I said, then changed my mind. "Well, come to think of it, if you've got nothing better to do, sure." Unless you're burdening yourself like the White Knight, it's just as well to carry an extra weapon, and that's what Tennetty was. Pretty good one, too.

She smiled. "Nothing to kill here but time."

I would have been a lot happier if she hadn't meant it. I was going to spend the morning bowhunting, in part to stay out of trouble, but mainly for practice, and effect. I don't mind killing my own food—back when I was majoring in meat science, I slaughtered and butchered more than a lot of cows—but it doesn't give me any thrill. It did give Tennetty a lot of pleasure, which is why I was nervous about going hunting with her.

Frankly, I'd just as soon have skipped it all. Playing with weapons is an inadequate Freudian substitute, no matter how big and manly the bow is, or how far and fast it can shoot.

Jason frowned. Sometimes I can almost read minds: giving Tennetty permission had been easy, but it was harder for him to decide whether his sense of duty prevented, permitted, or demanded that he go along.

He finally came down on the side of having fun, although from which angle I wouldn't have wanted to bet.

"I haven't been hunting in a long time," Jason said, tossing the weight of the world from his shoulders for a moment. He relaxed, just a trifle.

I was tempted to turn this into a lesson about not assuming an invitation, but decided to let it pass. Ever since Jason had traded the silver crown of the Emperor of Holtun-Bieme in on the barony, he hadn't had a lot of time to relax, and he deserved it.

"Sure," I said. "Come on."

"Good morning," Aeia Cullinane said as she walked into the breakfast room, my daughter Janie at her side, the two of them complicating my day while they brightened it.

"Morning, Daddy. Morning, all." Janie bent to kiss me on the cheek. Short black hair and bangs that always try to cover the eyes, thin limbs fleshing out almost daily, mannish leather breeches covered by a muslin shirt belted tight to show slim waist and slender curves: my teenage daughter. Sixteen, barely but This Side sixteen, not Other Side sixteen. They seem to grow up faster here than I remember them doing there.

"Morning, Sweetness," I said.

She slipped into the chair next to Jason and reached for a hunk of bread while Aeia struck a pose while pretending to decide where to sit. I didn't mind; I was enjoying the view.

There's a sharp mind behind the bright eyes that have just a touch of a slant to them. Part of her sunbleached hair was bound behind her in a ponytail, leaving the rest to frame her face, wisps of hair touching at high cheekbones. She was

11

dressed, to the extent that she was dressed, in a short white silk robe, its hem cut diagonally, about knee-length on the left side, mid-thigh on the right. It was a great view, but a bad idea, probably; the guards were a rough lot.

Jason frowned at his adopted sister. "Do me a favor?"

She tilted her head to the side. "Depends."

"Put some clothes on before you come out of your room, eh?" The master-of-the-house voice didn't quite fit, not yet, but it was getting better.

"What do you call this?" she brushed a hand down one side.

"Trouble. I don't know what you've been doing in Biemestren, but that doesn't go here."

"Oh," she said, dismissing the point rather than acknowledging it. She smiled at me as she sat down next to me, resting warm fingers on my arm for a moment as she pressed her leg up against mine. Not teasing, just touching.

Explain something to me: why are women two degrees warmer than men are?

And why do I keep getting in trouble over women?

It's real simple, most of it: I *like* the ones I sleep with, whether or not they've got their clothes on, whether or not they're willing to take them off. Add to that a certain amount of grooming and, er, charm, and subtract the sense of desperation that most men have around pretty women, and I do okay, or get into trouble, depending how you look at it.

Tennetty eyed her own fingernails. "I wouldn't worry. If there's anybody here who doesn't know what happens if he lays a hand on Aeia or Janie, I'll explain it—"

"Thanks much, Ten," Janie said from around a bite of bread, "but I can explain things myself."

"—and if I need help, Durine, Kethol, and Pirojil are always available." Tennetty considered the edge of a knife I hadn't seen her draw. Like I say, I'm too slow in the morning.

"I don't think I'll need help."

Jason brushed the objection away. "That wasn't what I meant. I don't want to have Bren jumping up and down every time somebody looks crosswise at her."

"Not to worry." Aeia smiled, amused by the thought of Bren Adahan being jealous. "Maybe he'll be too busy watch-

12

ing me to put his hands on Janie's bottom. It's important to keep the menfolk busy, Janie told me last night."

She glanced over at Jason, then turned to me, to see if I noticed. I pretended not to, which only made her smile more.

Jason didn't quite blush. Janie, on the other hand, had a great poker face; she had taken the smile from her face by the time she had turned back to him.

I guess I was supposed to be upset, but there's part of being a parent that appears to have been left out of my makeup: the thought of my daughter having sex doesn't bother me. Sorry. Long as she visits the Spider or the Eareven priest twice a year and gets herself taken care of—something I made sure she did for the first year after menarche—I just hope she has fun.

Somebody trying to force her or hurt her would be different, but that's not sex, dammit. I'd do to that kind of slime the same thing I did to the last ones that raped her mother. (And no, I wouldn't do it slower. Doesn't make it any better, and it doesn't make them any deader.)

I wasn't supposed to know what was going on between Janie and Jason, though. It made things simpler. Jason and I already had enough to argue about.

Aeia went on: "But if I need any help with my social life, I'll be sure to let you know."

Jason didn't suspect anything; he wasn't good enough an actor not to glance from face to face if he knew. Janie didn't seem to pick up on it, either, which meant nothing.

I smiled back at Aeia in a sort of avuncular way, I hoped. We needed a long talk, her and me, and that would have to be orchestrated just right.

Forget the orchestra, though—what tune did I want to play?

A friend of mine who was acting major used to say there was an old saying in the theatre: "Drunk and on the road don't count." We hadn't been drunk, but we had been on the road. And, if the truth be known, it had been awfully good, for both of us.

Compare that to a woman who didn't let me touch her anymore, who claimed that she loved me but never laughed or smiled in my presence, whose shoulders shook in the night with silent weeping. You tell me how you'd rather sleep next to *that* than to one who sleeps in your arms, her breath warm on your neck, her legs intertwined with yours, matching you heartbeat for heartbeat.

But you don't leave your wife of almost two decades because she's an emotional cripple, and you don't dump her for a younger woman just because when you touch her, it makes you feel twice as alive.

All that seems reasonable. I don't know what you actually *do*, though. That makes me feel awfully old.

When I was younger, I always knew what to do.

I pushed back from the table; that seemed right for the moment. The ground didn't open up and swallow me. Always a good sign.

"Jason, Tennetty, and I are going hunting," I said to Aeia.

She either didn't take the hint, or dismissed the idea. "Have fun." She made a moue as she reached for a sweetroll. "Bren up yet?"

I shook my head. "Haven't seen him."

I wondered for a moment if that was a red herring for my benefit, if she was sneaking off to sleep with Bren the way that Janie was to be with Jason, then decided that I wasn't going to get anywhere guessing. I don't care who plays musical beds, as long as I don't have to sleep alone. Which had been the trouble, of late. One of them.

Besides, there's Slovotsky's Law something-or-other: Don't accuse your mistress of cheating on you with her future fiance.

To hell with it. I was spending too much time musing about musical beds. I stood up. "I'm out of here, folks."

Tennetty hacked off a fist-sized hunk of bread, dipped it in honey, and stood. "Let's go kill something."

The castle was quiet in the golden morning light, probably a holdover on the part of Karl's staff. He used to insist on— well, try to insist on—sleeping late, and U'len was probably keeping things quiet in his memory, or maybe just out of habit.

14

"Meet you at the stables," I told Tennetty and Jason. She nodded and sprinted for the back staircase, while Jason maintained a dignified walk. I headed up to the two-room suite my wife and I shared. Well, maybe it was three-room suite, if you included the secret passage to the room next door, although the room next door was unoccupied, and the passage was barred from our side. I like the idea of having a back way out; I'm cautious enough that I don't want anybody else to have a back way in.

Kirah lay stretched out on the bed, the blankets having slid aside, revealing one long leg almost to the hip. Sunlight splashed on her long, golden hair, her breasts rising and falling with her gentle breathing, her arms spread wide, her mouth just barely parted, all trusting and innocent and vulnerable and lovely.

I felt cheated: I wanted to reach over and hold her for a moment before I left, but I couldn't. Not while she was sleeping, ever. One of the rules. Not mine. Kirah has her own way of enforcing her rules. Call it passive-aggressive, if you like—but it *hurts* her when I push things.

Damn.

I exchanged my cotton trousers for leather ones—you can get cut by the brush—and after I'd buttoned the fly I shrugged into a hunting vest, and then the double shoulder holster that Kirah had made for me. I belted my shortsword around my waist, tucked a couple braces of throwing knives never mind exactly where.

An oak box with a trick catch—you have to press down on the top of the box while you press up on the latch—held my two best pistols, loaded, oil-patched, and ready to go; I slipped them into the holster. A nice design: it held one pistol a bit too high, but the other, held in place by a U-shaped spring hidden in the leather, was held slantwise under the armpit, butt-forward. Draw, cock, and bang.

Me, I'd rather store most of my guns safely unloaded, and eventually I'd be able to. Jason's twin sixguns were the first on this side, but they wouldn't be the last. With Jason's revolver and speedloader, it's flip, slip, slam, and blam—flip the cylinder out, slip the Riccetti-made speedloader into place, slam the cylinder shut, letting the outer shell of the speedloader fly where it may, and then *blam*. And that's worst-case; most of time, I'd keep the revolver loaded, trusting Lou Riccetti's unlicensed modification of the Ruger transfer-bar safety to keep the gun from going *bang* unexpectedly. On the other hand, it takes more than a minute to load a flintlock, and I've never, *ever* been in a situation where I've said to myself, "Gee, it'd be nice to have a loaded gun in about a minute."

Never. It's either *nah*, or it's *now*.

A small gunmetal flask of extract of dragonbane sat on the bureau, carefully sealed with wax, secondly because I don't like the reek of the gooey stuff, but mainly because a good friend of mine is highly allergic to it, being a dragon. While creatures with the sort of magical metabolisms that can be harmed by dragonbane had long been driven away from the Eren regions—humans and magical creatures tend not to get along—there had been rumors about things coming out of Faerie, and out on the Cirric Jason had seen a few creatures he couldn't identify.

So I slipped the flask into my vest.

Last but not least, I tucked two Therranji garrottes into their separate, leather-lined pockets. Vicious things—the slim cables were made with springy barbed wire, the barbs canted backwards so that the garrotte could only be tightened. Just tuck the handle through the loop, then slip the barbed-wire noose over a head, give the wooden handle one hard jerk, and let go—in order to get it off, the poor slob would have to remove the handle, then slip the loop off the butt end. Can't get it over the head? No problem—whip it around the neck, put the handle through the loop, and pull.

Trust the Therranji to come up with a weapon that mean—elves can be nasty—and somebody like me to carry two of them on his person.

Still, peace is nice. You don't have to take a lot of precautions before going out for a simple walk in the woods.

I wanted to take one last look at Kirah sleeping, and I wanted not to take one last look at her, so I hung a quiver from my shoulder, grabbed my best longbow and a couple of spare strings, and headed down to the stables.

Jason was already in the saddle of a huge red gelding—another one of Carrot's foals, I think—and the stableboy was finishing saddling a stocky roan for Tennetty. I picked a smallish pieblad mare and saddled her myself, earning a broad, gap-toothed smile from the stableboy, touched that the great Walter Slovotsky would handle his own horse.

Well, it didn't hurt anything for him to think that.

Water and field rations are always kept ready in the stables. Until they string the telegraph to Biemestren and out to Little Pittsburgh, there's no way to know when a messenger will have to be dispatched in a hurry. I slipped a canteen over the saddlehorn, and a pair of saddlebags in front of it.

We rode out through the main gate and into the day.

The gently rolling land around the former Castle Furnael, now Castle Cullinane, had been cleared at least a mile in each direction, in part to give the baron some farmland of his own, I suppose, but mainly to prevent any large force from sneaking up on the castle. The western road cut through at least two miles of wheat fields before it swung north toward the woods that countless Furnael barons had used as their private hunting preserve. That was down the road almost two miles away, just enough distance to warm the horses.

Hooves clopped quietly on the unpaved road, while above, soft white clouds scudded across a deep blue sky, something that only soft white clouds ever do. Below, waist-high stalks of young green wheat bowed gently in the breeze. The air was still cool from the night, with none of the afternoon tang of sunbaked fields, but the day was young.

"Nice day," Jason said.

"That it is," I said, hitching at my holsters. Nice days make me nervous.

Jason had one of his twin revolvers in a holster on the left side of his chest, the butt facing forward, just about even with his left elbow. Not a bad placement, actually—it would be a bit clumsy to get at it with his left hand, but it could be done.

I envied him the weapons. If a messenger from Home didn't show up soon with a pair for me, I'd have to ride over and have a word with Lou. After all, I was the one who built the first flintlock on This Side, and seniority should count for something, no?

Tennetty chuckled. "Always ingratiating yourself with the help, eh?"

"Eh?"

"The horse," she said. "You saddled it yourself." She snorted. "That dung-footed stableboy looked at you like you were, I don't know, something special."

"Well . . ." I shrugged, as modestly as possible, under the circumstances. "I am, Tennetty."

She was disposed to leave it be, but Jason couldn't. "So why did you do it?"

I shrugged. "I used to trust other folks to saddle my horse, but I've found that I take a more active interest in my cinch straps than any stableboy possibly can."

Tennetty nodded. Jason frowned. We set off in a walk down the road.

"So," he finally said. "You think we're settled in enough, yet?"

I nodded. "Sure. You're going to have to let the staff problems sort themselves out, but looks like everything's okay here. You itchy to get back on the road?"

He nodded. "Ellegon's due tomorrow, or maybe the day after. I think we'd best go find Mikyn's trail. I'm worried about him."

Mikyn was a good kid, but he was on his own, as far as I was concerned. Yes, he was one of Jason's childhood friends, but it was more important to me that he was a *gotterdammerung* looking for a place to happen, and I've been around enough of those in my time. No rush, thanks. Besides . . .

"Let's hang on for awhile," I said. "Ahira had a word with Danagar before we left Biemestren—he's put some more feelers out."

Mikyn was somewhere, perhaps in the Middle Lands, perhaps elsewhere in the Eren regions, searching for the man who had enslaved his family. The odds were poor that Mikyn was on a warm trail; they were only fair that his disguise as a traveling farrier would hold up.

Odds wouldn't stop him from looking, the young idiot. Well, hell, odds wouldn't have stopped me, either.

Jason pursed his lips. "I should have done that."

"Maybe." Actually, it would have been a bad idea; the last thing that Emperor Thomen Furnael needed was for Jason to be telling his best field agent what to do. Thomen's seat on the throne was probably precarious enough as it was; his only title to it was as a gift from the usurper's son. I'm not condemning, mind; *usurper* is a technical term, and Karl was my second best friend.

"In any case," I said, "we're probably best off waiting until we hear something, then hitching a ride on Ellegon. It'll likely save time. Besides, truth to tell, I'd like at least a few more days of rest, food, and good light exercise before we go back in harm's way." Still, I wondered about Mikyn. "You know if he's any good with fire and iron?"

Jason nodded. "Better than me. Nehera gave a bunch of us the short course, a few years ago. I don't think anybody would confuse either of the two of us with a master farrier, but I could do a good, clean, quick job, and Mikyn was better."

"In any case, we wait. We'll hear soon enough." Or more than soon enough.

"Very well." He nodded. "Wouldn't we be better off waiting at Biemestren?"

Tennetty snickered. "Oh, a great idea." She drew her sword, a short, cross-hilted rapier, and gave a few tentative swipes through the air. "Why not just hack Thomen's legs off for real?" She slipped the rapier back into the sheath with a decided *snap*.

"Eh?" Jason was bright, but he was still young.

"Think about it," I said. "Imagine yourself riding up to the castle. In Biemestren. What happens?"

"What do you mean, what happens?"

"Just what I said. Tell me what happens. What's the first thing you do?"

He shrugged. "I'd pay a call on Thomen. I'd ride through the gate, and leave my horse out front."

"Right," I said. "You'd ride right through the gate. Without asking permission, because you spent most of your childhood living there, and it still feels like home to you, and nobody there would think of stopping you, right?"

He caught it. There was nothing wrong with Jason that a few years of growing up wouldn't cure, assuming he had the time to grow up.

His lips twisted. "And what his royal highness, the Emperor Thomen, formerly Baron Furnael, doesn't need is Karl Cullinane's son suggesting that the throne doesn't really belong to him."

"Exactly." I nodded. "You stay the hell out of Biemestren until and unless you're sent for, just like all the other barons. And when you go, you walk just a bit more humbly than they do."

He smiled. "And, say, occasionally flash a bit of temper, only to be silenced by a single look from the Emperor."

Tennetty laughed. "He catches on fast." She turned to him. "Now, in the interim?"

He raised his hands in surrender. "I guess we stay here, eh?"

"For the time being," I said.

"Good.—Now let's get some exercise." Without a polite word of warning, or even a curt one, Tennetty kicked her horse into a canter; it took a good half mile for the two of us to catch up.

Where the road swung north to give a wide berth to Benai Hill, a path into the forest broke through the plowed ground and met the road.

The path was well-maintained, even after it entered the forest—overhead branches were hacked off, some brush cleared by the side. I wouldn't have wanted to gallop down it in the dark, or even canter in the light, but it was perfectly fine for a nice, quick walk.

Kind of pleasant, really: stately oaks and elms arching high above, keeping things all cool and green and musty, even though the day was already heating up. My hearing's awfully good, for a human's, but I couldn't hear any animal sounds over the clopping of the horses' hooves.

A nice quiet day.

Something rustled in the bush toward the side of the road.

I had a throwing knife in my left hand and a cocked pistol

in my right as a rabbit scampered across the path, losing itself in the woods.

Tennetty was only a little slower with a flintlock; Jason was third, his revolver, one of the only two that existed, carefully pointed toward the sky.

"What—?"

"Ta havath," Tennetty said. *Take it easy.* "Just a rabbit." Tennetty glared at me as she carefully holstered her pistol and slipped her rapier back into its sheath. "What was *that* about?"

I shrugged an apology as I reholstered my own pistol and slipped my throwing knife back into its sheath. "Sorry."

The two of them were kind enough to let the matter drop.

It was a nice day, so why was I coming close to jumping out of my skin at every sound? Yes, there were those rumors of things coming out of Faerie, but we were solidly in the Middle Lands, far from Faerie.

Not good enough. I mean, it was true, but it wasn't an excuse.

I could have argued that Tennetty and Jason were just as jumpy as I was, but that would have been just for the sake of arguing—the two of them were operating under the sound principle that when somebody quickly draws a weapon, he's got a good reason. Which I hadn't. A rabbit within shooting range is a good reason to draw a hunting weapon slowly, carefully, without alarming the rest of your party. It is *not* a reason to suggest by word or action that the shit's about to hit the fan.

We rode in silence and I kept my jumpiness under control as we followed the path in for maybe half an hour—remember, every step you take in has to be taken out—until we came to a small clearing, where I called for a break.

I dismounted, more stiffly than I liked, and rubbed at the base of my spine.

Getting a bit older every year, Walter.

Tennetty either didn't hurt or didn't want to show it. I wouldn't have bet either way.

"Leave the horses?" she asked, sliding out of the saddle as she did.

"Sure." I uncinched the saddle and set it on the spread-out horse blanket, slipped the bridle, and tied the horse to a tree, just the rope and hackamore to hold him there. Jason did the same.

Tennetty just slipped the bridle and dropped the reins. "Stay," she said. I guess that if her horse couldn't stay ground-hitched, she was willing for it to be her problem.

I slipped into my shooting gloves and leathers—I'll cut my fingers and scrape my arm when it's for real, but not when it's practice, thank you very much—then strung my bow, a fine Therranji composite that had cost me more than I like to think about. I'd have to show this to Lou; I doubted even he could have improved on it. Nicely, elegantly recurved, it was made from three pieces of almost black wood, a long strip of reddened horn sinew-bound to its belly, the whole thing covered with a smooth lacquer. The grip was soft, thick leather, gradually molding itself to my fingers with each use. About a fifty-pound pull—which is plenty, really.

"I've always seen you favor a crossbow," Jason said, stringing his own longbow. He slung his quiver over his head, then hitched at his swordbelt. He thought about it for a moment, then unhooked the swordbelt, leaving it around the pommel of his saddle.

I nodded. "Usually do," I said. "Hey, Jason?"

"Yes?"

"What would you say," I said, quietly, "if I told you that there's six Holtish rebels hiding behind those trees over there and that they're about to jump us?"

He edged toward his horse.

Tennetty snickered. "What you should say is, 'I'm sorry, Holtish rebels, let me drop my pants and bend over for you, so you can stick my sword up my backside,' that's what you should say." She jerked a thumb toward his horse. "Wear the sword."

He buckled the sword on with good grace. I've known people who take direction worse than Jason. Lots of them. I've seen one of them in a mirror, every now and then.

I fitted a practice arrow to the bowstring—I don't waste killing broadheads on trees.

Now, I like crossbows. You can fire them with one hand,

from the saddle, or from a prone position, three things that you can't do with a longbow. You can do two out of those three things with a short bow, but you give up range and striking power. Not a good compromise. A longbow has greater range than any crossbow without a good winding gear, and a much greater rate of fire. The only trouble is that it takes a lot of practice to get good at it, and more practice to stay good at it.

Across the meadow, maybe twenty years away, an oily crow sat on a limb, considering the silly humans below.

Well, let's see if I can still do zen archery. The trouble with being a stranger in a strange land is that you have to be your own zen master. I brought the bow up, keeping my form perfect, not aiming with my eyes, not exactly, and visualized the release, the string leaving my finger in perfect form—smoothly, evenly, instantly, not with a plucking loose.

I let go, and in less than a heartbeat, the arrow was quivering in the limb, a full three feet to the right of where the crow had taken flight.

Jason snickered. "Off by the full arrow's-length. Not too good, Uncle Walter."

Tennetty caught my eye; the corners of her lips were turned up. If it had been anybody else, I'd call the expression a smile. "See how close you can come to his arrow, Jason Cullinane. I'm curious."

Jason brought up his bow and loosed too soon, the string loud against his leathers. The arrow disappeared into the forest.

Tennetty laughed out loud, and Jason started to bristle, but caught himself.

"Well," he said, "let's say we start hunting in that direction."

"After," I said. "Let's fire some more practice arrows first."

Hunting, like fishing—and sex, for that matter—is one of those things where you really have to be there to understand it.

Except for the killing part, I like it, a lot. At least the way he did it. You stalk across the floor of the dark forest, the comforting rot of leaves and humus in your nostrils, listening, watching intently—and without worrying about somebody jumping out from behind a tree and killing you. It's a good thing.

At my side were people I trusted, because I don't go hunting with people I don't trust.

There are other ways to do it. One of the best ways to actually catch food involves finding a good spot and waiting for the game to pass by. You sit, conserving energy, and wait. Eventually, if you've picked your spot right, your rabbit comes into view, or your deer, or antelope or whatever. But that's survival hunting.

This was more fun. Back on the Other Side, I never could move this quietly. I'm not complaining, mind, but being one of the big guys isn't all that it's cracked up to be. Trust me.

Besides, we weren't really hunting. What we were doing was relaxing, and by the time we'd worked our way into the forest, firing a few practice shots here and there, I'd managed to get rid of my jumpiness. For now.

Just as well. "Jason, you see that stump over there?" I asked, pointing to one about forty yards away.

"The one just behind that fallen tree?"

"Right. Bet you I can put an arrow into that root, the one that bends up to the right."

He shrugged. "So can I."

"From here?" I raised an eyebrow. "A silver mark to who gets closer?"

He nodded. "Sure."

"Tennetty?"

"No, I don't need to donate to the cause," she said.

"No. We need a referee and judge."

"Yeah, sure." She took up a drill instructor's stance. "Awright. Nock your arrows. Draw your bows. Three. Two. One. *Loose.*"

It was a tricky shot, trickier than it looked, if I was right—the leaves from a lower branch of an old oak blocked the top of the parabolic flight of the arrow. You have to remember that your shot does not travel in a straight line, but in an arc. The trick was to aim so that the arrow's flight would take it through a gap in the leaves . . .

I released, smoothly. I was a bit off, but more lucky than off: it barely nicked a couple of leaves, not slowing it enough to make it miss. It *thwok*ed comfortably into the root, while Jason's arrow buried itself in the ground, easily a foot short.

"Pay me," I said.

"Put it on account," he said.

"Sure."

I retrieved my arrow, and nocked it, looking for another target.

"Er, Uncle Walter?" Jason frowned as he examined the head of his arrow, but I didn't think he was frowning at it.

"Yeah?"

"How come I get the feeling that we're not really after deer?"

Tennetty chuckled. "Maybe because we're too busy shooting up the trees?"

"There's a perfectly good archery range behind the barracks," Jason said.

"If you know anything more boring than spending a morning firing arrows at a bull's-eye, you be sure and don't let me know."

Me, I'd much rather pretend to go hunting and shoot up a few trees. I never really practice with my throwing knives— I just use them, every once in a long while, to assure me that I still have the Talent for it. But that's deeply imprinted. I don't have to practice that any more than a fish has to practice his scales.

My learned skills are different; if I don't put in at least a few hours with the longbow every tenday or so, I start to go real sour, and there have been more than a few times that would have been unfortunate. Unfortunate in the sense of Stash and Emma Slovotsky's baby boy getting himself dead. As Woody Allen would say, death is one of the worst things that can happen to somebody in our line of work, and many of us simply prefer to pay a small fine.

So I practice. I've spent far too much of my life practicing at how to shoot some things and cut with some others, but there you have it. Part of the dues.

25

But you don't tell anybody everything.

"I like this better," I said. "Out on a nice day with some good company, clean air, maybe the chance of making a few marks . . ."

". . . off some sucker," Tennetty said, with a smile.

But it wasn't a nice smile, and it almost ruined the morning.

CHAPTER TWO

In Which I Discuss Some Family Matters

Chi fa ingiuria no perdona mai. (He never forgives those he injures.)

—ITALIAN PROVERB

MOST OF THE TIME, things go from bad to worse, but every now and then the human universe shifts for the better: it's clear that something bad's going to happen, but then something else entirely does, something gentler.

Sometimes it's nice; sometimes it's just something bad that declines to happen. Either is just fine with me.

The first time I remember it, I was about seven, I guess. My parents had gone out for the evening, and my brother, Steven, had a date, so they'd hired a baby-sitter. Mrs. Kleinman, her name was; she lived on some sort of widow's pension in a set of funny-smelling rooms in the red brick apartment building down the block from our house. Ugly old biddy, who really didn't like kids. Never wanted to play, or talk; all she wanted to do was turn on the television, take off her shoes, and fall alseep on the couch with one hand in a bowl of potato chips.

Well? What would you do? I'd done the obvious thing,

and there had been trouble when Stash and Emma got home. Whenever old Stash—it's an old Polish nickname, okay?—got angry, there was this tic in his right cheek; it would twitch with every pulsebeat.

He came into my room, the light in the hall casting half his face into shadow, his fists unclenching. Stash was a short, broad man, but he had huge hands, and they made huge fists.

He wouldn't have punched me, but he was going to spank me. His face was so red from the chin to the top of his balding that I thought he was going to blow up, and the tic was pulsing two to the second, the speed of a fast walk. I was worried about him more than me, I swear, as he loomed over me.

"Walter . . ." he always called me Cricket, except when he was angry at me, and he was furious.

And then he swept me up in his huge arms. I could smell the whiskey on his breath. Gales of laughter rocked me. *His* laughter.

"God, Cricket, I guess that old biddy *did* deserve to have her shoes nailed to the floor."

I guess that's why the smell of whiskey on somebody's breath doesn't bother me.

I was currying the mare when I heard Bren's footsteps behind me. The cleaning stalls at Castle Furnael—Castle Cullinane, that is—were well designed, with a low, calf-high open wooden box in the center of the stall. You stand the horse in the box, with inhibits it from moving around, and prevents you getting kicked.

I wasn't worried about being kicked. There wasn't any good reason to be concerned about anything at all, eh? One of the stableboys and two of the horse soldiers were just outside, reshoeing a stubborn gelding; the other stableboy was across the way, working on Jason's horse, and the house guard was within a quick shout. If we were going to have a problem, it wasn't going to be here.

Besides, Bren Adahan would hardly be here to give me a problem, eh?

"Hello, Baron," I said, turning slowly, resting my hand on the partition separating the cleaning stalls. It's reflex—ever since my first day on This Side, I've always looked for a place to run. I've always had a reason. I haven't always *had* a place to run, mind, but I've always looked for one. "Where've you been keeping yourself?"

"All over, Walter Slovotsky," he said. "I spent the morning at two of the tenant farms. Then I came in and did an inventory at the farm. Then the kennels, and now here."

"Inventorying the baron's livestock?" A good idea, and something I should have thought of. I tended to think of the walled keep itself as being Jason's new home, although really it was the keep and the huge chunk of land it sat upon, including the livestock managed at the clump of buildings down by the pastures, a couple of miles away.

"Somebody ought to," he said. He was in tan today, in a pale, almost snowy doeskin tunic and leggings, the effect picked up by an antler clip that held back the hair that otherwise would have fallen over his right ear.

Very stylish, but then again, Bren, Baron Adahan was always very stylish. I've always been more fond of substance, myself. No, that's not fair. I had been out in the field with him, and he had gotten as down and dirty as the rest of us. A good man to have at your back in a fight, something both Jason and I knew from experience.

Perhaps to remind me of that, he wore a very ordinary leather combo belt tight on his hips, his shortsword on the left, a dagger and a flintlock on the right.

"Have you a moment?" he asked.

"For you, Baron, I've always got a moment," I said, not meaning it.

He smiled, as thought there was no hypocrisy in his voice, or in mine. "I'll be leaving tomorrow; there are matters in my barony that need my attention."

"Little Pittsburgh?" I said. There's always something happening in the steel town.

"Yes. Not just that, but yes." He nodded, and then, for no reason or other, it happened: we were friends again, even if only for the moment. "Let me give you a hand." He stripped off his tunic, then unbuckled his sword and hung it on a post. It already had the brush ready for him before he had his hand out.

He stroked the harsh bristles with his thumb. "Ranella's

29

devoting her attention to the railroad, and somebody has to take care of the administration," he said, as he ran the brush down the other side of the horse, steadying her with sure fingers in her name as she whickered and pranced just a little. "Something I was trained for, no?"

"Each to his own, Bren."

His smile was forced. "I'm going to ask Aeia to come with me."

"Don't blame you at all," I said. "I would, if I were you."

He was silent for a long time. We sometimes have to live on the silences. "Maybe she'd be better off here, with the others."

I nodded. "Maybe. She's going to have to decide for herself."

"There is that." He dropped the subject. "I see you didn't come back with any game today. Enjoy your hunt nonetheless?" he asked, taking up a firm grip in the mare's mane with one hand while he reassuringly stroked her neck with the other.

"It was pleasant enough."

"The doing, not the prey, eh?"

"Something like that." I tucked the hoof pick under my left arm, and stooped to pick up the mare's front hoof and scraped it out. It was packed full of horseshit and dirt, much like life itself. I would have liked to let it slide by—I am a lazy bastard, and there are standards to maintain—but all sorts of hoof diseases can get started if you don't clean them out properly.

Bren held out his hand for the pick. I handed it over and steadied the horse while he did the right front hoof, then moved back to do the rear one on that side. I finished with the final hoof, then gave the horse a solid pat on the flank as I closed the stall door.

"Leave her there, in the grooming stall, an' it please you," the stableboy called out. He was working on Tennetty's horse across the way. "I've got to muck out her own stall, and I'll do it just as soon as I finish with this horse, Walter Slovotsky."

"She'll need some fresh straw," Bren said.

"I'll get it, Baron—" the stableboy cut himself off; Bren was already partly up the ladder toward the loft. I swarmed up after him.

There was a skittering at our approach, but you almost never see the stable rats.

Stables are stables: bales, tied with twine, lay brick-stacked against the front wall, four rows deep. Bren hacked through the twine with a hayknife while I used the pitchfork to pitch it to the stone floor below.

"It's difficult," he said, standing at the edge, considering the edge of the hayknife, "to be a disciple of the late, great Karl Cullinane."

"So I hear."

"You have to change, you see." His smile wasn't friendly anymore. "In the old days, it would have been simple. Nobody not of my station would have thought to take, oh, anything I wanted. But if someone did, there wouldn't be a problem." He patted the spot of his belly where the hilt of his sword would have been. " 'All men are created equal', eh? Didn't used to be that way. Anybody short of my class wouldn't have had the time to get as good with a sword as I was. Am."

He thought about it for a long time, then he turned and stuck the hayknife back in a bale, and vanished down the ladder. He had gotten some horsehair and sweat and dirt on his chest and breeches, I guess, which was why he left carrying his tunic in his hands, without looking back for a moment.

I looked at his retreating back for a long time, even after it wasn't there.

I went up to our rooms to find Kirah, but she wasn't there, and she hadn't left a note as to where she was going to be. I came to This Side illiterate in Erendra, and put in a lot of effort first changing that, then teaching my wife her letters. Damn inconsiderate of her not to even leave a damn note.

I probably should have gone looking for Kirah, but I looked for a couple of friends instead.

I found Doria with the dwarf and my younger daughter over in the blacksmith's shop, next to the bathhouse.

31

"Daddy!" My baby daughter's face lit up and she ran for me; a father is always a hero to his daughter, even if he doesn't deserve it.

I swept Dorann up in my arms. "Whatcha doin', kiddo?"

"Aunt Doria and Uncle 'hira are showing me how to smith," she said, suddenly becoming serious as she raised a finger. They're very serious at three and a half. "Now don't you touch the metal. It's *hot*."

"Okay, Dorann," I said, giving her a quick kiss on the top of her head. "I'll be careful." My daughters are always watching out for me. It's nice. I ran my fingers through her hair. "Isn't it about your nap time?"

"Don't need a nap," she said. Which settled that.

Both my daughters ran to stubbornness, once they get their minds made up. Kirah used to claim that it came from me, and I used to claim that it came from her, and we used to argue about it constantly, if never angrily, until she finally gave up; so I guess I was always right, and the stubbornness *does* come from Kirah's side of the family.

"What's that in your ear, sweetie?" I palmed a piece of rock sugar from my pouch as I set her down. It was wrapped in a twist of paper, so it was easy to trap it with the back of my forefinger and middle finger as I clapped my hands to show that they were empty, then pretended to pull it from here ear. "You hiding candy again?"

Sleight of hand is related to pickpocketry, and the latter is one of my talents. It's never gotten me a jewel brighter than Dorann's white smile and squeal of delight as she popped it into her mouth.

Ahira had chased the smith out—or more likely, given him the day off—and was bent over the forge, doing some minor repairs to a mail shirt. Tricky work—you want to be sure to weld each ring tightly shut without welding any ring to the other. During the time we were working for King Mah- erralen over in Endell, he had picked up some of the art.

So had I, actually, although not as much as he had, which isn't fair, given my head start—back on the Other Side, before all this started, I spent a summer apprenticing at Sturbridge Village. It would say something about genetics versus environment, but with Ahira, it was pretty hard to decide what was what.

I'm not sure whether Doria was legitimately interested, or just being sociable. Dorann, on the other hand, was interested in everything.

I remember when Doria used to wear her Hand cloak: a big, bulky dull white thing that made her look old and shapeless. I hadn't seen her wear it since Melawei; she probably put it away with all of her other Hand memorabilia, and maybe memories.

Today, Doria had tucked the hem of a white cotton pullover shirt into her tight pair of Home jeans, and was looking fresh and immaculate as she held Doria Andrea's hand.

"Looking cute today, Dore," I said.

Doria and Ahira looked too young. He had stripped to the waist for the work, and the muscles beneath the skin of his hairy, barreled chest were like rope beneath the scars. One weal on his right shoulder still stood out, red and angry, and it looked like somebody clumsy had played tictactoe with the point of a knife just under his left nipple. Which was pretty close to what had happened, so I understand. He didn't talk about it much.

If you ignored the scars, though, Ahira hadn't changed one whit in the years we had been on this side: while the top of his head barely came to the middle of my chest, the shock of thick brown hair—thick both ways—held no trace of gray. It probably wouldn't for awhile; dwarves live long lives.

The fingers that held the tongs in the forge were thick and strong, the joints like walnuts. His face was flushed almost crimson from the heat, and sweat poured down his forehead and dripped down his cheeks; with his free hand he took a dipper of water from the cooling trough and dumped it on his head, to an accompaniment of giggles from Dorann.

Save for the eyes, Doria still looked like she was in her early twenties: her skin was still creamy smooth, her short blond hair shiny with youth. Beneath the mannish shirt, firm breasts bobbed invitingly. (Okay, I admit it: I like woman. Sue me.)

Doria slipped her free arm around my waist. "A-*hi*-ra's

get-ting *twit*-chy," she sang, leaning her head against my shoulder. "Too much coming-out-of-retirement, I think."

"Too much above-ground, maybe." Shaking his head to clear the last of the water from his face, he pulled the tongs out of the forge, and considered the color of the glowing ring before clamping it into place and hammering it down. *Wham. Wham.* "Truth to tell, we haven't been making enough trouble of late."

Doria's eyes twinkled. "Not major trouble."

The dwarf smiled. "Oh, that. Well."

The phrasing and timing were off, just a trifle; they weren't hinting that they'd been sleeping together, but up to some innocent deviltry.

The major-trouble theory was Ahira's theory, not mine. He thought that Lou Riccetti, the Engineer, was the real revolutionary, that the technological advances coming out of the Home colony in the Valley of Varnath were the real challenges to the established order, that everything that the rest of us did was just a distraction, a diversion to keep everybody's mind off the real game. Karl had agreed.

I'm not sure. What put an end to slavery in the United States? Was it the Union army, or the industrial revolution?

Me, I don't know; I only *act* like I know everything. I like things complicated, a lot of the time, but not always. Far as I'm concerned, we should have been sticking to the original plan: kill off the slave traders, thereby raising the price of human chattels to the point where they become prohibitively expensive.

So far, so good. It gets harder every year, but slaves get more expensive every year, too.

Part of the plan is to make it look doable, and that means staying alive. I've always thought that my personal survival is the centerpiece of a good plan.

I laughed. "Hey, we got half the world thinking that Karl's still alive and out there, somewhere."

"True." The dwarf pursed his thick lips for a moment. "I guess it still makes sense, though, to wait around here until we get some word about Mikyn." His broad face split in a smile. "We dwarves are patient folks."

"Shows." Sarcasm is wasted on Ahira. I don't mean

that he doesn't get it—he does—but it doesn't bother him. "Still . . . Mikyn's bitten off a big chunk; he might need help chewing."

"Possibly, but I'm in no rush." Ahira picked up another piece of wire stock, about six inches long, and tossed it into the forge. "If Ellegon's available, though, we might want to hop over to the coast and snoop around Ehvenor." He said it casually, as though it was something he was just considering, but he and I had been friends for too many years for it to go over my head. Ahira wanted to investigate, and was going to try to talk me into it.

He looked at me, and smiled weakly, then rubbed at his shoulder.

Doria has the bad habit of asking questions when she already knows the answer. "Perhaps you want to look up whoever did that to you as well?"

He shook his head. "Life's too short."

For a moment, a dark cloud passed over his face, and I knew that something important had happened to him after we split up outside of Ehvenor, but one thing I learned long ago about James Michael Finnegan is that he will talk about his problems only when he wants to. I doubt that there's anybody he trusts more than me, but even I would hear about it some other time, if ever.

"Life's too short, and so are you." Doria's mouth twitched. "I'm not sure that whatever's going on near Ehvenor is any of our concern."

It could have been anything, or nothing. There had been stories of some strange killings closer to Ehvenor, of animal mutilations that reminded me of ones we had in the western states on the Other Side, or more dragons issuing from Faerie, of other large magical creatures, most of whom had been gone from the Eren regions since the coming of Man.

Some of the stories were probably true—Jason and his crew had killed some huge creature while they were in the Shattered Islands. I didn't sound like anything I'd ever heard of.

He looked up at me. "What do you think?"

"I think Doria's right; I think we have enough to do without biting off some magical problem."

And, besides, he wasn't thinking it through. A magical problem wasn't something that just he and I could look into by ourselves.

In the center of the city of Ehvenor has long stood a building that has been an outpost of Faerie in the Eren regions—probably the only outpost of Faerie in the Eren regions. I'd seen it a couple of times, from a distance, a huge, glowing white building that seemed to have a subtly different shape every time you looked at. I hadn't tried to get close, and didn't want to. Call it the Faerie embassy, or the Faerie outpost, or whatever—call it whatever you want; it's nothing I had any need to rub up against. There's something about being around Faerie that drives people crazy, and the outskirts of Ehvenor are wild and crazy enough. Trust me.

I rubbed at the back of my left hand, at the place where a long-healed scar should have been, would have been, if I hadn't had a flask of healing draughts handy that last time.

He wasn't thinking it through—it wouldn't be just the dwarf and me. Add Jason, and we were still short. But enough of that for now. If we could put it off long enough, maybe we wouldn't have to do it. Let it be somebody else's problem.

"Think it over and let me know," he said.

"I can tell you now," I said. "It's none of our concern, and we have enough else to do."

"Perhaps," he said, Doria echoing him with a curt nod, Dorann holding out her arms for Doria to pick her up. It was a dismissal.

Doria, my baby daughter, and my best friend had been having a fine day without me.

I found Andrea Cullinane in her new workshop, unpacking.

Ideally, a wizard's workshop should have been built up against the wall of the keep, somewhere out of the way. I'd done that when Lou and I were laying out Home, and Karl and Andy had had something similar done in Biemestren, but Castle Cullinane was small, and most of the space within the walls was claimed.

Andrea had taken the last one in a row of continuous storerooms in the dungeon, a dank, cold end room of a series lit only by barred windows, simple unglazed openings, at the juncture of ceiling and wall. The only way in was through the storerooms, weaving through musty stacked barrels of wine, past plump bags of grain, ducking underneath green-crusted hams hanging from ceiling hooks, walking through the sunlight-striped dark and damp.

I don't like basements. Back home, back when I was a kid, I could always hear the scrabbling of rats every time I went downstairs. I remember going after one with a baseball bat once, but I swear it reared back and hissed at me and chased me the hell upstairs.

Cellars and dangeons on This Side tended to be worse than home—some special efforts I'd taken to cut down on the Endell rat population long justified what King Mahertalen of Endell used to pay me.

But there weren't any rats here. Or mice. Just musty, damp, cold silence.

I shivered.

I stopped at what passed for the door to her workshop: a sheet of undyed muslin hung across the opening, damp to the touch.

"Andrea? It's me."

A pause. "Just a moment, Walter," she said. I listened hard for the sound of syllables that I could only hear and not remember, but there weren't any. Just a rustling, as though of paper and then cloth. Then: "You might as well come in."

I pushed through the muslin, shuddering at the touch of it. The room was lit by several sputtering lamps in addition to the barred sunlight streaming down, although none of the light managed to dispel the gloom. Wooden boxes, some open, others still nailed shut, stood stacked on the stone floor or on tables. I don't care where you are—This Side, the Other Side—moving cuts into work seriously.

Skin damp from a sponge bath—some of the water was still heating in a blackened copper vessel over a lamp—she was just finishing buttoning her fly.

I would have been happy to help her with her clothes. On or off. Andrea Andropolous Cullinane: black hair, no longer salted with gray; high cheekbones; elegant nose; tongue playing with the lower full lip; slick black leather vest

37

cut high and matching black leather jeans that looked like they'd been applied with a fine brush (I admit it: I imprinted young on women in tight jeans)—all tight at full breasts and trim waist, leaving her long midriff bare.

I could see vague lines of stretch marks on her flat belly if I looked real hard. Not that I minded looking hard; even so, she looked *good*. Maybe too good.

I fingered the amulet hanging from the leather thong around my neck. The diamond-cut crystal was pulsing through a superficially reassuring progression of dull green and amber. No red, no indigo, no bright colors.

Which didn't mean anything, not really. Andy had built all of our amulets, and could have defeated any of them.

"How's the work coming?" I asked, with just the slightest overemphasis on "work."

She smiled. "Unpacking gets you dirty. No sense in getting clothes dirty, too."

Even if that meant working naked in the cold and damp of a dungeon? Just maybe, catching a quick glimpse of herself from a shiny surface or two wouldn't bother her.

I reached for her crystal ball, stopped myself, and then continued the motion at her quick nod of permission. A neat bit of equipment: its stand was a brass snake, impaled on the pole.

Colder to the touch than it should have been, and heavier. Like life itself, don't you know.

I looked into the perfect crystal, but all I saw was my own reflection, widened and distorted. I hadn't expected anything more, and didn't get it.

Just as well.

"We could try to get him out here by way of having him inspect Little Pittsburgh," she said.

It took me a moment to realize that Andy had picked up our conversation from the night before, about how to get Lou Riccetti, the Engineer, out for a visit. Lou hadn't been out of the Home settlement in years and years, and it would probably do him some good to travel a bit, see the world. Her new idea was to invite him to inspect Little Pittsburgh, the steel-making town in Barony Adahan, the next barony to the east.

Not a bad idea, but I hate that sort of parenthetical leap, when she assumes that I'll follow the train of thought back to the previous conversation.

"Possible," I said. I wasn't going to try to change Andy, not over something just irritating. Better to change the subject. "What have you been up to?"

Her smile was a little too knowing. "Sleeping. Dreaming. Working. Unpacking. The usual, you know?"

Her voice was just a hair too light, too casual, or maybe my own bad dream had oversensitized me, which would be a first; nobody's ever accused me of even being sensitive.

"Dreams?" I asked.

"Dreams," she said. "You know: stories that you tell yourself when you fall asleep. Sausages chasing bagels through tunnels, stuff like that."

"Is that all?" Look: my dreams are just dreams, Jungian archetypes cut open and dribbled into the creases of my mind. But I deal with magic and a wizard's dreams as little as I can.

"No," she said, raising a hand to dismiss the subject, then letting it drop. "No, that's not all. I've been having dreams of running through endless streets, always lost, always looking for a way out. Not good." She sighed. "But they're just dreams." She looked down at a book and stroked a short nail against its plain leather cover. "I probably shouldn't drink any wine before bed. It makes me dream too much." She looked down at the book again.

There is a way for a wizard to enter somebody else's dream. It's risky for both parties; it's also one of the classic ways for wizards to duel, for one to try to bend another's will.

She looked up at me. "What aren't you asking me?"

I pursued my lips. "I'm not sure whether you're worried about somebody attacking you through your dreams, or whether you're wishing there was another wizard around to dream with you."

Her smile might have not have been irresistible, but I wouldn't have wanted to bet. "Neither. I'm wondering something else entirely." She fingered the book. "I'm wondering why I'm getting interested in location spells again, in direction magic. I was already pretty good at them, but lately I've had a taste for the stuff." She toyed with a slim steel needle. "If you want to put this into a haystack, I can give you a good demonstration."

"Thank you, no."

That was not good; trying too hard to locate Karl—a wizard can bash his or her head against the wall of death as much as he or she pleases—was what had driven Andy to exhaustion, and she was just barely recovering. Alternately, perhaps it had driven her near madness, and she never would recover, but merely learn to hide it better.

I changed the subject. "Have you seen my wife today?"

She nodded. "She was somewhere around," she said, gesturing vaguely. "Is that why you're down here?" she asked. "What's going on?"

It felt like I was missing something, but I wasn't sure what. "I was just talking to Ahira. Just for the sake of discussion, how would you feel about a field trip?" I asked, hoping she would say no.

If we were going to look into whatever was happening on the edge of Faerie, we'd need somebody capable of working magic. If I could get Andy to turn us down, it shouldn't be a problem turning Ahira's notion off—there were perhaps half a dozen minor wizards in Holtun-Bieme, all of whom had the typcial wizard's nervousness about going in harm's way, none of whom I'd trust anyway. That would leave Henrad, formally Andy's apprentice, but Henrad had been out in the field with Ahira and me before; I suspected that he hadn't regained any taste for it. Things had gotten a bit messy for sensitive types like Henrad—and me, for that matter.

"Where?" She asked.

"Toward Faerie, maybe as far as Ehvenor."

"Check out the rumors?" she asked, just a touch too eager. At my nod, she smiled. "I'd love to." She reached over to her worktable and fingered a gem, working it between thumb and forefinger. "With some study, I could work up the spells that would let me take some readings and, just maybe, see what's going on. But it wouldn't be a good idea—I've been trying to cut down, and you know how that goes."

There Are Some Things Man Is Not Meant To Do. You can tell which they are because they're bad either for you or for somebody else. Nobody ever is better off by doing heroin, and doing magic seems to affect some people about the same way: they get hooked on it, go crazy for it. Stable magicians can hold themselves to a maintenance dose, but maybe Andy had overdone it, trying to Locate Karl. More likely grief—compounded by lack of exercise, food, and sleep—had overwhelmed her.

Still, she was looking good.

"You're wondering if it's a seeming," she said, standing hand on hip.

"No." Not if she had been working naked—a fascinating notion in and of itself. I didn't know enough about magic to know if her seeming would delude her as well as others, but it didn't matter. I knew Andrea: she wouldn't have been working without clothes if the sight of her real body bothered her, and even if she had put up a seeming, she would know what she really looked like.

I guess I didn't sound convincing: she shook her head, denying an accusation I hadn't made. "It's no seeming, Walter. Rest, food, exercise and—"

"The hair didn't come from exercise."

"—and a bit of dye," she said, taking a steap toward me. "I don't like the look of gray. Turns the men off." She reached up and touched my temple, just where I was going rather, well, handsomely gray. "It looks better on you."

I guess that was my cue to reach for her or something, but I'm not sure that either of us really wanted to. We'd been lovers—once, or twice, or five times, depending on what you're counting; I'd rather enjoy than count—almost twenty years before, and there was still something between us.

I was tempted, for a of reasons. Forget hormones for a moment—although I think I spend too much time thinking with my testicles for my own good. Andy and I had quite properly loved each other for years and years, and her husband, my friend, was dead, and maybe we needed to celebrate his life in a very private and personal way.

But not under the same roof as my wife.

It occurred to me that I was being noble, silly as that idea sounds, in trying to talk her into staying off the road. Both Andy and I knew what was likely to happen if and when

41

we were out in the field together, and perhaps I had just persuaded her, albeit indirectly, to stay safely home.

I took her hand in mine, her fingers soft and warm, and brought them to my lips.

"Old friend." I said, "it's good to see you looking good."

Screw nobility. Just remember that Walter Slovotsky is somebody who cares for and about his friends. Andy was, apparently for the first time since Karl was reported dead, doing well. I wasn't going to fuck around with that. In any sense.

Well, when you don't know what to do, it's probably a good idea to take a nap, eat a meal, or go to bed with somebody you like. Some combinations work well, too.

Kirah's and my rooms were empty; I stripped to the buff and stretched out under the down comforter and fell asleep.

The Dream Is the Same

THE NIGHTMARE IS AL-
ways the same:

*We're trying to make our escape from Hell, millions of us
streaming across the vast plain. Everybody I've ever loved is
there, along with faces familiar and strange.*

*Behind us, stretching across the horizon, there's a scream-
ing pack of demons, some in cartoony shapes, some that look
like misshapen wolves, all of whom have me scared so bad I
can hardly breathe the freezing air.*

*The exit is up ahead, the gold ladder up through the
clouds, and already there are people climbing it, a steady
stream that reaches up into the fluffy whiteness, and beyond. I
can't tell who's gone through, but I can only hope that my kids
are among them. Please let it be my kids.*

*Some have already climbed through the clouds, but there's
no way that all of us are going to: the demons are approaching
too quickly, and they're going to catch some of us.*

And then I see him: Karl Cullinane, Jason's father, stand-

*ing tall, face beaming, his hands, chest, and beard streaked
with blood and gore.*

"We're going to have to hold the perimeter," *Karl says.*
"Who's with me?"

*He smiles, as though he's been waiting his whole life for
this, the fucking idiot.*

"I'm with you," *somebody says.*

*Figures push out of the crowd, some bloodied, some bent.
Jefferson and Franklin work their way through, accompanied by a thick old black woman, her shoulder stooped from
too many years of hard labor, her hair bound back in a blue
kerchief. Or maybe it isn't Jefferson—his hair is kind of a dusty
red instead of white. Doesn't matter—he belongs here.*

"Please, Madame," *he says, his voice tight,* "go with the
others."

She snorts. "I only spent thirty-seven years on my knees
scrubbing white folks' floor to put food on the table fo' six
children, and put those six children through school." *Her fingers clench into fists.* "Think I let them get at my babies,
motherfucker?"

Franklin chuckles. "He begs your pardon, Madame."

Jefferson bows deeply. "Indeed, I do."

*Another man, massive brows looming over eyes that see
everything, his walrus mustache white as snow, bites his cigar
through, then discards it with a muttered oath.* "We can hold
it," *he said, his voice squeakier than I thought it would be.
But he sounds like himself, not Hal Holbrook.* "But we need
more."

*Karl looks at me—they all look at me: Jefferson, Twain,
Ahira, mad old Semmelweis, all of them look at me—his
bloody face puzzled.* "Walter? What are you waiting for?"

Then I wake up.

CHAPTER THREE

In Which Hiccups are Cured, Dinner is Eaten, And An Excursion is Arranged

The blazing evidence of immortality is our dissatisfaction with any other solution.

—RALPH WALDO EMERSON

Wanting it doesn't make it so. If it did, we'd all learn to want harder. I can already want quite vigorously, thank you very much.

—*WALTER SLOVOTSKY*

IT'S CALLED THE PATHET-
ic fallacy, but that's only the technical term; nothing pathetic about it.

I remember when I started personalizing things—I was about maybe five, or six.

It runs in the family. Stash—I thought of him as Daddy, then—still had the Big Car, the 1957 Buick Starfire 98 he had bought in Las Vegas, on his one-and-only trip there. It was among the last and absolutely the best of the standard American bigmobiles, a huge car pulled around by a three-hundred-horsepower V8, easily enough for the job—a monster engine, it would roar like a lion. Two-toned, black and yellow like a bumblebee, wraparound windshield, curved fenders, and a rear deck large enough to camp out on.

The Big Car had bench seats like a couch. It was big as a house, and when I rode in it, held down by the big-buckled seat belts Daddy and his friend Mike had spent a weekend putting in, I felt as safe as I did on a couch in my house.

Sometimes, people in Volkswagens would honk at us, derisively.

Daddy would just chuckle. "They don't get it, eh, Em?"

And then Mom would give out her sigh, the deep one that meant *here he goes again*, and then she'd say, "What don't they get?"

He'd say something like, "How this metal all around us protects us, how if we're in a crash with one of them little shitmobiles—"

"*Stash.* Shhh."

"—it's going to spray them all over the landscape, but old Beauty here's gonna protect us."

It was kind of a mantra for the two of them, although I doubt that either of them would ever have recognized the word.

They stopped repeating the mantra the day that some idiot in a blue Corvair plowed into us head-on as we were coming home, just about to pull into our driveway. We were jerked *hard*—windshield starred all over in an instant; full ashtray flung its contents into the air, blinding me until I could cry the ashes out; the buckle of my seatbelt left bruises on my right hip that flared purple and yellow for weeks—but we were okay. The worst hurt of us was Steve, my brother— he had gotten bashed against the back of the front seat—and all he had was a bloody nose.

The idiot in the Corvair got taken away in an ambulance, so badly battered that I can't to this day decide whether it was a man or a woman.

Blood was everywhere, and the harsh smells of gasoline and smoldering oil hung in the air. Mom, one hand on the back of Steven's neck, had taken him inside the house, but nobody thought to chase me away.

46

I waited with Daddy while the man with the wrecker hauled away our car. Our car.

God, it was mangled. It wasn't just that the fender and hood had been crumpled, and the glass broken, but the front wheels twisted out at funny angles, as though the axle had been smashed, and the body overhung the frame on one side. The wrecker man shook his head as he pulled the lever that lifted the front of the car up and into the air.

"Buy it new, Mr. Slovotsky?" he asked, over the futile protest of the metal.

"Stash," Daddy said, absently. "Everybody calls me Stash. Short for Stanislaus. And yeah," Daddy said. "I bought it new. Ten years ago." He patted the mutilated steel, then pulled his hand away as though embarrassed.

The wrecker man shook his head once, quickly, jerkily, as though to say, *It's okay. I understand.* "Yeah. Good machines. Wish they still made them," he said, starting to turn away.

"It's just a machine."

"Sure, Stash." The wrecker man smiled. He didn't believe Daddy any more than I did.

Or any more than Daddy believed himself. Stash ran blunt, gentle fingers through my hair. "I drove your mother to the hospital in this car when we were having you, Cricket."

"Can they fix it, Daddy?" I asked, still clutching at my side, rubbing at my hip.

He shook his head, tears he didn't notice working their way down through the five-o'clock shadow on his cheeks.

"No," he said. "It's broken too bad to fix. But you and Steven and Mom are okay, Cricket, and that's what matters. That's the only damn thing that ever matters." He gripped my hand tight.

"No, I'm not okay," I said, probably whining. "I'm *hurt.*"

"Yeah. Just hurt. Bruised maybe. And I'm real sorry about that, Cricket, honest I am, but we all could be dead, dead, dead."

Muttering something in Polish, he let go of my hand and gently stroke the car's metal flank as the wrecker pulled it

47

away from the curb. I never learned much Polish, and I don't remember the words, but I know what they meant.

They meant: "Thank you, thou good and faithful servant." We watched until the wrecker turned the corner and the Big Car was gone, and then we just stood there and watched a long while longer, until our eyes were dry.

When I woke, Kirah was across from the bed, watching me. I had already been vaguely aware of her, but, suspicious though it is, my hindbrain didn't want to wake me for that.

A bit spooky: she is an overstuffed armchair by the window, her legs curled up beneath her, the sun through the bars striping her face in gold and dark. Only one corner of her mouth was visible, upturned in a smile that could have been friendly or forced. I couldn't tell; my wife learned her dissimulation skills before she ever met me.

"Good afternoon, darling," she said. She was sewing: white cloth heaped in her lap, needle darting in and out.

I stretched, then wiped at my eyes. "Hi there." I took a pair of shorts from the bureau next to the bed and slipped into them before I levered myself out of bed and padded across the carpet to bend over—slowly, gently, carefully—and kiss her, careful to clasp my hands behind me. She couldn't help it; and I had to.

She tossed her head, perhaps for display, perhaps in nervousness; I backed off a half-step and was saddened at the way the tension flowed out of her.

"Sleep well?" she asked me, in her ever-so-slightly-halting English.

"Nah. I've never been very good at it," I said. It was an old joke between us. Sometimes, when the center falls apart, you hold onto the old forms.

"You cried out a couple of times," she said. "I couldn't make it out."

That was just as well. I switched to Erendra. "Bad dream," I said.

I went to the washbasin and splashed some water on my face and chest, then toweled off my face in front of the closet while I picked out some clothes for a semi-formal supper, quickly settling on a short, loose-cut jacket of brown and silver over a ruffled tan shirt, and taupe trousers with silver piping down the seam. I like my formal clothes comfortable, and besides, the cut of the sleeves kept the throwing knife strapped to my left arm handy. Not the sort of thing I've ever needed at a formal dinner, but you never know.

I buckled my formal sword belt tightly around my waist, decided that it fit fine, then unbuckled it and slung the belt over a shoulder.

"Where have you been keeping yourself today?" I asked.

She shrugged. "Around." She bit off a thread and slipped the needle into the cloth, then carefully set down her work before she stood and came to me, gathering her long, golden hair at the nape of her neck.

She stopped just in front of me, not quite touching.

It wasn't just the dress, although that was spectacular: Kirah was in a long gown of white lace over red silk, scooped low in front and cut deeply in back, revealing a lot of soft, creamy skin. I swear, my wife was more beautiful every year. There's a richness of beauty that can come on in a woman's thirties, after all the traces of baby fat and innocence have gone, but before the years have dragged the elasticity from her skin and muscle.

And it was all for show.

No, that wasn't fair. "Really, where were you?"

"I spent the morning helping Andrea."

So, that was what Andy had been keeping from me. I didn't like the sound of any of this, but kept my disapproval off my face, I hope.

Andy was *supposed* to be keeping her use of magic to a minimum, on Doria's orders. Andy had spent far too much energy in her obsessive need to try to Locate Karl, and it's not good for humans, wizard or not, to be around magic a whole lot. Power is dangerous, even when you think you're controlling it.

Now, my own opinion was that Doria was being a bit too much of a Jewish mother, something she was only half equipped for. But even if Doria was right about the danger, it should be relatively safe for Kirah: she couldn't read magic. A page out of Andrea's spellbook would be the same blurry mess to her that it was to me. If you don't have the genes for it, you can't do wizard magic; if you don't have the right relationship with the gods or powers or faerie, you can't do clerical magic, like Doria used to do.

She cocked her head to one side. "I was just starting to debate whether or not to wake you for dinner, or just let you sleep through." She smiled as she took a step back, then one closer, every move a step in a dance.

"Dinner soon?"

She shook her head. "Not for a while yet. But you always take so long to wake up."

I reached for her and felt her stiffen in my arms. "Sorry." I let my arms fall to my side.

She put her arms around me and laid her head against my chest. That's okay under the rules, sometimes. "No. I'm sorry, Walter."

"You can't help it." I started to bring my arms up, but caught myself. It wasn't her fault. I had to keep reminding her of that.

My hands clenched. It wasn't her fault. It wasn't her fault that if I held her, she'd tense, and if I reached for her she'd scream.

But it wasn't mine, either. I've always done my best by her, but whatever I am, I'm not a healer of psyche and spirit. At best, I'm an observer of psyche and spirit.

" 'This, too, shall pass,' " she said, quoting me accurately, not Abe Lincoln inaccurately. I used to say it when she was pregnant, kind of as a mantra. Kind of funny, really: I'm always politically incorrect. Here, for suggesting that women ought to have roughly the same rights as men; on the Other Side, for—only rarely, rarely, and usually with bad results—pointing out that pregnant women go crazy for about a year, or longer.

Maybe it's not their fault. Maybe nothing's nobody's fault.

"Sure." It could happen. I'm skeptical, mind, but it could happen.

Slowly, carefully, I put my arms around her, not quite holding her, and kissed her on the side of the neck. She took it well: she flinched, but she didn't cry out or push me away.

Some victory, eh? I let my arms drop. "I'll see you at dinner."

It hadn't always been this way. Back in the beginning we'd spent more time in bed than out, in my memory if not possible in reality.

Hell, our first time had been within a couple of hours after Karl and I had pulled her out of the slaver wagon and freed her, along with the rest of that bunch of slaves. Like I always said, this business has always had its fringe benefits.

Even in the early days, though, there had been hints— times when I reached for her in the night and she would shrink away, only to explain that she was just tired, other times when I would come up behind her and put my arms around her affectionately and she would stifle a scream, only to smile in apology for being startled so easily.

But those times had been few and far between, then.

It had come on slowly, few and far between becoming occasional becoming not infrequent and then frequent so gradually until I realized that we hadn't made love for almost a year, and that she couldn't bear to be touched.

I needed a drink.

I found a shiny gray ceramic bottle of Holtish brandy and a pair of earthenware brandy mugs in the sitting room on the second floor.

Well, the staff called it the sitting room—I thought of it as a brag room. The rug covering the floor was a patchwork of pelts, the walls decorated with heads of various beasts that various Furnael barons had killed: a few seven-point bucks, several decent wolf- and boar-heads, and one huge brown bear, its jaw opened wide, yellow teeth ready to chomp. I doubt that the teeth were as polished and shiny in real life as they were now.

Among all the predators, high up on one wall, was one small rabbit—the whole thing, mounted on a plaque sideways, stretched out as though frozen in mid-bound. I'm sure that there's a family story behind the last, but I've never found out what it is.

A bit spooky of a place, but not because the animals looked like they were ready to come alive. They didn't; Bie-

51

mish taxidermy was substandard, and there's never been great glasswork in most of the Eren regions. Instead of glass eyes, there were the here-traditional white spheres of polished bone. It was like having a room full of little Orphan Annie's pets staring down at me. Takes some getting used to. Brandy helps.

Only trouble was, I had started hiccuping, and I hate drinking with the hiccups. Gets up the nose.

I had quickly gotten a fire going in the fireplace, and had settled myself comfortably into a low chair in front of the flickering flames when Doria tapped a fingernail against the doorframe.

She had dressed for dinner in a long purple dress made from a cloth I always think of as velour, although I know that's not the right name for it. The top was fitted tightly from low-cut bosom of her hips, where a pleated skirt flared out underneath a woven golden belt, the golden theme picked up by filigree on the bosom and arms of her dress and the strap of her pouch.

"Well?" she said.

"Nice." I said. "Pull up a throne."

She looked at the two brandy mugs warming on the flat stones in front of the fire.

"Expecting me?" she said, as I stretched out a lazy arm and gave each mug a half-turn.

I hiccuped as I shook my head. "Nah. But it doesn't cost anything to heat two mugs. You never know when a friend's going to stop for a drink."

"Or to cure your hiccups." She smiled as she folded herself into the chair and leaned her head against the high back.

"Yeah." I was a bit sarcastic.

She pulled what looked like a piece of quartz out of her pouch. "Suck on this for awhile."

I shrugged and popped it into my mouth. Sweet—"Rock candy," I said, from around the piece. Demosthenes, eat your heart out.

"Very clear, Watson."

I raised an eyebrow, as though to say, *And this is going to cure the hiccups?*

She nodded. "Ninety percent. Hiccups are caused by an

electrolyte imbalance in the blood; sends the diaphragm into spasms. Usually acidosis. Sugar or salt will push things the other way; if this doesn't work, it means you're alkalotic, and a bit of lemon will do. Hang on a moment."

I was going to argue with her, but the hiccups went away, probably of their own volition. "Where did you hear about this? From the Hand?"

"No. It's an Other Side thing. Friend of mine name Diane. Don't know if you ever met her."

"Mmmm . . . maybe. I don't know."

"Nah; you never met her." She smiled. "You'd remember.—How are the mugs?"

"Hang on a sec." The mugs were warm enough: just this side of too hot to hold, the ideal temperature for drinking Holtish brandy. I uncorked the bottle and poured each of us a healthy slug. I was going to get up and give hers to her, but she rose instead and settled herself down on the arm of my chair, her arm around my shoulders. She smelled of soap and flowers.

"L'chaim," I said, almost gargling on the Hebrew *ch*-sound.

That earned a smile. "L'chaim," she repeated, then drank. I did, too. The brandy burned my throat and warmed my belly. Not a bad trade.

"Something bothering you?" she asked.

"Just the usual," I said, keeping my voice light. "You're not the only one who worries, you know."

She chuckled. "What are you worrying about now? Your chances with the upstairs maid?" Her fingers played gently with my hair.

I faked a shudder. "Have you *seen* the upstairs maid?"

"Seriously."

I shrugged, gently enough not to dislodge her. "I shouldn't complain. Things are going well. Andy's looking a lot better, and the dwarf is pretty much healed up. Jason's a good kid. Greener than the Hulk, but—"

She silenced me with a finger to my lips. "We are going to get to Kirah, aren't we?"

I didn't answer.

Doria waited. She was better at waiting than I was.

"Not her fault," I said, finally. "What would you call it, post-traumatic stress disorder?"

She shrugged. "Two years of psychology classes, and you'd have me be the local psychiatrist?"

"I won't tell the AMA." I raised my little finger. "Pinky swear."

"Well, there is that." She considered the problem as she sipped, then dismissed it with a shrug. "It doesn't matter, Walter. Slapping a label on it doesn't mean you understand it, or know how to fix it. She's in bad shape . . . or at least your relationship is." Doria sipped, then sighed.

I rasied an eyebrow. "I didn't know that it showed. You've still got enough power to detect it?"

"No." She shook her head. Had the Matriarch stripped her of all of her power, or were there a few spells lefts in the back of her soul, awaiting need? Doria wouldn't say. "But I always thought of spells as a way of augmenting other sensitivities, not as a substitute. How long has it been for the two of you?"

"Since what?"

One side of her mouth twisted into a wry frown. "Guess."

"Hey. I don't tell. Remember?"

"Yes." She smiled. "Usually."

I thought of the last time, and tried to forget it, remembering instead one wild, warm night at Home, years ago, shortly after Karl and I had gotten back from a raid. I think it was the second night—the first was Karl's Day Off, so it must have been. We'd left Janie, then just a baby, with Karl and Andy, and taken blankets away from the settlement, through the woods, and up the side of a hill. We had gotten incredibly drunk on a small bottle of wild huckleberry wine, and made love under the stars all night long.

I mean, really, no shit, my hand to God: all night long.

If I close my eyes, I can still see her, her hair floating in the breeze above me, framed in starlight. . . .

But that was a long time ago, in another country, and the wench would rather be dead than warm in my arms again.

I changed the subject. "Andy's looking a lot better, lately. I don't think it's a seeming."

Doria sat silently for a moment, then smiled, dropping the matter of Kirah and me. "It's amazing what a bit of exercise and food and general activity can do, eh? Not to mention laying off the magic."

"She—" I stopped myself.

"She hasn't given it up?" Doria shrugged. "I'm not surprised. The disease model never *quite* worked for alcoholism, and putting it all on magical addiction probably isn't exactly right."

"I was surprised to hear her talk like that. Doria had been beating the drum for keeping Andy the hell out of her workshop, by anything this side of force.

"But it's *close*," she said. "I wish the rest of you would believe me. There's a seduction there, a constant temptation. I was an awfully chubby girl," she said, as though changing the subject, although she wasn't. "I finally managed to, most of the time, keep my weight down to something acceptable by controlling what and how I ate. Just so much—and always so much; if you starve yourself now, you'll binge later—and no more."

I took her hand in mine and kissed it. Gently, gently; you always have to touch Doria gently, and that's the way it's always been, and one of the things I've always liked about her. "You had other problems, but you've come a long way, kid."

She sighed. "One would hope so." Her fingers toyed with my collar and then with my mustache. "We'd better go down to dinner, eh?"

The trials of the life of the ruling class are something you learn to bear up with after a while, even if you're only a member of the ruling class by association. Everything's a trade-off. You tend to eat well, but you can be interrupted for or dragooned to help out on any of a number of things.

In this case, I was helping entertain two newly arrived village wardens on a formal visit. Not a bad idea, really, having the village wardens come in, to be wined and dined; I'm glad I'd suggested it to Jason.

We took our seats formally around the table: Jason at the head; Andrea at the foot; Ritelen, the senior of the two wardens, at Jason's right; then Kirah, Dorann, and Janie down the side; Doria, me, Aeia, Bren Adahan, and finally Benen, the other warden, down the other, giving each warden a seat of honor at the right of either Jason or Andrea. It gave Kirah a chance to engage in some formal chitchat with Ritelen, a barrel-chested, walrus-mustached man, as only she and Jason were within quiet conversation range of him.

It looked silly, is what it did. The formal dining table was meant to seat thirty, and less than a dozen people were spread too thinly.

Personally, I would have liked to set us down in two clumps, one at each end. Four to six is about the right number for a dinner conversation. Any more and the group will tend to split into several conversations, and most people will have the deep suspicion that they're in the wrong one. (Not me, mind. The conversation with me in it is by definition the most interesting.)

Or it can turn into a monologue.

Naturally, it didn't turn into a monologue from either of the two village wardens; that would have been too sensible, and too interesting. I would have liked to hear more about the wheat rot they were having in Teleren village, and would have wanted to pitch both of the wardens on the value of mung bean sprouts as a nutritional supplement.

But it didn't work out that way. Over the soup course—a thick, meaty turtle soup, heavily laden with cracked pepper and pieces of carrot that were just barely firm to the bite, served with hot rolls, still warm, firm, and chewy-crusted from the steamer; U'len does good work—Bren Adahan was holding forth on some fine point of horsemanship, Aeia following with rapt attention, the rest listening with a reasonable simulation.

"—the trick is to get the animal not to anticipate, but to react instantly. Any idiot can canter a horse at a fence and find himself taking it without wanting to; most good horsemen can anticipate early that the horse is going to want to go; but for the very best, nothing happens until you tell it to. I remember a time . . ."

Aeia and Janie paid very close attention, and all of the other women were listening almost as closely.

Except for Andrea. Gorgeous in a long dress of jet and crimson, she tented her fingers in front of her mouth and pretended to listen closely.

I think I understand the connection between women and horses, but I don't care for it. It's almost sexual—or maybe I should drop the "almost," and no, I don't mean any crass joke about women and stallions. (In fact, all of the women I know have the sense to stay the hell away from stallions, as do I. An uncut male horse goes absoluteley apeshit if he smells a mare in heat, or gets too close to a menstruating woman.)

Look: I don't have anything against horses. During the last twenty years I've walked thousands of miles and ridden easily twice as much, and I wouldn't want it the other way around, honest. I'd prefer cars, and I *much* prefer traveling on Ellegon when he's available, but I don't have anything against horses, not really.

On the other hand, they're remarkably dumb animals. They don't have any sense at all—you can ride them to death if you push them too hard, and you don't dare get too attached to them, because when it all hits the fan you *have* to be able to leave them behind. I once spent a full day hiding crouched in a rain barrel, breathing shallowly through a piece of tubing. I don't think a horse would have fit in there with me, and if I hadn't been willing to abandon my horse—a sweet little mare who used to nuzzle me affectionately, like a dog; I hope she found a caring owner—at a moment's notice, I would have been dead, dead, dead.

So don't talk to me about horses.

Particularly not about taking a fence when you didn't intend to. I almost broke my fucking neck.

Ahira's lips quirked into a smile. "Possibly we could talk about something else at dinner?" he asked, as U'len entered, bearing the next course on a silver salver.

"By all means, talk instead of eating my fine capons," U'len said. She was an immense woman, all sweat and fat and muscles, an almost permanent sneer on her face.

I'm not impressed with the local tradition of serving the meat course before the fish course, but I was impressed with the three birds resting on the huge serving plate: they were huge, plump, and brown, starred with cloves and bits of garlic and onion, crisply skin still crackling from the oven.

They smelled like heaven ought to.

"Take it easy on me," Jason said, easily slipping into his father's role as U'len's verbal sparring partner. "I know good food when I taste it. We'll see if this is."

"Hmph." She set the bird platter down in front of Jason, then began to wield the carving knife and fork herself.

Aeia was unusually lovely tonight in a ruffled blouse over a long, bright Melawei sarong that left her left leg bare from ankle to mid-thigh. She smiled over her wine glass at me, earning me a glare from Bren Adahan, but no particular glance from my wife.

Sit still, Bren, I thought. *You're going to make life difficult for all of us.*

"What do you think of the wine?" she asked.

I took another sip. "Not bad." It would have been nice to sit close to her, to feel her leg against mine, to feel a woman press harder against me instead of pull away.

I drank some more wine. A bit too tannic for my taste, but it was still young—the Biemish style of winemaking gives you wine that needs long cellering, although the result can be worth it. Winemaking was one of the things Bieme had to give up during the war years, and almost all of what the Furnaels had put down had been drunk during the siege. In the whole country there was nothing really ready to drink.

U'len started carving. I don't know about you, but I've always had a fondness for watching anybody do just about anything they're good at.

Blade flashing in the candlelight, in less time than it takes to tell it she had the first bird cut up, Eren-style: skin cut into palm-sized squares, each topped with a spoon-molded hunk of stuffing; breast sliced into thick chunks; thigh separated from drunkstick; top part of the drunkstick neatly removed from the meat; back and the rest of the carcass on its way to the kitchen for soup stock, carried with a swagger by the fat old woman as a pair of her assistants brought in the turnip greens and chotte to accompany the bird.

While she started in on carving the second bird, Jason speared a piece of skin and stuffing, and took a tentative bite.

"Well?" she asked, not pausing in her slicing, no trace of deference or even respect in her harsh voice. "How is it?"

"Not very good," he said.

I thought Benen's jaw was going to drop off and fall on his plate, although Ritelen, having figured out what was going on, hid a smile behind his walrus mustache and napkin.

"It isn't, *eh?*" U'len set her massive fists on her even more massive hips.

He looked at her for a long moment. "Nah. We, er, can save everybody else the, uh, problem of eating this. I'll just take care of it all."

"Uncle Jason's ly-ing, ly-ing," Dorann chanted, silenced momentarily, a moment later, by a mouthful of stuffing, Kirah's timing is sometimes very good.

U'len had served out the fish course—stream trout baked in sorrel and cream; okay, but I know a much better way to cook fresh trout—and was in the process of serving dessert when Kethol, Durine, and Pirojil walked in.

Not exactly the three musketeers. Kethol: lean, raw-boned, red-headed; Pirojil, chunky and pleasantly ugly; Durine, a quiet bear of a man. They had been Karl's surviving companions in what was becoming known as the legendary Last Ride, and two of the three of them had been with Jason in the search for Karl, the one that had turned up, well, me.

Pirojil spoke for the three of them. "Baron, we got a peasant outside, says he wants to see you. There's been some trouble out toward Velen."

I guess it was the night for Benen to be shocked, first at three soldiers interrupting the baron's formal dinner without so much as a with-your-permission; second, at the reason they'd interrupted the dinner; and third, at the way Jason was already out of his chair, and buckling on his swordbelt as he walked toward the far entryway.

"Well, let's see what the problem is," he said. "Baron Adahan, please take my place."

I would have been impressed with Jason's courtesy to the Holt, but I sort of figured it was more an attempt to keep Adahan's nose out of the problem than to avoid getting it out of joint.

"Be right with you," Tennetty said from around a final bite of trout, seemingly unbothered; Tennetty's never been much for desserts. She stood, reflexively feeling for the hilt of her knife before belting her sword about her waist.

I wasn't disposed to accompany them—the three musketeers knew enough to search the peasant, and Tennetty was along. Besides, I was looking forward to U'len's raspberry tart, even though the seeds always get caught between my teeth. But Jason was leaving, and Ahira was following him, so I did, too.

I guess my own sense of egalitarianism would have called for inviting him in, but nobody had asked.

We met with him in the courtyard, under the watchful eye of the keep guard, a dozen flickering torches, and a starry night sky.

The peasant wasn't what I'd expected, although I should have thought it through. Velen was a good two days' walk away—the peasant farmer had sent a son, not gone himself. Yes, he was short, dirty, smelly, and not too bright, and not so stupid as to not be nervous. He knuckled his forehead incessantly as he spoke, grunting out his complaint that somebody or something had killed his father's cow.

He actually wept.

Yeah. A cow. Not a big deal, right? Wrong. To a one-plot, two-cow peasant family, it probably represented the difference between getting by and starving. A good milk cow would go a long way to keeping a small family fed, between the milk and a calf every year or two. Cows aren't a terribly efficient way to deal with edible grain—if you know enough about balancing proteins, vegetarianism is efficient by an order of magnitude—but a lot of what they can get by on just fine isn't edible for humans.

Grazing rights on some of the baron's pasture wouldn't help out the peasant's family. Peasants don't eat grass.

"Sounds like wolves to me," Jasons said. His lips twisted into a frown. "The population went way up during the war."

Ruling classes are good for something; keeping the number of other predators low is one of them. In Bieme, it's also one of the traditional jobs of the baron.

Tennetty shrugged. "We can handle wolves," she said. "The four-legged kind, or the two-legged. Shotguns all around?"

Durine nodded. "Not for chasing them down, but for chasing them away."

"Took the cow out of his paddock?" Ahira shrugged. "Possible." He looked at me and raised an eyebrow about halfway, spreading his palms just so.

I pursued my lips and shook my head. "Nah."

Ahira nodded.

"You don't think it's a wolf pack?" Jason was irritated.

I sighed. "You missed it. Ahira just asked me if I thought it was too likely to be a trap, or if we ought to go out and take a look at the corpse before the wolves finish it off."

"You did?" he said, turning to the dwarf.

Ahira nodded. "Actually, I did." He smiled. "Pretty disgusting, eh?"

Jason frowned; I smiled.

It happens with old friends: you spend a lot of time with somebody over a number of years, you have some of the same discussions over and over again. Then one day you realize that when you're doing some things, or talking about others, you're leaving out most of the words, or even all of the words. You don't need to guess how they're going to deal with a situation: you *know*. A gesture, a word, or even less than that—and it's clear.

But that's not something you can explain to a seventeen-year-old, even a very responsible, precocious seventeen-year-old. They won't believe you.

In this case, though, it was easy. It wasn't necessary for Ahira and me to involve ourselves in an ordinary wolf hunt, but if it was something else, it could be connected to those stories of things coming out of Faerie, and anything involving magic could involve Arta Myrdhyn, and us.

Look: I don't know why Arta Myrdhyn—yes, *the* Arta Myrdhyn of tale and legend—sent us across. It's even barely possible he did it so that we'd open the Gate for his return, as he claimed. Me, I'm skeptical. I guess it's partly that I don't like people I don't like pushing me around—my friends do enough to that. I've never liked jigsaw puzzles, and like even less being a piece in one.

Or I'm afraid that the universe might do to me what I was always tempted to do: bash the piece into place, even if it doesn't quite fit.

Tends to be hard on the piece.

The trouble with life is that none of it comes with a manual, and you always have to decide what involves you and what doesn't. After more than twenty years of friendship, I knew that this was the sort of thing that Ahira would sleep better after checking out, and that he wouldn't want to sleep until we were closer to checking it out.

As usual, he was nagging me into doing something that I had misgivings about.

Well, we were trying to teach the kid about life and such, so I might as well continue the lesson.

"Equipment," I said to Ahira. "Tell him what I think we'll bring."

He nodded, and beckoned Jason over, whispering in his ear.

Actually, this might be a bit tough.

"Okay," I said. "Figure one flatbed wagon and a team to draw it." That was easy; everybody knows I prefer a padded bench to a hard saddle. "Rations, and standard road gear—just grab a couple of packs in the stables. But we'll take a quick run up to the supply closet and grab one net hammock each." They were of elven silk, light as a feather and strong. Given the right geometry, I'd much rather sleep a few feet off the cold, cold ground than on it. Or in it, for that matter. "Signal rockets, five fast horses—just in case. Boar spears, grenades, shotguns plus personal weapons for all. But I bet he forgot the sprouting box."

Ahira's smile widened. "A lot you know. I told him two."

"Fine." One of my less-than-crazy theories is that for people eating peasant food anywhere—which is largely pick-your-starch-and-beans—taking some of those beans and sprouting them is going to increase the nutrition they're getting significantly, at little effort and no extra cost.

Hence the sprouting box. Johnny Appleseed, eat your heart out. "That isn't all."

"So I told him." Ahira laughed. "Go on."

"All that's too utilitarian—you told him to be sure to throw a couple of extra blankets the flatbed, so I don't have to rest my tender butt on a hard bench. Add a *clean* teapot, and some tea. And a bottle of Riccetti's Best." I don't tend to get drunk on the road, but an occasional swig of good, smooth corn whiskey before bed cuts the dirt real well.

Ahira nudged the boy. "See?"

Jason frowned. I think he was looking for the trick, but there wasn't one, other than twenty years of being friends. I'm tricky, honest, but I hadn't set this up.

Tennetty snickered.

The peasant wasn't following any of this, which was reasonable—a lot of the conversation had been in English, and he probably only spoke Erendra.

Jason turned to him. "You can show us where?"

"Yes, Lord, I think—certainly come daylight."

Jason beckoned to Durine. "Find Maduc dinner, and a place to sleep for the night, see that he's fed and ready to leave at dawn."

"Yes, Baron Fur—Cullinane."

"Yup," Jason said, with smile. "Baron Furcullinane, that's me. Your other cow? How do you know it's safe?"

A good deduction: the peasant, young or old, wouldn't leave his only other cow endangered for the day and a half to it had taken him to walk in.

"My father keeps it in the hut with them, Lord."

Ahira looked at me, spreading his hands. Durine led the peasant away.

"You'd better go get some sleep, Jason," I said. "Going to be a long day for you, tomorrow." Andrea was busy sneaking up behind us in the dark, trying not to be noticed, so I didn't notice her. Let her have her fun.

"You, too."

Ahira shook his head. "Nope. It's a bright enough night. Walter and I are heading out now."

"Missing a night's sleep," I said.

He shrugged. "Won't be the first time. We'll say good

63

night to the family and be off." He turned to Tennetty. "You coming along?"

"Sure." Tennetty sighed. "Probably won't be anything to kill." She turned to me. "How do you expect to find it in the dark?"

Ahira shrugged for me. "We won't be there before dawn, and by then it'll be well marked. Buzzards." He thought about it for a moment. "The three of us ought to do."

Jason cleared his throat. "And how about me?"

I smiled. "But you're leaving tomorrow, aren't you?"

He spread his hands. "Fine. I'm being taught a lesson. May one inquire as to what it is?"

"I thought it was obvious." Ahira sighed. "When we're *here*, you are Baron Cullinane, and we're guests in your house. Fine. No problem. But once we step outside that house, or even plan on doing it, we're not your guests, or your servants, or anything less than your partners."

"Make that 'senior partners,' " I added. "And add 'teachers.' The dwarf and I don't just have a few years on you; there's a lot of experience, too."

He stood silent for a moment, and I honestly wondered how it would go. I mean, when I was seventeen, I didn't take being chastened in public all that well.

Come to think of it, I still don't. I don't even take being corrected in private all that well.

"Have a good trip," he said, turning and walking away.

Tennetty spat on the ground. "Asshole." I was curious about whether that was addressed to Jason or to Ahira and me, but I didn't ask. Don't ask a question if you don't want to hear the answer.

"Not fair," Andrea Cullinane said from behind me. "But thank you."

I jumped a bit, as though she had startled me. Tennetty cocked her head suspiciously, and Ahira didn't have to.

I chuckled. "I didn't do it so you could have him around a bit longer. I did it for my own tender skin. If Jason's going to be working with us, he's going to have to be reliable." Besides, he had the village wardens to keep entertained.

And maybe I was still remembering that the boy had once bolted when it counted—okay, right after it counted—

64

and that had brought a whole world of trouble down on a lot of heads.

She was in her new leathers again, covered by a matching black leather trailcoat, its surface dark without being glossy. She had a bag slung across one shoulder, and beneath the open buttons of the coat, a flintlock pistol was holstered on each hip, the one on the left hip butt-forward.

"What are you dressed up for?" I asked, as though I didn't know.

Her eyes went all vague and distant, a look I didn't like. "I need to get out of here; I'm going stircrazy." She shook her head as though to clear it.

"There've been stories," she went on, "about things coming out a Faerie, about animals bit in half. And then there was that huge thing, whatever is was, that Jason and Tennetty ran into on one of the Shattered Islands. You may need me."

"Wolf pack sounds a lot more likely."

Magical creatures and humans don't tend to get along, and few at all remain in the Eren regions. There are always stories, but most of the time they're just stories. I've been in on the creation of enough legends to know what nonsense they can be.

She cocked her head to one side. "What if it isn't just a wolf pack? What will you do then?"

What the fuck did she *think* I'd do? "I'll run like hell, that's what I'll do."

I had worked this all through earlier in the day, and everything had come down on the side of leaving Andy out of it. Forget Doria's theories.

Look: given the world we live in and the situations we've been in, it's no coincidence that a lot of the women I know have been raped. Relative freedom from the likelihood of that kind of assault is a relatively modern invention—in most societies, the only question is who, other than the woman, has been affronted. (It's customary for us to talk about the Other Side as though everything worked right and well there, but in the country where I was born, assaults are a crime against the state, not the person, and it's the state that decides whether or not to prosecute it. Yeah, I know.)

Everything leaves scars. Kirah has her troubles; it turned

65

Tennetty into a barely controlled psychopath; Doria came damn close to ending up permanently between the lettuce and the broccoli, if you catch my drift; and while I think she's made the best adjustment of them all, there's a trace of madness around the edges of Aeia's eyes. Just like the trace around Andrea's.

No. One crazy, Tennetty, was bad enough on the field—even if we were only going to be chasing down a few skinny, scared wolves. We didn't need somebody else marginal, and we particularly didn't need a borderline magic addict. Okay, maybe she wasn't a magic addict; Doria is perfectly capable of being wrong.

But Andy had been out of the field for years and years, so after all my talk about how we can practically read each other's mind, I feel like an idiot for having to report that when Ahira said, "Okay. Let's say a quick goodbye and get out of here," it came as a complete surprise to me.

And not a pleasant one, either.

CHAPTER FOUR

In Which I Think Unwise Thoughts and Say Some Farewells

The course of true love never did run smooth.
—WILLIAM SHAKESPEARE

Nothing is more annoying than somebody who has a keen eye for the obvious.
—WALTER SLOVOTSKY

I MANAGED TO SAY goodbye to all my family, starting with the youngest one.

Doria Andrea takes after her father—she's a late-night kind of Slovotsky, like me and Stash, unlike Emma and Steve and her mother and sister—but when you're that age, staying up late means making it through a long dinner, and that's about all.

"Sleep well, little prosecutor," I said as I tucked her in, in a private joke that only the originals among us would have gotten, and nobody but me found even mildly funny.

D.A. wrapped her little arms tight around my neck as I leaned over. "Come back soon, Daddy. Please."

"Will do," I said, gently prying myself away. I rested my hand on her head for a moment, on the soft baby-hair that was getting more golden each day, like her mother's. "G'night, Sweetheart."

Janie was waiting for me out in the hall, leaning against the wall. She started to say something, but cut off when I put a finger to my lips. I shut the door gently and followed her over to the landing.

"Trouble is, Daddy dearest," she said, ignoring my grimace, "you're getting *too* tricky in your old age."

"Oh?" I asked, trying to sound casual. I *hate* it when she calls me "Daddy dearest."

"You've managed to teach my boyfriend not to push you around—to not *try* to push you around. But it looks to me like you gave up a cheap little dry run that would have been good for the lot of you. Doesn't sound like a good trade to me." She shrugged. "If my opinion counts for anything."

Since that had been bothering the hell out of me anyway, I found it as hard to disagree with her as it would have been to admit that it was wrong, so I didn't do either.

"It counts, kid," I said, hugging her for only a moment.

She smiled. Why is it that my daughters' smiles brighten the whole world?

"Be good," I said.

Kirah was sitting in the overstuffed armchair, a lamp at her left elbow, her sewing set aside as she worked on some knitting or tatting or whatever; I don't know the difference and I don't much care.

"You're going," she said, her voice flat, as though to say, *I won't ask you not to go.*

"So it seems." I smiled. "Hey, not to worry. I know how to duck."

She forced a smile. Either that, or her real smile and her forced smile had started to look the same to me. I should have been able to tell, after all these years. I really should.

"That's good," she said.

It getting chilly out, and it was already chilly in. I shrugged out of my finery and padded over to the closet, dressing quickly in undershorts, black leather trousers, blousy black cotton shirt, and—lest I look like Johnny Cash—a long brown cloak, fastened loosely at the breastbone by a blackened brass clasp. I took a rose from the vase on our nightstand, sniffed at it once, and stuck it in the clasp, examining myself in the dressing mirror.

I'm not entirely sure I liked the sharp-eyed fellow who looked back at me, although he was good-looking enough.

Pretty darned handsome, in fact, the features regular, and there was kind of a pleasant Eastern cast to his eyes. Nice farm jawline, and clever mouth under the Fu Manchu-style mustache. He was well into his forties, but there were only hints of lines at the edges of his eyes, although the touches of gray at the temple were pretty nice—too bad that the gray was as lopsided as the smile.

It was clear from that far-too-easy smile that he spent too much time being entirely too pleased with himself, but it wasn't clear to me that there was enough character in his face for that to be at all reasonable.

It was entirely possible that he was thinking about how he was going out on the road with a particularly attractive old friend of his, and how—what with her son having cleverly been talked out of joining him—he might arrange to get his ashes properly hauled.

It was also possible that he was thinking about how wrong it was to be thinking about that in front of his wife. I doubt it, though. Like I say, I'm not entirely sure I liked the guy.

"What are you thinking?" she asked, as though we were a normal husband and wife, the kind who could ask each other that kind of question and expect an honest answer.

Kirah, I thought, *what happened to us?* "Well," I said, putting on my reassuring smile, "I'm thinking I'm practically naked." Close enough.

I went to the dresser and put on my weapons: throwing knives properly stowed, pistols in their holsters, master belt holding both shortsword and my long, pointed dagger. I know that a bowie is a better weapon, but I like the dagger better. Tradition, and all that.

Besides, I'm used to it.

I rolled up my hunting vest and stuck it under an arm. The Therranji garrottes were in two of the pockets.

She put down her knitting or tatting or whatever it was and walked to the chifforobe in the corner.

"Here," she said, handing me a full leather rucksack. "Clothes, some dried beef, a few candies, everything you need." She smiled up at me. "Almost."

I stuffed the vest inside, then slung it over a shoulder. "Thanks." I kissed the tips of my fingers and touched the air in front of her.

She leaned toward my hand and swallowed once, twice, hard. "You'll be back soon?"

Of course, I should have said. *Don't worry.* "Do you want me to?"

"Yes." She nodded. "Oh, yes. I do."

"Then why not—good."

She waited expectantly, her face upturned. No matter how many times it went wrong, I always thought that if I moved slowly enough, gently enough, she would be okay. This time it would be okay.

Asshole.

"It's okay, Kirah," I said, putting my arms around her. For a moment, just a moment, I thought it would be okay now, that she could let me touch her again.

But she shook her head once, emphatically, and then again, violently, and then she set her hands on my chest and pushed me away. "*No.*"

I walked out of the room, ignoring the whimper behind me.

Dammit, it's not my fault.

There was a farewell committee waiting for us down in the stables: Doria, Aeia, Durine, Kethol, and Pirojil. Bren Adahan had been left to keep the village wardens company.

The riding horses had already been saddled, and the two-horse team hitched to the wagon.

I settled for just checking my cinch straps and finding a carrot for the dappled mare that Tennetty had picked out for me before hitching the horse to the back of the flatbed wagon. I was going to drive the flatbed, but I wanted a riding horse, too. You never know when you're going to need to get away quickly, or across country. Flatbeds and fields don't get along.

Ahira was already on the back of his small gray mare, and as I walked through the wide doors, Tennetty swung up to the saddle of a nervous black gelding with a white blaze across his face, and kicked him into a clomp past the lanterns and out into the dark of the courtyard.

70

Andrea folded a blanket neatly across, twice, and set it down on the flatbed's seat before climbing on. "Let's go," she said, patting the seat next to her.

Doria, still in her purple evening dress, looked at me, pursed her lips and shrugged. "Take care of yourself, Walter," she said. Her fingers kneaded my shoulders for just a moment, and then she kissed me gently on the lips. "Watch out, eh?"

"For who?" I shot her a prizewinning smile she didn't return.

"All of you," she said. "Particularly Andrea."

I didn't know how things were going to break with Aeia—hell, I didn't know how I wanted them to break—until I heard myself saying, "Walk me to the gate—the rest of them will catch up in a moment."

I caught the dwarf's eye; I spread the fingers of one hand wide for a moment. *Give me five minutes, okay?*

He repeated the gesture and nodded. *Not six*, that meant.

Aeia and I walked out of the stables and into the dark. I could almost feel hostile eyes on my back, and wondered what window Bren Adahan was looking down from. Torches ringing the keep crackled in the still air, sending clouds of dark smoke into the dark sky. Above, a gazillion stars stared back at us. hanging intently on our every motion, every word. Or maybe not.

She was still wearing the Melawei-inspiraed outfit she had worn to dinner; I mentally worked at the complicated knot at ther left hip.

"You're scared about this," Aeia said.

"Always am." And that was true enough. "Wake up scared in the morning, go to bed scared at night."

She laughed, a warm, coppery sound like a carefully bowed cello. "You couldn't have persuaded me of that when I was a little girl. My Uncle Walter scared? Nothing could scare my Uncle Walter, any more than . . ." she grasped at the air, iooking for the right analogy, ". . . it could scare my father."

I chuckled. "Well, half right. Karl was too dumb to be scared."

She took my hand and we walked in silence, holding hands like a couple of schoolkids. "Just a couple of days?"

I shrugged. "Probably. Could be a few more. Or things could really heat up and we might be gone for awhile. You never know." It was like in the old raiding days, when a team would head out on the road, looking for trouble, usually finding it in the form of a slaver caravan. Slavers have to move the property around, particularly new property. People have a tendency to form relationships with other people, even if they own them. Bad for their business.

I never really liked those days, back when I was seconding Karl. Yes, there was a certain something to them; the parts that Karl didn't participate in were often kind of nice. See, not all of the folks we freed over the years were men. Some of them, quite a few, were women, and some of those were more than a little attractive. It's amazing how grateful a woman can be when you've just freed her, and often spectacular how she'll show her gratitude. You could ask my wife about that.

Besides, the money was good.

But . . .

"Bren's asked me to go with him over to Little Pittsburgh," she said. "What do you think I should do?"

"Little Pittsburgh's an interesting place," I said. "A bit dirty and sooty, but interesting."

"That wasn't what I meant."

"I know." Her hand was warm in mine. "You meant that we're going to have to make a decision sometime," I said. "Bren won't wait forever. Kirah won't not-see forever. We're going to have to decide what we are."

She nodded. "You can add that I won't wait forever. But I wasn't asking for forever, I wasn't asking about eventually. I was asking for now. What are we to be now, Walter Slovotsky?"

I rubbed my thumb against the softness of her hands. "Friends, at least."

She stiffened and let go of my hand, and touched herself above the waist at the right side. The air between us chilled, and I remembered Aeia holding a rifle straight, cheek welded

72

to stock, squeezing the trigger gently, ignoring the red wetness spreading across her waist, at the right side.

"Comrades-in-arms," she said, her voice holding a trace of that Cullinane coldness. "At least."

"Of course." I gestured an apology. "Always," I said. The coldness broke into a smile. "Better." She put her hands on my face and kissed me hard.

As we rode through the gate, Andy started to say something but caught herself. Just as well.

CHAPTER FIVE

In Which I Ride at Night, And Rediscover What a Pain in the Ass It is

I will not give sleep to my eyes, or slumber to my eyelids.
—PROVERBS 132:4

R<small>IDING</small> DOWN A COUN-
try road in the dark was interesting at first. Ahead, the road
curved and bent, twisting gently through fields and past vil-
lages, as the horses clopped through the dark, the rhythm of
their hooves always in awkward syncopation; someday, I'm
going to get a string of horses with matching legs and strides.

It was dark, yes, but not cloudy; the stars above shone
their pale light over the landscape, turning it all delicate
shades from the palest of whites to a rich, velvety black. The
night was rich with sounds and smells, from the distant hoot
of an owl and the skritching of insects to the quiet *whisshhh*
of wind through the trees. Night near a forest always smells
vaguely of mint to me, and this was a cool night.

But it all palls quickly.

Ahead, the road did just what roads do: it went straight
for awhile, then it bent, then it went straight again. The stars
above shone their pale white light over the landscape, robbing

it of all colors except a hint of sickly blue, turning the night into something seen on an old black and white TV set.

And all the while, the horses just clopped on down the road, every once in a while relieving themselves, filling the air with the scents of manure and horse piss.

Rather have a Buick, thank you much.

Actually, just for the entertainment value, I would have settled for Ahira's eyes. Dwarves can see deeper into the infrared than humans can, and not only does that give them two colors the rest of us don't have, it's a huge benefit in the dark. (It's also why their warrens are usually lit by glowsteels rather than heat sources—a torch puts out a *lot* of IR.)

We kept quiet, generally. It really would have been perfectly reasonable to talk as we rode, except that I had a vision of somebody lying in ambush chuckling over how easy we were making it as we rode under a tree. Without the distraction of conversation, either Ahira and I might be able to pick up some stray sound, if there was some trouble ahead.

Now, if I'd really thought that there was going to be trouble ahead, we wouldn't have been out here; I would have been safely in my bed at the castle instead of sitting on the hard seat of a flatbed, each rut in the road bashing the back of the seat against my kidneys.

By the time we arrived in Velen, my eyes were aching from lack of sleep, the sun was hanging mockingly over the horizon, and there were buzzards in the air to the southwest.

CHAPTER SIX

In Which We Encounter Some Wolves

There are no compacts between lions and men, and wolves and sheep have no concord.

— HOMER

How come you can never find a dragon when you need one?

— WALTER SLOVOTSKY

BY THE TIME WE GOT TO the buzzards, it was well onto midmorning. The buzzards had settled down both onto the carcass and onto the corn field surrounding it.

Heedless of the damage she was doing to the calf-high corn rows, Tennetty rode hard at the buzzards, scattering them into flight.

I guess they didn't know about her; they took her seriously enough to beat their wings lazily into the air, but half a dozen took up residence in a neighboring oak, squawking out complaints and abuse. Middle Lands buzzards are smaller than I'd always thought Other Side buzzards are (I've never actually seen an Other Side buzzard, so I'm not sure)—about the size of a big crow, huge ugly wattles hanging under wickedly curved beaks. Hideous things.

Bones aching, I set the brake and climbed down from the flatbed.

What we had here was the typical local setup: a dirt road

ran diagonally across a vaguely rectangular piece of land, vanishing into the dark of the forest on either side. The woods could be only a strip of a few dozen yards, left mainly as a windbreak, or they could be much deeper.

The road was edged with a low stone retaininG wall that raised it about two feet above flat ground level. I'd seen better-maintained retaining walls; these were a bit fallen down. But that wasn't my problem. It was the baron's problem, and his tax collectors'—they were supposed to be sure that the farmer was maintaining his well and roads.

The house, such as it was, was a half-timber, wattle-and-daub shack next to the road. A hedged privy, a dubious chicken coop, and the ubiquitous stone well were the only other structures.

There was some movement over in the crofter's shack, and that would have to be attended to, but I wanted to take a look at the cow first.

Or what was left of it. The wolves had done a good job, and the buzzards had been working hard to finish it. They—the wolves; buzzards don't eat take-out food—had dragged it about thirty feet through the field, doing even more damage to the young corn than Tennetty had.

The cow was a stinking, bloody mess.

I was kind of relieved. Back when I was majoring in meat science, I had to slaughter a lot of cows, and the part I hated most was the killing, and dealing with the fresh-dead. You have this pneumatic stunner—looks like a bull-barrel shotgun, sort of, connected by hose to a compressor—and you put it up against the cow's forehead and pull the trigger. The air pressure sends out the hammer—basically, just a piston—which gives the cow a sharp rap on the skull, hard enough to knock it unconscious at the least, break bones more often. At which point you hoist it, cut it and let it bleed out.

Messy work, but within just a few minutes, you don't have something that looks like a cow anymore; you've got parts. Sides of beef, viscera, tongue. Skin flayed off, waiting to be tanned.

We had even less than that here. The wolves had eaten about half the cow. Actually, they had eaten or carried off the rear half of the cow, legs and all, leaving the front half more mutilated than eaten.

It didn't make sense. It wasn't that it was too messy; it was too neat—in too many places, the flesh had been bit through cleanly. Possible for a wolf, I guess, although he would have had to be trying hard to be neat. And why would that be? Who would teach a wolf to play with his food?

But it *was* wolves—their prints were all over the soft ground. The pack had headed off to the northeast, into the woods.

Ahira and Andrea had left their horses hitched to the wagon; they joined Tennetty over the bloody mess, the three of them waving clouds of flies away.

The dwarf's brow furrowed. "It looks like the rear half of this thing is gone, bitten clean away."

Andy raised an eyebrow. "You mean, like what Ellegon would do?"

Ahira didn't answer.

There was more movement inside the shack. Tennetty stalked over and pounded on the door with the hilt of her shotgun.

"Out. Everybody *out. Now.* We need to talk to you," she said. You can always trust Tennetty to know just the right way to put everything.

I would have sworn that the ramshackle building wouldn't have held more than a couple of people, but in a few minutes a family of seven stood nervously on the dirt, the mother holding a baby in her arms, the youngest daughter—cute despite the dirt; they can do cute real well at that age—holding a struggling chicken tightly.

Tennetty ducked inside. I wished that she would talk things over before she did them; these sorts of things can be death traps.

But she came out laughing—not just giggling, but laughing *hard,* one hand holding her stomach. I thought she was going to drop the shotgun. "Yeah," she managed to wheeze out, in between gales of laughter, "they've got a . . . cow in there. And a goat, and I think there's some, some chickens in the cellar."

Ahira and Andrea were over with the family, trying to

calm them down. I had the impression that having a bunch of strangers with guns around wasn't either normal or comfortable for them.

On the other hand, when she turns on her smile, Andrea can charm bark off a tree.

"Greetings, all," she said. "We're just here to look into your wolf problem. The baron sent us."

"Old or new?" the woman asked, suspicious of us, if not of the notion of the nobility looking into predators.

"New," she said. "Baron Cullinane. We work for him. Tennetty, Daherrin, Worelt, and Lotana," she said, indicating us in turn.

I'd had a moment of nervousness. Andrea's always had an unfortunate tendency to honesty, and the three of us have gotten fairly famous through the Eren regions. That can be handy, but more often it's a problem: more than a few idiots would like to see what holding onto the former Empress of Holtun-Bieme would get them. (Dead is what it would get them, I hope. But maybe they don't know that. Or maybe they don't care what I hope.) And lots of folks would like to find out if they're better with a shortsword than One-Eyed Tennetty or faster with a knife than Walter Slovotsky. (Yes, there are both; but you'll understand that I'd prefer not to demonstrate that.)

Andy's instincts were right on the money: she had picked out false names for the three of us, but not for Tennetty. Tennetty was fairly famous in her own right—women warriors weren't common, particular one-eyed ones—and giving her a false name might be a clue that the rest of us were traveling under false colors.

The man ducked his head. "Begging your pardon, but—"

His wife shook her head, quickly. "No."

"I saw them," he insisted.

"How many?"

"Half a dozen, perhaps more. Wolves, yes, but . . ."

"But what?"

"There was something else," he said.

Andy's gentle smile broadened. I think she was trying to look reassuring, but she came off as amused. "And what might that be?"

He gripped at the air in front of him. "It looks like a wolf, just like a wolf, but it isn't." The words came fast, as though stumbling out. "I saw; I know. It isn't. It is larger, it moves strange, it isn't a wolf, it just looked like one."

I gave it a try. "What do you mean, it wasn't a wolf, but just looked like one?"

His fingers twitched in frustration. "It didn't *move* right. It bends in the wrong parts."

"A wolf that bends in the wrong places," Tennetty said. "Doesn't sound like a major problem to me." Tennetty dismissed them with a gesture; they filed back into the hut, although we could feel their eyes on us.

"It was a day and a half ago," Ahira said, *sotto voce*. "Wolves can cover a lot of territory in a day and a half. If they want to."

I wish I'd taken that zoology class. What was the dynamic of pack wolves? Did they have a territory, or—

Andrea knelt next to a pile of turds, one hand in her wizard's bag.

"Hang on a moment," I said, irritated. "I don't—"

"If you can come up with a better way to find them than with a location spell, Walter," she said, "then let's get to it."

"I'm a fairly good tracker," I admitted. Traditionally, it's the job of the nobility to protect the peasants, whether it's from invading raiders or wandering wolves. We weren't the local nobility, not really, but we were sitting in for him.

"Not good enough." Tennetty shook her head. "In a few days, if they're holed up and not on the move, you should be able to find them. In the meantime, not only do they fatten themselves on the local cattle, but we have to sleep during the heat of the day and hunt through the night."

"On the other hand, Andrea's supposed to keep her use of magic to a minimum. It's not healthy—"

"—for you to be talking about me in the third person." Andy said, her smile wide, but not particularly pleasant.

Ahira held up a hand. "We are all tired. But let's think it through." He ticked it off on blunt fingers. "We've got no problem with having wolves around, as long as they know enough to stay away from people. These don't." He added a finger. "They aren't going after cattle because other game is scarce: it isn't. They have a taste for beef, and aren't frightened enough of humans. So they have to go. It's cool in the woods—we'll duck off the road the woods and pitch the sleeping tarp, everybody gets some rest, and then a hot meal, and then we hunt late in the afternoon."

He frowned. "With the location spell."

No point in putting it off any longer. The horses were saddled, the guns loaded and lashed into place. My bow was only half-strung, slung over my chest, two dozen widebladed hunting arrows stuck into the quiver on my back. (Yes, stuck—you don't want the arrows falling out even if you take a fall.) A flask of Eareven healing draught was strapped to my left calf—my scabbard kept banging into it.

My hand was sweaty where it gripped the boar spear. It's the best hand-to-hand hunting weapon ever invented: six feet of shaft, grip points wound with leather and brass, topped by a long, fist-wide blade. About two feet back of the blade was the crosspiece. The classic crosspiece is just that: a piece of brass intended to hold whatever you've just stabbed at arm's length. Some genius—no, not one of us; we don't have the patent on genius—had modified it into kind of a U-shaped staple, points sharp, but unbarbed.

The result looked like a trident with a glandular condition.

Tennetty held four of the horses. They stood prancing, waiting, while Andy, in a ring of torches, crouched over the wolf shit.

There was something in her face that took me way back.

Once, a long time ago, I saw a little corgi who had just been hit by a car, about half a block from the vet's. My brother Steven and I were walking home from school and just came in at the end of it. Dr. MacDonald, a comically rotund little man, came running, a black bag like a real doctor's in his hand. He knelt over the little dog.

I don't remember much about the dog itself—I looked away.

But I do remember the look in Dr. Mac's face as he loaded the syringe: not only a kind of sedate compassion, but a raging unhurried competence. I misread it, and I grabbed for Steve's arm. "He's going to be able to save it."

Steve shook his head. "No. He's going to make the dog stop hurting."

There was that same something in Andrea's face as she silently knelt on the dust, oddments of bone and beak and feather spread out in front of her in the shape of a run-over bird.

With medical precision, she cleaned the ball of her left thumb, then pricked it with the razor point of a knife she had borrowed from Tennetty, letting one, two, three fat drops of blood well up, then fall into the dirt and the wolf turds.

The fire flared higher as she spoke, first in a quiet mumble, the volume growing steadily as her voice became clearer, uttering words that could only be heard but never remembered, smooth sibilants that vanished on the ear and in the mind. The torches flickered higher as she screamed out the vanishing syllables.

For a moment, just a moment, I thought that nothing would happen. There's a part of me that doesn't really believe in magic.

But then a feather twitched, and a piece of bone began to vibrate, and the twitching feather was joined by a white, ghostly one, as was the bone, and then another and another. Bits of feather and bone, both real and pale simulacrums, assembled themselves into bird, and flapped into the air.

Ahira and Tennetty were already on their horses, the butts of their spears resting in their stirrups.

Andrea rose, her face pale and sweaty in the firelight. "Quickly, now," she said, her voice a husky hiss. "The bird will try to keep itself halfway between me and the wolf. Let us hurry."

We cantered off toward the setting sun.

Just to show you what an asshole a kid from New Jersey can be, I used to think that riding a cantering horse was sort of like driving a fast car. Yes, I thought, you have to worry about bumping into stuff, but physically demanding, nah. Except on the horse.

Well, a lot I knew.

We clopped down roads, cut across fields—yes, careless of the damage to crops, but conscious of the damage a pack of wolves can do to the local livestock—avoiding cutting throught the woods.

Ahead, the bird fluttered just barely visible, constantly slowing, but always flying just a little too fast, just a little too far for us to ease up on the horses. Riding a fast-moving horse is hard.

Yes, my mare would jump over a drainage ditch, but I had to hang on to her back as she leaped the ditch, and landing was every bit as hard on me as it would have been if I was doing the jumping. Not to mention the way the saddle of the usually-cantering and sometimes-galloping horse kept threatening to slam the base of my spine into the base of my skull.

I was about to call a halt, using as my excuse that I didn't think the horses could take it, when the bird stopped at the edge of a field, perched itself neatly on a gnarled limb, then dissolved into a shower of feathers and bones.

I looked over at Andrea.

She nodded; the spell had dissolved because we were close, not because it had run out of magic.

The woods blocked out the setting sun, loomed dark and menacing.

Ahira was already on the gorund, his boar spear in his hand. He planted it solidly in the ground, then reached for his crossbow, quickly cocking it and slipping in a bolt.

"Tennetty, keep your spear ready, but get your rifles and bow out. Andrea, shotgun on the half-cock—"

I slipped from my saddle and started to string my bow.

Ahira shook his head. "Nope; Walter, you work your way around and drive them toward us." He tossed me a pair of grenades.

I chuckled bravely as I stowed the grenades in my vest. Well, it was supposed to be a brave chuckle, but it sounded forced to me; I just hope the others weren't quite as perceptive.

"And what if they decide to run toward me instead of you?"

He chuckled back. "Then I'd suggest you climb a tree. Do it now."

*   *   *

Skulking through the woods is partly art, but mainly craft.

It doesn't matter who or what you are: if you try to walk on the floor of a forest—twigs, dry leaves, and God-knows-what-else underfoot—you will make noise. The trick is to stick to hard-packed dirt, to flat rock and green grass. This can get a bit complicated when you're also being damn sure to stay within dashing range of a tree.

I circled around downwind of where the wolf pack should have been, making more noise than I would have liked, but not enough to carry very far. The idea was to spook them after all, and drive them in the direction of my friends.

Nice thing to do to your friends, eh?

Well, it was Ahira's idea, not mine. And it shouldn't be a problem—that's what the guns and the bow were for. Not that that was my problem, not now. My problem was keeping myself alive and unbit while I located the pack.

Hmm. If I were running a wolf pack, I'd have posted scouts some distance away from the body of the group. It would be an interesting mathematical problem—the further away the circle of watchers, the more warning they could give, but the more of them you'd need. Probably susceptible to some sort of minimax solution, or game theory analysis, but I don't guess that wolves do either.

The other way, of course, would be—either instead or in addition to posting scouts—to have some roaming watchmen making regular tours.

I don't know whether it was a hidden watchman or a roamer I'd missed that jumped me. With barely a rustling of leaves and twigs, two hundred pounds of coarse fur and awful stink lunged out of the dark brush for me, teeth unerringly aimed at my leg.

—Which wasn't there.

Emma Slovotsky's baby boy doesn't wait around to get bitten by a wolf. I danced out of his way and kicked him as he passed—it didn't hurt him, but it made his lunge carry him past me.

By the time he had spun around, I was already up the nearest tree, chinning myself on a thick branch, my stomach left somewhere behind me on the ground.

As I clambered the rest of the way to the branch, shouts and shots echoed off in the distance, but they seemed less important than the way the wolf scrabbled at the bark of the tree as he tried to get at me.

He howled once, then went silent—he didn't snarl, didn't growl. The silence was more frightening than snarling would have been. The way he crouched down in preparation for a leap was even worse.

I know I'm supposed to be completely cool and calm at all times, but it's only in the job description—it has nothing to do with reality. My fingers trembled as I pulled a grenade out of my vest, and tried to strike the fuse on the patch of roughness on its side. From the shots and shouts off in the distance, it sounded like the other part of the fight had already taken off, but it still made sense to scare any remaining wolves in their direction.

Meanwhile, my new friend was eying me silently, in between leaps up the side of the tree that brought his awful yellow teeth within inches of my ankles. I thought about trying to pull myself up to where I was standing on the branch instead of sitting on it, and decided that I could too easily lose my balance trying. I thought about kicking at his face, but I only thought about it.

It took three strikes until the grenade's fuse sputtered into life, and I pitched it hard in what I hoped was the direction of the pack, and then turned to deal with the lone wolf.

I wish I could report that I did something clever or heroic, but all I did was pull one of my brace of pistols, and cock it. The next time he gathered himself for a leap it gave me a stable enough target to aim at, and I gently squeezed the trigger. Shooting down is supposed to be hard, but that's only when you're shooting out and down—you tend to compensate for the distance to the target instead of the horizontal component of the distance.

But with wolfie ten feet directly below me, I just laid my iron sights low on his chest and pulled the trigger, rewarded by a bang, a cloud of foul smoke, and a gout of flesh and gore from the base of his neck.

He took a half dozen wobbly steps back, then fell over, watching me with glassy eyes as I clambered down.

It wasn't anything personal, not anymore. Wolfie was just protecting his pack, the way I was protecting mine, and I'd happened to be equipped with weapons he wasn't genetically prepared to deal with. I'd say I was sorry about that, but I really wasn't.

What I was sorry about was that we were on opposite sides. He reminded me of an old friend as he growled at my approach, yellow teeth bared for one last try, wanting a last taste of an enemy's blood in his mouth.

I slipped one of my throwing knives into my hand and flung it hard, burying the point in his throat, slicing through the jugular. Blood wet his chest and darkened the ground.

He died quickly.

I know that the grenade had gone off sometime during all that, and I know I'm supposed to be able to pay attention to everything that's going on, but I honestly don't remember when it happened. Look: I'm no hero, but it wasn't cowardice that kept me there with the dead wolf for a long moment.

I guess what it was, was that I felt like shit.

I felt like giving the dead body a pat, but that wouldn't have done any good, so I ran off into the forest.

Thick brush clawed at me in the dimming light. My sense of direction is unerring, so I knew that I was just feet away from where the strip of forest broke on cleared land, but for the life of me I couldn't see it.

I broke through, into soft dirt and a battlefield lit by the red and orange light of a setting sun.

It was too bright for stars, but the faerie lights were already out in force. Under their pulsations, wolf bodies and parts of wolf bodies lay scattered across the ground, most with arrows protruding from their immobile sides, others chewed by leaden teeth. One had fought his way through the rain of lead and steel to reach Ahira; it lay on the ground, still struggling at the end of his boar spear.

Only one stood, squared off against Andy and Tennetty.

Ahira freed the boar spear with a wrench that sent the wolf into a final spasm, and turned to face the last wolf.

Except that it wasn't a wolf.

It *looked* like a wolf, all right, albeit an overlarge, gray one. I would have assumed it was just the alpha male—until it moved. It didn't bend at the joints, the way any animal did—it flowed, liquidly, legs snaking instead of bending as it moved.

Tennetty fired a pistol into its side, but either she missed or it didn't do anything important: whatever it was just shuddered, and braced itself for a leap, no sound escaping through its bared teeth.

Andy brought up her shotgun, but she's never been much of a gunner: the blast dug up a spray of dirt to one side.

The wolf-thing lunged for her.

That was when Ahira, grunting with the effort, drove his boar spear down into its chest, shoving the tripartite head of the spear not only through the wolf-thing, but a full two feet into the soft dirt, pinning it to the ground like a bug on display.

Its legs squirmed like snakes, and ripples shook its body from nose to tail, and its bright eyes went dull and glassy, then dark, as the spasms subsided.

Ahira gave one last shove to the boar spear and then released it.

I had been running toward them across the soft ground, staggering more than once as I almost fell flat on my face, although God alone knew what I could do. Now I let myself ease into a slow walk. You don't have to run when the enemy's dead.

Tennetty let her swordpoint drop and wiped it on her leggings before putting it away in her scabbard. She walked over to where another boar spear protruded from the body of a dead wolf, set her booted foot against the wolf's side, and wrenched the spear loose. She leaned on the spear like a farmer leaning on his hoe.

"Shit, Walter," she called out. "You missed all the fun."

Things had gotten closer than they should have. The wolves should have just run away, and been picked off with bow and guns, not charged en masse. Ahira and his boar spear had been intended to be a sort of free safety, to pick off any problems that the guns and bow missed.

Ahira staggered away a pace or two. He squatted on the soft ground, then sat down hard, breathing heavy.

I stood over him. "A bit close, eh?" I offered him a hand, but he shook his head.

"Too close," he said. "They were working as a team; it was like that thing was directing them." He gestured at the wolf-thing lying on the ground, his spear still stuck through it.

Andrea smiled as she wiped her brow. "Now I remember why I've always let the rest of you do field work." She gestured toward the wolf-thing. "What *is* that?"

Ahira shook his head. "There's been talk of strange things coming out of Faerie; looks like we've just killed one of them." His mouth pursed into a line, then relaxed. It didn't matter what it was, now that it was dead.

I was going to say something, no doubt something clever, but Andy's eyes widened and her mouth opened.

"Ohmi*god.*"

The wolf-thing rose, its formerly dull eyes now glowing, its body flowing around the boar spear like water. It shook itself, like a dog, sending the boar spear tumbling end over end into the air. The spear left behind no mark in its dark fur.

Oh, shit.

It took a growling step toward Ahira, flattening itself for a leap.

Tennetty danced toward it with her own boar spear, but she overcommitted herself: a grizzled paw, moving bonelessly, slapped the spear out of the way and out of her hands. She was clawing for her sword when the thing leaped on her.

Ahira was too far away, and he was between Andy and the ground where the wolf-thing was savaging Tennetty; it was up to me.

The right thing to do, the only sensible thing for me to do, would have been to stand back and put a throwing knife in the right place. The only trouble with that plan was that the two of them were rolling around so fast, that there was no way of doing that—I'd be as likely to put the knife into Tennetty as into it. Still, there was that flask of dragonbone extract in my vest; I could drip some down the blade, hoping that this was one of the creatures with the kind of magical metabolism that dragonbone screwed up.

In any case, the silliest thing to do would be to leap on its back and try to plant a knife in just the right spot, but only an idiot would try it, and I'm not an idiot. Karl was an idiot—that's the sort of thing he would have done.

Me, I'm too smart.

My reflexes, on the other hand, were stupid: before I quite knew what I was doing, I had pulled one of my Therranji garrottes from my vest and had leaped for its back.

Tennetty's arm, through deliberation or accident, was jammed in its teeth. It was the only time I had ever heard Tennetty scream. The creature had flattened its chest and torso, cupping Tennetty's waist, threatening to flow over and engulf her.

I flung one arm around its neck and clung to its back like a rider on a runaway horse, but it was like clinging to hard jello: there was no hard muscle, no bone against which to gain purchase. Somehow or other—damned if I know how—I was able to lock my ankles together beneath it as I tried to slip the garrotte around its neck, but Tennetty's arm was in the way.

"*Let's go,*" I shouted. "FortheloveofGod, leggo."

Somehow, I managed to get the wire in around the neck and to work the handle through the loop.

I jerked hard; the garrotte disappeared into the dense fur. Now it was supposed to writhe uselessly, trying to remove the garrotte from its neck, while it died, this time for keeps. But the wolf-thing didn't stop—if anything its struggles intensified, as it rolled over, slamming all of us hard into the ground.

Things got a bit vague there for a moment, but I tried to hang on as, with a hard shake, it dislodged Tennetty, and then the neck turned impossibly far around for me as we rolled around the ground together.

I *think* I remember slipping a throwing knife into my free hand, and then into the thing's side, but I don't think that would have been quite possible.

Somewhere in all that it managed to dislodge my dagger, but I managed to cling to its back . . .

. . . until a double-bending flip that a creature with a real spine wouldn't have been able to pull off flung me out and down, hard.

Some gifts won't ever leave me: I hit the soft ground with a proper slap-and-roll, my left arm numb from the shock. I staggered to my feet—

"It's mine," Andrea Andropolous Cullinane said, her quite voice piercing through the shouts and growls.

She had dropped her smoking rifle to one side. Now she shrugged out of her cloak, dropping it negligently to one side, ignoring the chill air as she faced the wolf-thing, the sun over her shoulder, framing her in all the colors of fire. Ahira was at her side, his axe now in his hands, but he moved away at her gesture.

She faced off against the wolf thing.

"Be gone; you will not harm me or mine," she said. "I tell you once." She tossed her head, clearing the hair from her eyes. Her tongue snaked out and touched her full lips once, twice, three times.

The wolf-thing took a hesitant, flowing step toward her.

Her smile was thin as she raised a hand, strong, slim fingers stroking the air in front of her. "Be gone, now and forever. I tell you twice."

A low thrumming filled the air as she thrust her arms out in front of her, fingers spread, but cupped forward.

The light of the setting sun started to take liquid form, threads of gleaming honey rolling across her fingers, splashing on the ground all about her. At the touch of the liquid light, sticks and bits of stray straw flashed into flame, and the earth itself began to smolder.

The heat flashing on my face was hotter than a forge.

"Move back, move back," the dwarf said.

His face red and sweaty, Ahira scooped up Tennetty in one arm and seized my waist, dragging me backwards, although I really didn't need any encouragement. Still, I couldn't turn my back.

Andrea took a smooth step forward, toward the wolf-thing, one foot swinging out and planting itself firmly in the dirt, her hips swaying, grinding with an intensity that was almost sexual. Or maybe not almost; I don't know much about magic.

She let the strands of light play through her fingers as it crouched for a leap.

"Be gone, I tell you a third and last time."

She lowered her voice and the stream of light began to darken, and at first I thought that the spell wasn't working, but no: the thrumming grew louder and higher, the volume and pitch and violence of the sound growing, until it screamed like a Jimi Hendrix guitar riff.

The sound pressed the thing back.

Andy spread her fingers wide, and gathered up gleaming strands of golden dusk. Deft fingers, inhumanly powerful and delicate, wove the strands into a stream of braided ruby light that flowed from her fingers, splashing hard against the wolf-thing. Where the stream touched the wolf-thing, it burned, spattering flaming gobbets of flesh off into the air.

I tripped Ahira and forced him and Tennetty down.

Andrea screamed harsh syllables that could never be remembered, as the sound grew louder, pressing down on the world, the light so bright I had to cover my eyes.

Just in time. Even with my lids squeezed painfully tight, the flash dazzled me, and heat washed over me in a wave.

Worst thing in the world is to be blind during a fight—I forced my eyes open.

Sweat streaming down her face, Andy stood on a mound of dirt that poked above one of two irregular puddles of lava. A cloud of darkness hovered above the other, already dissipating.

"Be gone," Andrea said, quietly. "It's done."

"For here and now," the cloud said, its voice deep, but airy. "But you have ruined my fun. Perhaps I shall ruin yours some time."

She muttered something, then looked up, expectantly. Nothing. "Who are you?" she said.

The voice laughed. It wasn't a nice laugh. "Not all your rules work on me, though some do. I'll not give you a handle with which to hold me, or turn me. Call me, oh, Boioardo, though that never was and is not now my name."

She muttered another spell, and started to raise her hand, fingers crooked awkwardly.

"Oh, let me have a few more moments," Boioardo said.

'Perhaps you'll appreciate it, should we meet in a Place with different rules."

Faerie? I thought. "No, Andy. End it now."

Tennetty was starting to come around; I gathered her up in my arms, ready to run. I'm better at running than the dwarf is—although if Andy couldn't hold the thing, we were all cooked.

"Ah. So clever, Walter Slovotsky of Secaucus. Will you be so clever in the Place Where Trees Scream, or the Place Where Only That Which You Have Loved Can Help You?"

"Of course." I forced a smile; bravado is always a cheap thrill. "I'll be even cleverer; it's part of my charm."

Perhaps it wasn't going to be a cheap thrill—the darkness started to move toward me.

"*No.* Be gone," Andrea said, straightening her fingers. She muttered another word, and wind blew the darkness away, into the light of the setting sun.

It was gone. We stood alone in the dusk, wisps of smoke rising from the field. Ahira was bent over Tennetty, dealing with her wounds; Andrea stood on the mound of dirt rising above the darkening pool of lava, her face reddened, her whole body beaded with sweat.

Smoothly she turned, balanced like a dancer. "I think, dear friends, I'll take an attaboy on that one." She leaped lightly across the puddle of lava, took three steps toward us, and fainted dead away.

CHAPTER SEVEN

In Which Ellegon Shows Up and Points Out an Obligation

I was gratified to be able to answer promptly, and I did. I said I didn't know.

—MARK TWAIN

I'd always liked Robert Thompson's idea of avoiding compromise, of letting the person with the strong convictions have his own way . . . and then I realized that encouraged people to have strong convictions when they don't have enough data.

—WALTER SLOVOTSKY

THERE WAS A BRIGHT golden haze on the meadown. The corn was as high as an elephant's eye—granted, it would have had to have been a small elephant, and maybe the critter would have had to squat a bit. And—no shit, I was there—it looked like it was climbing clear up to the sky.

"Fuck you, morning," I murmured, *sotto voce.* I hate mornings. Never cared for Oklahoma much, either.

Well, we needed to keep somebody on watch. Tennetty had been banged up, and she had been loath to waste more healing draughts on herself than necessary—that stuff is expensive. Certainly worth more than my night's sleep. Andy was drained, and, besides, she's never had the kind of alertness to her surroundings that the dwarf and I have.

By the process of elimination, that left the dwarf and me, and, as usual, left me pissed off. (I shouldn't complain; for once it didn't leave me in deep shit.) Ahira and I had split the night, and while I think I'd gotten the better of the deal, I'd not gotten much the better of it.

We were camped on the edge of the woods, a few tell-tales protecting us from somebody or something sneaking around behind us, a single watchman—me—protecting our front. Field work is an exercise in applied paranoia.

Time to sit, and watch, and think, as the dawn brightened into morning.

A lot to think about in the night. Too much.

Whatever was happening on the edge of Faerie was no longer just somebody else's problem. It had struck close to home. It's not that I don't care if magical monsters mess with people elsewhere, but it's a big world, and I'm only one person. But my wife and kids were in Barony Cullinane. Boioardo, whatever he/it was, had mucked about in Barony Cullinane. That made it personal.

Still, it wouldn't hurt to spend some time around the barony instead of rushing off into trouble. Let the castle settle down, keep our ears open for a bit of news, let Tennetty heal on her own instead of using up expensive and rare healing draughts. Let me spend some more time with bow, sword, and pistol. I'd rather sit than run, run than fight, but I'd rather fight than die, thank you very much.

Maybe there was some way out of it. Sometimes, if you leave a problem alone long enough, somebody else solves it for you—President Reagan diddled and twiddled his thumbs over the Osirak reactor outside of Baghdad until the Israelis took it out for him.

I would have been perfectly happy if the equivalent happened this time. Magic and humans don't tend to get along, I think; it's one of the reasons that we developed in other ways on the Other Side, and why the mundane tended to drive out the magical in the Eren regions. There was an age of dragons, when, if you believe the tales, clouds of them darkened the skies.

I didn't see what Stash and Emma's baby boy could do to halt the return of that sort of thing, even if I did want to put myself in the middle of it. Like trying to stop an oil spill by sticking your finger in a hole in the pipeline.

Sometimes, if you leave a problem alone long enough, somebody else solves it for you.

Like the Kirah?

You've been really fucking clever in leaving that *alone, Walter,* I thought.

What should I do? Drop her, in favor of Aeia? Right; that's be guaranteed to be good for Kirah's mental health. Try to force the issue? I wasn't about to lay my hands on a woman who shuddered when I touched her, and if somebody doesn't want to talk about something, there's no way to make them.

I sighed. I didn't see any good way out of it.

Maybe, just maybe, if I left her alone, if I kept the pressure off, if I didn't make it a matter of public record and public discussion, she'd work things out herself.

It was, at least, something to hope for.

Sometimes you have to settle for that.

Far off in the blue sky, a distant speck stopped moving erratically, and started down toward us.

Ellegon? I thought, trying to shout with my mind.

If it was him, he was too far. Karl and particularly Jason have always had an unusually tight bond with the dragon, and could mindtalk with him at fair distances, but he and I have never been that close. Not possible, really—Ellegon knew Jason before Jason was born.

If it wasn't Ellegon, than it was trouble. There was that flask of rendered dragonbane in my vest; I got it out and pried the top off.

"Okay, everybody, we've got somebody or something inbound," I said, getting to my feet. "Battle stations, people."

Fight-or-flight is always a fun decision to make, and when it's just me, I tend to vote with my feet—he who fights and runs away lives to run away another day and all that. But I couldn't outrun something that flies, not without a lot more than a bikini-wide strip of woods to hide my privates in.

I dipped three arrows in dragonbane and laid them gently on the rock in front of me. I could fire them quickly, and then flee even more quickly, if necessary.

The speck grew.

The sleeping bodies, all of them, had broken into a flurry of motion—Ahira shrugging into his clothes and armor, Andrea reaching for a rifle, Tennetty, her left arm bound up in a sling, bringing a pistol to the half-cock and tucking it in the front of her belt.

A familiar voice sounded in my head. *Walter, I would take it as a personal favor it you'd be kind enough to avoid killing me.*

At this distance, I could make out the familiar shape: large, saurian, huge, leathery wings beating the air.

I could practically hear the twang of my anus unclenching.

"And it's good to see you, too, Ellegon," I muttered, knowing that a whisper was as good as a shout at this distance.

Always a pleasure to be near the center of the known universe.

Eh?

The center of the universe—that spot just behind your forehead. Or just south of your belt buckle. You keep changing your, er, mind.

Just wait until you hit puberty.

In another century or two I'll be just like you. Sure. Once every dozen years or so. If I can even find a female dragon.

I muzzled a comment about "did the earth move for you, too"—

Just as well.

—as I unstrung my bow and set it aside. Accidents can happen—a quick flaming in the campfire burned the dragonbane from the arrowheads, without costing me the arrows. Good arrows are expensive.

I looked up; the sky was clear.

Where are you?

Behind you, on final approach—passengers don't like my hard landings.

I rubbed at my tailbone. *So I recall.*

Chickenshit.

A dark shadow passed overhead; leathery wings snapped in the breeze as Ellegon braked in for a landing, slamming down hard enough on the road fifty yards away that I could feel the ground shake.

Ellegon: more tons than I care to count of gray-green dragon, the size of a Greyhound bus studying hard to become a Boeing 737; long tail at one end, alligator head at other, with the usual vague wisp of steam or smoke issuing from between the dagger teeth.

The huge, saurian head eyed me with cold, heavy-lidded eyes. I guess Ellegon hadn't liked the 737 thought-slash-comment.

Good guess. The head turned away. A brief gout of fire issued from the cavernous mouth, red tongues of flame licking the dirt road.

The dragon lumbered forward a step and slumped to the ground on the warmed spot—I couldn't tell whether in fatigue or to make it easier for his passenger to climb down from the rigging on his back.

It's purely out of consideration. As we all know, I am the most considerate of dragons. The fact that I've spent most of the past three days with my aching wings pounding the air has nothing at all to do with it.

The passenger, of course, was Jason Cullinane. Some things are eminently predictable. He waved genially as he walked across the field toward us.

"Good morning," I said.

We could have used you yesterday, I didn't say. He'd work it out by himself. Eventually.

He hitched at his swordbelt, and at the shoulder holster that held a gun butt barely visible under his short jacket. "I thought, maybe . . ."

Ahira shook his head. "Don't 'think maybe', next time. Think for sure."

I couldn't have put that better myself. I gestured at the log where I'd been sitting. "In the meantime, have a cuppa."

Back when we were both college students, a friend invited me up to her dorm room one Thursday to sit in on her weekly electronic conversation on one of the electronic information services—I can't remember for the life of me whether it was Compuspend or the Source, or whatever. We sat in front of her Osborne cute little machine typing at the bunch of other folks, people from all over the country who were sitting

97

typing at us. We occasionally wondered if they were sitting there naked . . . too.

The thing I remember most about it—well, the thing I remember second-most; it was a pretty good evening—is that the best, the most interesting parts of the six- or ten-handed electronic talk were the ones sent privately, below the surface of the public conversation, from one user to another.

Having Ellegon in on a meeting is kind of like that, even if the meeting is taking place while you're breaking camp.

Ahira tucked a folded tarpaulin carefully into his rucksack. tied the rucksack shut, then pitched it over to me; I tossed it into the flatbed wagon.

Tennetty took a tighter grip on the reins of the harnessed horses, who were prancing, snorting, nervously pissing, and otherwise indicating that they weren't happy. Horses tend to be nervous around Elegon, probably for the same reason that a hamburger would tend to be nervous around me. Which is why Andy had already taken the saddle horses down the road.

Jason was sitting on the ground, his back against the base of a tree. his knees up: he set his cup of tea gently down on the soft mass. "We do have to look into what's coming out of Faerie. Ehvenor. eh?"

The boy has a keen eye for the obvious. The Ehvenor part, not the part about looking into it.

You're being too harsh, Ellegon said, his mental voice taking on that extra clarity, that particular brassy timbre that told me he was talking to me only. *Although he does have his father's subtlety, such as it is.*

The dwarf pitched me another bag of gear, then picked up a gnarled stick and took a last nervous stir at the ashes of the campfire. "Somebody has to." He pursed his lips for a moment. "I don't like it. Magic." He shuddered.

I chuckled. "You complaining about magic?" If it wasn't for magic, Ahira would still have been crippled James Michael Finnegan.

"Sure." he said. "And back on the Other Side. I would have complained about nuclear weapons, antibiotics, automobiles, and all other mixed blessings, too." He looked over at Andrea. "How close do you have to be to find out what's going on?"

She gestured at a spot on the log she was sitting on. "Put somebody or something who knows right there, and I don't have to be any closer than here."

Ahira raised an eyebrow. "Some sort of mind spell?"

"No, I'd ask him." She smiled.

"Very funny. Seriously. How far away from whatever is happening would you have to be to figure out what it is?"

She shrugged. "That would depend on what *is* going on. I might be able to read it anywhere from, say, three days ride to, maybe," she said with a squint, as she held her thumb and forefinger together right in front of her eyes, "this far from it."

"No way to do it from here? No matter what it is?"

She snorted. "Sure there is, if what's going on is broadly focussed *and* powerful *and* highly kinetic *and* unsubtle *and* unshielded, plus a couple more adjectives that wouldn't mean anything to you. But if it was, you'd have half the wizards throughout the Eren regions already alerted to it, and there would be . . . manifestations of that. So it isn't. So, if I'm going to find out what's going on, I've got to go see. The closer we get, the less I have to push myself in order to find it."

Ahira nodded. "I'll think it over." He looked over at me.

I knew what he was asking, but it was the wrong question. He was asking *when* instead of *whether*.

I shook my head. "No need to rush off without thinking. If we give it a couple of days, not only will we have time to pack intelligently, but we might be in better shape to hit the road."

"You sound too persuasive." Tennetty took a sip of her tea, and spat it out into the fire. "Gone cold on me." Her lips twitched. "You're not eager to go," she said.

"I'm not convinced we should go," I said. I hadn't liked the way Boioardo had looked at me, but I wasn't in any rush to go haring off after him. I've never seen the point in galloping toward my appointment in Samarra. (Well, that's not quite true. I used to date a girl named Samarra Johnson, who was well worth a gallop or two, but I digress.)

Tennetty scratched at herself, grimacing at the way her

99

bruised body protested any movement. "I'll take the flatbed and the horses back, if the rest of you want to go by air."

Fair enough. I may as well eat the cubs, then?

"Cubs?"

I forget. Not only can't you hear with your mind, your ears are handicapped, too. The wolf cubs. A gout of flame pointed out a direction. *Thataway.*

I sighed. There *would* have to be wolf cubs, wouldn't there? Hell of a note. You can't even save some innocent peasants from a ravening pack of wolves without having to clean up after, and feeling guilty as all hell about it.

There were two of them, and they were cute as anything, hungry to the point of starvation, and smelly as a pail of shit.

The small burrow under the rock wasn't much of a den, but it had probably been the best thing that mother wolf could dig in a short while. The pack was moving, under the influence or control of Boioardo, and long-term dens would have to wait.

The dwarf wasn't going to let me off the hook. "Well, you could always leave them to starve to death and just feel bad about it later."

Jason looked over at him. "That's the stupidest idea I've ever heard."

Andy crouched down and reached out to stroke one. It nipped at her, then nuzzled at her hand, probably trying to nurse. "Or you could slit their throats."

Tennetty knelt down beside the rock. "I'll do it. Not fair to leave them to starve." She drew her bowie and reached for the nearest of the cubs.

Jason grabbed her wrist. "What's your rush?"

"They're hungry." She shrugged her hand away. "They're no enemy of mine; I don't need to see them suffer."

He held up a hand. "Just put it away for a minute. Let's think this out."

I already had. Damn, damn, damn.

Sometimes, coming from the background I do is a burden, and it looked like Jason had inherited some of it from Karl. In a primitive society, people don't tend to be suckers for cute animals; interspecies empathy is a luxury, and people

100

who are scratching for existence don't tend to spend a lot of time and effort on it. You can't, say, raise all the puppies that your bitch breeds, and you don't have the expertise to spay her. So you have to either drown in litters of pups, or drown most pups.

Look—I've *had* to be hardhearted at times; there's situations where it's necessary to say that something's just natural, that there's nothing you can do about it. I've run into a lot worse than this. Cute baby animals die all the time out in the woods, and in a lot of cases it's just part of nature. And I've run into a lot worse than that.

But this wasn't part of nature. Boioardo had brought the mother of the cubs down out of the hills, and we had killed the pack, and that left the orphans with us. With me.

Ellegon's bulk loomed off in the distance, through the trees. *It would be awfully convenient if we had to take to our heels now.*

It would also be convenient if we had a proper canine milk source back at Castle Cullinane. "Jason," I asked, "any chance there's a nursing bitch in the kennels?"

"No." He shook his head. "Not mine. Bren insisted on showing me the inventory, and that didn't mention it. On the other hand," he went on, "there's got to be a village warden somewhere around with one. You ever know a warden not to keep dogs?"

"There's the cows," Ahira said. "Cow milk might be worth a try."

Tennetty spat. "Silly idea. Just make it quick; that's the best you can do."

Jason shook his head. "I don't think my father would have, do you?" A thin smile played across his lips for just a moment. He reached into the den and scooped up one of the cubs. It nipped and wriggled as he handed it to me. It wasn't interested in sitting still.

He grabbed the other one, and ignoring its yipping and wriggling, headed down the path toward Ellegon. "Anybody who wants to come with me had better move it; we're heading back to the castle, on the double."

I looked down at the pup in my hands. Its fur was harder,

denser than I would have expected a puppy's to be, and its eyes were glassy with hunger and thirst.

Shit, shit, shit. "Let's roll it."

"Okay." Ahira shrugged his pack onto his shoulders. "Let's give the boy a hand."

"I thought you wanted to leave them to starve to death and worry about it later."

"No, you didn't."

By the time we got back to Castle Cullinane, Aeia, Bren, and their entourage had left for Little Pittsburgh.

CHAPTER EIGHT

In Which, Surprisingly, Neither My Wife Nor I Are Urinated Upon

To sleep, perchance to dream.
—WILLIAM SHAKESPEARE

Bill, your mother swims after troop ships.
—WALTER SLOVOTSKY

THE COMPLEX PROBLEMS sometimes have simple, easy solutions—it's the simple problems that drive you crazy.

Like feeding the wolf cubs. The complex one was *What the hell do you feed them?*

The way I'd figured it, there was a huge chance that we wouldn't be able to find the cubs enough to eat, and that we'd have to put them out of their misery. I wasn't looking forward to that, mind, but it would have made things simpler.

But it turned out that what to feed adopted wolf cubs was already a solved problem, and so was taking a shot at domesticating them. It had been done before, in the old days, and the methods had been passed down by the dogkeepers. Some of the literate ones—and, in the old days, dogkeeping was a respectable profession, often taken up by petty nobility—had kept notes on the subject.

It was Fred (don't blame me; that's his name, okay? It's a variant of Fredelen, a common Holtish name) the

103

dogkeeper's firm belief that the Nyphien sheepdog was a mixture of the blood of wolf and the large Holtish dog called a *kalifer*, the oversized canine I always think of as a hairy mastiff.

Still, there were differences. According to Fred, a dog bitch would have done for the first few tendays, but after that, the pups would have savaged the poor thing's teats. Takes a mother wolf to keep baby wolves in line.

The standard baby wolf food was goat milk and whey, with the addition of one part bull blood for every ten of milk, and some herbs that Fred wouldn't identify.

. . . and more attention than a newborn human baby gets. If you want them coexisting with humans, you'd better have them smelling them constantly.

The next ten days were not fun.

The nightmare is always the same:

We're trying to make our escape from Hell, billions of us pushing our way through the damp curtains that hang down from infinity, obscuring the endless surface.

Everybody I've ever loved is there, along with faces familiar and strange.

Behind us, sometimes visible down the endless rows of curtains, the screaming pack of demons pursues. I don't want to look at them, and I don't have to, not anymore. We're almost out, almost safe.

But almost is never good enough.

The exit is up-ahead, clearly marked with glowing green letters. And some are pushing their way through, thankfully. I think I see my wife and kids go through, and out.

I hope so.

The demons are approaching too quickly, and they're going to catch some of us. And then I see him: Karl Cullinane, Jason's father, standing tall, face beaming, his hands, chest, and beard streaked with blood and gore.

"We're going to have to hold them back," Karl says. "Who's with me?"

He smiles, as though he's been waiting his whole life for this, the fucking idiot.

"I'm with you," somebody says, and he waves whoever it is into their place next to Clint Hill and Audie Murphy.
"It's your turn," Karl says, turning to me. He's covered with blood, some sort of yellow-green ichor, and wolf shit. He tosses his head to clear the blood from his eyes. "Your turn, Walter."

"Your turn, Walter," Jason said. He shook me again.

I woke up slowly, half in the here and now, half in the nightmare, still watching Karl's face superimposed over his son's.

Didn't like that at all—somebody in my line of work is supposed to wake up quickly, and before being touched at all. I don't care if my hindbrain thought me safe in bed next to my wife; the door was open, and an armed man had gotten in and next to me.

Not good, Walter.

Fast asleep, Kirah lay on the far side of the bed, curled under her blankets into a fetal position, her feet poised to push me away.

A dirty, smelly woolen shirt and pants lay on the floor next to me. Clothes to feed wolves in. Shudder. I levered myself out of bed, and shrugged into my wolf-feeding clothes—they were still vaguely moist with wolf drool—and a few oddments of weaponry before following Jason out into the hall.

My mouth had the metallic taste it gets when I don't get enough sleep. For some reason, I hadn't gotten enough sleep in the tenday we'd been back. Funny about that.

I stopped at the top of the stairs to look out the window.

Ellegon lay on the cold stones in the courtyard below, sleeping, his massive legs tucked underneath his body, his huge head resting on the cold stone, like a cat. Cute as a bus.

Too bad. I could have used the company. Being up and alone at night isn't any fun.

Jason handed me one of his two lanterns. The castle tradition, probably going back to the siege, was to keep too few wall lanterns burning in the middle of the fucking night, and everybody had to carry their own light sources with them.

"How are they doing?" I asked.

105

He shrugged. "Nora's been hiding under the stove; Nick's been eating enough for three of them." He raised a hand in farewell. "And I've got to get some sleep," he said, padding down the carpet toward his room, not bothering to throw a quick glance over his shoulder.

I made my way down into the inner ward, and the shack we were using as a wolf-kennel.

"Back-back-*back*, you vicious beasts," I said, as I unlocked the wire-mesh door and hung the lantern on the hook.

Obediently, the two pups bounded out of their hiding places, Nora almost making it through the door before she bounced off my foot and ran, yipping, back into the shed; Nick snuffled around my feet silently as he wagged his tail.

The locked cabinet held a fresh jug of Fred's foul-smelling wolf-baby food mixture; I took down a clean wooden bowl, and poured some for Nora. Nick hadn't gotten the idea of lapping out of a bowl as quickly as his sister; by the time I got some into one of the feeding bottles and a rag half-stuffed into the mouth of it, he was whimpering.

Another week or so and he'd be able to eat out of a bowl.

Or I'd wring his thickening neck.

I plopped myself down on a pile of straw—stupidly but harmlessly (this time) trusting Jason to have cleaned out the place before he left. The little monsters could have—and certainly would have—dirtied it up, if they'd gotten around to it.

Nick couldn't keep himself still; I had the usual trouble getting the pup tucked under one arm and getting the bottle to his mouth. He ate greedily, like he hadn't been fed in minutes.

Basically, as Fred had explained it, the way you have a fair chance with wolf cubs or wild dogs is to catch them young enough—which he thought we did—and to basically spend all your time rubbing against them.

Make them members of your family, he'd said. Imprint them, he might have meant.

We'd see how it went over the long nights.

I understood why Fred didn't want to have to do it—

the smell of the pups scared Fred's dogs shitless. I was beginning to think that a spray bottle of wolf urine would be a wonderful invention for making a territory as offlimits to domestic dogs.

I'll tell you, this would have been the perfect time for young Baron Cullinane to exercise a bit of baronial authority and tell one of the scullery girls she had a new job, as nurse to a pair of cubs.

But the Cullinanes are a stubborn breed—this was additional work, not expected, and Jason wasn't going to dump it on the castle staff, not if it wasn't absolutely necessary. No, that was for those of us who had taken on the responsibility: him, Ahira, his mother, and me.

Look: I like dogs, I like playing with dogs, I like hanging out with dogs for a few minutes now and then. Throwing a stick and having a dog fetch it is one hell of a lot of fun, the first couple of dozen times you do it.

But I didn't like spending six hours out of every day endlessly feeding and petting a couple of puppies, mucking out their kennel, and missing sleep.

Shit.

I had until dawn; Ahira would take over then. Hours of misery ahead.

Still, they were kind of cute.

I leaned back against the wall. Nora, always the less affectionate, retreated back into the shadows when she finished eating, while Nick kept sucking and licking at the bottle and the rag until he whimpered a bit, and fell asleep on my lap.

A long shift lay ahead, with nothing much to do but reflect on how the universe sucked.

Where had I gone wrong with Kirah? Was it something in how I touched her that had ruined sex for her? I don't mean to brag, but I've had relatively few complaints over the years. It isn't always ummeasurably wonderful or anything, but I'd always thought that I had more than a vague idea about what-goes-where.

No, I was being silly.

I rubbed at Nick's head, and he stirred for just a moment, then fell back asleep.

It's amazing how the same life can look good during the day and like a black cesspit in the middle of the night.

During the day, it was more important that I was living and working with friends who I cared for, and who cared for me; that the work we did was important to more than ourselves; that I had two beautiful, healthy daughters, both of whom were fond of me; that I was in good health and managed to keep up good spirits . . .

. . . and, at night, all I could think about was that my wife wouldn't let me touch her.

I guess I feel asleep, but I came awake suddenly. Nick, awake in my lap, had stiffened into immobility.

The drill is always the same: you get yourself armed and ready, and then you decide whether or not you're going to have to use it. I dumped the pup to one side and had my dagger out of its sheath—

"Walter?" It was Kirah's voice.

"Yeah." I slid the knife back in its sheath. "Just me," I said, bending to give the puzzled puppy a pat.

Balancing a serving tray on the palm of her one hand, she let herself in and knelt in front of Nick, who decided that she was okay, and demonstrated by wagging his stubby tail vigorously, then nipping gently at her face when she picked him up with her free hand.

"Hi there. What are you doing up?"

"Feeding you." She handed me the tray: half a loaf of U'len's garlic bread, in slices thick as my thumb; a huge mound—easily a pound—of cold, rare, roast beef, sliced thin enough for carpaccio, accompanied by a white clay mortar (as in ". . . and pestle") of freshly ground mustard and horseradish sauce; a wedge of blue-veined goat cheese surrounded by apple slices (try it!); a mottled brown pot of steaming herb tea, with two mugs.

My wife knows how to scrounge in a kitchen.

"I couldn't sleep alone." She smiled, aware of the irony. "I missed you, I guess."

"What time is it?" I asked, spreading a huge dollop of mustard and horseradish sauce on one slice of the bread, then heaping a restrained half of the beef on top of it before setting the tray up on the table. I'd leave some for her. At least until I finished my sandwich.

"Half past first hour." She set Nick down, and he immediately started chasing his tail.

"Pull up a seat," I said. I'd come on at midnight. "I've only been on for a bit more than an hour." Enough time to get seriously depressed, that was all.

I bit into the sandwich. The horseradish brought tears to my eyes, but it was worth it. There's something to be said for cold roast beef, thinly sliced, seasoned with just a little bit of salt, some cracked pepper, and mustard and horseradish sauce, served on coarse brown bread with little bits of garlic scattered through it . . . but I'd much rather eat it than say it.

Kirah seated herself just out of my reach, then leaned back, tugging at the hem of the light cotton robe she wore over blousy pants and slippers.

Nick went hunting for Nora, who just huddled deeper into her improvised nest in the far corner of the shack. Kirah started to get up, but desisted at my head-shake.

"Leave her be," I said, from around another mouthful. "Won't do any good to go chasing after her; she'll come out in her own time. Or not."

When something that can't be helped is bothering you, one cure is to think of something else that can't be helped that bothers you.

So I wished for a good Other Side reference book. Common sense and old records can only go so far. I remember something about most wolves deferring to alpha males, and that the way a human successfully deals with them is by persuading them that he's sort of a super-alpha male, but how did you do that? Growl and nip at them? Slap them on the snout? Pin them down with one arm and make them behave? Or was gentle firmness the way to go?

Common sense doesn't make it; all animals—homo sap definitely included—have their ways, and you violate them only at your peril. Doesn't matter how much you reason, or threaten—you can't get a cow to walk down stairs, a cat to point out game, or a horse to fetch.

I did remember from an ag ecology class that wolves

mainly live off rodent pests, and that farmers who hunt them aren't doing themselves any favor. Back when I was working for King Maherralen in Endell, I'd stopped the dwarf wolf-hunt cold. (Okay, okay: I strongly recommended to the King that he stop it, and he did.) There were much better things for the king's people to do, no matter how much bad blood there was between dwarves and wolves.

Would it be possible to return these guys to the wild? Damned if I knew.

Nick came over and started nuzzling and nipping at my hand. I tried to pet him into quietness, but it didn't work—he just kept at me. Sharp little teeth. "*No.* No biting."

Kirah giggled. "That's exactly the way you used to say it to Jane."

I laughed back. "I probably did." I gestured at the tray with my free hand, offering to make her a sandwich.

She shook her head. "No. I made it for you.—What do you think this Boioardo of yours was?" she asked.

I shrugged. "Something from Faerie. Something dangerous."

She pulled Nick over to her; he settled down in her lap and went promptly to sleep.

I raised an eyebrow.

"You just have to know how to talk to them," she said. She tossed her head to clear the hair from her eyes.

I spread a blob of goat cheese over a slice of apple and bit into it. It's one of those combinations that seem ridiculous until you try them, like prosciutto and melon, or raw oysters and hot sausage—the sweetness of the apple softened the bite of the ripe cheese, and crunch of the apple complemented the gooeyness of the cheese.

I made another one, and offered it to Kirah, who surprised me by accepting it.

"I was talking to Andrea about it, about him," Kirah said, licking at her thumb for the last of the cheese.

"Nick?"

"No. The fairy."

Sometimes, I know just what to say to a woman: "Oh? She have any ideas?"

"No." Her look said that one of us was an insensitive idiot who would probably need both guesses. "*I* do."

"Well? What do you think?" Gee, maybe I could of sounded a bit more stilted, a little less condescending, if I'd tried. I don't know. When a relationship goes sour, there's nothing right to say.

"Hmm. You talked about how he moved sort of like a wolf, but sort of not, like he wasn't bending in quite the right ways, at the right places."

She had been listening closely. I nodded. "Yeah."

"Well, it reminded me of something. I was just watching Dorann this afternoon, and she was down on all fours playing with Betalyn—Fona's daughter? They were playing horse."

I smiled. "Who was on top?"

For once I'd said something that wasn't wrong: Kirah smiled too. "Betalyn—Dorann wanted to be the horse. But she wasn't bending in the same places that a real horse would. And when she reared back, she didn't toss her head the way a real horse would—she was playing at it."

Analogy is tricky. It can lead you to a useful truth, or right past it, and onto a landmine. "So, you think Boioardo is a baby fairy, out playing at being a wolf?"

"What do you think of the idea? Is it possible?"

I don't know why my wife cares so much about what I think, but she was watching me like everything hung on my next words. "Maybe. You could easily be right." Which she could have, although that's not why I said it.

Her shoulders eased; I hadn't noticed how tightly hunched together they were. I miss a lot. "I'm not sure what good that does," she said. "But I thought . . ."

"It's worth sharing." But who knows about Faerie? What would that mean? Were all these rumors of magical outpourings from Faerie just the equivalent of a vicious kindergarten class out of recess? "I don't know if it does any good, mind," I said with a smile, "but it's worth sharing."

There were two obvious places to find out—Pandathaway and Ehvenor. Ehvenor, because Ehvenor was the only Eren-region outpost of Faerie. Pandathaway, because if there was any movement out from Faerie, no matter how subtle, the Wizards Guild would surely be looking into it, sooner or later.

111

I didn't like either choice, particularly Pandathaway. There was still a price on my head on Pandathaway—with a bonus if it was delivered in small slices.

That left Ehvenor. I never much liked Ehvenor. It's an outpost of Faerie, and the rules of the Eren region don't entirely hold fast there. It's not too bad out near the edge of the city—I've been there, and come out with nothing worse than a nervous tic that went away after a while. But they say that the further in you go, the more the fluctuating, positional rules of Faerie apply, and the less the solid ones of the rest of the universe do.

There was a solution that worked for a lot of problems: stay out, and let somebody else handle it.

That looked like the best one to me. I'm not bad at what I do, but I'm not a magician. I don't like magic, and I've found it far healthier to stay out of the way of magic, no matter what the source.

"It scares you, doesn't it?"

I don't mind my wife thinking I'm not an idiot. "You *bet* it does," I said. "Anyone can get a reputation for being invincible. It's easy: to start, you go out and into harm's way and survive. Repeat, and you've got a reputation; do it a few more times, and you're a legend. But reputation doesn't make you invulnerable the next time. It doesn't matter how good you are, either; there's always a chance you're going to get unlucky. If you keep rolling the dice, eventually you're going to roll snake eyes too many times in a row."

"Like Karl did."

I nodded. "Like Karl did, like Jason Parker did, like Chak did, like . . . like we all will, eventually. Maybe."

We had been ignoring Nora too long; she came out from her hiding place and started in on playing with my shoe.

"This is how the whole problem started, you know," I said, playfully—very gently—kicking at her. She responded by seizing the toe of my shoe between her teeth and shaking it back and forth, like a dog with a rat.

"Oh?"

"Slavery." I reached forward and took the pup by the scruff of the neck and held her firmly for a moment. "When you fight with another tribe—doesn't matter who starts it—

and you win, what do you do with the survivors? Kill them to the last man, the way Chak's people would? Let them go, nursing a grudge—"

"Which they may have a right to."

"Sure. But it doesn't matter." I shrugged. "Right or wrong, you don't want to buy trouble, and if you just let them go, you're buying trouble. So, do you kill them—do you kill them all? Or do you take them in?"

And if you do, can you take them in as citizens or tribesmen, or whatever you want to call them? Of course not—even assuming you're willing to play that game, it takes two.

Slavery wasn't the only choice, of course; there were all sorts of ways short of that—colonization springs to mind. Karl had coopted Holtun, after Bieme had won the war. The difference was a matter of permanence and scale; he had taken the Holts in, with the promise of earning co-equal status in the Empire, eventually.

"So, you're saying that the slavers who burned my village and took me when I was just a girl were just a bunch of nice people. Misunderstood. Did I ever tell you about the time that six of them, that six of them—"

"Shh." I started to reach for her, but stopped myself. "Come *on*, Kirah." I shook my head. "Not talking about what it became; I'm talking about how it started." I patted the pup. "Maybe out of the best of intentions, eh?" Maybe, in the long run, it would have been kinder to let Tennetty simply put them out of their misery.

That wasn't enough for Kirah. Her lips pursed into a thin line, and then she turned away. Damn her, she was always turning away from me.

"Kirah," I said, "I don't ever forgive anybody for ever hurting you. Deliberately or not." I wanted to reach out and take her in my arms and tell her that I'd make everything all right, but that's the kind of lie you can't tell a woman who screams if you hold her.

For a moment, I didn't know how it was going to break. Anything could have happened, from her taking a swing at me to her coming into my arms.

But she just picked Nick up, letting his lower legs dangle.

"Sure," she said, coldly, dismissing me. "Go away, Walter."
There was a tremble in her voice, but I was listening carefully
for it. "I'll handle things here. You need some sleep."

The perversity of my sleep patterns tends toward the maxi-
mum—I couldn't get back to sleep.

CHAPTER NINE

In Which We Leave on a Trip

I am always at a loss to know how much to believe of my own stories.

—WASHINGTON IRVING

Slovotsky's Law Number Nineteen: When telling a story, effect trumps truth.

—WALTER SLOVOTSKY

STASH USED TO SWEAR that it really happened, but lying runs in the Slovotsky family. Me, I don't believe it.

Story goes like this:

Once, when I was real young—three or so—Stash put me on a kitchen counter, and held out his hands.

"Jump, Walter, jump," he said. "Don't worry; I'll catch you."

"No, you won't," I said. "You'll let me fall."

"Jump, Walter, jump. Really—I'll catch you. Honest."

We went back and forth for awhile, him holding his huge hands out for me, me scared, knowing that this was some sort of test.

I jumped. And he stepped back and I fell on the floor, hard.

I lay there crying. "But you *said* you'd catch me."

"That will teach you not to trust anybody," he said.

I've thought about it, over the years. I've thought a lot

about it. Doing it would have been cruel, and my father would have cut his hands off before being cruel to me. But pretending that he had done it, maybe that's different. What he was telling me was true: guaranteed, if you live long enough, and trust people even casually, somebody you've trusted will let you down.

They're only human; everybody's fallible, including me. Particularly me.

Is it better to learn that through a childhood calamity that maybe never really happened or to risk learning it when it really matters?

Don't tell me that lies are always cruel.

Jason found me down in the fencing studio, a large room at the east end of the barracks annex. A light and airy place: one wall consisted mainly of shutters open to the daylight, the other wall was regularly whitewashed.

I'd taken out a practice saber and a straw dummy and—after a good stretch; you need those more and more as the years go by—I was practicing some lunges, working my thigh muscles so hard they practically screamed.

As a friend of a friend used to say, "After forty, it's patch, patch, patch." The maintenance costs on the physical plant keep going up, but the infrastructure keeps wearing down. My right knee had developed what was looking like a long-term ache, although it only got real bad when I overdid things. Still, not good. I thought about ice, and I thought about heat, and I thought a lot about traveling over to Little Pittsburgh to see the Spider, and find out if he could put some whammy on my cartilage.

"Mind if I join you?" Jason asked. He was dressed in a white cotton tunic with matching pantaloons, bloused into the tops of his boots: good workout clothes.

"Why? Am I falling apart?" I gestured at the rack of practice weapons. "Sure. Pick a toy."

"Thanks." He selected a pair of mock Therranji fighting sticks and gave a few practice swats at my favorite sparring partner: a wooden pillar, covered with hemp matting that ran floor to ceiling. He blocked an imaginary blow, parried another, then hammered out a quick tattoo against the covered wood. *Thwocka-thwok-thwok-thwok-thwok.*

"Want some free advice, worth what you pay for it?" I asked, taking up an on-guard stance opposite him.

He nodded. "Sure." He moved one stick back defensively, and thrust the other one out tentatively.

"Don't try to be able to do everything. Balance yourself between overspecialization and not being able to learn anything." I moved in and gently parried an experimental thrust, beat his stick hard aside, then withdrew.

"Nice," he said. He tried a complex maneuver that I didn't quite follow, which probably foreshadowed an attack against my sword arm; I parried easily and moved to the side, letting his lunge take him by me, blocking his attempted slash with his left stick.

"Thankee much, young Cullinane." I faked a slash at his right wrist, then turned the movement into a thrust that would have skewered him through the chest except for two things: one, we were using practice weapons; two, Jason blocked—too nicely by half!—with his left stick.

It had taken me too long to figure out what he was doing—he wasn't trying real Therranji stick play. He was fighting two-swords style, using his left stick as though it was a dagger, his right like a saber. Close in, the dagger is a killing weapon—if you go corps-a-corps against a two-swords man, you'd best not already have something interesting to do with your free hand. At normal fighting distance, it's a decidedly annoying additional blocking device and threat, particularly the ones with the pronged hilt that can trap your blade.

The classic one-sword solution to the two-sword problem is straightforward, in both senses. You maneuver your opponent into taking a square stance—all attack and little defense—while you're in a three-quarters or side stance, very effective on defense. Block hard on the long sword, then attack the long-sword arm, hit it hard, withdraw enough to be sure that he's lost the weapon—that's not the point to get eager—then skewer him.

Forget fencing targets, forget one-cut finishes. All those pretty lunges in an attempt to get through to the body aren't worth half as much as a good, deep cut down the forearm, a slice through muscle and tendons that leaves a weapon dropping from a bloody hand.

I was thinking about too much theory, I guess; Jason worked his way through my defense and gently bounced what I was thinking of as his blocking stick off my head.

"Damn." I backed off, rubbing at the sore spot. It hurt. He smiled. "Another point?"

"Nah."

He set the fighting sticks back in the rack, then turned to face me. "You don't think much of the idea of sniffing around Ehvenor, do you?"

"No, I don't." I shook my head. "I don't like messing around with magic."

He nodded. "I understand that. I agree. But a messenger just arrived. Seems there's other things going on near Ehvenor, too—there's been a 'Warrior lives' killing in Fenevar."

Complete with note. In English, apparently.

I hadn't heard from the dragon for hours.

"Mikyn?"

He shrugged. "Possibly not. It's our only lead."

Now, that was something reasonable. I mean, handling an outpouring of the magical was out of my league, but following a clue toward a lost friend was something I could handle.

"One party or two?" he asked.

Two parties was the obvious solution. One to look into Faerie, one to chase after Mikyn. One party to contain me, one not. But, still, what would we do when we caught him? Arrest him? For what?

Mikyn, you're under arrest of suspicion of being crazy because we haven't heard from you for too long.

Nah. On the other hand, if he had gone over the edge . . . well, it needed somebody relatively senior and trustworthy. There was a relative shortage of those. "I dunno. Let me talk it over with Ahira."

Jason nodded. "Sure. Let's go."

"Now?"

"Is there some problem with now?"

*　　　*　　　*

The dwarf was in the darkened smithy, again, his finished mail shirt hanging from a frame on the wall. Light from the coals reflected from his eyes, making them all red and demonic. He had a piece of work going in the forge. It looked like the start of something: a piece of thumb-thick bar stock about the length of my forearm, with another, shorter piece welded perpendicularly onto it, about a quarter of the distance from one end.

"What's that going to be?" I asked.

He smiled as he slipped the joint back into the forge, and worked the bellows, hard. Heat washed against my face in a solid wave, while rivulets of sweat worked their way through the hair and the scars on his naked chest. He had been at it for some time; the thick hot air in the smithy was filled with the not-unpleasant reek of fresh sweat.

"Don't you remember those newfangled nightsticks the police were starting to wear, back on the Other Side? I figured I'd give one a try." He tapped the hammer gently against the end. "The handle's supposed to spin—I've got Kayren whittling a collar for this. I'll slip it over, then flare out the end just a trifle."

"I remember them," I said, "but those were made of wood."

Ahira smiled. "I figure I can handle the extra weight." He was silent for a long moment. "You're trying to decide whether or not it's one party or two."

Jason looked disgusted. "Oh, come *on.*"

"Hey, kid," I said, "you have a friend for more than twenty years, and spend most—"

"Too much, anyway," the dwarf put in.

"—of your waking life with him, and he'll read your mind, too."

Trouble was, Ahira was only close, this time. I was more thinking about keeping the hell out of the Faerie matter than I was about who would be looking into it.

The dwarf shrugged. "It's pretty obvious. The Faerie matter is more important, but the likelihood that it's something we can affect, one way or the other, is small. On the other hand, Mikyn is one of ours, and so is the Warrior myth we created. We have to look into that." He was silent for a moment. "One party," Ahira said. "Mainly to check out Ehvenor; that takes priority over looking for Mikyn."

"That seems awfully clear to you," I said. I can't always read his mind—Ahira's smarter than I am. Sometimes I can divert him.

"Andrea's necessary for Ehvenor," he said, ignoring the objection, "and I'm not going to let her wander around without us."

"Is that an issue?"

He pursed his lips for a moment. "Yes. She's going, she says, and Tennetty's going with her. Tennetty is dangerous without proper supervision—so that means at least one more of us."

Jason cocked his head to one side. "How about two parties? We've got more people available. Durine, Kethol, and Piro, for a start."

"We could let you take Kethol and company and go haring after Mikyn," Ahira said, as though considering it.

"Well, yes."

"Bad idea," the dwarf said. "I want them around, keeping an eye on the family." That's how Ahira referred to my wife and daughters: *the* family, as though none other mattered. I understand that. "If Daherrin was here, we could get some help from his team, but he's not. We don't have enough for two parties." He smiled at Jason. "The lesson begins: pick the party."

Jason made a fist, and stuck out his thumb. "Me."

"Who's going to take care of the pups?" I asked. "I thought you were going to take responsibility for them."

Jason smiled weakly. "I guess I have to add the job to the scullery maids' roster—and Jane says she'll take a turn."

I grinned back at him. "Handy to have a bit of rank, eh?"

"I *tried* to handle it without delegating it to them. Okay?" Not waiting for a smartass answer, Jason added the index finger. "Second is Mother—you're right that we have to have a wizard in on this, if we're going to look into the Faerie matter." He was missing the point: Andrea was already insisting on checking out Ehvenor. The only question was who would go with her, not whether or not she would go. "Then there's you two." He rubbed at the side of his nose with his middle finger. "You don't like the idea of trying to do two things at once, do you?"

I snorted. "I sometimes have enough trouble doing one thing at once." I cocked my head to one side. "Don't you have any misgivings about taking your mother along on this?"

She had handled herself well in Velen, and I'd been watching her closely since. She looked fine, not much different at all, although maybe there was a bit more of a rosy glow to her cheeks than usual. But going out in harm's way wasn't something Andrea had been doing, not since the very beginning. And if it required magic?

Again, it was all academic—Andrea was going, and that was that—but Ahira and I were teaching Jason; "academic" doesn't mean "irrelevant."

"No," Jason said. "I don't." Jason's expression wasn't one of unconcern; it was a cold and distant look, the expression of a chessmaster who knows the value of his pieces, and will push them around the board into the right place, no matter whose face the piece wears.

Even his. "It's necessary," he said. He added his little finger. "Tennetty." He held out his hand, fingers spread. "Five of us. Small enough not to draw unnecessary attention, small enough to hide with a little cover, large enough to handle some trouble. Ellegon to drop us off and pick us up. Just outside of Ehvenor, I'd think."

"No," Ahira said. "If there's something really sticky going on there, we don't want to drop right in on it. Better to work our way up to it, and sniff around as we go. The locals may have done some of the looking into things for us."

Better, yes. Best was to keep the hell out of it. I didn't say as much, but I guess my face showed it.

Ahira turned to Jason. "Give us a minute, will you?"

"But—"

"Now will be fine," he said, gesturing to the door of the smithy. "You can get my saddle from the stable. I want to put a few more equipment rings on it."

He stood in the doorway, watching the boy walk away, then turned back to me.

"Give it up, Walter," Ahira said. "You don't have to go,

nobody's going to hold an axe to your throat. But you know you're going, just as well as I do." His chuckle was hollow in his barrel chest. "Three reasons; take your pick. First," he said, "because while this whole thing about creatures coming out of Faerie was distant, as of about ten days ago it became local, it became personal. Your wife and kids live in this country, in this barony, and you're no more going to leave that kind of menace uninvestigated than I am."

He looked up at me. "Second reason: Jason, Andy, Tennetty, and I are going. You're not going to let us go into this alone," he said, as though daring me to dispute it.

"Noble guy, aren't I?" I smiled.

He didn't take the bait, not directly. "One last reason," he said, not looking me in the eye. "Your wife won't let you touch her, and if you can get away for awhile, you won't have to deal with that. You can put off handling that for as long as we're on the road." He turned back to the forge.

I wanted to be angry, to be furious with him for mentioning it. If he'd said it in the presence of anybody else, I know I would have been.

But he was right. On all three counts.

Damn, damn, damn.

Jason walked through the doorway, a saddle slung over his shoulder. "Where do you want this?" he asked.

"Just dump it on the floor," Ahira said. "You'd best go pack. We leave in the morning."

As we walked away, Jason's brow furrowed. "What was that all about?"

"What?"

He gestured clumsily. "Ahira. It was like he was . . . I don't know. Not there. Angry, maybe. Was it something I said?"

"Nah. It's not you. Game face," I said.

"Eh?"

"Never mind."

He frowned at that.

I thought about explaining that even when you look at the football game as a job, as a way to pay for school, you get yourself psyched up for it, and that when you trot out on the field, your heart pumping hard, the ground springy beneathy your feet, ready to, say, grab a quarterback and slam him down so hard that his descendants will still ache, there's a kind of glare you wear, whether or not you intend to.

And then I thought about how he probably didn't have the background to appreciate it, and how I didn't feel like explaining football to a This Sider.

And then I thought about how if I kept saying "Never mind" to the kid he was going to slip a knife into me someday, so I just smiled.

"Honest," I said. "It's not important."

I'd said goodbye to the kids, and to the pups, so I went over the list one more time. Weapons, clothes, food, money, miscellaneous. Miscellaneous was, as always, the largest category. Packed for running, if necessary—the most important stuff was in either my belt pouch or my small rucksack.

Grab and run, if I had to. When the shit comes down, you grab your friends, and—if time—your essentials. Leave the rest be.

There was a gout of fire below in the courtyard.

They're waiting for you. So am I.

So wait a bit longer.

My big rucksack was packed solid; I took it to the window and tossed it down to Ahira's waiting hands. *Thunk.*

I turned back to Kirah. "Like the old days, eh, old girl?" I asked, smiling.

She didn't smile back. "I don't want you to go."

Walter Slovotsky's advice to wives whose husbands are packing for a trip: be nice. Let problems lie.

Look—trivial problems can wait, or you can solve them yourself while your spouse is gone. That's why we call them trivial, eh? They're not important. Anything serious you can't solve between the time he takes his rucksack down out of the closet and heads out the door. That's not the time to try.

All it can do is screw up his mind while he's gone. So leave it be. This wasn't a time to be discussing that; it wasn't the time for either of us to be discussing anything.

The obvious thing, the right thing for me to do was to ignore what she'd just said.

"Right," I said. "And you don't want me to stay, either. You can't stand to have me touch you, remember?"

"Please. Don't blame me for that." She faced me in the doorway. "It's not my fault, Walter. I try, but every time you touch me, it's like . . ." she raised her hand in apology, as a shudder shook her frame. "I'm sorry."

Walter Slovotsky's advice to husbands leaving on a trip is ever the same . . .

I gripped her arms tightly, ignoring her struggles. "It's not my fault, either, Kirah. I didn't do that to you, and I won't be blamed for it. I won't—" I started, then stopped, and let her go. She gripped herself across the middle and turned away. Her shoulders shook as she fell to her knees.

"No." *I won't live my life in penance for harm others have done to you*, I didn't quite say.

It's neither of your fault, if you want my opinion, Ellegon said, his voice pitched only for me.

Thanks. I think I needed that.

All parts of the service. Should we get going, or do you want to have a few more tender moments with your wife?

I kissed the tips of my fingers and held them out toward her back. "Goodbye, Kirah."

Ah, parting is such sweet sorrow . . .

The sun had shattered the chill of the earliest morning, but clouds were moving in, and the sky to the east was slate gray and threatening. Time to get going—flying through rain is not fun at all.

Jason and Andrea had already climbed up and fastened themselves into their seats on the rigging we'd lashed to Ellegon's broad back, while Ahira was under the dragon's belly, giving the knots a last check. I'm as safety-conscious as anybody else, but riding Ellegon isn't like riding a horse—he'll let you know if things start to give.

Alternately, if I do have it in for you, a few strands of rope aren't going to make a difference. The dragon snorted, startling the honor guard of soldiers who had gathered to bid us good journeying.

124

Doria was taking her duties as Steward seriously—she had a piece of paper with a list sticking out of her blouse pocket.

"Going to have this place in good shape by the time we're back, eh?" I asked, with a knowing smirk.

She smiled and shrugged. "I lost my old profession when I defied the Mother; I'd better find something else I can do." She knew better. If nothing else, there was always a job open at the Home school, teaching English, civics, and pretty much anything else; besides, Lou Riccetti would be glad to have her around.

"Home ec majors," I sniffed. I gave Doria a quick squeeze goodbye, then climbed up and belted myself into the saddle behind Tennetty.

She turned in her seat and gave me a quick glare. "You took long enough."

"Leave it be." Andrea frowned her into silence.

"Everything okay?" Ahira asked, as he levered himself into his seat and belted himself in, too firmly; dwarves dislike flying almost as much as they do traveling by boat.

Jason felt at the butt of his revolver, from where it projected under his jacket. "All set."

Tennetty folded her arms in front of her chest and leaned back against the pile of gear lashed between the two of us. "Fine."

Andrea gestured in impatience. "Let's go."

"Ducky," I said. "Let's get the fuck out of here."

Hang on . . .

PART TWO:

ROADWORK

CHAPTER TEN

In Which We Reach Fenevar, and the Trail Heats Up

'Tis the men, not the houses, that make the city.
—THOMAS FULLER

Health hint for the traveler: Don't throw rocks at guys with guns.
—WALTER SLOVOTSKY

I'VE ALWAYS TAKEN THE ideas from where I could get them. Hey—I'm not as inventive as Lou, or as anybody else; I do the best I can.

I got the "Warrior lives" notes from my big brother, Steve. It was one of the few Vietnam stories he ever told me. (When he wasn't drinking, that is. Two beers and he'd start with the stories, and wouldn't stop with either the stories and the drinking until he was totally wasted.)

It wasn't something he'd done—he had spent most of his time in Vietnam as a door gunner on a sort-of-unarmed helicopter, what they called a slick—but it was a habit that some of the ground soldiers had: they would leave the ace of spades, the death card, on dead enemies. The way he explained it, it supposedly started when somebody had a short deck of cards on him, and thought it kind of funny. Eventually, a lot of the outfits had their own cards printed up, with the name of their unit on them.

"Now, let me understand this," I had said. "They'd expected Charley—"

"You weren't there," he had said, softly. "Call them the Vietcong, or the NVA, or the enemy."

"—they'd expect the enemy to run across dead bodies of their own people, and get spooked because they had a *playing card* on their heads?"

He'd shrugged. "I didn't say it made sense. I said that's what they did. But it did make sense. It made the whole thing more personal. There was a way to make it even more personal," he had said. "But we didn't do that most of the time."

"I thought you flew all the time," I said. If he was going to reporach me . . .

"Just flew *most* of the time," he had said. And then he wouldn't say any more.

The ideal place to have Ellegon take us would have been as far away from Ehvenor as we could get, if you asked me; the right thing to do would then be make tracks in the opposite direction from Ehvenor.

That, however, wasn't the plan. The plan was to be dropped off down the coast from Ehvenor; Fenevar seemed about right. It would have been convenient to be dropped off behind some outcropping near the rocky shore of Fenevar. The only trouble was, there wasn't a rocky shore.

The land near Fenevar was flat and at water level, more swampy than lakeshore. There wasn't much forest or other cover; as was true of much of the arable land around the Cirric, farmers had long cleared and planted well up to the edge of the freshwater sea, and beyond, growing kelp and wild rice in the shallow, swampy water.

The dragon had to leave us back up the road, in the rolling foothills, a good half-day's walk down to the city.

As we had learned back in the old raiding days, the danger when Ellegon touches down is directly related to two things: how isolated the area appears, and how long he is on the ground. We did the best that we could with both.

How's it look? I asked, as Ellegon banked hard in a tight circle.

The wind beat hard against my face, pulling tears from my eyes. I could barely make out the hill below in the gray predawn light, but Ellegon's eyes were better than mine; he had spotted the road that bisected it neatly, cutting through the dense wood.

Nobody around, as far as I can tell. Coming in.

Air rushed by as the dim ground rushed up. Ellegon, his wings pounding the air hard, slammed down on the dirt road.

Their safety straps already off, Jason and Ahira slid to the ground below, while Tennetty and I pulled straps loose and tossed packs and rucksacks down. I lowered Andy down to Ahira's waiting arms, then slid down a loose strap to the ground.

Ellegon took a few steps down the road, then leaped into the air, climbing in a tight spiral before flapping off into the sky.

I'll start checking rendezvous points in a couple tendays. Until we meet again, be well, he said.

White light flared as Ahira pulled a glowsteel from his pouch. He already had his huge rucksack on his back. "Let's go folks. We've got a full day's march to Fenevar."

Tennetty, shrugging into her rucksack, nodded. "At least. And nothing more than sour beer to look forward to at the end of the trip."

While a modified direct approach—distract, grab, and go—is one way of getting something specific, it's a lousy way to try to find any information.

There's any number of strategies to use when you're snooping around for intelligence—and I can always use some more intelligence.

One of the best is also one of the simplest. Any town along a trade route—and, for obvious reasons, we've always tended to work around trade routes—has at least one travelers' inn. If it's a sizable town, usually more. Travelers—no matter what they trade in—almost always like to talk. Not always honestly, mind.

Then again, who am I to complain about a bit of dishonesty?

All we got out of the first two inns we tried was a mild buzz.

The talk in the Cerulean Creek Inn, the third inn of the

evening, flowed like the sour beer; it tended to slop over on the floor and turn it into mud.

The general practice along that part of the coast is to sell ale by what they call a pitcher, although it's barely half the size of a common water pitcher. Some drink right out of the pitcher; others use a mug. I poured Tennetty another mug full, then tilted mine back, barely wetting my mouth.

She took a long pull. "Well?" she asked.

"Well, what?"

"What brilliant things have you found?"

I had debated bringing Tennetty along this evening. There were plenty of problems: women warriors were rare in the Eren regions, and she was relatively well known. She was moderately famous as Karl Cullinane's one-eyed bodyguard, her temper was never fully under her control, and she scared me.

On the other hand: her glass eye was in place, visible and entirely convincing under a fringe of hair, and nobody would have mistaken me for Karl, either in truth or in legend.

She was the obvious choice for this, despite the minuses— she could be counted on to keep her mouth shut, unlike Jason; she wouldn't look out of place in the drinking room of an inn, unlike Andrea; she wouldn't draw the wrong sort of attention, unlike Ahira.

Maybe I would have been better bringing Ahira along. He wouldn't have stood out: over in the far corner, a dwarf and his human companion sat, sharing a loaf of almost black bread and a bowl of thick stew of unlikely ancestry. By the cut of his leather tunic, I decided the dwarf was from Bener-ell—the Benerell style has always been for clothes that barely fit. The human could have been of any origin, although you'll find more of that wheaty blond color in Osgrad than elsewhere.

Changes happen, even while you don't look for them. Or maybe particularly when you don't look for them.

I hadn't answered Tennetty. I turned to her, raising my voice ever-so-slightly.

"I don't know, either," I said. "That . . ."—the line called for a long pause—"*thing* we saw this morning was one of the strangest things that have ever reached Tybel's eyes, and that's a fact."

The broad-faced fellow down the bench from me pricked up his ears.

I picked up our empty pitcher and turned it over, empty. I'd buy more in a moment, unless somebody took the hint.

"Yeah," Tennetty said, not helping much. I don't know about her, sometimes. This was the third time we'd tried this routine, and her side of it was no more polished than the first.

I'm afraid I glared at her.

"That it was," she added, chastened, trying to bit more. "Really, strange."

It took all I could do not to raise my eyes toward the ceiling and implore the help of the gods, or of heaven.

"Very strange."

"Begging your pardon, traveler," the fellow whose attention I had caught said, "but did you talk of seeing something strange?" He half-rose, courteously gesturing with his own, full pitcher.

Several times, I thought. *And pretty darned clumsily.*

"I guess I might have," I said, beckoning him over. I guess if a fish is hungry enough, he'll bite a hook with a plastic bug on it.

He splashed some ale into each of our mugs, then politely sipped at his own first.

"Lots of strange things been seen of late," he said. "More and more over the past few years. Travelers report many things, although tales do grow in the telling."

I nodded. "That they do. But this was something that didn't grow. It was a wolf that wasn't a wolf."

We were gathering an audience, or at least some company; the drinking room of a tavern isn't the place for those who prefer solitude. The dwarf and human pair wandered over as I launched into a seriously edited version of our encounter with Boioardo and the wolf pack: I cut out the fight, had it eating a deer instead of a cow, and placed it outside of Alfani rather than back in Bieme. I've always been a stickler for details, just never for accurate ones.

The obvious way to find something out is to go around and ask questions, but that invariably raises the question of who you are and what you're after. Given that there is a price on my head—the Pandathaway Slavers Guild is no more fond of me than I am of them—I'd rather not answer the first question honestly, most places I go.

So the obvious way was out. A better way is to talk about something interesting, something related to what you're interested in, and let everybody else impress you with what they know about it.

A little bald man, a trader in gems and gold who had given his name as Enric (and who must have been a lot tougher than he looked, given his admitted profession and lack of a bodyguard) ordered a round for the table. "It's coming from one of the Places of the other ones, perhaps, they say. Or from," he made a sign with his thumb, "*there*."

"Places of the other ones?" I tried to look puzzled. "There? You mean—"

"I mean just as I say, traveler. It's an old belief that it is dangerous to mention either by name. My grandfather, long dead though he is, used to talk of them as only *them*, and while I thought that strange, he did live to sixty years."

Another man spat. "Faw. Just a superstition."

"Maybe it was, and maybe it wasn't. Maybe they know when their names are spoke, and maybe they don't. What with strange things happening, with something or other having wiped out that little village up near Erevale, I'm not one to take chances." He turned to me. "What do you think, Tybel?"

I shook my head. "I've never been one to take chances, either." Without a damn good reason. Wiped out a village? I hadn't heard about that.

"A wise man," he said. "And with the Warrior about, turning visible only to kill? I used to own a servant, had her for ten years—Venda, her name is. Stout as a stoat, and loyal as a good dog. But with the Warrior about—and there are many who say it's Karl Cullinane—murdering honest men who own such, I'll tell you that I sold her, for good coin and without apology."

Tennetty frowned. "One moment. The way I've heard it is that Karl Cullinane and his people will leave alone all but slavers, and Guild slavers in particular."

Enric shook his head. "That's the way it used to be, for

sure. For years and years. I've met some of the Home raiders and traders—I even camped for an evening with a bunch of his men one night, in Kuarolin, up along the edge of the Katharhd? Tough-looking bunch, but I felt perfectly safe among them, and they were welcome in most towns—nobody thought they'd be hunting for any but slavers, and slavers are none too popular anyway.

"But there's been word of it changing. There was a hostler murdered in Wehnest, for nothing more than having a bought servant."

"Not just off in Wehnest, either." A burly man slapped his fist down on the table, causing mugs and pitchers to dance. "Just outside our own Fenevar, not forty days ago, Arnet and his brother were murdered in their beds, and one of those notes left behind. Englits all over it, they say." He shuddered. "Dangerous language, I hear—they say that you don't have to be a wizard to write spells in it."

"That's nonsense. Pfah." Another spat.

In Fenevar, you can tell the locals by their habit of spitting as punctuation. "You have to be one of their wizards to do it, to make their gunpowder."

I listened with more than half an ear for the next hour, buying just a bit more than my share of the rounds. That's the key to being inconspicuous. You don't have to be average—you just have to seem like you're typical.

I guess I drank too much. But I do remember hearing a fragment of a phrase from Reil the baker, one I didn't want to inquire into too closely.

"—and that's what Alezyn said. You know, the new farrier, the one who was through about five tendays ago?"

Bingo. Alezyn was Mikyn's father's name. It was possible, of course, that there was a real farrier going by the name of Alezyn, but I don't believe in coincidences—somebody with that name near a killing.

It all made sense. Many smiths—most, easily—and a lot of hostlers did some shoeing on the side, but like anything else, shoeing horses is something you get a lot better at it if you do it regularly. On the other hand, outside of the largest cities, there simply wasn't enough work for a fulltime farrier, and it was a respectable and likely profession for a smith or horseman to take up, if he had a bit of money for tools, and the taste for the road.

Didn't take much in the way of tools, either. A small anvil and maybe a portable forge if you were extravagant, although you could build a firepit for that kind of work. Hammers, tongs, various trimming knifes and clippers, plus some bar stock, and you were in business. You could put all of it on the back of a pack horse, if you were pressed, although you'd probably want a wagon.

Home raiding teams usually carried at least one traveling farrier's rig with them. It always was a good idea for a raiding team to send scouts out, and one of the best covers we had used, back during the raiding years, was that of a farrier.

Mikyn had separated from the rest of the team, taking the traveling farrier rig with him.

We were getting warm, perhaps. Possibly we could wrap up the Mikyn matter quickly, before investigating Faerie. Not a bad idea, all things considered. We had a double objective, after all, if we could manage it: sniff around Ehvenor to see if we could find out what was happening with Faerie, and see if we could track down Mikyn.

Which was more important? Okay, Ehvenor. Fine.

Which was more urgent, though? That was another thing.

Maybe a better question was: which could we handle better?

And why ask questions when there was beer to be drunk. Er, drank?

Enric refilled my mug. "You're decidedly good company, Tybel," he said. "It's been a pleasure meeting you."

"That's because I listen well."

Somehow or other, Tennetty got me back to our rooms.

I don't remember dreaming that night, although I do remember getting up once to puke into the thundermug next to my bed. (If I hadn't, the smell would have reminded me.)

In the morning, I had the godfather of all hangovers.

Anything for the cause, eh?

CHAPTER ELEVEN

In Which I Have a Hangover

It is only the first bottle that is expensive.

—FRENCH PROVERB

Mrmf. Gack. Urpffff.

—WALTER SLOVOTSKY

TRYING TO GET SOMEthing decided over a hangover is no fun at all. Trying to do anything over a hangover is no fun at all.

I couldn't see it, not with my eyes closed, but there was a thumb-sized flask of Eareven healing draughts at my elbow as I lay stretched out on the settee in our common room. Tennetty had placed the filigreed brass flask at my elbow when she and Ahira had hauled me out of my room and set me up on the settee. A damp cloth lay across my eyes, easing the dry burning of my eyeballs to mere agony.

Sadistic bitch. She knew that I wouldn't take it, not for something like this. Healing draughts are for medical or personal emergencies.

"You okay, Walter?" the dwarf asked.

"Peachy keen." Each word hurt. There were little men with big knifes carving on the inside of my temples, and demons with spiked shoes and flamethrowers walking up and down every tendon in my body. Never mind what was going on in my stomach. I don't like to think about what was going on in my stomach.

At least the settee was overstuffed and would have been comfortable if even softness hadn't hurt. The luxury was not unexpected—we had taken a large suite of rooms at the Krellen Inn. When you're paying with real Pandathaway gold—even if you get back a lot of local coins as your change—you can usually get a spot of luxury.

I would have settled for a jot of comfort.

Ahira bit into a red, round apple; the crunching sound hurt my forehead.

My mouth tasted of sour vomit. Every time I turned to look at something I could feel my neck bones squawk, and the grit behind my eyes grated as I lay there.

There is a cure, but I couldn't use it. Wouldn't use it.

I forced myself up to one elbow and fumbled for the stone mug of too-hot Holtish herb tea that Andrea had brewed up for me; it was supposed to be good for both headaches and menstrual cramps. This is one time that I can swear that one out of two isn't good. I had to remove the damp cloth from my eyes to find it.

I eyed the flask of healing draughts. It would be wrong to take it, just to cure the hangover. It's not just that healing draughts are expensive—although they are—it's worse: they're rare, hard to get hold of. We're supposed to save that stuff for serious hurtS, for emergencies.

Granted, I once downed a half bottle when I was fleeing from a town—I've shown my heels to so many that I don't recall just which one now—but I had sprained my ankle, and while that's usually a minor injury, it would have gotten me killed then, and by my definition, an injury isn't minor if it gets you killed.

In all the times I've been banged up, and there are a lot of those, I've never used the stuff promiscuously—I've always preferred saving promiscuity for other contexts.

The wind was blowing hard from the west, in through the window; the frest air helped just a little. Jason had been dispatched for food, and had returned with a basket of fruit, a dozen sticks of roasted pork, peppers, and onions from the market down the street, and a pail of ale from the eating room below.

The smell of food made me gag. The aroma of roast pork and a hangover don't mix.

Well, the tea was a loser. Maybe the ale would be better. I accepted Jason's offer of a battered pewter tankard, and sipped at the flat brew, hoping it would clear the painful fog behind my throbbing eyes.

It didn't. I've never had much luck with the hair of the dog as a hangover remedy.

Healing draughts are expensive, and hard to come by. Hangovers hurt. Balance the two in the scales, and the supply of healing draughts was still meager, and hangovers hurt like hell.

Put it in proportion: I could lie here in pain for the rest of the day. In a day, tops, I'd be back to normal, and if we were going to leave Fenevar, we'd need at least a day to get horses and provisions, never mind about which direction.

The trouble, of course, is that even if it was Mikyn, he could have gone anywhere, in about three directions. On the other hand, while things in Ehvenor weren't likely to stay in one place, the city itself was considerate enough to stay in one place, and maybe that solved the problem for us.

How to travel was easy: we'd go by land. Fenevar isn't a major shipping center—the shoreline is too swampy and shallow.

"At least we don't have to travel by water," Ahira said, repressing a shudder.

Andy patted his knee. "Just as well, eh?"

Dwarves don't like water any deeper than what they wash in—and the traditional dwarvish wash house is a small room, concave to a drain in the center, ringed with chest-high (to them) wash basins. Ahira was the only one I've ever known to use a bath tub.

It's obvious why, when you think of it—a human with a lungful of air is lighter than water. Swimming, for us, is just a matter of working with natural forces, sometimes bobbing up and down to rhythmically clear mouth and nose from the water in time with breathing. Dwarves, on the other hand, are denser than we are. Their bones aren't only thicker, with the correspondingly larger joints that confer a greater mechanical advantage, they're made of a slightly different, more compact calcium matrix than ours. Their muscle fibers are smaller and much more numerous, and they carry a smaller fat-to-muscle ratio—that's one of the reasons they're so fond of ale: starch and alcohol are good sources of quick calories.

Drop a dwarf in water, and he'll sink like a stone.

I trotted out Lou Riccetti's old joke: "How do you make a dwarf float?" I tried to grin, but the effort hurt.

Ahira smile dutifully, while Andy answered. "Two scoops of ice cream, one dwarf, and fill with coke."

Yup; because that's the only way. I guess you have to be an Other Sider to find it funny.

Jason wasn't having any of the humor. "I don't like any of it, but we've got to find him."

Tennetty sneered. "Wanting doesn't make it so. He left several tendays ago. He could be anywhere."

Andy shook her head. "Not if he's maintaining a cover as a roving farrier."

"We need to find him."

Jason was right. It was one thing to kill slavers. Nobody shed tears for them. Fear them, sure; deal with them—well, what else was there to do with a conquered neighbor?

But express sympathy? Identify with them? Consider Home raiders a common threat?

Nah.

The trouble with creating a legend is that people will believe it. Ahira and I, and later Jason, had gone to some trouble to keep Karl's legend alive in the stories about the Warrior, and Karl was the archetype of a Home raider. By murdering the locals and leaving the note, Mikyn was fucking with the legend. I'm not sure whether I was more surprised or annoyed. Both, I guess—Mikyn had been raised in Home, and he should have *known* better.

I sipped some more of the hot tea and lay back. Just reach out, take the small brass bottle in my trembling hand, then break the wax seal with my thumb, and tilt it back . . .

No.

Ahira had been thinking. "Any chance you can put a location spell on him?" he asked Andrea.

140

She shrugged. "Perhaps." She shrugged. "Certainly. I've gotten very good at location spells."

I was going to ask how, but I caught myself. Back when she thought Karl was alive, she had labored long and hard to locate him. You do it a lot, you get good at it.

"I will need something of his," she said, "preferably some hair or nails, or something he's interacted with intimately."

"They say the note was written in blood."

"His?" Ahira was skeptical.

"Not likely, but it's a start." Andrea stood up. "There's a hedge wizard in town. As I understand it, he's a confidant of Lord Ulven. I think it's time for a bit of professional courtesy." She wasn't wearing wizard's robes, of course, but equally of course she could quickly demonstrate what she was, if necessary.

"Hold on, please." Ahira held up a hand. "You haven't done this for awhile."

"Magic?"

A frown twisted its way across his face. "No. The rest of it." He pursed his lips for a moment, then bit another chunk of meat off his skewer. "If you're going to brace a local, we'd best be able to get out of town quickly. That means horses."

Tennetty nodded. "Me. You part with gold too easy. Looks suspicious."

"Fine."

"Hmm . . ." she cocked her head. "One each, and two spares?"

"Three, if you can. We also should try to learn as much as we can about the local situation—there's a dwarf smith; I should go and see if he wants some word from the Old Country. Jason, it's you and me for that one."

Jason scowled. "Why me?"

"Because you speak dwarvish, and with a thick Heverel accent. Tall Ones who can speak the language, accent or no, are rare enough that you'll charm him. If he happens to be from Heverel, all the better." He turned to Andrea. "Which leaves you and Walter for the wizard. You need somebody to watch your back." He nodded at me. "You'd best leave now."

141

"Now?" I asked.

"Now," he said.

"Well," I said, each word a painful effort, "a bodyguard has to move around."

"True enough. Better down that stuff," he said.

My hands trembled as I examined the wax seal perfunctorily, then broke it, tossing the cap aside. I the flask to my cracked lips, each movement hurting.

A spasm of nausea washed over me, but I fought it down successfully. The too-sweet liquid washed the vomit and sand from my mouth, replacing it with a warm glow, like good brandy. In between painful beats, my headache disappeared, various aches and pains sparking away, disappearing.

But I really hate magic. Honest. I just hate hangovers more.

"That feels better," I said, my voice deepening and strengthening as I tossed the damp cloth aside and swung off the couch and to my feet.

No pain, not even any morning aches. The air was just chilly enough to be bracing, and filled with the enticing smell of roasted pork, peppers, and onions. I was twenty again—strong, arrogant, and horny, ready to deal with anything the universe cared to offer up . . . starting with a stick of roast peppers, pork, and onions that Jason had left on the serving platter.

As I bit hungrily into the cold meat, Ahira caught my smile and returned it.

In divvying up the jobs, he was still looking after me, the way it had always been. He could easily have assigned himself as Andrea's bodyguard, even if that meant she would have to wait until he got back from the smith.

Tennetty scowled. "What are the two of you so proud of yourselves about?"

Ahira shrugged. "Private joke."

142

CHAPTER TWELVE

In Which I'm Too Smart For My Own Damn Good

A hasty judgment is the first step toward recantation.
—PUBLILIUS SYRUS

Figure it out fast—and so what if you're wrong? You might get lucky, and implement the wrong one so that it works.
—WALTER SLOVOTSKY

The sign read—

REMNOR
Magician, Wizard, Mage, and Seer

—IN TYPICAL CONVOLUTED ERENDRA LETtering, although runes and symbols were scattered across its surface.

Andrea stopped five steps before the doorway, and reached into the bag at her waist.

I started to reach for her wrist, but stopped myself. "Hang on a second," I said.

She turned, her face creased in irritation. "What *is* it?"

"Look," I said, "I'm no expert on magic—"

"That's for sure."

"—but I do know that it's a risk for you. You've overdone in the past. Doria thinks you've been hooked on it."

She dismissed it with a frown and a wave. "You don't, or you wouldn't have let me come along."

I had been thinking about that, and I'd been thinking about how convenient it had been for me to think Doria wrong, and decide that Andy was safe to travel, because if I didn't, I don't know what we would have done for a wizard.

She tossed her head, sending her long black hair flying as she struck a pose, one hand on hip. That's who Acia got that habit from, I guess. "I don't intend to spend the rest of my life living that down. I had a problem. I pushed myself too far, and made it worse by not taking care of myself. I've got it under control now."

I guess I didn't keep my skepticism off my face—not surprisingly, because I wasn't trying to.

Also unsurprisingly, that didn't calm her down. "Dammit, Walter, you know you need a wizard in on this, at least the Ehvenor and Faerie part."

I had to admit that was true. "Sure, but—"

"But nothing," she said. "Just navigating around the middle city takes magic. By some perspectives, it doesn't have a diameter."

"Eh?"

"I mean," she said, "looked at one way, there's a fleck of Faerie in the middle of the city, and the rules of Faerie are . . ." she grasped for a word ". . . indeterminate, by your standards. Not entirely determinate, by mine. When you get close natural laws break down.

"Well, no, they don't exactly break down; they kind of get neurotic. They don't apply in the same way, and there's a whole new set that you're not equipped to learn. You'll have to trust me there and then, and you have to trust me here and now."

An old friend of mine used to explain that what most women want from the men in their lives is loving leadership. I guess he hadn't met Andrea. Or Tennetty. Or Acia. Or Kirah, for that matter. Or probably Janie.

Argh. Slovotsky's Law number whatever: a generalization that doesn't apply to anybody means you're missing something. Doria, maybe? Dorann, please?

"For now," Andrea went on, "you'll have to trust my judgment about when magic is necessary. Understood?"

She didn't wait for me to answer; she dipped two fingers

into her bag, and pulled out a handful of dust and tossed it into the air, accompanying it by a pair of muttered syllables. Stubborn old habits die hard—I tried, once more, to make sense of what she was saying, to remember the words, but I couldn't.

Dust motes turned to a million points of light, and then dimmed to redness, and then further until all they left behind was a dazzle in my eyes.

She stopped. Her eyes closed, her lips moved slowly, silently for a full minute.

That's a long time to stand and wait.

Passersby stared at her out of the corner of their eyes, and then hurried on. Most normals—present company certainly included—tend to want to be away from a working wizard, preferably as far away as possible.

Finally, her eyes opened. "Okay; he's waiting for us. Let's go in."

"Hmmm . . . can I ask what was for?"

"The first was just checking for . . . a certain class of trap. As to the second . . ." She smiled. "It's an old wizard's trick. You know how a spell is a collection of syllables, each in its right order? Well, if the spell is built right, there's often stopping points, short of the whole thing. You go almost to the end of the spell, and then leave the last few syllables—sometimes even one—unsaid. Sort of like building a car, then putting the key in the ignition—but not turning it. Then when you need it, out come the last few syllables." She gestured with her fingers. "And *vroom*. Lightning shoots from your fingertips, or whatever."

"I've never had lightning shoot from my whatever; it just felt like it once." I was trying to keep things light and friendly, but I didn't like her tone. There was a shadowy undercurrent in her voice, something dark and deadly, and I didn't much like it. I took her arm. "Excuse me, old friend, but you've missed the point—we're not here to fight with the local wizard."

She raised her eyes to heaven and rolled them. "I know that. Silly. I didn't want to walk into Rewnor's shop with an almost-built spell hanging over his head, and mine. Not a friendly thing to do. I was busy," she said, and her lips split in a remarkably sexy smile, "eating my words, eh?" She patted my shoulder. "You handle the being clever and the sneaking around; leave the magic to me."

She pushed through the curtains; I followed.

Some day, if I'm lucky, I'm going to walk into a magician's shop or workroom that's lit like a library, clean as MacDonald's, and sterile-smelling as a hospital.

I wasn't lucky today.

Rewnor's workshop smelled like a gym locker, redolent of old dirt, unwashed sweat, and variously related funguses eating away at toes and crotches.

Just like a gym locker room. Ugh.

No, the standard history of me is right, but I'm not a witling; I decided in junior high that football was to be a way of paying for college without slashing a four-year hemorrhage in Stash and Emma's savings. What I did in the fall was a job, and that's all. The stink of unwashed sweat holds no whiff of nostalgia for me. I spent too many hours in gym lockers, back on the Other Side, and don't miss the stench at all.

What light there was came from a pair of sputtering candles set into reflective holders high on the wall. Not even a glowsteel. What light there was revealed a smallish room lined by workbenches, an open door at the far end leading to immediate darkness.

The day was heating up outside, but the air was dank and chilly in here.

Shaking her head, Andrea walked to a workbench, picked up a fist-sized copper bowl and took a sniff. "Myrryhm, hemp, and cinnamon? *Really?* I am unimpressed." She turned to me. "I've always been unfond of love potions, but if you're going to do them, it's perhaps best to *do* them. A simple increase of libido is hardly the same thing, don't you agree?"

There was no answer.

"Oh, *please*," Andrea said to the empty air, with a sniff. "I know you're here just as well as you know that I am, and for the same reason. Trying to hide your fire is useless, you know; you're being *very* silly, and that's starting to irritate my bodyguard. I wouldn't want to irritate him, and I suspect you don't, either."

A bronzed god of a man strode out through the doorway, into the room. He stood a head taller than me, and I'm not a short man, and his wide shoulders threatened to split the seams of his wizard's robe.

"I was doing nothing of the sort," he said. "I was busy with a preparation in my back room." His voice was a baritone rumble, almost smooth enough to be singing. He clasped his hands in front of him and bowed his head slightly. "I am known as Rewnor; you are welcome to my humble shop."

Andrea returned the salute. "Call me Lotana, although that is not now and never has been my name."

He raised a protesting hand and tried to smile ingratiatingly. "Please, please, dear lady. Name spells are beyond such as me, and I'd know better, in any case." He squinted, as though looking at something hovering over her right shoulder. "I can't tell quite what it is, but it's about one syllable away from eating me, eh?"

"Or something." Her smile seemed genuine. "I thought I'd hidden it well."

"I thought you said you'd swallowed all your spells," I whispered, not particularly afraid of Rewnor hearing.

She crooked a smile. "You'd have been telling the truth, if he'd put a truth spell on you, wouldn't you?"

"I don't see the need." Rewnor spread his hands broadly. "I've recogized you as my better, good Lotana, but that doesn't make me blind. You're here for some purpose, and I doubt it's for love philtres of guaranteed harmlessness and questionable efficacy. Can I be of help?"

"Possibly," she said, idly picking up a tool from the table, a fairly serious violation of wizard etiquette, as I understood it. It looked more like a dentist's probe than anything else, except for dim glow at the point. She tested the point against the ball of her thumb. "There've been rumors of things coming out of Faerie. I'd wondered what you've heard."

Rewnor looked down at her, and over at me, his face studiously blank, as though he was forcing himself not to take offense at the cavalier way she was handling his tools. "Things

147

have been happening, Mistress Lotana, and that's the truth. As to what, you'd have to ask the likes of better than I."

"There was a murder here, a few tendays ago. A note was left behind. We would like to arrange to see it."

"How did you know I had it here?" He frowned. "You *are* good."

Well, actually, we hadn't known it was here. We were going to ask his help getting access to it.

Andrea started to say something, but I stopped her, "You know that Lotana is better than you are. You perhaps don't want to know how much, or all that is involved." I made a mystical sign. It didn't mean anything, not on This Side, although Sister Berthe of Toulouse—the nun we used to call "Sister Birtha de Blues"—would have been proud at how easily I did it.

Rewnor raised a hand. "Ah. I see."

Andrea glared at me, irritated at how I was interfering, but I spread my hands in apology. "I'm sorry, Lotana, but there was no avoiding it. Rewnor was always going to see that there are great forces involved. Friend Rewnor is safest just giving us the note and staying out of all this."

"Well . . ." A ghost of a smile kissed her lips, and I wouldn't have minded joining it. "If you think so. I would have preferred to enlist his help, despite the danger, but . . ."

We were out of there, the paper in hand, within two minutes.

It wouldn't have taken so long if I hadn't panicked him.

The note was written in the blocky printing that Andrea used to teach at her school in Home, for both English and Erendra.

The Warrior Lives

—it said, in big brown Erendra letters, now flaking. And below, in English, just:

Don't try to find me. Please. I'm getting closer.

"No, dammit, there's nothing I can do with it. He just dashed it off, and while he used blood, it isn't *his* blood. I can't use things he's only casually interacted with for a location spell, or I'd be able to track anybody, anywhere, just by sorting through a few quadrillion oxygen molecules and find one that the quarry breathed."

Andrea was not happy.

Neither was I, as I stood next to the window, trying to fan the fumes outside. Andrea's attempt to see if the note could be used to trace Mikyn had involved some odorous compounds, and I didn't need for any of the inn's servitors to smell the sulfar and hellfire of a magician's preparations.

Below, the horses were saddled, and the others waited. We didn't absolutely have to get out of town right now, but in whatever direction he was traveling, Mikyn was heading away from us as time went by, and we wouldn't be able to catch him by standing still.

Wait for word of another Warrior killing? That was possible, of course, but dangerous. Why would some travelers— ones with suspiciously too much money in their kip—be hanging around Fenevar? A good question—so best to be sure it wasn't asked. Much better to move along the coast in either direction, and see if a farrier named Alezyn had been through, and when.

We took the back stairs down to the alley, and to the horses.

Tennetty had brought a fairly broad selection, from a dull, listless gray gelding pony for Ahira—who never liked a horse to have a lot of spirit or speed; I think he would have preferred a lame one, really—to a prancing pinto mare for herself.

I checked the cinch strap, then swung to the broad back of my chestnut gelding, his torn right ear suggesting that he'd lost out to a stallion at some point before he'd lost out to the gelder's knives and irons. He wanted to move faster than I was interested in, but, thankfully, Tennetty had equipped him with a fairly vicious twisted-wire bit, and we quickly agreed that we'd proceed at my pace, not his.

"So?" Jason asked, coming abreast of the dwarf as we started off in a slow walk, down the main street toward the coastal road through the swamp, maybe a mile ahead. "Where are we going?"

Ahira shrugged. "Tromodec is about two days that way, Brae three the other way. What we have to decide—what I have to decide—is if we let the search for Mikyn trump looking into the Ehvenor matter." Ahira was, by common consent, including mine, in charge strategically—and that's in part because he didn't make decisions unnecessarily arbitrarily. "Anybody got any advice?"

"Brae," Andrea said. "It's one step closer to Ehvenor." At that moment a cloud passed in front of the sun, so that a shadow quite literally fell across her face. But there was something else in her expression, something I couldn't quite name. Obsession, perhaps? Compulsion, maybe? I dunno.

"Tromodec," I said. "A couple days probably won't make much difference, we can catch up with Mikyn quickly. Tromodec is closer; it means knowing something sooner. By at least a day." And we'd be two days further away from Ehvenor, and Faerie. We could probably find out all that was known about the things coming out of Faerie anywhere along the coast, and I had little preference for examining the buzzsaw close up.

Besides, if the matter of Ehvenor was all that important, there were likely other folks than us, other wizards than Andy looking into it. Let them get in the way of the axe for once.

"Brae," she said. "The matter of Ehvenor is more important. Didn't you hear the rumors of a village that had been wiped out?"

"I never believe rumors. I've started too many myself. Tromodec."

"*Brae*," she said, her petulance only partly an act. There was more than insistence in her manner; perhaps a touch of fear? Or obsession?

"Tromodec." I smiled my most charming smile, no doubt dazzling her from scalp to crotch. "Wanna wrestle over it?"

"Later, maybe." She returned the smile like she meant it, earning both of us a glare from Jason.

I wasn't any too pleased with him, either; it had occurred to me more than once that if it wasn't for his presence, I'd likely be bunking with Andy instead of Ahira. I could have stood consoling the widow a couple of times.

Ahira turned to Jason. "Baron?"

Jason's chuckle sounded forced. "Oh, you mean me?" He was irritated with me; no doubt he'd side with his mother. "I favor Tromodec," he said.

Well, you could have knocked me over with a quarter-staff—I wouldn't have thought to duck. I should have thought it through, though—Jason was more interested in the search for Mikyn than the investigation of Ehvenor, which put us on the same side.

"If it works right," he went on, "we're closer to Mikyn; if it's wrong, we've only lost four days instead of six, the way it would be if we wrongly go to Brae."

Tennetty snorted. "I've got a better way. Just figure out which way is more likely to get us into trouble, and pick that one. It's what always happens, anyways."

"By which you mean Brae," I said.

"Sure. One step closer to Ehvenor; one foot further in the grave. I say Brae."

Ahira tugged on his reins, hard; his pony wanted to canter, and he didn't want that. "We have two for Tromodec, two for Brae. Which means that if this was a vote, I'd cast the deciding one, and get to decide. Since this isn't a democracy, and it's my call anyway, I get to decide."

Jason started to open his mouth, then stopped himself.

Ahira sighed. "I remember him, too, Jason. I remember how mad Karl and I were when we saw how his father had beaten him." He lowered his head for a moment, perhaps to bid farewell to an abused little boy, but when he raised it, his game face was back on—cold and merciless.

There was a time when Ahira could have gone up against anything with a smile on his face and a joke on his lips, but that time had passed.

"On one hand, we have the fact that Mikyn's moving around," he said. "Tromodec is the right move if we want to chase him down. Ehvenor and Faerie will stay where they are. On the other hand, the matter of Ehvenor and Faerie is more important than the problem of a rogue Home warrior, no matter who he is." His axe was bound across his saddle with quick-release ties that would let it go from both the saddle and sheath with one quick tug. He rested his free hand on it, as though asking it for help.

"If we knew for sure that we could find him quickly," Ahira said, "I might think differently, but, as it it, I say Brae. Ehvenor's more important; we head for Ehvenor."

When I was a kid, I always thought of a swamp as of necessity something like the Florida Everglades or the Maevish bogs—brush lightly covering a few spots of damp land and water, but mainly immense patches of quicksand that would suck you down forever if you stepped in the wrong place.

It's just as well that there's no guaranteed penalty for being wrong; I'd have paid it too many times over, in my life. Which probably would have been shorter, a lot shorter. I'd rather be lucky than right—there was a time I got involved in a small political mess in Sciforth, and definitely picked the wrong side. The good guys would have, as it turned out, stuck my head on a pole, while the bad guys and I split a pot of gold.

The swamp road twisted across the cluttered ground, seeking the ridge line, probably build up where there was no ridge. To the right and left, the ground fell, through tangles of vines and creepers, to an impenetrable morass of cypress and willow, the mess punctuated by infrequent stretches of open water and a rare sodden meadow.

The odd jay—there is no other kind—would occasionally perch in an overhead tree, either to crap on us or taunt us, or both, and every so often I would hear the sound of slithering on dead leaves, but while the swamp should have been teeming with life, most of the life had learned to avoid humans, and wasn't going to make an exception for a quartet of them just because they were accompanied by a dwarf.

There were a few exceptions. At one point, the road twisted in hairpin turns down the side of a coastal ridge, and the last of the turns revealed a small lake, maybe a mile across, rimmed by rushes and cattails. A small doe had been drinking at the edge of the water; at our approach, she lifted her head, eyes wide as saucers, and vanished off into the brush with swooping bounds, startling a covey of swans from concealment and into flight.

Tennetty, always alert for game—or at least a chance to kill something—brought her loaded crossbow up, but didn't take the shot. My guess is that she didn't have a clear shot, and a crossbow has little stopping power—if you don't nail a deer through the spine, heart, or (much more likely) lungs, you've got a long chase ahead of you.

"So much for a good dinner tonight," she said.

We camped that night by the side of a straight section of road, hanging hammocks between paired trees rather than trusting the ground. Snakes and all.

Even I couldn't have crept through the brush silently, and the road stretched out straight a quarter mile in either direction, so we lit a cookfire and relaxed, knowing that we'd see anybody coming up on us in plenty of time.

Jason took first watch, while Ahira sat up with him, the boy nervously stirring at the fire, the dwarf rewinding the leather and wire wrapping of his axe-hilt. Me, I couldn't sleep, not yet, so I improvised a pad of blankets in front of my saddle, and sat with them, stropping my dagger. It's hard to have too much of an edge on a knife.

Tennetty's eyes were sleepy as she joined the three of us, a brown blanket wrapped around her shoulders.

I looked up at her. "You look tired."

She nodded as she dropped a folded blanket to the ground next to me, and seated herself tailor-fashion on it, huddling in her sleeping blanket.

"I feel tired," she said. "Just too wound up. I guess." She stared off into the dark like she was expecting something to leap out of it, then shook her head. "Happens, sometimes."

She looked too tired to be sitting up, so I scooted over a bit, to let her use my saddle as a back rest. She gave a quick Tennetty-smile—lips together, their ends barely curling up—and leaned against it, and against me. I could feel the warmth of her body through the blanket, which told me that it had been far too long since I'd been with a woman.

Still, I guess those are the times that I most like out on the trail—the end of the day, when there's nothing to do but sit and talk until sleep drives you to your bed, whatever it is.

Tennetty's arms were folded under her blanket. Knowing Tennetty, each hand would be resting on the butt of a loaded pistol. I don't mean to be condescending; it felt reassuring.

One thing I could always count on is that Tennetty would be ready for sudden violence. Too ready, maybe, but ready.

The dwarf was rewinding the leather in some sort of intricate weave that I couldn't quite follow, his thick fingers moving with their familiar delicacy, while his eyes and mind were elsewhere. On the ground in front of him was a fresh spool of bronze thread—combined with the leather, it would give a good, solid grip, be the handle or hands wet or dry. (Whenever it all hit the fan, my hands were always wet, as soon as I noticed them.)

Picking up the theme, Jason had his revolver and cleaning kit out, the cartridges, bottles, cleaning clothes, and other paraphernalia neatly lined up on the blanket in front of him, steel and brass flickering in the firelight.

He cleaned and oiled the pistol in just a few moments—doesn't take much if you haven't fired it—then wiped it down with an oily rag before reloading it and slipping it back into his holster, thonging it into place.

"Other one in your bag?" I asked.

"Eh?" He looked over at me. "Other—oh: the other revolver." His smile was a trifle too easy. "I doubt it. I left it with your daughter."

"Jane, I trust, and not Dorann?"

He decided to take that as a joke, which it was. "Just in case," he said.

Tennetty, her eyes still sleepy, nodded in approval.

I stropped my dagger some more. Nehera, the master smith, had made it from a single piece of iron, lightly sprinkled with just enough charcoal, then heated and folded over, hammered on hundreds of thousands of times, making it strong despite the thinness of the blade. It would bend rather than break, but it could still hold enough of an edge to cut through muscle and cartilage. The surface was covered with the marking of the process: dark striations, like a fingerprint. I could have recognized the pattern among a hundred similar knives.

I tested the edge of the blade against my thumbnail; even with a light touch, it bit hard into the nail, which was more than good enough, so I wiped it down with oil and slid it back into its sheath.

154

When I looked up, Jason was eying me, perhaps a bit skeptically. I tried to decide whether he was thinking that I was acting out some nervousness, or just unable to keep my hands still, but I've never been much good at mindreading, so I slipped one of my throwing knives out of its sheath and started to work on that. I don't *have* to keep my hands busy, mind; I just like to. Can quit any time I want.

Jason caught Tennetty's eyes and smiled tolerantly.

Ahira had caught the byplay. "You make the common assumption, Jason Cullinane," he said. "You assume that the objects we live and work with are just that: objects, and no more."

The boy shrugged. "Useful objects," he said, "but sure." He patted at his holster. "I mean, this is more useful than six flintlock pistols, but it's a thing, and that's all."

"No. It's never just a thing. Not if you listen," Ahira said, with a sigh. "I spent a lot of time making this battleaxe," he said, taking another turn of bronze wire around the handle. "Only part of my smithing came with the territory—I had a lot to learn. It took me three tries to get just the *right* steel, and I had an expert steelmaker helping me. It took me more than a tenday to hammer that blob of metal into shape, working carbon and brightsand into the edge just deep enough. I had picked up ten pieces of ash and oak in my travels, and it took me even longer to whittle them down to thin laths, then glue them together so that they would hold, never splitting."

He rubbed the flat of his hand against the dark metal. "You work on or with something, some thing, long enough, and there's part of you in it. Not just for now, not just while you live, or even while you and it exist together, but for forever."

His eyes grew vague and dreamy. "There was a door, one night. It led to a room in which three children lay sleeping, two of them as dear to me as children could ever be. There had been assassins about that night, and while we thought them all dead, we could have been wrong. So your father and I sat in front of the door that night, perhaps just in case we were wrong, perhaps because we wouldn't have been able to sleep."

Tennetty leaned her head against my shoulder, her eye shut but her expression that of a little girl listening to a favorite bedtime story. I put my arm around her; she started, just a trifle, then relaxed. If I didn't know better, I'd swear she made a vague rumble, almost like a purr.

Ahira stroked the axe head yet again, then ran his rough fingers affectionately through Jason's hair. "And all night long, this axe whispered to me, saying, *Don't worry. Nobody will ever get past us to hurt them.*"

I don't understand it, not really, but for the first night in longer than I care to think about, my sleep was deep, dark, warm, and dreamless.

Breakfast the next morning, as sunlight began to break through the brush, was bread, cold sausage, and cheese for the humans, accompanied by a clay bottle of resiny local wine; it was oats, carrots, and apples for the horses, washed down with stream water for all.

I bit into another hunk of sausage, and swallowed. Spitting it out would have been uncouth, and probably slightly less nutritious than swallowing. Look, I like garlic—I like it a lot; I swear to God—but I don't think of it as a breakfast spice.

A cookfire probably would have helped the taste, but we needed to be on our way.

I really wanted something hot, though. A mug of tea would have warmed my hands and middle quite nicely. I thought about having a nip from the flask of brandy in my pack—that would have done it too—but decided against it.

Ahira, Andy, and Jason broke camp; I helped Tennetty with the horses.

"I've ridden on worse," I said, just to make conversation.

She smiled. "Not too bad," she said. "I checked them over as carefully as possible—Ahira's pony is slightly spavined, but he's the worst of them. Not really bad. Mostly freshly shod, all saddle-broken. I'd like to see how they handle gunfire," she said, with a sigh, as though she knew how they would, which she did.

They would run like hell, that's what they would do.

For a horse to hold still when there's lightning cracking somewhere just above and behind his head isn't something that comes naturally, or in one afternoon. The way you shoot from any but the best-trained horse's back is to dismount, tie the horse to something that won't move, walk away, and then do it.

Either that, or be sure that,

a) your first shot hits, and

b) you have a great need to be somewhere else quickly right after, and you don't much care where.

"The hostler must have had a large stock," I said. Supply&demand works even if you've never heard the term.

"Yeah. More than he needed." She nodded. "He bought a big string from an upcountry rancher, about eight, nine tendays ago; expecting a trader a few tendays back."

I know, I know, it's obvious—but nobody else had seen it, either. It's one thing to play armchair quarterback; it's another to be out there, calling the plays yourself.

"Andy?"

She swallowed a mouthful of bread before she answered. "Yes?"

"In order to locate Mikyn, you need either something of him, or something he's interacted with intimately, right?"

She didn't get it either, which is understandable. If you haven't ever made something from cold iron and fire, you won't understand how very much trouble it is, how every hammer stroke puts something of you in it, even if all you're making is something as humble as, say, the barbeque fork I'd made in ninth-grade metal shop, the pail hooks we used to churn out by the dozens during my summer at Sturbridge . . .

. . . or a horse shoe.

Jason was quicker—he had already approached his horse, and lifted its front hoof. "Nope—this one could stand a reshoeing, in fact."

"Try another one," I said, reaching for my own horse's left front leg. Tennetty, one hand flat against the side of its neck, kept it calm while I lifted the leg.

Nope. You can often tell a farrier by his style, and dwarf-trained smiths had a distinctive one, a lot cleaner than that of whoever had shoed this horse.

157

Two down, and no go.

Ahira had checked his pony, and then Andy's nervous black mare.

"I think we're on to something. Eight nails," he said. "Nice dwarvish style." Ahira's broad face was smiling so hard I thought it might split. "Walter, you may take one 'nicely done' out of petty cash." He turned to Andy. "How long? And do you need me to get it off the horse?"

She shook her head. "Not if you two will hold it still. And ten minutes, if that."

It barely took five, although it left her face sweaty, and ashen. Like mine.

Her quivering finger pointed back the way we had come. Toward Fenevar. Toward Tromodec. Away from Ehvenor.

Ahira shook his head. "Damn it," he said, as he looked up at me. "We've got a rogue on our hands, but the reasoning still holds. Ehvenor is more important. We leave Mikyn for after Ehvenor; we head toward Brae."

Shit. Magic scares me.

CHAPTER THIRTEEN

In Which We Are Welcomed to Brae

Joint undertakings stand a better chance when they benefit both sides.

—EURIPDES

Hey. The ruby was just sitting there. Okay?

—WALTER SLOVOTSKY

THROUGHOUT MOST OF my childhood, Stash's best friend was Mike Wocziewsky, a local cop. He had been either a detective or maybe just a plainclothes investigator, but he'd been caught in a wrong bed, and rather than taking a hearing on Conduct Unbecoming, he'd gone back to a blue uniform, and the streets.

I liked Big Mike. He was built like a big blue barrel, smoked cigars that looked and smelled like dog turds, and never stopped telling stories. He gave me my first jackknife, an official Scout knife. No, they weren't the best the money could buy, but there was something wonderful about having the real equipment. I loved that knife.

And the stories Big Mike used to tell.

"There are these five scuzzballs hanging around on the corner, and I know for sure that they are the same scumbuckets that had hit old man Kaplan's liquor store the week before and left him bashed up pretty bad.

"Now, you gotta understand: I *don't* like old man

159

Kaplan. The cheap bastard doesn't believe in a policeman's discount—well, didn't. These days I have trouble getting him to take my money. You should see the case I got for Christmas, Stash . . .

"—But never mind, even though I wouldn't give a shit if he'd fallen down the stairs at home, when he's on my street he's one of my people, and I don't like having one of the people on my block lying in a hospital bed with one tube running up his nose and another out of his shlong, understand?

"Back to the douchebags on the corner. I don't have anything to pull them in on, and besides, I'm a bluesuit now, not a shield, and so it's none of my business. Bluesuits don't investigate. Except, well, I don't let dogfuckers shit on my people, not on my block. So I go up to one of the cuntfaces, and pull him away.

" 'Pretend like you don't want to talk to me,' I say, kind of low, but just not quite low enough. He's not slow, and he gets the idea real quick, and shouts out something as he sort of swings at me. But I've got about a hundred pounds on him, and he knows better than to really slug me—I mean, if he does that, he knows I'll put in so much stick time that his *descendants* will hurt.

"But while he's swinging on me, I grab his arms, and shove him up against a wall, real gentle, just hard enough to distract him while I slip the hundred I'd palmed into his pants pocket.

"Now, the other dingleballs are watching all of this, and one of them sees it, which saves me some trouble. I just let him go.

"I didn't know how far it would go, and I didn't much care, but a couple of days later I visit the dickhead in the hospital, and he's in even worse shape than Kaplan, and very willing to talk. Lay a hand on him? Nah. I just offered to give him another payoff. For some reason, he didn't want that.

"Hundred bucks a lot of money? Sure is. To a cop. I got paid back. I bet old man Kaplan thought it was the best hundred he ever spent."

*   *   *

I'd been expecting to hit town in midafternoon, but we must have been making better time than I'd thought.

It was noon when Brae came on us suddenly, or vice versa, depending on how you look at it. The way I see it, the center of the universe is a couple of centimeters behind the middle of my eyebrows. The center of the universe just moves around a bit.

In any case, we rounded a bend, and there it was, a collection of one-, two- and three-storied wattle-and-daub buildings and twisty little streets sprawled across the coastal hills, running from the crest of a ridge all the way down to the Cirric.

Not much of a city.

"Reminds me of an old joke," I said. "Waiter comes over to the table. Says, 'How did you find your steak?' 'I just looked under the parsley, and there it was.' "

Andy laughed dutifully, as did Ahira. Neither of the other two did. I guess you have to be raised speaking English in order to get the jokes—and Tennetty wasn't. And you've probably got to have a sense of humor, unlike Jason Cullinane.

At first, Brae stank of fish. Not surprisingly; the water in that region are rich with fish, and dried alewife—ugly fish—is a major export. Despite the smell, my mouth watered as the thought of fresh spotted trout over an open fire, seasoned only with salt, peppers, oil, and maybe a squeeze from a small, sweet, Netanal lemon.

Ahead, straddling the road, was a guard staation at the entrance to town—of antique construction, but freshly manned.

"Strange," Ahira said. He was handling the horse better than I'd expected, although I knew he would have preferred his pony. I had another use in mind for the pony.

I nodded. Along the Cirric, most danger to the locals comes from the sea, not the land. The domains tend to be on good terms with each other, generally saving their hostility for pirates and islanders.

"Okay, everybody," Ahira said. "Let's take things nice and easy; I don't see any need for a problem. Nice slow walk toward the guard station. Walter, you're on."

This is why we get along well—Ahira knows when to let

me be, and when not to. Actually, I'd been working up another cover story, but Ahira pointed out that we had met some of the travelers in Fenevar, and could easily be exposed as somebody with something to hide if we changed out story. Not that that would necessarily be horrible; a lot of folks who travel through the Eren regions aren't quite what they seem, and anybody who automatically believes what a traveler says is too trusting by more than half.

I turned in the saddle, and gave everybody the once-over. The rifles were lashed in a bundle with the bows, and the pistols were safely stowed away. Andy was dressed in her wizard's robes, but had, as she put it, "dimmed her flame" to that of a minor wizard, much less powerful in appearance than in reality. I'd have to take her word for it.

She looked too good, dammit, and the smile on her face, while not too eager, was just a notch off.

Tennetty, a blue cotton shift over glossy leather riding breeches, was her maid, and if a maid carried a largish dagger, that wasn't particularly surprising.

Nor was a three-person bodyguard for a wizard, even one of them a dwarf.

We looked the part, I supposed. Except for Jason. There was a bulge under his tunic, which was okay; lots of people carried an extra knife or purse against their body, but the butt of his revolver peeked out. Which wasn't okay—while slaver rifles and pistols were becoming increasingly commonplace as time went by, I didn't want to have to explain what we were doing with something that was so clearly the product of Home.

"Lace up your tunic a bit," I said. "And when you put the holster back on, shift it around so that the butt isn't visible, eh?" If everything hit the fan, I'd be more than happy for Jason's revolver, but I'd be less than happy if that's what made everything hit the fan.

We couldn't stand a search, but a search isn't a common custom when passing into an Eren town.

Last but not least . . . "Andy?"

She closed her eyes for a long moment. "Two local magicians. Not particularly bright flames; not terribly powerful or

accomplished. Or they're doing the same thing that I am."
She smiled. "Only better."

I would have shivered, but it was too warm out.

The guards at the station had been stamped out of the same
mold: medium-sized, stocky men, with walrus-style mustaches
and sharp chins, large hands that held on to the stocks of
their spears either for support or out of readiness. Me, if I had
to stand guard, I'd want a spear, too—gives you something to
lean on.

About three-quarters of a wagon wheel had been stuck
up on the side of the guardhouse, for reasons that escaped
me for the moment.

"Names and purpose in Brae?" one asked.

"Tybel, Gellin, Taren," I said, indicated me, Ahira, and
Jason. "Bodyguard to Lotana, wizard. Duanna," I said, indicating Tennetty, "wizard's maid."

Now, I won't swear that it's true, but I've always thought
of bodyguards as non-talkative types, and bet most people do.
A few clipped words might save us a lot of fast talking. "Passing through, or passing by—your choice; no trouble wanted.
May stay one night, two, three, or none. Planning on trading
further down the coast. We don't discuss what, where, or
who."

They would figure out that further down the coast meant
Ehvenor, but it wouldn't be in character for me to discuss it.

The two guards shrugged at each other. "By command
of Lord Daeran, be welcome in Brae," one said formally,
with a slight bow.

"The town is laid out like this," the other said, indicating
the broken wagon wheel. "Town square here." He tapped
the hub with the point of his spear. "Lord's residence here;
if you're looking to buy fish in quantity, you negotiate that
with the Valet." He did say "Valet," honest—it was the same
word as for the fellow who lays out your clothes and cleans
your room for you.

"You'll find inns along High street," he went on, tapping
a spoke. "Fish markets along the docks." He tapped against
some of the broken spokes. "Ride through Main street."

163

another tap, "and through the center of town and by the Posts of Punishment on your way."

Andrea cocked her head to one side. "Wouldn't it be quicker to take the Street of the Eel up the hill to the Old Avenue?"

He looked at her suspiciously. "I hadn't realized you'd been in Brae before, Mistress Lotana."

She gave him a chilly smile. "I haven't."

She made a brushing gesture with her fingers, something halfway between a gesture of dismissal and the sort of finger movement a wizard often makes when throwing a spell. I didn't like it, but there wasn't much I could do about it, or even a good reason to argue about it. Andrea was, after all, good with location spells, and it couldn't hurt for one of our party to know her way around Brae.

It could, however hurt for one of our party to shoot off her mouth, and I resolved to discuss that with her later.

The soldier decided to drop the matter. "By the Lord's direction, everyone is to pass the Posts of Punishments," he said. "Any other needs?"

I would have asked about the Posts of Punishment, but with Andy already having shot her mouth off, more curiosity didn't seem called for.

I jerked my thumb at the pony, trying to keep things casual. "Could use a good smith. Useless, there, threw a shoe this morning."

Shoeing a horse takes some tools and effort—removing a shoe takes a lot less.

A look passed between the guards, and one walked to the rear of our group, examining the gray pony's foot closely for a moment, then nodding.

The fact that I was ready for all of this didn't mean that I liked any of it, although as the guard let the hoof drop, the chill in the air warmed up. I wasn't born yesterday—I had pulled both front shoes the day before, to be sure that the hoof would be properly dirtied, and the sharp edges worn a bit.

"Smith? Not a farrier?"

I spread my hands. "That would be fine, too." I shrugged, calmly, casually, but not too casually. A bodyguard with no connections to Mikyn wouldn't be upset at the question, but would think it a bit strange. "I wouldn't have thought Brae large enough to need a fulltime farrier."

That must have passed muster, because he nodded and said, "You'll find Deneral the smith on the Street of the Dry Creek," he said, returning to his tour-guide persona, "at the base of the hill. He does fair shoeing, so they say. Again, welcome to Brae."

We rode past the wattle-and-daub houses of merchants and town-bound tradesmen, toward the center of town.

"Posts of Punishment?" Jason asked.

I shrugged. "Common along the coast."

There's an Other Side variant of it called crucifixion—basically, you tie somebody up on a stick, don't let them have food or water, and let them die of thrist and exposure.

I frowned. Maybe I haven't seen enough death and suffering, but I really didn't need the local lord ordering me exposed to some more.

Ahead, the street narrowed; we shifted from riding two-two-one abreast to a single line, with me, as chief bodyguard, first, Ahira last.

Across the square were six posts, each about the size and shape of a telephone pole, each topped with a vaguely cigar-shaped iron cage barely large enough to contain a person. What amounted to a siege tower stood nearby, rolled just out of reach of the first cage.

That one, and three others, were occupied by motionless forms, all rags and bones, slumped up against the metal.

From that distance, I couldn't tell if any of the four were alive, but then I saw an arm move.

Tennetty grunted. I thought she had a stronger stomach than any of the rest.

Ahira hissed at her to shut up. So did I. I wasn't too worried; being nauseated by the sight of this wasn't particularly a break in character.

"Fine," she said, her voice low. "But I know one of them. I recognize her from Home. She's an engineer, name of Kenda. And the one in the far cage. That's Bast."

Ohmigod. I remembered Bast as a skinny little boy.

Jason's horse took a prancing step as he walked it up to my side. "What do we do?"

"Nothing quickly," I said. "Nothing at all, until Ahira and I say so. If we say so. Understood?"

His face was white, but he nodded.

CHAPTER FOURTEEN

In Which I Go for a Stroll

There are usually aleph-nul ways to do something right, but aleph-one ways to do it wrong.

LOU RICCETTI

Lou always makes things complicated. What he means is that if you choose how to do it at random, you will screw it up. What he's leaving out is that if you're careful about how you do it, you'll probably screw it up. Still, "probably" is better than "will."

—WALTER SLOVOTSKY

I'VE ALWAYS TRIED TO both keep and avoid a sense of proportion. Ever since the freshman philosophy class that James Michael and Karl and I were in together.

There's lots of ways to teach ethics. Professor Alperson tried a complicated one.

"Okay, he said. "Classical ethical problem, with a twist. You're in a specific city on a specific date and time, and you're walking along the railroad tracks. You hear the whistle of an oncoming train.

"Now, ahead of you, you see two people stuck to the tracks; each is wedged in by the foot. One is an old man, who you know to be a good and saintly type; the other is a young boy, who you know to be the worst brat in all of . . . well, never mind. You only have time to save one. What do you do, and does it matter what you do?"

We batted that one back and forth for awhile. I, of course, challenged the parameters he had laid down—never take a problem at its own face value—but he held firm. No, there was no way either was going to free himself, the train was not going to stop, and I knew that for sure, and we'd discuss epistemology some other time.

James Michael tried to take the long look, but rejected it. "In a hundred years, they'll both be dead, so it doesn't matter? Is that what you're getting at?"

Alperson shrugged. "Maybe. Maybe I'm not getting at anything."

Karl took it seriously. "You save one. Either one. You save the old man because he is good and virtuous and because virtue should be respected, or you save the boy because no matter how much of a brat he is, he still deserves to grow up, but you do save one of the two."

Alperson smiled. "What if I were to tell you that the date is August 6, 1945, and that the city is Hiroshima, and that in two minutes, the bomb the Enola Gay is about to drop will kill all three of you? Would that make any difference?"

Karl shook his head. "Of course not."

Alperson's smile grew larger. "Good. I don't know if I agree, but good. You've taken a position. Now support it."

It took us the rest of the day to put it all together, but the locals were still talking about it, and evincing curiosity didn't make us seem, well, curious.

There had been a murder just outside of the city of Brae, but well within the domain of Lord Daeran.

There had also been a contract team of engineers from Home here, laying out a glassmaking plant. Canning—well, jarring—of fish in glazed clay pots was one of the ways of putting down a larger-than-usable catch. While overcooked and oversalted lake alewife fillets in a sealed pot of brine was not my idea of a good time, there were folks inland for whom that was a great if expensive treat, and a very good supplement to a diet that consisted largely of bread and onion, with too little protein.

Real glass canning, though, would have been an improvement—safer, faster, cheaper. Good glassmaking was something that Lou Riccetti wanted, and the Cirric shore was the right place to put such a plant. So he had sent out an engineer team to negotiate and reconnoiter, led by Bast, one of his senior engineers. Bast was a good fellow, who I still, deep within my heart of hearts, thought of as a skinny boy who drew more than his share of guard duty.

A new idea of Lou's, contracting out labor.

Not a great one, as it turned out.

Farm slaves were increasingly rare these days, horses and oxen increasingly common. Of the circle of farms surrounding Brae, owing fealty to Lord Daeran, only a handful had even a single slave; most were worked by large families and their horses and oxen.

Except for one, a small plot worked by an old man named Heneren, his childless wife, and a superannuated slave, name of Wen'red. They had been visited by a traveling farrier, who was traveling through the arc of farms, reshoeing as he went.

He had swiftly murdered Heneren and his wife, announced to Wen'red that he was now free, and left the old slave alone as he headed off toward the city.

Wen'red had waited a day before he had started in toward the city, on foot. It took him several days—he hadn't been off the farm in thirty years, and got lost. But he knew his duty to his late owner, and reported the murders to a city armsman . . .

. . . the day after Bast had been seen helping the farrier book passage away from Brae.

The afternoon of the morning that Mikyn had sailed way.

Two days before an armsman returned to town, bringing word of the state of Mikyn's victims.

It was only natural that Bast and company would offer help and shelter to a Home raider, even one in a farrier's disguise that they would have pierced easily.

It was equally natural for Lord Daeran to try Bast and company for conspiracy in the murder of Brae subjects, and to stake them out in the hot sun and cool night, providing them only water, and only enough to keep them alive, until they would die of starvation and exposure.

Nice folks, eh?

*   *   *

"Just about midnight," Ahira said. "Guard will be changing any time."

My time. No matter how much intelligence you have, you can always use good intelligence, if you catch my drift.

We had taken conspicuously rich rooms that were even more conspiciusouly secure. They were on the third floor of the inn, with but a single door entrance, and two balconies, neither of which would be easily accessible from below, and only barely from above—the overhanging roof would prevent somebody from simply dropping down from roof to balcony.

There was nothing that would prevent me from rappelling down the side of the building into the edge of the square below, except the possibility of some passersby seeing what was going on.

But local light-discipline was lax, and two of the lamps on the street were out, the residents not yet braced by armsmen demanding they be lit.

More than enough shadow for the likes of me.

Walk out the front door? Sure, I could have done that—but it's always better to have the option of being officially somewhere else when there's skulduggery going on.

That's me, Walter Slovotsky: skulduggger.

I sat tailor-fashion on the floor, Andrea behind me, fingers kneading at my shoulders hard, just this side of bruising. I might turn down a massage from a pretty woman, but only rarely from somebody who is good at it, and never from a pretty woman who is good at it.

Jason scowled. I had a blindfold over my eyes, but I could hear him scowl.

"I should go too," he said.

Tennetty snorted. "Like you could get him out of trouble?"

His voice was too quiet. "Yes," he said. "Like I could get him out of trouble."

He was right—he had saved my life last time out—but it was irrelevant. We weren't configured for violence or flight, and I didn't see any way to change that, not tonight. If we had been more cold-blooded, we would have left the engineers in the hot sun for another day before I went reconoitering—

giving the rest of the group time to get beyond town, ready to run if things went sour.

But no. They had all been up there for days and days, slowly burning to death and starving in the hot sun, and while I didn't see any possible way I could get them out tonight, the sooner we knew what we were up against, the sooner that we could get them out.

If we could get them out.

Look—truth is that the important of something doesn't have a lot of effect on whether or not it's doable. I've had too many lessons on that already; I hope this wasn't going to be another one.

Time for a quick sneak around, to find out whether rescue for the engineers consisted of a breakout, or a merciful death.

Or nothing at all. If you can't do it, you can't do it.

"Time," I said, rising to my feet. I opened my eyes, and could see through the blindfond that the lamps were still on in the room. "Lights out."

I heard several puffs of air, and then. "Lights are out."

The best way to see in darkness is to be born a dwarf— not only do they see better with less light, they can see three colors down into the infrared, and can find their way at a dead run through territory and conditions where you and I wouldn't have a prayer.

The best way wasn't open to me. The second best way to see well in darkness is, first, to have the heredity that gives you decent night vision; second, to eat your carrots, whether you like them or not—I don't; and third, to give your eyes enough time in darkness before you venture out into it.

Black is one of my favorite colors, particularly at night. The trouble is, it's the classic color of a thief. Similarly, it would have been nice to rub some black greasepaint over my face and hands, but that would have labeled me as someone skulking about.

Ahira gripped my shoulder for a moment. "Don't get too close, and don't get into trouble." He was always trying to keep me out of trouble, and it was only through the obvious necessity of it that he had agreed to my night walk.

171

"Trouble? Me?" I smiled. "How could anybody who looks this good get into trouble?"

He didn't chuckle, although his grim frown lightened a shade or two. "True enough. Don't try to get too close—you're much too high class to be concerned about the fine details of the Poles of Punishment. Just make a quick survey of the situation, then get back here."

"Sure."

What the well-dressed thief was wearing this year: black cotton breeches of a nice thick weave, neatly bloused in plain leather boots that were somewhat better made than they looked; a dark tan shirt, jauntily slashed to waist, all that covered by a brown cloak whose collar would work fine as a hood, if need be. A particularly short shortsword, suspended from the swordbelt with cloth linkages, instead of metal—no clanking when I walk, thank you. A fine leather sap tucked into the belt—a footpad's weapon, but something a bodyguard might carry. Two braces of throwing knives hidden here and there, and a largish pouch slung pertly over the right shoulder, containing some money, a couple of flasks of healing draughts, and a few oddments. Gloves of the softest pigskin, which gripped the short woven leather rope quite nicely as I tied it into a rappelling rig, then passed one end of the long climbing rope through.

The street was quiet. With Ahira holding one end, I threw the other end over the edge, and stepped out into the night.

There's basically two ways around a city—you can stick to the main roads, or try to keep in alleys and back streets. I passed down several alleys before I found what I was looking for: a tavern across the street, its open door belching sailing songs into the night, and on this side of the street a raised walkway.

I pulled some dirt out, then stripped off my shoes, socks, gloves, cloak, belt, sword, and shirt, wrapped everything else tightly in the cloak, and stuffed the bundle under the walkway, patting dirt back into place over it.

Ahira was right. Somebody who looked the way I had wouldn't have any business skulking about the center of town, past the Poles of Punishment, alone or in company.

Shirtless, I straightened and slung the bag over my shoulder and strutted across the street toward the tavern.

First, a bit of beer. No, first, a *lot* of beer.

The street was cold under my feet as I walked across the street, and through the broad door, into noise and light and singing.

"Hey," I said. "Is there nobody who will drink with a sailor?"

CHAPTER FIFTEEN

In Which an Old Acquaintance Is Briefly Renewed

He is the best sailor who can steer within fewest points of the wind, and exact a motive power out of the greatest obstacles.
—HENRY DAVID THOREAU

It's always seemed to me that most sailors spend most of their time making up funny names for things.
—WALTER SLOVOTSKY

THE FIRST TIME I WENT sailing. I don't think it went terribly well. Some people have no sense of humor . . .

I had a summer job at a Y camp in Michigan—just driving a truck, actually, although that was more fun than it sounded like. What I got to do was haul campers out on expeditions—canoeing down a river in Canada, hiking through the forest in the Upper Peninsula, survival camping in a national reserve, like that—and hauling them back. All in the back of slightly modified trucks. Grossly illegal—all the laws specified school buses—but as long as there weren't any accidents, nobody was going to bother the Y.

There were two neat things about the job. One was the scenery. That part of the world is pretty. The other one appealed to my laziness: when there weren't campers to be driven around, I didn't have anything that I had to do.

So I hung around the camp. Ran five miles a day to keep my wind up; rebuilt a few forest paths and such, but mainly just goofed off around and read—Stash and Emma would send me a CARE package each week with five packs of M&Ms, ten new paperbacks, a couple pairs of socks, and a totally useless dozen condoms. (I didn't find any need for condoms in an all-boy's camp.)

One day, one of the campers—a sixth grader, I think—asked if I was willing to come out and skipper an E-scow for him and a few of his friends. It was a single-masted racing shell with twin daggerboards, fast and lovely as it skimmed across the lake, but if you didn't handle it just right, it could capsize in a breath of wind. Seems that while all five of them were very experienced sailors, the camp rules required an adult in charge, and I was considered one, being all of nineteen at the time.

It was strange. Mickey, the kid who was really in charge, would address me very formally—"Skipper, I think we should stand by to come about," and then I'd say, "Stand by to come about," and they'd framish the glimrod and farble the kezenpfaufer, or whatever needed to be done, and wait for me to respond to Mickey's nod with a "come about."

The only part they didn't like was when I told them stuff like, "All right, let's hoist up the landlubbers and batten down the hatches."

No sense of humor.

Particularly when I said, "Stand by to capsize."

"The thing is," my new friend said, his thick arm thrown across my shoulder, "is that the *Watersprite* may *look* like the slowest scow on the face of the Cirric . . ." actually, he said "Shirrick," but you get the idea ". . . and it may *smell* like the least-bailed excuse for a floating cesspool ever to dishonor the sewer-water in which it floats, and it may be *captained* by the stupidest man ever to risk falling overboard and poisoning the fish below, but, once you get used to her and to her ways, she's even worse. Havanudda beer."

He was a broad, thick man, with a rippling sailor's beard that spilled down both cheeks, across his neck and down into his chest. Beneath the beard, his face was sweaty and dirty in the light of the sputtering candles that dripped wax onto the filthy surface of the rough-hewn table. Absently, he crushed a beetle with his thumb, then drained some more beer, one hand on my knee.

I think he was about to launch into another long, drunken monologue—drunks do that, a lot—so I interposed another suggestion.

"So," I said, weaving in time with him, "you think I should not think about thinking about signing on." My slur was worse than his, but not much.

"Welen, my pet . . ." he waved a finger. He was trying to point, probably. "I think you'd be crazy to entertain the thought of considering contemplating the idea of thinking about signing on."

"Aw, it can't be as bad as all that, now can it?"

"Can't it now? I see right through you, Welen, and don't you think I don't. I know what you're up to."

I forced a warm smile. "Oh, you do, do you?" I didn't look toward the door, but with a bit of luck I could make it out into the night with a kick, a leap, and a dash.

"Don't you think I don't—been too long with dirt instead of a deck under your feet, eh? It shows, man, it shows. A man's got to eat—and drink, eh?—and a sailor's got to sail. I don't doubt that, Welen-pretty, but you can do better than the *Watersprite*, is all I say, except to add that you can't do worse."

He rose, wobbly as a newborn colt. "No time like the present—just let me finish this, and we're off. Hey, Tonen, Rufol—I'm off. Are you with me, or against me? Swear to the Fish, I do, you'll not find your way back alone. I think you are drunk, the two of you, the both of you are drunk."

"Drunk, us? No, just reefed a bit too tight," another sailor said, as he and yet another lurched to their feet, and we all lurched out into the night.

We staggered down the street, down the hill, toward the center of town, belting out a very pretty harmony on a sailing song usually used to time the pulling of a rope.

I took the baritone lead; I'd spent a fair amount of time impersonating—no, *being*—a sailor; it was one way to move along the coast and among the Shattered Islands without drawing any attention, and ships are always in need of crews.

The light-negligence that I'd seen higher up the hill

wasn't echoed in the center of town. The poles were ringed by a dozen lanterns, and a ten-man squad of soldiers stood guard from nearby. If I had to, I would have bet there was another troop in the dark of the lord's house, across the way, and certainly plenty more within call at the barracks. Coastal cities had always been subject to pirate raids, and local lords knew to keep troops handy.

"—so haul them hard, sailors,

"Pull them down and away,

"You'll work hard for your money,

"No drinking today.

"So haul them hard, sailors—"

One of the troop broke away and stalked across the darkened ground toward us.

"Be still, the lot of you," he said, smiling, "M'lord sleeps with his windows open, and if you wake him you'll not be finding him amused."

My new friend threw his arm companionably about the soldier's shoulders. "He doesn't like singing? What kind of lord is this?"

The poor soldier gagged at the smell of his breath. I didn't blame him. The sailor released him, then staggered toward the nearest of the posts, dragging me by the arm.

"Come look at what we have here. Eh, but what *do* we have here? Skinny little birds on their perches. Hello, skinny little bird? Would you like to come down from there and perch on my face?"

From the cage, Bast's skeletal face looked listlessly down, his eyes dull. There was no sign of recognition; I doubt he could even have focused properly. I wouldn't have wanted to bet he could take another day. Kenda looked ever worse, and the two in the cages beyond were unmoving, perhaps already dead. The cages were secured by locks, not apparently welded shut.

No, not welded shut at all—as Kenda shifted position slightly, the door squeaked against its catch. Not good, but not as bad as it could have been—it was possible that they had been welded in there. There isn't a This Side lock I can't open, given the right tools and a few minutes. I had the right tools in my pack—the few minutes would be a problem.

Never mind that for now. Just get information.

One guard sat in the door at the base of the siege tower, a tall, thick column probably concealing a circular staircase—it was thicker than would have been needed for just a ladder, and it would be much easier to manhandle bound prisoners up a staircase than a ladder.

"Heyheyhey," the guard said. "No talking to the condemned, eh? Be off and on your way."

We staggered off into the night, belching out another chorus.

Dockside, my thick-fingered friend let the other two on first. "I want to have a little, oh, talk with our new friend, eh?" he said.

The other two laughed as they reeled off down the docks toward the narrow gangplank. They knew about his predilections.

I'd worked them out a while back, but I wasn't ready for it when he clumsily threw his arms around my neck and said, "Was that good enough, Walter Slovotsky?"

He didn't sound drunk at all.

It was suddenly colder.

His smile was crooked. "Did we find out enough, I asked you," he said quietly, then raised his voice. *"What's the matter with you? I jus' wanna be friends, don' you wanna be friends?*

"You should ask how I know you," he went on, lowering his voice. "You don't remember me, but we met once before. Years ago."

He fingered his neck, at the base of the black beard that ran down his chin and neck and into his chest. Perhaps it was the flickering lamplight, or maybe I did see, almost hidden beneath the mat of beard, white scars that an iron collar would have left behind.

Clumsy fingers groped where his collar would have been. Had been.

"Push me away now, Walter Slovotsky," he whispered. "A quick curse, too, if you please."

"I do it with women, damn you—keep your hands off

178

my pants, or I'll geld you," I shouted, as I shoved him, hard, "I swear I'll cut your balls off and stuff them up your nose."

"*Aw, let's be friends.*" And, again, *sotto voce:* "We sail in the morning. I'm not a brave man, or I'd stay and help you and your friends." He backhanded me across the face, hard enough to sting, no more. "*That* for your shyness." And, again, quietly: "If you're leaving by water, the two fastest ships in dock are the *Butter* and the *Delenia*, but careful of both captains. They do much business here." He raised his hands in defeat.

"*I* know when I've been told no," he said, staggering away into the dark, gesturing a farewell with a casual wave as I walked off in the other direction.

I didn't even know his name.

CHAPTER SIXTEEN

In Which a Hearty Breakfast Is Eaten

In skating over thin ice, our safety is in our speed.
— RALPH WALDO EMERSON

Audacity is a virtue that should always be practiced with caution.
— WALTER SLOVOTSKY

THE OTHERS WERE ALL up waiting for me. Ahira hauled me up into the window so fast it felt like flying.

"How did it go?" he asked. "Did you find out what we need?"

"Maybe." I nodded. "I'll need to think about it."

"See," he said with a relaxed smile. I liked that smile. I hadn't seen it for awhile, not since Bieme. "You didn't have to get all that close, eh?"

I shrugged. "I guess I should have listened to you."

"Sometimes things are real simple," I explained to three others, as we gathered around breakfast in the central room the next morning. "I know the easy way to get them out."

Down in the town center, our friends were spending another day starving and frying in the hot sun. Tennetty was off running an errand.

Here, outside, sunlight splashed in through the breeze-stirred curtains, onto the four-person dining table and the silver trays heavily laden with rashers of bacon, chicken pies, and little ceramic ramekins holding coddled eggs, among other things. Breakfast is traditionally the biggest meal of the day in Brae, which is fine by me.

Ahira cooked his head to one side. "Sure." Using a pair of silver tongs to protect himself from the heat, he took the lid off a baking pot, and sniffed. "Some sort of stew, I think." He slopped some onto his plate, and mopped at it with half of a golden fist-sized roll. "Hmmm . . . not bad. Kid, I think."

I reached for a roll—it was still warm from the oven— then tore it in half, and dipped one end into a crock of raspberry preserves. It was delightfully sweet, with maybe just a touch too much tartness, and the seeds crunched between my teeth.

Andrea wasn't having any of it—she and her son were only picking at their food.

Ahira crunched into a thick rasher of bacon, then washed it down with a swallow of deeply purple wine. "So tell me how we do it the easy way," he said, a suspicious twitch to his grin.

"You and Jason take over the siege tower, climb up, and run a cable through all four cages," I said. I dipped the other hunk of bread into a cup of golden butter, and bit into that. Hmm . . . it was hard to decide which way was better—I downed both halves of the roll in two bites. "We splice one end to the other, tying them together. Meanwhile, I wrap det cord around the base of each pole, and light the fuse.

"Just before it all blows, Ellegon swoops down out of the sky, and grabs the whole mess just as the explosives cut the poles free."

Jason frowned in disgust. Andy shook her head, tolerantly.

"I think I see some problems with that," Ahira said, dryly.

"Only a few," I said. "One, we don't have a cable. Two, last time we talked about it, Lou figured he's about five years away from being able to produce det cord or any other good plastique equivalent, so that part doesn't work—the closest thing we have is a handful of grenades, and they won't do it.

"Three, there's no rendezvous set up with Ellegon for another eighteen days, so we can't count on him for this.

"Four, there's too many soldiers out there, and they'd cut us down before we got anywhere."

There was a pyramid of three tiny roasted chickens on one of the serving plates; I took the top one and tore off the drumstick. It came off too easily—either the bird had been overcooked, or I was more pumped up than I was trying to affect. Not that it matters: the skin of the drumstick was crisp and garlicy; the meat was rich and firm.

Tennetty burst through the doors, shut them behind her, and gave a quick nod as she took her seat at the table and tore into a loaf of bread. "Passage for eight on the *Delenia*," she said, from around a huge mouthful. "We leave at noon, tomorrow."

"Boarding?"

"Any time in the morning, from first light on. One problem, though—she's riding too low for her dock space, and they're moving her out to a mooring today so they can finish loading her. Long Dock needs work—it's been silting up underneath, and Lord Daeran had a problem with his last set of silkie workers."

"Launches?"

She nodded. "Her own. Two. Each can carry eight, including crew. Both will be tied up at Long Dock from sundown on."

Andrea had caught on. "We've done this one before," she said. "One day after arriving on This Side."

Once we were safely on the ship, we would have a common interest with the captain in getting the hell out of here, just as we had done, long ago, with Avair Ganness and the *Ganness' Pride*. "Almost makes me feel nostalgic." Her smile brightened the whole room as she reached for a chicken breast and tore into it with strong white teeth. "How about the other part?"

"All a replay." I shrugged. "Ahira and I did that one, too, the time we ended up having to put your husband on the throne." I shook my head. "This time, though, it's a solo."

It would have to be me, and me alone. I'm not a hero or anything, but Ahira wouldn't be able to get in. It was totally not Andy's sort of thing; Jason was just too young to pull it all off. Tennetty could do the threatening part of it—and well—but not the rest of it. I sat back, trying to think of a way I could make this work with a fortyish woman wizard, a reliable dwarf, a still-green kid, or a one-eyed psychopath in the lead role, but couldn't.

"Uh, excuse me? Last time you did this?" Tennetty cocked her head to one side. "As I recall, last time you went face-to-face with royalty was the time you got Baron Furnael killed, no?"

"Close enough." I nodded. "Hey, I'll have to do it better this time."

Jason looked from Ahira to me, and back to Ahira, and then back to me. "You love this, don't you?"

"Truth to tell, Jason-me-boy, I do. Consider it a personality defect." It also scared me shitless, but not out of an appetite. I reached for another piece of chicken.

One does have to keep a sense of proportion about such things.

While our friends baked in the hot sun, we spent the day preparing, and resting, and eating.

I had to get up too early for breakfast the next morning. It was important to be at the residence early.

CHAPTER SEVENTEEN

In Which I Have
a Pleasant Chat
with Lord Daeran

The same man cannot be skilled in everything; each has his special excellence.

—EURIPIDES

There's a balance you have to learn, between being able to do a little of everything, and therefore nothing at all real well, and becoming overspecialized and completely useless outside your specialization. Learning that balance is, I've always believed, part of becoming an adult. I figure I'm about twenty years overdue to learn it.

—WALTER SLOVOTSKY

Oᴸᴅ FAMILY STORY—and it's one of the few that my mother used to tell, so it could be true. Nah. But . . .

It seems that when my parents were trying to have me, there was some trouble conceiving. The doctors didn't know much about infertility then, and were trying whole bunches of things, some of which made sense, others of which were just patent nostrums. Schedules, diets, temperature taking, boxer shorts—the whole bit.

Finally, according to Mom, the doctor said, "Look. Stop trying so hard. It may just be a matter of relaxation. So take it easy, don't worry about schedules, don't worry about time of the month. Just do it whenever you feel like, okay?"

"That's why," Emma would say, her mouth quirked into a smile that caused Stash to blush just a bit, "we can never, ever go back to Howard Johnson's."

The way to a man's heart is through his stomach—or his rib-
cage, if you're playing for keeps; the way into a lord's residence is through the kitchen.

It only stands to reason—the formal front door is for
formal visitors, and is well-guarded by people wanting to
know the reason for somebody entering. There was a lot of
traffic, mind; Lord Daeran wasn't just idle royalty, but like
most of the rulers of the small domains along the Cirric, the
equivalent of the village warden, as well—his time was spent
in negotiating rates for dock space and bargaining over the
cost of potted fish.

On the other hand, given the local refrigeration problems—there isn't any—there are constantly people arriving
with food deliveries.

Particularly in early morning, before the sun is fully up,
before even those who are up and working are really awake.

Well, give them credit—this isn't the way an attacking
army would work its way in.

The trick was to look like I knew where I was going, and
to be sure that I didn't end up in a closet.

Fairly straightforward, actually—the kitchens occupied
the alley side of the residence, and there was only one open
door, through which I could hear the clanging of pots and
shouting of cooks. (Why all cooks shout is a mystery to me.)

I was through the outer kitchens and into the cooking
room itself before anybody braced me. It was a burly woman,
who vaguely reminded me of U'len, although this one had an
even meaner expression on her face, if that could be believed.
She had been stirring a huge stockpot filled with bones and
carrots and onions, but she stopped to look up and glare at
me.

"Sweetmeats for Lord Daeran," I said, bowing deeply,
holding out a small wooden box and a piece of parchment to
her.

She didn't take either. "What am I supposed to do with
these?"

"Lady, I've ridden all of a day and a night to bring this
from Fenevar and Lord Ulven." I spread my hands. "The box
is to be properly presented to Lord Daeran; the parchment is

to be imprinted with the mark of Lord Daeran's Valet, attesting to my having delivered it in good order." I gestured at the parchment. "Good lady, I am sure that you can mark it for him, if you would be so—"

She eyed the broken wax seal that my carelessly spread fingers didn't quite obscure. "And what am I supposed to do about this?"

I smiled innocently. "Which?"

"This seal. It appears to be broken. Will I find some sweatmeats missing inside?"

"Please, please, good lady—do I look like the sort who would steal a sweetmeat from the likes of Lord Daeran?"

She nodded. "Yes, you do. Now, do I look like the kind of fool who would sign for something I knew to be short?" She shooed me away. "Now, now, Lord Daeran is normally a patient man, but be along with you," she said, brushing me toward the inward door. "Find somebody else to sign for it. Our lord has little patience."

"Oh, please." Pleased don't throw me in that briar patch.

"Be along with you."

One down.

I made my way up the service stairway, cold stone rough beneath my naked feet. Bare feet are quieter than shoes.

The next part was going to be easy. We knew where the lord's room would be—when you've got an appearance balcony outside, it's not hard to guess.

Security might be tightened up shortly, but it would be a while. Word of what he was doing to the engineers would get back to Home, but it would take tendays; Daeran would want to tighten things up soon, but he wouldn't want to put everybody on full war footing *too* early, for fear that his troops would lose their edge.

Alternately, he might assume that Lou Riccettie would think of contract engineers as Lord Daeran might think of a subject—labor to be hired out, but nobody to fight a war over.

In the last, he was right. Too much land and too many countries and domains lay between Home and Brae over which to fight a war.

In any case, Lord Daeran's quarters were going to be on the second floor, and there wern't going to be any guards in front of his door, although he would probably sleep with the door locked.

I stopped at the beaded curtain across the entryway to the second floor, listening at the beaded curtain that hung over the doorway. Listening for the sound of feet padding down the hall, anything.

Nothing. Cautiously, slowly, gingerly, I pushed a strand of beads out of the way. There was no reason at all for there to be a guard standing in front of the door. So, there would be no guard standing in front of the door.

All I had to do was convince the guard standing in front of the door.

I eased the strand back and stood there too long, thinking. Not good, but harmless this time.

The obvious thing to do was to pull out the pistol and point it at him, because everybody knows that when somebody points a gun at you, you just do whatever they say, right?

Well, no.

A Grateful Dead fan once got backstage by buying a pizza and walking past all of the security stations loudly proclaiming, "Pizza for Jerry Garcia. Pizza for Jerry Garcia." It worked just fine, and, so I hear, the band was kind of nice about it, and let him hang out backstage for the rest of the show. And they ate the pizza, too.

On the other hand, some would-be presidential gatecrasher once tried just that with Jerry Ford—"Pizza for President Ford. Pizza for President Ford" and he didn't even get to the Secret Service. He was arrested at the first police checkpoint and spent the rest of the weekend in jail while the lab checked out the pizza to be sure the pepperoni wouldn't explode or something.

All of which goes to show that impertinence can work for you or against you.

The box held my finery—I had been intending to change in Lord Daeran's room before waking him, figuring that the plain muslin tunic and leggings of the lower classes might not intimidate him.

I dressed quickly.

The very best guards are the most literal-minded. If they have specific orders to cover a situation, they obey them; they show no initiative at all.

On the other hand, rulers, particularly harsh rulers, tend to want to have things both ways. They punish any violation of orders, but they also hand out punishments for violating unwritten, unvoiced orders—regardless of what the literal orders were, regardless of any conflict between the written and un-. Keeping quiet around a sleeping lord would be an unwritten, but enforced order.

I walked right through the beaded curtain, gesturing as imperiously as possible to the guard.

"Don't you have ears, man?" I asked, loudly. "Didn't you hear me call you?" I asked, slapping my hand hard against my thigh as I walked toward him. "Look at this mess," I said, gesturing back toward the hall. "Have you ever seen anything so—"

Either they don't hire terribly bright men as guards in Brae, or he wasn't a morning person. He hadn't decided what to do when I hit him hard in the throat with one hand—no windup; I'm good at that—and then slammed the box into the corner of his jaw—a blow to the chin gives a nice shock to the brain stem—before his panic circuits cut in. By then, it was too late. His eyes rolled up, his knees buckled, and he collapsed.

I didn't quite catch him before his head bounced on the floor—ouch!—but I quickly hauled him through the darkened doorway and into Lord Daeran's room. I've gotten pretty good at tying people up—the basic trick is to start by wiring the thumbs together, tight.

The room was large, light and airy, plaster walls newly whitewashed, the expanse broken by an occasional painting. A black-and-white striped Nevelenian rug covered the floor. Thick, too; I sank to my ankles. Lord Daeran lay snoring on the broad bed. Alone. Good.

The broad window to the balcony were secured by a bar. I carefully lifted the bar and set it down on the floor, then pulled the windows open with one hand while drawing my dagger with the other.

Lord Daeran's bed was a huge canopied fourposter, silk ropes secured to each post. Hmmm . . . it was obviously for him, but which way?

I smiled. Nah. I'd never get away with it.

It only took me a minute to set myself up.

Well, no point in wasting time—I turned him over, and stuffed a wadded end of blanket in his mouth and set the point of my dagger under his nose as he came very, very quickly awake.

"One loud word, Lord, Daeran," I whispered, visibly trembling, "one shouted syllable, one raised voice, and I'll discuss this with your successor." I moved the point of the knife from his nose to his throat, and kept up a nice, vibrato quaver. I do a good tremble. "Understood?"

My voice cracked a bit around the edges, which I think scared him more than anything else. I wouldn't want a nervous man holding a knife to my neck, either.

Under other circumstances, I suspect Lord Daeran would have cut a better figure, but sleep had splayed his long goatee and bristly mustache, and fear had his eyes wide.

He didn't really want to nod—not with the knife ready to cut his nose off—but managed to move his head up and down a fraction of the inch.

I pulled the end of the blanket out of his mouth, and replaced it with the neck of a metal flask. I thumbed the flask open.

"Have a drink," I said raising the flask to his lips and the point of the knife to this right eye.

It was pretty foul stuff, but he choked it down.

"Swallow good, now," I said, still obviously scared shitless.

I let out a sigh as I moved away from the bed. I set the flask down on the table, took a small glass vial out of my pouch. The cork came out with a loud *pop*.

"That's all over." I raised a hand as I relaxed into a chair, a man whose work was done. "Just keep your hands away from your mouth for a few moments, and we don't have to worry about you purging yourself. In the alternate, if you want to find out how much your successor loves you, just let out a yell. I'll dump the antidote out on the rug or shatter the vial against the wall. By nightfall you'll have died a particularly horrible death."

I tapped the point of my knife against the glass, and he winced. It was starting to get to him.

I smiled. "Careful. Don't get any on the bed." I didn't turn my head decently aside as he vomited onto the floor, a quick stream of green foulness. "Stage one. Even if you get to a bottle of healing draughts now, it won't do you any good. This mixture is special—the Matriarch of the Healing Hand could probably cure you, or perhaps the Spidersect Senior Tarantula, or whatever they call him. I don't think your locals can manage it."

Wiping his mouth on the back of his sleeve, he was able to summon up more composure than I would have had in his situation. "I take it there's an alternative." He tried to smooth his beard and hair into place.

"Yeah," I said. "You can get my friends out of your cages, down to Long Dock, and all of us away from here. You've changed your mind—they're going to be banished, not slowly executed."

I had been hoping for some quietly blustering threats, but he just nodded. "Who are you?"

I bowed. "Walter Slovotsky, at your service." His eyes widened marginally; he had recognized the name. "Or the other way around, eh?"

"So," he said. "I free your friends, and then I get the antidote? Enough to counteract the poison?"

"Sure." I nodded. "It doesn't take much—this is easily three times as much as is needed. To cure you, that is. You will still hurt some. Probably spend half your next tenday squatting over a thundermug—but it'll be loose stools; at least you won't be shitting out your whole insides."

He looked at me out of narrowed eyes. "I'm not sure I believe you."

I had been counting on selling him on the story.

It only stood to reason—I had taken a huge risk in sneaking myself in, and for what? Just to feed him a mixture of water, iodine, pepper oil, ipecac root, and some slightly raunchy mayonnaise we had pilfered from yesterday's breakfast and let sit out in the sun?

Of course not.

The bigger the bluff, the better chance it has of working, and this was about as big as I could arrange on short notice.

Hmm . . . we could always fall back on Plan B. The only trouble was, I had been counting on this one, and I didn't have a Plan B. I mean, I had the general outlines, but none of the nuances, and the nuances are always the best part. It ought to start with a thrown knife in his throat, to stifle his screams, and I could take it from there. The window? Not for me, but yes—strip the guard's tunic off, and throw him out the window. He would be the assassin, killed while trying to escape.

There was a desk next to the window; I could probably hide under it while everything went to hell, and maybe slip out during the confusion.

I'd gotten out of worse, but not often, and one of these days I wouldn't. When you're playing table stakes, you can't always push everything you have into the pot, and I had, and the son of a bitch was going to—

A universe was born in a cloud of gas, grew to a majestic spectrum of stars, and then aged and died to cold iron stars in the moment between when he said, "I'm not sure I believe you" and "You'll have to take the rest of the poison to persuade me that the antidote works."

Slowly, he picked up the flask and held it out to me. "I want to see some of it pour into your mouth."

I swallowed the horrible, thick stuff—God, we had done too good a job on it.

"See?" I said, as my gorge rose. I hate ipecac root. Waves of nausea dropped me to my knees as my stomach purged itself, but I held the flask out, threatening to throw it, as he retrieved a dagger from somewhere next to his bed.

I wiped my mouth on his sheets, then carefully, deliberately swallowed a third of the antidote, such as it was. It burned its way down. Just what I needed on a nauseous stomach: a shot of Riccetti's Best corn whiskey.

He hesitated for a long moment, then dropped the point of the dagger. "I guess I'd best get dressed," he said. He was already planning to betray me, of course. I hoped I was one step ahead of him.

Two soldiers lowered Bast to the dirt of the town square, laying him next to where Kenda was already recovering—a dose of healing draughts was not going to do Mardik or Veren any good. There's nothing you can do for the dead.

It was a good time to think about that, and to think about Bast and Kenda, about Tennetty, Jason, Ahira, Andrea, and myself, for that matter. A horrible way to die.

I looked Daeran in the eye. It would be a mistake to move my free hand toward a knife. I had to remember that I had the antidote to the "poison" that even now still had his stomach a bit queasy, and that was weapon enough.

The fact that something isn't true has nothing at all to do with your not remembering it.

Daeran kept staring at my right hand, the hand that held the flask, measuring his chances of securing it in one leap, and deciding that he didn't like the odds. I kept my eye on the hefty soldier behind me who kept trying to circle back behind me so that he could move in and grab my arms. Eventually, he might try it. Or maybe not. I'd have to be ready to toss the antidote aside, and tell Lord Daeran that there was more on the boat already, but I wasn't at all sanguine about that working.

People would have gathered in the square, but squads had been detailed to close off the base of the streets.

Kenda was able to sit up by herself, and raised the bottle to Bast's cracked, bloody lips.

He swallowed once, convulsively, and the all-too-familiar miracle happened: pink washed most of the ashen color from his face, and the black hollows that were his eyes filled out. He was still half-starved—there was only so much that a healing draught can do. It would be days before he could walk by himself, and weeks before he could fight. If he could fight—self-defense was part of an engineer's training, but I don't remember Bast as being terribly good at it.

"No more than ten soldiers," I said to Lord Daeran. "One each to carry my friends, eight more to make you feel secure."

The fullback behind me took a step forward, his foot scuffing the gravel. I was supposed to turn around and look at him, while the free safety to my left dived in and grabbed the flask. Granted, the flask didn't contain anything important. Just my life, and my friends' lives. That made it easy for me to forget that the liquid was only a gill of corn whiskey.

I raised the flask above my head, ready to dash it to the ground. "Tell them, Daeran."

He motioned them to desist. "Corporal Kino, pick out ten men. Two to carry Walter Slovotsky's friends." He included the two football players, of course.

Under a sky filled with puffy, peaceful clouds, a cool wind blew off the Cirric, blowing the scent of my own fear away.

Tennetty and Jason were waiting at the end of the dock. Jason's pistol was at his side, his finger near but off the trigger. Tennetty had her sword out in one hand, a flintlock in her other hand, and another brace of pistols in her belt.

Maybe three hundred feet off the end of the dock, the *Delenia* floated, secured at bow and stern by anchor and mooring. She was getting ready to leave. Her mainsail and mizzen were up, their booms swung out by the wind, sheets hanging loose as they flapped and cracked in the stiff breeze. The jib had been raised, but was bound to the foremast. Setting it would take only a few moments, though. Raise anchor, drop the mooring, haul in on the sheets, and the ketch would be off. It was rigged for several additional sails—they're called staysails on the Other Side; This Side the term is "leach sails"—but that would just add a little speed.

Andrea and Ahira stood on the high rear deck, talking with the captain. I don't know exactly what they were saying, but I hope they were being persuasive.

I don't think the sailors in the two launches were any too pleased. A Cirric sailor has to be able to fight as well as run, but the *Delenia* was a fast ketch, and they were undoubtedly much more practiced at running than fighting.

"The flask, if you please," Daeran said, holding out his hand, "and then you may load yourself and your friends in the boats and go."

I laughed. "Really? Do I look that stupid?" I held the flask out over the water. "We'll all go out to the ship, and then send the flask back in one of the launches."

"How do I know you won't simply kill me once we're aboard?"

Jason spoke up. "You have the word of a Cullinane."

There are parts of the Eren region where that would have settled it all.

Brae wasn't one of them, apparently. "No," Daeran finally said. "I don't trust any of you. You will go out in one launch, and six of my men and I will bring the prisoners along in the other. We will get on board, and then make our exchanges, and then each of us will go our separate ways."

I thought about it for a moment, and then shrugged. "Sure."

CHAPTER EIGHTEEN

In Which I Make a Trade and We Seek to Bid Farewell to the Friendly Natives of Brae

Crescit amor nummi quantum ipsa pecunia crescit. (The love of money grows as the money itself grows.)
—JUVENAL

So I said to myself, a two-way split can be profitable, but a one-way split might even be more than twice as good.
—WALTER SLOVOTSKY

LOGISTICS, FORMAL OR in-, has never been something that I've found terribly interesting. It's always been somebody else's department. Riccetti, now . . . hell, Lou would have worked out the problems just as a matter of practice. Logistics was why we put Little Pittsburgh in Holtun, rather than Home—Home is out of the way, and too near elven lands for the comfort of many, myself included.

That's Lou. Me, I had been vaguely wondering how they had managed to load the ship, but I hadn't really thought much about it until the launch pulled around the far side of it, revealing the floating dock.

Well, actually, it was more of a small, thin barge, stabilized at either end by floating barrels lashed to the water line, which presumably didn't let it dip or rock much that way. A wooden frame hung over the railing of the boat, basically locking the barge into place at the waterline. Clearly, the goods had been placed on it back on dockside, and then the whole thing poled out to the *Delenia*, the frame tied into place. That way, the barge could be emptied into the cargo net and the net lifted up by the winch with some reasonable amount of security for both crew and cargo.

Above, two crewmen were finishing securing the cargo crane, the cargo netting already having been neatly folded over the rail and lashed into place. They were late with that. You can't actually use the crane unless you've got the sail booms either stowed or, more commonly, lashed to the other side of the ship—they both swing through the same space, as the long-arm crane's boom has to be long enough to swing through a huge arc to provide the mechanical advantage that will allow one or two seamen to move a ton of cargo from dock to deck.

During my time at sea, working my way from port to port, I always used to like running the winch and crane. It's hard work, which I grant is atypical for me, but there's something special about being able to handle such massive forces, even by indirection.

Then again, maybe not.

I thought for a moment that it was all going to break loose as Tennetty leaped lightly from the launch to the floating dock, then helped me up, the flask still clasped carefully in my hand, as though everything depended on it.

Which it did.

Daeran and his soldiers followed us onto the floating barge, two of them carefully lowering Bast and Kenda to the ground. Above, the captain, his hands on the rail, leaned over.

I disliked him at first sight—from the neatly trimmed beard, framing the lips that were parted in an exhibition of straight, white teeth, down to the v-shaped torso of an acrobat or bodybuilder, all the way to treetrunk legs. All nicely bronzed, rather than browned.

Pretty man bother me.

"Greetings," he said, his voice deceptively calm. Or maybe not. Maybe maybe he was just an idiot who hadn't figured out how easily, how quickly everything could go to hell. "I am Erol Lyneian, captain of the *Delenia*."

I nodded. "Walter Slovotsky. Captain of my own soul."

"Oh, shit," Tennetty muttered. "I thought you were going to react like this."

"What?"

"You don't like competition, Slovotsky," she said. "Pay attention."

"I see," he went on, "that we have a problem. Why don't all of you come up and discuss it?"

It was just as well that Tennetty had cautioned me—it had been my intention to make the final exchange aboard ship, but something in his voice made me want to change my mind.

It was still the right move. "Very well," I said.

Ahira was waiting for me at the top of the ladder. "I think," he said, "that we may have a problem." His voice had taken on that level, overly calm tone he only used when things were just about to break. "*Delenia* and Erol Lyneian have been trading here for too long, and they're on good terms."

"How good?"

"Good enough that Erol Lyneian isn't even scared."

That was bad. Part of the plan involved the captain being sufficiently frightened of the local lord that he would want out of there, and quickly, not trusting Lord Daeran to believe that his involvement with us was innocent. It's sort of like Big Mike's routine with the stoolie, except Lord Daeran played more for keeps than any bunch of New Jersey street hoods.

Andy's eyes were glazed over, almost completely. If I'd had the genes for it, I suspect I'd have seen nascent spells hovering over her. But if everything went off, she would be like a flamethrower operator in combat—everybody's favorite target. She might have time to get a muttered, unrememberable syllable out, but she might not.

What we needed was something that would be worth more to Erol Lyneian than the ability to trade in Brae. A lot more. He only had a crew of five—it doesn't take many to run a well-designed ketch, and the more labor you have, the narrower the profits—and things didn't look like an even match, even with them on our side.

On the other hand, if everything hit the fan, he would know there was no guarantee he would make it out alive.

I smiled at him, as though to say *You can count on being the first to go*, and he smiled back and made a gracious gesture, as though to say, *After you, my dear Alphonse.*

Okay. I know: there were twelve of them against five of us, and I've faced worse odds than twelve to five.

On the other hand, Daeran's soldiers looked like they knew what they were doing, both singly—which was bad enough—and worse, collectively. As though to underline that, three of Daeran's bruisers leaned their heads together and started divvying up targets.

Bad, bad, bad. We could probably take on the six, but it would be close, and if the seamen came in on the other side . . .

I did a quick sum of the party's possessions, including coin, gem, potions, and everything, and decided that wasn't going to do it, even if we threw in my charm. A sea trader has to be something of an adventurous type, but his ship comes first, unless—and maybe not even if—you've got enough to buy him another ship.

Lord Daeran had decided that wasn't going to do it, either. He held out his hand. "The antidote, please," he said, smiling, his men gathered around him in a semicircle. "Then we'll all leave," he said, lying, thinking that I would have to decide to believe him.

That's how a Mexican standoff ends. With somebody making a fatal error.

"What would you trade for passage on your ship, Erol Lyncian?" I asked.

"Oh," he said, idly, "you've already paid for passage." He didn't expect me to believe him, and I didn't.

Well, we'd been saving this for years. It was even a secret that anybody but the Engineer knew how to make it, although all of us Other Siders did.

"I will tell you how to make gunpowder," I said. "Not the magical slaver imitation. Real gunpowder, black powder.

It's very cheap to make. I'd tell you right now, except that they would know how, too."

Ahira's jaw dropped, and Jason's eyes grew wide. I wasn't looking at Andy and Tennetty, but I don't imagine I would have seen them beaming approval.

Look. It wasn't the best idea in the world. Maybe it wasn't even a good idea. The best I can say for it is that I'd just given Lord Daeran and Erol Lyneian a huge conflict of interest. One of them as the source of real gunpowder would mean an immense shower of wealth; two would mean just another competitive business. As the sole non-Home possessor of the secret, Erol Lyneian would be a happy ship owner sailing from port to port, selling cheaply-made gunpowder at high prices; if it could be bought competitively, it was just another commodity.

If I'd had a day or more to think it over, I can't imagine anything else I could have said that would have made Erol Lyneian want to side with us, rather than with Lord Daeran. I've thought about it since, and I still can't come up with an alternative.

There was only one trouble in this admittedly brilliant piece of improvisation: I could see by the look in Erol Lyneian's eye that he didn't believe me.

I only realized that Lord Daeran did believe when he lunged for me, wrestling the flask from my hand as he shoved me up against the rail.

In retrospect, of course, it only stands to reason. I'd spent some time persuading Lord Daeran of my sincerity, and it had worked—he went for the flask of supposed antidote, after all. He was disposed to believe me; I could have sold him the Brooklyn Bridge, even thought he wouldn't have had the slightest idea what a Brooklyn is. Erol Lyneian, on the other hand, had just met me, and had yet to discover what a charming and reliable fellow I am.

Things went to hell quickly.

One reason that wizards need good bodyguards is that in a fight, a wizard is everybody's first target; having Andy free and operating would have ended things in our favor quickly.

Two soldiers jumped at her; out of the corner of my eye

I saw Andy collapse from a blow to the head, and Tennetty hack down at the soldier who then tried to pin her against the deck, but I was busy with my own fight.

This would, in the old days, have been a great time for Karl to be there.

Once, when a trap we set for slavers went suddenly sour, he ended up inside a circle of four swordsmen—and good ones, too—armed with nothing more than an improvised quarterstaff. In about eight seconds, it was all over—he had hit them hard, and fast, and they were down.

But Karl was dead and gone, and all we had was me.

I did the best I could—I flung a throwing knife into Lord Daeran's belly, and lashed out with my foot at the nearest of the soldiers, sending him crashing into one of his fellows.

That gave me enough time to get my sword free.

I batted a knife out of the way and slipped my blade in between another's ribs. His bubbling scream cut off as he twisted spasmodically away, my blade jamming in his ribs, taking my sword with him. Ten years before, even five years before, I would have moved fast enough to extricate the blade, to twist it loose, before it was caught, but I was getting old and slow.

We would have had no at all chance if it hadn't been for Jason's revolver and for Ahira. The dwarf somehow got hold of a huge boarding pole, and flailed it around like a quarterstaff, hitting one of Lord Daeran's men so hard that he actually broke through the railing and slammed down hard on the floating dock below.

Jason's revolver spat flame and smoke at one of the soldiers, echoed by a gout of blood and gore from his thigh. Screaming, the soldier fell heavily, across Bast.

Bast's arms moved spasmodically, clumsy hands flailing away at the soldier's face. He was doing the best he could, but he wasn't going to be any help.

I ducked under a butt-stroke from a spear and lunged for the owner of it, drawing one of my Therranji garrottes as I did. I faked at him with my left hand, then neatly looped the garrotte over his head with my right, drawing it tight with a jerk that should have taken his head half off.

Face already purpling, he staggered away, fingers clawing

uselessly at his throat. It would take a bolt cutter to save him now, and I wasn't about to go digging in my kit for ours.

But there were so many of them; even without Erol Lyneian and his sailors taking part, there were just too many of them for us to take at such close range. I should have thought it out better. I should have insisted that Jason stand back, out of range, before everything hit the fan, but that sort of thing had always been Karl's department, and Karl was dead.

One soldier reached Jason, pulling his revolver down, his body shuddering at the shot that ripped through his belly and out his back, but before Jason could free the weapon two others were already on him.

Tennetty had just fired one of her flintlocks, although I didn't see what, if anything, she hit. Moving even faster than I'd have thought she could, she was on the back of one of the soldiers wrestling with Jason, her shiny bowie rising then falling, then rising and falling again, now redly wet.

Jason managed to free himself and fire off two more quick shots, but his rovover clicked empty.

The revolver.

It fired cartridges, filled with the smokeless powder that Lou Riccetti and his top assistants had spend years perfecting; for now, it was one of two, one of only two repeating pistols, the most advanced weaponry in the world.

Jason was Karl's Cullinane's son, and Karl Cullinane would have done his damnedest to make sure that a weapon that advanced didn't fall into foreign hands. Jason Cullinane tossed the pistol over his right shoulder, over the railing. A priceless piece of blued steel tumbled end-over-end through the air, arcing outward.

I think that was when I heard Tennetty scream, as a sword pinned her by the shoulder to a mast, her knife falling from her useless fingers. I know that was when Jason went down under a rush of bodies. It was too late for him to get his sword free—

Something caught me upside the head, shaking the whole universe for a moment. I staggered, tried to recover as I drew my belt knife and stabbed backwards, rewarded by a scream.

"Walter, we—" I didn't get to hear what Ahira was trying

to say. The largest of the soldiers hit him with a flying tackle, neatly knocking the dwarf, his arms spread wide in helplessness, backwards through the hole in the railing, like a cue ball smacking into the eight, and the eight into the pocket.

Except that the pocket here was deep water.

Very deep water.

"No."

No, it was going to be okay. Ahira was tough. When he hit the floating dock, his superior masculature and thicker bones would protect him. But he had been hit hard, and at a sharp angle, and it arced him out past—

I can still hear his scream of terror, a high wailing cry. I can still see him falling backwards, out of control, his fingers reaching for the floating dock, missing it by inches. I can still see the splash he made, and see his wide eyes, and the panic written on his face as the water closed over it.

Dwarves don't float.

Dwarves can't swim.

Dwarves sink like a stone.

"No," I shouted. Asshole. You'd think that a man would learn, well before he's my age, that wanting something not to be so has never, ever changed it, that it doesn't matter what you want, what you desire, what you need, but what you do.

Reflexively, foolishly, idiotically, uselessly, I reached out a hand, but it was useless. The water was eight, ten feet below the rail, and Ahira had already vanished from sight.

Something hit me alongside my right ear, I think.

CHAPTER NINETEEN

In Which A Friend Has A Few Final Words With Lord Daeran

Pride, envy, avarice—these are the sparks have set on fire the hearts of all men.
—DANTE ALIGHIERI

I can think of two things I've been waiting my whole life to say. A friend of mine recently stole one of them.
—WALTER SLOVOTSKY

My KARATE TEACHER, Mr. Imaoka, gave me the best lesson on fighting that I've ever had.

"The most important lesson in karate is running," he said, as the lot of us reluctantly strapped our sneakers on. "The first thing you do in a fight," he said, "is to turn and run away.

"Run for at least a mile, preferably two or three. If he's still chasing you, he's probably out of breath by then. If it's still worth fighting about," he said with a smile, "you turn around and beat him up."

When next I could follow what was going on, Lord Daeran was looming over me, looking none the worse for wear, his hair and goatee now neatly combed, his face glowing with health and vigor.

He had gotten to our healing draughts, it appeared.

I would have rather had a hangover, thank you much.

There was a constant stabbing pain under my left shoulderblade, where I was sure that I had been stabbed. I had to breathe shallowly, broken ribs grating at even the slightest movement.

Not that I could have moved a lot. Lord Daeran had saved me that trouble by tying me to the rail near the stern, between Tennetty and Jason, my hands behind me. Andy, Kenda and Bast lay tied on their sides on the hot deck, a soldier looming over each of them, although I don't know why.

Tennetty and Jason were cut in dozens of places, and while they hadn't bled out, neither of them was in any shape to fight: Jason was battered badly, and while the fingers of Tennetty's right hand were feeling around for the knots, her whole left arm hung limp—the sword she'd taken in the shoulder must have gotten to a nerve center.

Not good.

Over her gag, Andy's eyes were wild, even the heavily bruised right one, swollen almost closed.

Ahira was dead.

Our gear had been spread out across the deck, clothes scattered haphazardly, weapons and other stuff carefully laid out for Daeran's examination. Stooping over our gear, he fingered an unmarked gunmetal flask. I wouldn't mind if he drank that—it was a liniment for saddle sores, and the main ingredient was wood alcohol.

"First matters first, Walter Slovotsky," Daeran said. "The antidote. You have more of it, I'm sure."

Well, yes, we did—the more of it was in another flask, just out of his reach. I like an occasional nip to cut the dust of the trail.

I didn't answer, and I was very careful not to look either at the flask of Riccetti's Best or away from it. He didn't get angry. He just stalked over to me and carefully hit me across the face twice, first time with his palm, then with the back of his hand.

Not torture. Not yet. This was just to let me know that he was serious.

In my mind's eyes, I could see Ahira taking the bastard in his broad hands, fingers crushing the life out of him.

But Ahira was overboard, in thirty feet of water.

Dead.

Only one chance, although not much of one. Things hung in a balance here, perhaps too delicate a balance. With the damage we had done to his party, Daeran and Erol Lyneian were at rough parity on the ship, and Daeran would know better than to endanger that by sending for more troops right now, threatening to cut Erol Lyneian out totally.

The two of them would come to terms before they could afford to torture the secret out of me; they would have to set up a cozy little arrangement that would have landed them with an antitrust suit on the Other Side.

I could think of only one card to play. We had managed to keep the secret of black powder for close to twenty years now, through the time that Pandathaway wizards had invented their expensive substitute, through Riccetti's re-creation of the smokelees power for cartridge weapons, through all of it.

But it was now, or never. I voted for now. "Saltpeter—the crystals you find under old piles of manure."

"No," Bast shouted. "Don't tell him. In the name of the Engineer, shut your mouth. Don't—."

"Saltpeter," I said. I wasn't going to be stopped. "Five parts by weight. Powdered charcoat—willow works best—three parts. Sulfur—two parts."

"That's the antidote?"

"No, no, no," I said. "That's *gunpowder.* Black powder. Manufacture is tricky, but those are the ingredients. Saltpeter, charcoal, sulfur. Five, three, two."

A stray smile crossed Erol Lyneian's lips. "I think that Lord Daeran is more interested in the antidote to the poison right now. You managed to spill all but a drop."

I tried to shrug, regretting the effort instantly. "There wasn't any poison," I said, spitting out each word through a red cloud of pain. "All a bluff. The idiot went for it."

Think, dammit, think. I was just going through the motions. All I had done was my usual part if it: try to buy some time for Ahira to figure us a way out of this mess, to pry up some loose edge of the trap we found ourselves in for him to work on, but Ahira was gone.

Dead.

I'd have to do his job. Or somebody would.

No. There was another solution. We could all die.

Daeran took a step toward me, but stopped at Erol Lyneian's gesture. "You're lying."

"Then have some more out of that flask," I said, pointing with my chin. That hurt, too. "It's just corn whiskey, but enjoy. It'll taste the same. Enjoy. Compliments of the Engineer."

Below his angry eyes, Bast's lips were pulled back in a snarl. If he could have worked his way loose, he would have gone for me, not for them. The secret of gunpowder was the great treasure of the Engineer, and I had just given it away.

Well, my life and the lives of my friends were the great treasure of *me*, and I was hoping that I had just bought a better chance of survival for all of us. Neither of them would trust me, and Erol Lyneian now knew too much, as did all of his men.

But he wouldn't have to face that intellectually, not yet. Lord Daeran had three functioning soldiers aboard the *Delenia*, all of them with naked weapons, and Erol Lyneian had only his five crewmen, none of them visibly armed, all of them on deck. Erol Lyneian and his men could win a fight, probably, but only an extended one. He couldn't count on taking out all of Daeran's people before reinforcements arrived.

Daeran forced the mouth of the corn whiskey flask between my lips.

I took a large mouthful before he wrested it away. Last drink for the condemned man, although not be intention.

"Too eager, you are," he said. "I think you may be bluffing again. We'll wait and see what the effect is."

It wasn't going to work. I didn't have enough leverage to play Erol Lyneian off against Daeran. All I was doing was buying time. For what?

Maybe Tennetty could work her way free.

She clearly didn't understand the situation; she was smiling. Crazy, idiot bitch. Didn't she know how badly she had been cut, didn't she know that we were all dead, that I was just buying us some time for a miracle, and that it wouldn't come?

Jason started smiling, too. Imbecile.

Look, I don't mind people being heroic, but this was ridiculous.

Ahira was dead, we all were as good as dead, and the fucking idiot was grinning—

It was then that I felt the blunt fingers behind me, working on my knots.

Daeran saw something in my eyes, I guess. His brow furrowed, and he took a step forward.

I spat blood on the deck. Blood always makes a good distraction.

"Healing draughts," I said. "No more until I get them, for me and my friends."

"We'll see about it, after the details," Daeran said.

"Now," I said. "Or I bite my tongue off and you never know what the secret procedure is."

The secret procedure wasn't much—grind each ingredient separately, toss in a barrel, then wet it down with water (good), urine (better) or wine (best), then stir, stir, stir, until your arm feels like it's going to fall off. Then stir some more. Push the mixture, now vaguely dough-like, through a wire mess to mix it more—it's called corning. Repeat, dry *very* carefully, and there you have it. It's dangerous—kids, don't try this at home—but it's not complicated.

"You're bluffing. Again," Daeran said.

"Try me," I said, bluffing.

He didn't quite sigh. "Not this time, I think. This time, I'll let you win." He took a step toward me.

Behind me, the fingers went away. Ahira, somehow clinging to the side of the ship, probably standing on top of the molding surrounding a porthole or something, had ducked down.

"No, them first." I nodded at the others. They needed it worse than I did, Tennetty and Jason in particular, and I needed my hands free.

Daeran had decided to control his temper. There would be enough time shortly to punish me for my insolence, and just because he'd fed them healing draughts, it didn't mean he couldn't kill them later.

"Very well." He moved over to where Tennetty was bound, and brought the bottle of healing draughts to her lips.

The fingers behind me returned, and finished their work,

then pressed a knife hilt into my hands, but the hilt was withdrawn. The fingers put leather thongs into my hands and closed my fingers around the thongs, giving my hand a final quick pat before the blunt fingers went away.

Thanks a fucking lot, Ahira.

It was him. There was no question of it. I knew the touch of that hand, and I don't look a gift horse in the mouth, not when it's the only ride out of town. My best friend was alive, and operating independently, and—

Of course. Sometimes I'm such an idiot—he wasn't teasing me. He had just given me the inventory of our weapons, and assigned me the one he thought suited our situation best, trusting me to read his mind.

We had leather thongs—the ones that had bound my wrists, no doubt—and we had a knife.

Okay; that was a start.

The knife would go to Tennetty, and Ahira would try to work his way around, clinging to the side of the ship, trying to stay out of sight. No. He wouldn't. If he fell again, he might not be able to make his way up out of the water. He would stay right where he was, perched on top of the rudder or whatever. He would free me, Tennetty and Jason, and then expect me to start things off.

How the hell had he gotten out of the water? I had seen him hit the water, and seen him sink like a stone.

Later, Walter, later.

And what had taken him so long?

Andrea, Jason, and Tennetty had been treated with the healing draughts; it was my turn.

Lord Daeran knelt in front of me. "Your healing draughts. Then you will talk. I promise you, you will talk." He brought the warm lip of the bottle to my mouth, banging it hard against my teeth.

I didn't care. The too-sweet taste of the healing draughts washed the blood from my mouth, my aches and pains becoming distant and vague.

No time to enjoy that now. I tied a loop in one end of the leather thong, and slipped the other end through it.

Lord Daeran's eyes went wide as I whipped the loop over his head and drew it tight around his neck.

"*Now,*" I said, probably redundantly.

No time to finish him off—I kicked him aside then went low, toward our gear. Tennetty, the knife held in her outstretched hand, went high above me, bowling herself into a soldier who was reacting just a little too slow. I think she gutted him; his scream rang in my ears.

No time to think, either; I would have to do it all right, and by instinct.

I slid a sword hilt-first toward Jason, then tackled the soldier above Andy hard enough to have satisfied even Coach Fusco. Sonofabitch always thought I took it too easy on quarterbacks. Fuck him.

And to hell with the soldier, too—my rush carried him back to where the rail caught him across the kidneys. His arms flew apart as the tetanic shock hit him hard.

We were still overmatched, and even with Ahira back in action we wouldn't have had a chance unless . . . first, I'd have to get Andy free, and she would have to . . .

Of course. Trust your friends. I could see the boom out of the corner of my eye, and hear Ahira laughing about it in the corner of my mind.

"Tennetty, Jason—*down,*" I shouted. The dark shadow swept toward me; I ducked under it and went for Andy as the boom, propelled by impossibly strong dwarf muscles, swept hard across the deck, bowling over soldiers, the sailors reflexively ducking.

I scooped up a knife and reached Andy's side. A slice and a twist and she was free, fingers already clawing at her gag; a leg-sweep knocked down the soldier who had been lunging at her.

Her arms spread wide, she rose to her feet, uttering just one syllable.

Daylight reddened and dimmed, and the sky went dark above us.

Time slowed. I'd been hearing my heart thumping hard and fast, but now with each beat was a slow double moan.

Gwa-thunnnnnk.

Long pause.

209

Gwa-thunnnnnk.

I could still think. I could still see, but I couldn't even fall fast. We were all stuck in the same clear molasses: Tennetty, her knife rising, unable to see the saber inches from her back, about to skewer her; Ahira, one hand clamped on a bloody mess that had been the face of a soldier, his other arm squeezing another's chest further than bones could give; Jason, in full lunge through the belly of the largest of the soldiers, his face grim as he saw another blade descending toward him.

We were all trapped in the red time. Except for Andy.

Leaning hard, like she was walking against a strong but steady wind, she walked smoothly across the deck, pushing up on the saber menacing Tennetty as she passed.

She reached her son's side, and brushed the attacking blade aside, then set one finger on either side of the soldier's head, muttering a word I could not have remembered even if I'd heard it.

Sparks leisurely leapt from finger to finger, strengthening as they did. Her mouth was moving, repetitiously, but I couldn't quite read what she was saying. The sparks became a flow, and the flow became lightning, jagged forks piercing the soldiers' head until a cloud of smoke gathered about his forehead and ears.

Slowly, gracefully, she turned toward me and smiled. It wasn't a friendly smile.

Over to you, she mouthed.

As the light blued again, and time returned to normal, Ahira had retrieved his axe from our pile.

There were only two soldiers left alive on deck. Tennetty had snaked her arm around the throat of one, and Jason, his sword shining in the light, had squared off against the other.

All that left was Lord Daeran, lying on the deck, loosening the garrotte that I clearly hadn't quite tightened enough.

Hey, I was in a hurry.

Ahira raised his axe.

"What . . . *are* you?" the lord asked.

If it had been me, I would have been tempted to make a speech, about how Mikyn was one of ours, and if he needed stopping, we would stop him, and no locals need apply, and

210

about how putting friends and associates of ours to death for unwittingly helping Mikyn was just plain wrong, and wasn't going to be tolerated.

But Ahira didn't make premature speeches.

The axe fell, and then he spoke.

"Justice, you son of a bitch," he said.

I guess, back in the old days, James Michael and I saw the same movies.

Soldiers at the dock were loading themselves into boats, and two of the small boats were already on their way toward us.

"Captain," I said, "do you want to try to explain it all right now, or shall we get out of here?"

Erol Lyneian smiled as he gestured his crew into motion. "We still have an agreement, Walter Slovotsky. "The *Delenia* is to take you to safely where you wish to go; you are to give me the secret of making engineer gunpowder."

He wouldn't apologize for his having made a virtue of necessity earlier, for siding with the late Lord Daeran. Business, after all, was business.

Bast pushed himself forward, staggering, probably both from the rolling of the ship. "No. Don't tell them anything, don't let the secret out, don't—"

Tennetty caught his arm, twisted it up and around behind his back with an economical motion. "Not now. Later, if at all." She pushed him away, then drew her sword again and took up an *en garde* position next to me.

I nodded to Erol Lyneian. "We have a deal. Let's just move this ship, asshole."

CHAPTER TWENTY

Immediately After Which I Strike My Forehead, Quite Briskly, with My Open Palm

It ain't what a man don't know that makes him a fool, but what he does know that ain't so.

—JOSH BILLINGS

Sometimes, it's good to be wrong.

—WALTER SLOVOTSKY

THERE IS A THING A friend of mine once labeled the "rhinoceros in the corner." Maybe she was just repeating it, but I always associate it with Peggy.

"The rhinoceros in the corner is the idea that hangs over a conversation," she said, "but that you don't talk about. You find them all over the place, in a lot of situations."

"Like, say, the first time you go to dinner with a girl?" I smiled. It was, of course, the first time we'd gone out to dinner.

"Woman."

"Woman." Fine.

"You talk about school," she said, "and about majors, and jobs, and movies, and politics—anything. But what you're both thinking about is whether or not you're going to bed together."

212

"Oh?"

"I mean, like, you're thinking about that, and she's thinking about that, but you don't talk about it."

"You mean like we're not?"

"Well . . ." She smiled and sipped at her beer. "Yeah."

Ahira didn't want to tell me how he had survived, not unless I asked; and I wasn't going to ask him. Just pure stubbornness on both of our parts, but it's kind of a parttern we'd fallen into over all the years. Eventually, one of us would give in, but you wouldn't want to bet the farm on which.

Ahira and I stood in the spray, on the foredeck, near the bow. He sat on the step next to the anchor, one arm hooked over a safety line as he honed the edge of his battleaxe; I leaned against the rail, doing nothing much.

Ahira whisked his stone smoothly against the edge of his axe. *Fsssssst. Fsssssst. Fsssssst. Fsssssst.*

"You're going to get that sharp enough to shave with, if you keep at it," I said.

He shrugged. "No such thing as too sharp an axe." Yes, a too-thin edge could chip in a fight, but that wouldn't make much practical difference, not with Ahira's strength behind it.

At least Ahira was talking to me, even if the stubborn bastard wouldn't volunteer the information I wanted him to. I was *persona non grata* with Bast and Kenda, and Jason wasn't sure, yet, whether I had brilliantly bought us more time—thereby cleverly saving the day—or whether I had cravenly sold out everything that Home stood for, and for no purpose. I would have given him an argument, but I'm not sure which side I'd have taken, so I had given it a pass. Andy was asleep in her bunk, Tennetty watching over her, Bast, and Kenda.

"Feels faster now than it was before we tacked," he said.

"I know," I said. "But it just feels that way."

Running with the wind is fast, but despite the name it's stuffy and no fun. The faster the sailboat, the less pleasant it is—the more efficient the boat is at using the wind, the less breeze you have. You carry your effluvium with you. It feels like you're not moving, like the rest of the universe is moving around you. Slowly, and stuffily.

I much prefer sailing close-hauled, close to the wind, the rush of air in my face, occasional jets of spray refreshing me.

Magic and madness were loose somewhere out in the night, and we were sailing off into it all.

We talked, and kept watch on the night. Not the worst thing to do. The night was clear, the sky bright diamonds displayed proudly on the blackest velvet. To port, beyond where the starlight capered across the gentle swells, dark land loomed threateningly below the starry sky, the blackness broken only occasionally by the flickering of lanterns or fireplaces in some window ashore.

Off to starboard the roiling surface of the water, dark and glossy, shimmered and shattered the starlight.

A sailor only sees the surface of the sea, always is left to wonder what may wait below the surface. There's a lot you never know.

I guess I'd never know what the right thing to do about Kirah was. But maybe I didn't have to decide on the right thing, not in terms of effects. Maybe what I ought to do was accept the principle that if I wanted things to work out for me and Kirah, just maybe running around the Eren regions wasn't the way to cure it, that maybe the reason things had gone okay during the years in Endell is that I'd been there.

Or maybe not. Maybe what both Kirah and I needed was a long time away from each other.

I could still remember her, though, her hair floating in the breeze, her body soft and warm. Too long ago.

There comes a time when you just make a decision, when you stop fooling around pretending that what you're doing is weighing and balancing and considering and trying to decide, and you just decide. Fine.

I'd decide. Enough trying, enough whining and wondering and whereforeing. When I got home, I'd make things work between Kirah and me. Period. Never mind how, never mind why. I'd just do it.

"What are you thinking about?" Ahira asked. *Fsssssst. Fsssssst.*

"Just thinking that it's getting cold out here."

Straight ahead, perhaps only a few hundred yards, perhaps more than a few miles, a trio of faerie lights slowly

214

circled each other as they pulsed gently through the progression of blues and greens. The tempo picked up, and the lights orbited faster around their invisible center, becoming all red and orange, the pace increasing still further as they circled each other faster and faster, tighter and tighter, until the circle could not hold and first one, then the other two shattered into a shower of fiery sparks that blued as they fell toward the dark waters below.

"Magic and madness are loose somewhere out in the night," I said.

"True enough."

"And we're sailng toward it."

"There is that." *Fssssst. Fssssst. Fssssst.* He raised his head. "Where would you rather be?"

"Here's fine, I guess." Some of the best times are when you just sit and talk and think.

Erol Lyneian was very much a neat freak: the anchor cable, of that strange Therranji construction that left a brass-and-iron cable as flexible as rope, had been carefully flemished against the deck, not simply coiled in a heap.

Ahead of us, starlight danced on the water; the water rushed against the fast-moving boat. Above us in the dark, the jib strained to catch every whisper of wind, looming above us like a large vague ghost.

One of the crewmen worked his way forward. Vertum Barr, his name was: a short, bony man well into his fifties, naturally so thin that you could see his ribs despite the small potbelly, dark and wrinkled like a dried mushroom—the sort of sailor you find working all over the Cirric, from boat to boat. He would never own more than he could carry in his seabag, but as long as he could work he would always have a bunk under which he could stow his bag.

"Carrying a bit of weather helm as the wind picks up, eh?" I asked.

His face split in a gap-toothed grin. "How did you know that?"

"Please. I do have an eye for the obvious: she's heeling a bit. Whoever is back at the tiller keeps having to bear away. Costing us speed."

"Hmmm . . . and what would you be doing about it, were it yours to do?"

I shrugged. "Is this a test? Your center of effort's too far back. Me, I'd just crank the traveler leeward—flatten out the mainsail. Or maybe I'd heave to the reef the mainsail some. But I'm a lazy man. A captain who prides himself on every breath of speed is either going to fly one of those loose-footed sails you're rigged for, or more likely going to put on a bigger jib."

"He is, is he?"

"And somebody who has gone to the trouble of having the mainmast rigged with twin forestays isn't going to want to heave to and switch sails the easy way—it'll take at least four men to do the job, and I'll bet you'd like a couple of assistants to help with that huge mother of a jib."

"I wouldn't bet against you, truth to tell." He smiled. "Well, I could use some help, at that."

"Sure; we'd be happy to."

Ahira nodded. "I can finish this later." He stowed his axe in its sheath and then bound it to a rack of belaying pins. "What are you getting us into now?"

"Just a bit of work." I still wanted to ask him how he had survived, and he wanted to tell me, but the two of us have always allowed ourselves to be stubborn over things that don't matter.

His smile was bright in the dark. "That I can handle."

We surprised them. Ahira and I managed to haul the huge bag with the balloon jib—we would have called it a genoa jib on the Other Side—all by ourselves, even though Ahira grunted with the effort as he hauled the sailbag up the hatch. It must have weighed four hundred pounds, but Ahira can carry weights like that.

Me, I just steadied the thing. I'm only human, after all.

The rigging was a bit different than I was used to, and they had folded and packed the sail according to their own idiosyncratic system; I wouldn't have wanted to try to rig the sail myself, but Vertum Barr and Tretan Verr knew their jobs, and it wasn't all that long before we had the balloon jib up on the leeward forestay, and the smaller jib down, folded, bagged, and stowed.

We returned to our spot on the deck, the huge jib bal-
looning in the wind above us, luffing just a bit as the crew
worked to get the trim right.

"I don't know what you see in this," Ahira said. Not
criticism. Just observation.

"Guess you have to be born with a taste for it." I smiled.
"I had a bit of experience on the Other Side." Just a bit. "It's
relaxing."

"Hmm. "

"You've got something on your mind," I said.

He nodded. "That's a fact. I've been wondering if you're
getting too slow, Walter." Ahirda said, considering the edge
of his axe, as he resumed his sharpening. "You all do seem
to slow down, as the years go by."

"And not you?" I asked, maybe too harshly. "You
missed a step today." If Ahira hadn't been bowled over the
side, we might have won on the first round, instead of lucking
into another shot at the game.

I shuddered. The locals have ways of getting people to
talk, and I'm none too fond of even the *idea* of red-hot pokers
being shoved up my ass. We all have our peccadilloes, and
that's one of mine.

He shook his head. "No. Not me. I'm not aging like you
are, not as fast." He stared at me out of sad eyes. "If I was
losing it, bit by bit, I'd admit it. To myself."

I leaned back against the railing and closed my eyes. Possibly I was getting too old for this. I'd been saying that for
ten years, and maybe it was coming true.

Damn silly time to be growing old. Magic was loose in
the world and we were sailing toward Ehvenor, toward God-
knew-what. The situation called for not only the wisdom that's
supposed to come with age, but the reflexes of youth. We
needed a cross between Alvin York, Natty Bumppo, George
Patton, and Shadowjack, and all we had was me.

"Maybe," I said. "And maybe we just were unlucky this
time. I don't think we did too badly. Getting out of Brae with
all of us alive is about ten strokes under par, as far as I'm
concerned. That was too close."

"No," he said, firmly. "Just par."

We sat silent for a long time.

"Don't be angry," he said. "It had to be said."

"Maybe it did, and maybe it didn't."

"Would ignoring it make things any better?" A broad hand gripped my shoulder. "I seem to remember somebody telling me, one rainy Friday night, years and years ago, that I wasn't going to drive my wheelchair out of the dorm and into the rain, because I couldn't afford to risk getting a cold, not in my state. I remember him saying something about that it was fucking unfair, but the universe was fucking unfair, and we weren't going to pretend otherwise."

I shrugged. "Well, you couldn't."

It was hard to remember Ahira as crippled James Michael Finnegan, largely because I'd never really thought of James Michael as a cripple—his mind had always been sharp, sharper than mine. The body, sure, that was bent, but after you've known somebody for awhile, you learn to stop worrying yourself over it. It doesn't rub off.

"I also remember," he said, his voice low, "that you canceled a date to put together a poker game that night."

"Hey, I needed the money." I smiled. "Besides, I didn't really cancel it, we just pushed it back a week."

Bethany had been good about it; she had acted as James Michael's hands at the poker game, and had been amused at the way that the other players paid more attention to her cleavage than to their cards. Nice lady. Next weekend we had a nice steak dinner, complete with a bottle of Silver Oak Cabernet, paid for with my winnings.

"Now it's my turn," he said. "You've got to start taking it easy." He chuckled to take the sting out of it, the laugh a deep rumble in his barrel of a chest. "You can't afford to get your neck broke, eh?"

"Hey, I wouldn't do that. Deprive all the women of my charm? But leave it for later. Not now. I'm still okay."

He had finished with his axe; carefully, gently, he wrapped it in an oilcloth.

"Maybe so," he said. "Probably. But you will slow down too much, some day. We can push it back a bit, but there's going to come a time when you're not going to be able to go out and do things yourself." He bit at his thumb. "Next generation's coming along—Jason's getting sharper. We're

218

going to have to be sure that he's got the right kind of people to back him."

"Until what?"

The dwarf shrugged. "Until things change. However they change. Until the revolution that Lou is building takes off on its own; until the gather of Holtish and Biemish nobles becomes a true parliament, until Arta Myrdhyn takes a hand and screws up whatever the hell we think we're doing."

Starlight danced on the water, and a brief spray more chilled than refreshed me.

"In the meantime," he said, "you've got to do two things."

I knew what the first was going to be. "Practice, practice, practice."

"Yup. Starting in the morning. You and me . . . well, I can read your mind almost as well as you can read mine. Tennetty tends to bunt too much, and Jason can't coordinate with anybody."

I shrugged. "I keep thinking of him as his father. Karl would have ducked back and blown six of them away before getting into the fight, and then he could have taken out the rest."

Ahira looked me over, slowly, the way he always did when I said something stupid. "Not the last time. Don't buy into the legend, or you might start to believe you're just as legendary." He looked out over the water. "You've got to remember you're tricky Walter Slovotsky, and stop trying to be Karl. Swaggering through the town square on a recon was a Karl sort of thing."

Well, I didn't say, *I actually didn't do it Karl's sort of way. I did it my way.*

But Ahira was off on his you're-getting-too-old-for-this kick, and I didn't want to complicate the issue.

Besides, he was right. I've always been best at sneaking and indirection, not taking on half a dozen swordsmen. I should have thought out a way around it, not confronted Lord Daeran in some sort of Mexican standoff.

"I'll try," I said.

"Good," he said, rising. "We start practicing in the

morning. In the meantime, get some sleep. I'll keep an eye on things tonight; I can catch up on sleep tomorrow."

Screw it. "*Okay*," I said. "O-fucking-kay. I give."

"Eh?"

"I give in. You win. If you won't tell me, I'll break down and ask."

He smiled as he ticked his thumbnail against the anchor. "Ask what?"

"How it happens that you're alive."

He smiled, again. "You mean because dwarves can't float, can't swim, right?"

"*Yes*. That's exactly what I mean. Are you going to tell me, or let me die of curiosity?"

He shrugged and he hefted the anchor chain. "I think I'll ask Erol Lyncian for a piece of this, as a good-luck charm.— Anybody ever tell you that dwarves can't *climb?*"

CHAPTER TWENTY-ONE

In Which I Face Off with a Fanatic, and Spend Time with an Old Friend

There are truths which are not for all men, nor for all time.
—VOLTAIRE

I changed my mind, okay?
—WALTER SLOVOTSKY

OLD FRIENDS ARE GOOD to have around. There's a story or two about that, but they'll have to wait, just a bit.

We stopped to trade at Artiven, bobbing safely at anchor offshore, while the launch took Erol Lyneian and some trade goods ashore—a few bundles of Sciforth ironwood, a couple of hogsheads of horrible-smelling Fenevarian glue, and, surprisingly, fifty-or-so pounds of Home wootz.

Maybe that shouldn't have been so surprising—Artiven was known for its knives and swords, and it would have been hard to think of a better start than the high-grade weapon steel that Home produced.

He could have gone right past, I guess, except for two things: for one, crew provisions were low. There hadn't been quite enough time to load them in Brae. Taking to your heels usually interferes with something important; this was above par. Two: Ahira wanted Bast and Kenda off the ship, and away from us.

Erol Lyneian had been pushing me for more of the details of powdermaking, and I'd been supplying them.

Bast wasn't happy. We hadn't had quite enough healing draughts to bring him and Kenda up to full health; the aftermath of his ordeal had left him frail, at least for the time being. Rest, food, and time would do everything else. Although he couldn't rest.

He caught up with me as I was getting a lesson in rigging and ketch sailing from Vertum Barr—I'm no dilettante, but I like learning new skills and polishing ones I already have—while Tennetty and Jason were working out on the rear deck.

It was good to play sailor again, wearing nothing but a pair of blousy pantaloons and a headband—well, and a knife strapped to my right calf, concealed by the pant leg—worrying about nothing more important than how to get a bit more speed out of the shape of a sail, whether the bilge hold needed pumping again, or how to fly a complex set of sails.

The *Delenia*'s gear was unusual, even by the idiosyncratic nonstandards of Cirric sailing: she used a lot of lacquered, layered wood rather than iron (okay) and brass (better); jibsheet fairleads anchored, instead of track-and-slider; reefing claws that looked like bear paws. Strange stuff, but not bad.

Tennetty had stripped down to a thin cotton shirt and shorts, and Jason down to just a pair of ragged Home jeans. They circled each other, hands reaching out for a grip on forearms or waist.

"Now," Vertum Barr said, chewing on a piece of jerky as he talked, "you hear a lot about how the mizzens don't add much to the speed of a ketch, and there's some truth to that. But when you're close-tacking, the faster you can come about, the better off you are, and that's why we pay particular attention to the trim of the mizzen." He frowned at the horizon, his forehead creased leather. "Probably fly the mizzen trysail, if things look shaky."

Far off, probaby a storm was brewing. All kinds of storms.

Tennetty let Jason grab her by waist and arm, and as he

222

tried for a solid throw, she kicked her heel against his calf, knocking one leg out from beneath him, the two of them falling hard to the deck, Tennetty on top, her fingers stopping inches from his eyes.

She slapped the deck and rose. "Again."

"So why a ketch?" I asked.

He smiled. "*Delenia* used to be a fishing boat—and a fisherman has to be nimble more than fast. If it were up to me, I'd have her remasted and rerigged as a sloop, but Erol Lyneian likes the way she handles as is, and she's his ship, not mine, eh?"

This time, as Tennetty and Jason closed, their arms and feet moved so fast that I couldn't quite make out what they were doing, but when they parted, he was still on his feet, and Tennetty was lying at his feet, slammed hard onto the deck.

If it were up to me, the ship would lie at anchor here while the storm passed us by, but none of the crew seemed to think it looked threatening enough. You can pick up a lot of knowledge by working the coast, from boat to boat, but there's things that only years of experience teach you. "Now, if we have to run before the storm, we may be able to run quicker, without endangering ourselves, if we have a bit of cloth back here. Yes?"

I nodded. "That would seem to be so."

I'd heard Bast walk up behind me, but I hadn't done anything about it. Let him make the first move. Of course, if the first move was sliping a knife in between my third and fourth ribs, I'd probably regret it. I'm kind of funny that way.

Vertum Barr touched a bent finger to his brow and walked off.

"Walter Slovotsky," Bast said, as I turned. "We have to talk."

"We can't talk. If you want to argue about taking passage to Sciforth, talk it over with the dwarf, not with me."

Ahira was ashore, finding a ship for Bast and Kenda, a) which I didn't want to argue about, and b) with which I agreed.

"Not about that," he said. "About something more important."

I remembered Bast as a gangling kid, with an Adam's apple that used to bob nervously up and down his skinny neck, never really concealed by the soft, downy beard that couldn't grow long enough to cover it, or to conceal his soft face. He could never look me in the eyes on the old days, always looking away.

Now, his black beard was trimmed back, like an overgrown hedge; his skin was pulled taut at the bridge of his nose and above his cheekbones, and his unblinking eyes never left mine. He was dressed only in a blousy pair of sailor's pantaloons with thick rolled hems at his ankles—they were much too large for him—and carrying only a waterskin over his shoulder.

I knew what he was going to say before he said it. It's a minority opinion, but Lou's disciples have always seemed to me to tend toward the fanatical.

"We have to silence everyone aboard this ship," he said, his voice stubbornly level and reasonable, his eyes obstinately refusing to glow with fanatical fire. He dropped the waterskin over the rail, letting the coiled leather thong pay out from his hand until it splashed in the water below. He hauled it up and tied the skin to the rail, letting it cool in the breeze.

Evaporative cooling, and all that. I bet he even knew the name of it.

"Just because they overheard the secret of powdermaking?" I finally asked.

"Yes."

As Hassan ibn-al-Sabbah would have said, *Death to all fanatics!*

I shook my head. "The secret would have to get out sometime. May as well be now. If the choice is the secret getting out now or me cold-bloodedly murdering the *Delenia*'s captain and crew, then it gets out now." I reached down into my pouch and pulled out a stick of jerky, tore it in half and politely offered him his choice of halves. I wouldn't have returned the courtesy, mind—if he had done it, both halves could have been poisoned.

He thought about it for a moment, debating the propriety of eating with the greatest traitor that he'd ever known, then decided that it wouldn't stay his hand, if necessary. He bit into the jerky.

"No," I went on, "our edge is always going to be progress, not secrets. If the process for making slaver powder was cheaper, the secret of black powder wouldn't be worth anything. It could have been cheaper to make; hell, maybe it could be made that way; I don't know enough magic." I chewed some more jerky. Too salty. "No, our edge is going to be in staying ahead of the game, not in controlling who plays what pieces. For now, staying ahead means smokeless powder weapons replacing black powder. More bang for the volume, less smoke, slower burning."

His look was too controlled to be a glare, but just barely. I wasn't supposed to know the advantage of slow-burning powders in long barrels.

Tennetty and Jason walked up, both sweaty from their workout. Well, Jason had that sweaty-but-satisfied look that the younger folks get; Tennetty's breathing was still fast, and a vein in her neck pulsed in a rapid beat. She looked more drained than anything else.

"We're thinking about going ashore for awhile," he said. "Stretch our legs a bit, maybe ask around some." His face was too much a mirror to his thoughts; I could tell he was too eager.

"Tennetty?" I cocked my head to one side. "He's leaving something out."

"He told you."

"Tennetty."

"Well, maybe he could have been more specific." A smile worked its way across her face. "One of the crew came back with some rumors about things streaming out of Ehvenor. We thought we'd see what the local gossip is."

I turned back to Jason, not asking why he hadn't come clean with me. He still had a lot to learn—I don't insist on doing all the fun things myself. Besides, looking into rumors wasn't all that much fun. "You asking permission?"

He thought about that. He thought about the fact that he didn't like me much, and then he thought about the fact that he was perfectly capable of making errors, too.

So he said, "Advice, at least," his face going studiously blank. He had worked out that he didn't have to take advice.

Tennetty kept her smile small. Good; the kid didn't need to see her beaming approval. Might swell his head fast enough to burst the skin.

"You ask the dwarf?"

He shook his head. "Him next, and Kenda." He looked over at Bast. "Would you like to come along?"

Bast shook his head. "No."

Delicately put. Bast reminded me of an Other Side friend I used to have. Brian would always turn down an invitation to go out to dinner with a guttural monosyllable, implicitly trusting to his friends not to take offense. Not a good bet, not altogether. Eventually we stopped calling, most of us.

Jason was waiting with simulated patience, and the day wasn't getting any shorter. Artiven was a relatively safe town, but there was no sense in pushing it, either way.

"Sure," I said. "Go on in, but don't either of you try to nose around. Spend a bit of money, eat some local food, and keep your eyes and ears open, and your mouth chewing."

Jason and Tennetty walked away. Bast was still scowling at me.

Black powder wasn't as much of a secret as he thought. Andy had been around when Lou and I mixed up the very first batch, and helped stir, all the while chanting, "Bubble, bubble, toil and trouble." She knew the formula, and Ahira did, and I'm sure Doria knew what went into black powder, too, although I wouldn't have given odds that she knew the proportions.

Not that those mattered—you can get quite a distance from the classical mix and still get real gunpowder. The main secret is in knowing what to play around with, and going ahead and doing it. (Safely, that is; kids, don't try this at home.)

So, the simple argument went like this: Bast, don't worry about the secret getting out, because there's a bunch of us who have known it for years.

With Bast eager to slice the throat of everybody who had heard the secret, it was probably not a good idea to give him more targets; better to reason with him. "Did you know?"

He shook his head. "I had . . . hints, but I deliberately didn't follow them up. I didn't need to know how to make powder, and I didn't want to know. Master Ranella does, and there are . . . arrangements if she and the Engineer were both to die. But no, I didn't know how." He unfastened the water-skin from the rail and took a polite swig before offering it to me.

I thought about the waterbag, and I thought about the drinking to show that I trusted him, but then I decided that it was too big a risk, even though I knew there was no point in Bast poisoning me. Maybe he didn't know that.

We'd had enough to do with poisons recently, albeit fake ones.

"I don't think so, Bast," I said, handing him the waterbag back.

"You ask me to trust you, but you won't trust me?" he asked.

I nodded. "Well, yeah."

It was, after all, a fair statement of the situation.

The door to Andy's cabin stood half open. Inside, the slatted blinds over the porthole cast bands of light and dark onto her bunk, striping its rumpled brown blankets. Dressed in a pair of shorts and a halter against the heat of the day, she was sitting tailor-fashion on her bunk amid scattered items: a silver knife, its handle the dull white of new bone; a spool of impossibly fine thread; a small lenticular crystal clutched in a clay claw; a foot-long feather that pulsed through a rainbow of colors as she idly stroked at it.

You know: the usual.

She didn't notice me at first; she was concentrating on the thick, leather-bound volume. I glanced at the pages, and found that not only couldn't I read them, but that the letters blurred and swam in front of my eyes.

More magic. I shivered. I don't like magic.

I stood in the doorway, silently. I'm good at that. I once crouched silently on a tree branch for more than a day, motionless while the sun rose and fell and rose again, although my thighs and lower back still ache at the thought of it, even now, years later.

"Close the door and pull up a seat," she said, not looking up. "I won't bite."

"Oh, darn."

She raised her head into the bands of light and shadow, and the light caught her eyes and mouth as she smiled for a moment. Just for that moment, all the years fell away, and we were kids again, back in our twenties. She looked too young for all the years, maybe, or maybe it was just that the years had finally settled well on her. I never believed the common Other Side nonsense about how a woman was necessarily the most beautiful at twenty or so, and over the hill by thirty.

But it was only a moment; she moved her head back, one band of shadow turning her smile into a dark and distant smirk, another masking her eyes. "What's everybody up to?"

I sat down on the bed, the spell book between us. "Jason and Tennetty have gone into town, just to look around. Ahira's over in the docks, buying passage for Bast and Kenda. We should have the two of them out of our hair by tonight. What are you up to?" Translation: How much have you been using magic, and how much is it affecting you?

Her mouth quirked in the shadows. "Trying spells that are beyond me, without success." I guess my alarm showed in my face.

She waved her hand, as though to wave my concern away. It didn't work. "No, not dangerous ones—this is subtle magic. Information magic, not power magic," she said. She touched a fingernail to a fuzzy line on the page. "This one, for example: I could, say, accent the second syllable of the instigator, reverse the suffixes for any of the hegemonics, lisp my way through the dominitives, and all that would happen to the power is that it would randomize, and that wouldn't do much. It might raise the temperature in the room a few degrees, but that's about all."

"What's it for? The spell, I mean."

"Mapmaking," she said. "Directional magic. We'll need it in Ehvenor. We're getting close to Ehvenor. Tomorrow night?"

I nodded. "Morning after, at worst."

Or at best. This time I didn't shiver. Reflexively, I

reached toward the knife—I'm comfortable with an edged weapon in my hands—but pulled my hand back. Messing with wizards' equipment isn't a good idea.

"Sometimes a knife is just a knife," she said. "Go ahead; you won't hurt anything."

I hefted it in my palm, the silver blade cool against my skin, the bone handle too warm, as though she had been holding it tightly, too long.

She looked up at me, her eyes probing from the slatted shadow. Bars of light and dark cut diagonally across her face, striping it.

"I worry about you sometimes," she said. There was an extra note in her voice, something high-pitched, perhaps. It bothered me.

"Me, too," I said. "I'm getting too old for this." I ran my thumb along the edge of the knife. I'd seen sharper.

The edge of her mouth touched the light as she smiled. "Too old for what?"

"This running around, getting ourselves in and out of trouble."

"You still seem good enough at it," she said, leaning back, considering.

I shrugged. "The trouble with this line of work is no matter how good you are at it, eventually you get unlucky. It's like . . ."

That was the trouble. It wasn't like anything else. "Okay, try it this way. Karl and I used to spar, back in the old days. Now, back at our peak, he had the edge on me in strength, and I had a bit more speed, but his reflexes were just a touch better than mine. He couldn't move as fast, but he could react faster, he could get started moving just a hair before I did."

She nodded, her face impassive.

"So, given that he was better at hand-to-hand than I am, he should have won all the time. But he didn't win all of the time—just *most* of the time. Big difference. We were operating close to the limits of human reflexes, and sometimes you have to, say, commit yourself to a block before your opponent strikes—if you wait for him to make his move first, there won't be time for nerve impulses to travel to the brain and make the return trip before he connects, yes?"

"So?" she said. "What's your point?"

"My point, such as it is, is that we live in a world of both skill and chance. If you put yourself into a situation where there's a random factor operating, no matter how carefully you've scoped it out, no matter how good you are, sometimes you're committed to a path, sometimes you've already entered into a course of action, that'll smash you flat."

"Or blow you into hamburger," she said, her voice low but unnaturally even. She wasn't talking about me. "Turn his body into garbage," she said, her fingers digging into my arm, "and spread it across a filthy beach, gulls swooping down and pecking at threads of muscle and patches of skin, flecks and fragments of bone, and one eyeball, miraculously intact, lying on the sand, staring blindly at the sharp beaks, at—"

"Andy—"

"I can see him before," she said, the words coming faster and faster, "I can see him and I can feel it, except when the fire flares in my mind, except when the power plays through my fingers. I can see him smiling, not because he isn't scared, because he was never afraid to be scared, but because he knows that that will frighten them just a little more. I can see him lighting the fuse," she said, spitting out the words in a rapid-fire tattoo, "I can see him batting them away with his good hand while the fuse burns down, and laughing at them, smiling at them, maybe because they don't know enough to run, maybe because since he can't run he won't let them run, because he's decided that this is the end and they're all going with him." She looked up at me. "But sometimes he isn't wearing his face, because sometimes it's Jason's, and sometimes it's Ahira's, and it's been Piell's, and my God, Walter, sometimes he's wearing your face, sometimes he looks like you, sometimes it's you, Walter . . ."

"Shh . . ." I laid a finger against her lips. "Easy, Andy. Slow down."

With a visible effort, she stopped herself from talking.

Trembling fingers reached for my face, her touches tentative, light, like the brush of a cobweb.

"Sometimes it's yours," she said. "Sometimes he wears your face." Her breath was fast and ragged, and her voice was thick and liquid. "It's all getting so complicated," she said, "the closer we get to Ehvenor."

She touched my forehead with two widespread fingers and breathed out a spell, like she was blowing a bubble in the air.

Bright lights flared behind my eyes, in my mind, and I could see distant fires, to the horizon, and beyond. They burned too brightly; reds and oranges that intense, that vivid would have burned my eyes out of my head.

Off in the distance, beyond the horizon, the rolling waters of the Cirric roiled at the edge of Faerie, bubbling in places, freezing in others, while below the surface, immense dark shapes waited for release.

Somewhere far away but closer, a purple vein of magic had been cut open; strange things and strengeness bled out into the cold air, taking on a solidity that was nonetheless substantial for all its wrongness: a vision of a dagger-toothed, batwinged creature became real and flapped off into the night; a vauge, insubstantial hulking shape took on precision and substance as it shambled across the ground, scratching at its hairy sides.

Off beyond, beyond distance, barely visible yet crystalline in its clarity, a landmass stood waiting, bright lights pulsing across the twisting shoreline in a gavotte somehow familiar in pattern but unpredictable.

"Faerie," she said. "Imagine yourself with all the problems and sorrows a human could have. You could lay it all before the Faerie, and they could send you home healed and well, or broken and misshapen, better than you ever were, or worse than you ever feared you could be."

Chances?

She laughed, as she spread her hands in front of me, her fingers moving as though she was shuffling a deck of cards. "Imagine an infinite deck of cards, Walter. Each card has a number on it, from 1 to infinity. There is one one, two twos, three threes, four fours, and so on." She mimed fanning the deck. "Pick a card, at random, Walter, from one to infinity, and I will pick one, too, and what are the chances that my number is larger than yours?"

50-50, looked at one way; 100%, looked at another; zero, yet another.

"All are true," she said, dismissing the deck.

The inner vision turned away from the water, toward the land. We were used to thinking of powerful magical objects as few and far between, but I could see the flare of half a dozen charmed amulets or rings within the confines of Artiven itself. And not just the fire of an enchanted stone or piece of glass. Hiding, wrapped in long-rotted leather, an iron glove lay, its fingers thick worms of segmented steel, each finger tipped with a jagged blade like a shark's tooth, waiting while it lay beneath the sands at the shoreline, pushed down beneath the rotted piling of an old dock.

"Deathglove," she said. "It kills happily, it kills well, but it kills a bit of you every time you use it. Buried a long time ago, by somebody wise enough not to keep it. There would be those who would give everything they have for this."

Then how could it have lain there so long? I didn't voice the question, but she answered it anyway.

"Can't you see? It's hidden, it's hidden."

Not now it wasn't. But I don't need a deathglove, thank you very much.

"No, Walter, you idiot, not the deathglove, the rest of the picture, the summoning. It takes more power and control to find it, to see all of it. If I can just look deeper . . ."

The light started to clarify further, to brighten, but—

"No." I could feel the sharp clarity of the shapes cutting at my mind, sawing away at my sanity. I pushed her hand out of the way, and the light died behind my eyes. I wasn't meant to work magic, or to work with magic.

And neither was she, not at this level. Not like this.

"Stop it," I said. "Let it drop."

Her eyes had gone wide and unblinking, her jaw slack. A fat, red drop of blood hung at the swell of her lower lip as her lips moved rapidly, almost in silence, her breathing growing faster and more ragged.

"*No.*"

I shook her once, gently, then again, hard, but she didn't stop. I tried to shake her even harder, but I couldn't. I don't mean that I wasn't willing to shake her hard. I tried, but it was like trying to push her first through water, then molasses, then through a wall—there was a limit to how hard I could shake her, how hard her magic would let me hold her.

"*Stop* it."

I tried to slap her, but my hand slowed as it approached her face, turning what had been intended to be a sharp hit into a gentle cupping of her cheek. Whatever was moving her was protecting her on the level of physical attack.

"*Andrea.*"

I couldn't hit her, and nothing I could say was going to do any good, so I pulled her close, my mouth over hers.

Her eyes were wide and her mouth was wet and warm, salty with the taste of blood, perhaps mine, perhaps hers. Her arms snaked around my chest, astonishingly strong fingers locking tightly behind my back as she pushed herself hard against me, her tongue warm and wet in my mouth.

Old reflexes died hard while long-time inhibitions died easily: I swept the spell book and her gear off the bed and onto the floor, not caring about the damage.

Her eyes, now more insistent than mad, locked on mine as we fell to the bunk, fingers struggling clumsily with clothing.

The part of me that's always analytical mused that I used to be a lot more expert at this, but I told it to shut up, and for once it listened.

She lay in my arms for a long time, her head resting on my left shoulder, her breathing so slow I thought she was asleep, which is why I didn't move my arm from underneath her, even though her she was pressing against my biceps in just the right place to put the arm to sleep.

To tell the truth, the first time hadn't been all that good; we were both in too much of a hurry, or at least I was. The second time was better. Twenty years before, there had been a third time, but no matter how long it had been for me since I'd last been with a woman—and it had been *far* too long—I was years older, and was slowing down.

Well, I had seen this coming, and now it had happened, and the world hadn't ended, which was just as well.

What I hadn't considered enough was that Doria was

probably right, that Andy was overdoing the magic, and it not only was taking a toll on her, but was threatening to send her right over the edge, almost as though it was a personal force. I'd have to try to keep her away from magic, but I didn't have the vaguest idea as to how to do that. This worked once, but I didn't think that keeping it up twenty-four hours a day was a really live possibility.

I mean, assuming I was, er, up to it, how would I phrase the suggestion?

I smiled to myself, but it wasn't funny. Andy was pushing herself too hard, and I didn't see a prayer of stopping it. Maybe, just maybe, she could control it better. Maybe there was some other way.

I hate maybes.

I had thought she was asleep, but then she stretched and yawned, lifted her face to mine, and smiled as she stretched, one toe coming up and playing with the sheath still strapped to my right calf. I don't normally feel the need to be armed during sex, honest, but I hadn't spent a lot of time thinking this out.

Unsurprisingly, all the tension had gone out of her body. Even if you do it wrong, that still tends to happen, and while I hadn't been keeping score, I hadn't noticed a lot of mistakes on either of our parts, just the normal sort of first-time clumsiness. What did surprise me was that a lot of tension I hadn't known I'd had, had gone out of me. In my shoulders and right arm, particularly. (I suspect the tautness had gone out of my left arm, but it was numb, and I wasn't going to know about that for awhile.)

"What am I supposed to say?" she asked, her voice blurred with sleepiness. " 'Thanks, I needed that'?"

It would have been uncouth to observe that she obviously *had* needed that, even softened by an explanation to the effect that for an adult used to an active sex life, there were better things than having it cut off, as I could have explained from my own recent history.

Or I could have explained that I needed it too. No, not just the release; as much as I'd wanted that, I am more than skin and meat wrapped around a collection of gonads and hormones. What I had needed, what I had needed badly, was the touch of a woman who didn't shudder when I laid a hand on her.

But—

"Sure," I said. "That'll be fine."

Let me tell you two of the nice things about having old friends around:

You can do something that is at the very best morally ambiguous, and then, when questioned about it, you can try to shrug it off with a stupid one-liner, and all that will happen is that your old friend will stiffen for a moment, then relax in your arms and lay her head on your chest, and then she'll say with an affectionate laugh in her voice, "Walter, you are *such* an asshole." And then, quickly: "We'd better get dressed before my son gets back."

And, later, you can be standing next to a railing as a ship is blown through the night, watching the faerie lights dancing manically along the horizon, their reflections in the water shattered and dispersed long before they've ever reached you, and another old friend will walk up and rest a slim hand on your shoulder, lean her head against your arm, and say nothing, nothing at all.

CHAPTER TWENTY-TWO

In Which We Meet Three Slavers Snarling, Two Wizards Waiting, One Cleric Considering, but Skip the Partridge in the Pear Tree

Whoever loves, if he do not propose The right true end of love, he's one that goes
To sea for nothing but to make him sick.

—JOHN DONNE

Peer pressure is a pain in the ass.

—WALTER SLOVOTSKY

THE SUN HAD JUST SET, casting fading bands and threads of gold and crimson on sky and water, as the lights of Ehvenor drew over the horizon and started to peek out between the islands.

The cold gray waters around Ehvenor were scattered with rocky, wave-spattered islands. Some thrust stony fingers through the surface and into the sky, and made me think of underwater spires threatening to gut the ship. Others, their backs covered in moss and brush, rose only a few feet out of the water. Their dark bulks loomed dangerously beneath the waves, threatened the *Delena*'s bulk with grounding.

236

Mostly, they just got in the way.

Life's a lot like that.

Erol Lyneian pointed the *Delenia*'s bow high, toward what looked like a dangerously narrow passage between two islands, but he looked like he knew what he was doing, and I hoped he knew what he was doing.

"There's a landing on the other side of that. That's the closest I'm willing to go to Ehvenor these days."

There was a light behind Andrea's eyes—and no, that's not a figure of speech—as she laid a hand on Erol Lyncian's shoulder and said, "No. There is another. Further down, past the channel. Sail to that one." Her voice was a thick contralto, almost singing.

I looked to Ahira, and he looked back at me, but neither of us was going to say anything further.

Erol Lyneian started to protest, but she silenced him with a gesture. "Sail to that one."

The landing was a shelf cut into the side of the cliff, and three flights of steps carved up the side, zigzagging to the top above.

Delenia strained gently at her anchor as the onshore breeze tried to blow her up against the rocks, her sails flapping loosely in the wind. We unloaded our gear quickly, Jason and Tennetty descending first, Ahira and me throwing packs and parcels down to them and the four rowers in the launch.

I was the last one down. I turned to Erol Lyneian to thank him, but he hadn't gotten us out of Brae out of any goodness of his heart, but in return for a secret worth as much as a hull full of gold, perhaps. And worth nothing if I simply spread it around, telling everyone I encountered what gunpowder consisted of, how to make it.

Of course, it wouldn't be worth anything to me, either, but it never had been, not in the sense that Erol Lyneian thought of it. Which is why he hadn't thought of the possibility that I might spread the secret further—why would I give away something that I had so carefully husbanded all these years?

I smiled.

"Fare well, Erol Lyneian," I said, as I lowered myself over the side.

Only a few minutes later we and our gear were safely ensconced on the lower landing, watching the sailors row the launch all too quickly back to the *Delenia*.

Ahira looked at the lights brightening the sky overhead, obscured by the cliff, and then he looked at me.

"Walter," he said, "you're on."

Most of the time, the precautions you take are wasted, but you have to take them anyway.

A college friend of mine—she was a senior when I was a freshman—got married right after graduation. She wanted to get started on making babies, only to find after much effort and expense that she had a fertility problem, and that all the years and money she'd spent on contraception had been wasted. I don't want to count the number of times I've entered a room through a window, or perhaps an unexpected door, or poked my head in and out for a quick peek before going in. I can't begin to add up how often I've armed myself for the day or night without ever having to even touch a hand to a knifehilt or pistol butt. I won't try to remember the number of times I've loaded a pistol and hung it on the wall without having to fire it.

Still, you do it the right way, each and every time.

I crept up the steps slowly, carefully, hands feeling for any give as I slowly put my weight on each progressive step, eyes sweeping the steps ahead for a sign of anything out of the ordinary, happy that these were stone, and not wood. There's a thousand ways to gimmick a wooden staircase; a laid stone one is trickier, and a carved one is the toughest to rig, but it's not impossible.

The obvious place for a trap was at the top, where some idiot would poke his head and torso over the ledge, leaving himself an open target, so I paused at the last landing and gently straightened.

The plateau was overgrown by a thick vine that lay flat on the ground; it had long choked any grasses dead, so there was neither any obstruction nor concealment.

Still, in the dark, you wouldn't expect anyone to be looking for a forehead and a pair of eyes. You wouldn't expect there to be somebody right there, his eyes inches from mine.

Which is okay, because there wasn't.

What there *was* was a man, squatting easily, just out of reach, looking down at me, two men standing behind him. He was broad of shoulder and dark of hair and beard, and his thin lips barely split in a smile that held only a trace of cynicism, perhaps, or possibly just a hint of contempt.

The hilt of a saber hung near his left hip, canted forward, but his hands were clasped in front of him.

"Greetings," he said. Moving with exaggerated slowness, he unclenched his hands and gestured beyond, to the campfire, where three more shapes in dark robes huddled around a simmering pot. "They've been waiting for you, for all of you." He extended a muscular hand to help me up, but backed slowly away, palms up, when I didn't take it.

I looked beyond the three rough men toward the fire, toward the three hooded shapes there, watching us, not moving.

Six of them, five of us. I didn't particularly like the odds; the three robed ones sitting about the fire, might as well have been wearing signs proclaiming themselves magic user types.

The dark-bearded man spoke again. "Ta havath," he said with a smile. "We mean you no harm, not here and now." It was a genuine smile, but I didn't like it. "Even though I am called Wolkennen, and am a full brother of the Slavers Guild, as are my guild brothers here," he said.

Sometimes, everyone is lucky that I'm me, and not Karl—me included. Karl would have launched himself at Wolkennen, and damned be the consequences, figuring one down was a good start. Me, I just beckoned to the others to hurry the hell up the stairs, and straightened, slipping the hilt of a throwing knife to the palm of my hand.

I mean, I believed him, but I wasn't sure I believed that I believed him, if you understand what I mean.

Andy was at my side, one hand touching my arm to urge caution, a soft spell on her lips.

"Be easy, Walter," she said, walking up the steps and stalking across the mat of vines toward the campfire, and the three sitting around it. One of the slavers took half a step toward her, stopped by a glare from Wolkennen.

"No," he said. "Leave them be." The three slavers

backed off, away from us, away from the fire, toward the far end of the plateau where a pair of low tents stood pitched.

I walked the last few steps up the plateau. Down the slope, Ehvenor lay, waiting. Or maybe it didn't lie, and perhaps it didn't wait. Maybe it was doing more than lying.

Down the slope and below, Ehvenor flickered brightly in the night.

The last time I had been near Ehvenor, it looked pretty much like a normal city, except for the area around the Faerie . . . well, embassy, I always thought of it.

I'd say that part of it was unchanged, except that it had never *been* unchanged: that was the trouble with it.

It was a tall, dome-capped tower, rising perhaps four stories, seemingly woven of sunrise and haze, always best looked at out of the corner of the eye. When you'd look at it directly, it would seem to shift, to change, to melt from one shape to another, but always so subtly that you never could tell just what had happened, always knowing that something was different from what had been, but never able to tell whether the change had come on quickly or slowly.

It was still there in the center of the city, but now it was surrounded by three similar buildings, no, it was

a hundred buildings; silly, of course it had always been—
a thousand buildings, spread across
— no, tightly packed through
— miles upon miles of crooked
— no, curved
— no, straight streets.

I could have looked away, but its a bad habit to look away from things that bother you; you have to get used to it. So I looked, my jaw clenched so tight I'm surprised I didn't break any teeth.

Okay; fine. The outer parts of the city were still streets of cobblestone and mud, still buildings of wood and stone, but the center of the city, a mass of great brightness and indeterminate size, was something that my mind couldn't quite grasp, no matter how hard I tried.

Big fucking deal. Nothing to be scared about. I'd never been able to do integral calculus, either; not understanding something didn't have to scare me.

240

So why was I shivering? I would have guessed that it was cold on the plateau, but I don't like the looks of that kind of intellectual dishonesty on anybody, present company included.

Okay; it scared me. Big, fat, hairy deal. I'd been scared before.

Off toward the edges of the light, dark shapes shifted into and out of solidity, some evaporating in the flickering whiteness, others shuffling off into the darkness.

I turned back to the others.

Trouble was brewing, at least from one quarter. Andy had quietly joined the three robed ones sitting by the fire, but Tennetty and Jason had dropped their gear and squared off opposite the slavers. No weapons had been drawn, but maybe it was only a matter of time. Jason had already thumbed away the thong holding one of his borrowed flint-locks in place.

Silly boy. I thumbed away the thongs of *all* of my flint-locks. I was willing to take Wolkennen's word for his harm-lessness—until it all started.

Ahira stepped in front of Jason. "Let's not start anything we can't stop, friends," he said, mainly to Jason and Ten-netty, but maybe a bit to me, as well.

Something moved in the vines underfoot, and I started, stopping my hand at the butt of a flintlock.

"You know," I said, "this reminds me of a story I once heard about. Seems there were these two groups of combat-ants squared off against each other, trying to make peace. Only trouble was, one member of one party spotted a snake, and drew his sword to cut its head off. That's when it all broke loose. Not because anybody wanted it to, but because everybody thought it already was breaking loose."

Ahira nodded. "So we'll all stand very easy. Tennetty, you and I will just sit ourselves over there," he said, indicating a spot about halfway between the fire and the tents. "Jason and Walter, you join Andrea."

I didn't know whether to be flattened that he trusted me enough to back Andy on whatever was going on, or whether to be discouraged that he didn't trust me to either hold my fire or put it in the right place, so I decided to skip being flattered or discouraged and hurried over with Jason to where Andy was standing by the fire.

Well, I had long taken the position that if what was going on with Ehvenor was all that important, there would be magical types looking into it; I didn't know whether to be glad or disappointed to be proven right.

One of three robed ones stood, throwing back the hood, and letting the dark robe fall to his feet. Beneath the robe he wore tunic and leggings, both of a light yellow. My prejudices are always to think of wizards as small, wizened men and women—the more powerful, the smaller and more shriveled—but that's really silly, when you think of it. Somebody who can take on a better appearance may well choose to appear young and strong; somebody with enough power to make that appearance real may well choose to be young and strong, and by no means are all wizards human.

He was tall and just barely slender rather than skinny, his black beard trimmed neatly, the movements of his hands graceful as he beckoned to Andy.

"Join us, good wizard," he said, clasping his hands in front of him and bowing. "We have been waiting."

Andy said nothing, and the silence hung in the air for a long time while the city flickered and the fire crackled. In the crackling flames, a burning log broke in two, sending a shower of sparks into the air and off into the night.

Andrea raised a hand and breathed a spell, and the wizard stretched further until he was impossibly thin for a human, the tops of his ears losing their roundness, as his hair and beard became finer, softer, like a baby's hair.

"Well done, oh, well, done," the elf said, his words almost a song. "You have unmasked me, I do depose."

She tossed her head. "I don't need false congratulations. I couldn't have overcome your seeming id you hadn't let me."

"True." His look wasn't quite condescending; neither was the way he clasped his hands at his waist and bowed. The look was penetrating, the kind of stare that made me think he could look through not only my clothes and flesh, but maybe even my self.

"I am Vair ip Melhrood, long resident in glorious Panda-thaway, for these past two hundred years of the Wizards

Guild. I am known as Vair the Uncertain." His lips crooked into a smile. "At least, I think that's how I am known."

"You wear your age well," she said.

"Thank you."

The second rose, throwing robes aside in one rough motion. He came about waist-high on the first: a dwarf. My first thought was that he wasn't a wizard—dwarf wizards are rare—but when he seated himself tailor-fashion on the air, I decided otherwise. It takes a powerful wizard to use a levitation spell at all, and even more so to simply use it for the casual purpose of bringing his eyes to the same level as Andrea's—it could have been just showing off, but he was a dwarf, and dwarves don't tend to show off. No, he was a wizard, but he hadn't bothered with a seeming.

Dwarves don't mind how they look; there's no accounting for taste.

This one looked pretty ugly, even for a dwarf. He was only a little shorter than Ahira, but probably didn't weigh more than half as much. His skin hung off him in deep folds. The peeling skin didn't look particularly healthy, but I guess he didn't care about the heartbreak of psoriasis.

Where Ahira's big nose and massive jaw make Ahira look pleasantly homely, this dwarf's face was covered with deep wrinkles that made him look like shrunk leather.

"Nareen," he said, his voice a quiet rasp. "Nareen the Patient, Nareen the Glassmaker. I ask that you sit with us."

"I will hear you," Andrea said, "shortly." She turned to the third, who rose as the others had, pushing her hood back. Even though her hair was pulled back in a tight bun, she would have been lovely, except that her right eye stared unmovingly ahead, dead and unseeing.

She parted her brown robes to reveal pristinely white robes beneath. Despite the contradiction of the eye, I knew what that meant.

Shit.

"I have no name, nor am I called by one," she said, her voice a rich contralto. "But I am of the Healing Hand."

Double shit.

Shit: I don't like the Hand; it's personal. They took Dora away from us for years, and never really gave her back; she

243

had to break free, and was only barely able to. We had run into each other one time, her mind more melded than anything else into their collective conscious. I know that's part of how they relate to the Power they call the Healing Hand, and that's what enables them to act as a conduit for its blessings and providings, but I don't have to like it, and I don't like it.

Double shit: it seems that as Hand clerics develop more power, they give up more of their identities; the higher-ranking ones are known by their titles, having forsaken their own names. According to somebody who ought to know, the Matriarch herself no longer has any of her own personality, but is merely a reflection of the whole Hand consciousness, and that spooks me. I had a run-in with the Matriarch years before; she didn't find my rather charming self-centeredness, well, charming, and for some reason I'm uncomfortable being in the presence of someone of power who strongly disapproves of me. Always have been, ever since back in high school when I had a run-in with the principal about the awkward incident involving a hydrogen-filled basketball and a bunsen burner.

Call me picky.

Andrea gestured at where the slavers were camped out. "And these are?"

"They are with me," Vair said. "I required bodyguards. In Pandathaway, the Slavers and my own guild have a . . . standing arrangement." He cocked his head to one side. "You seem surprised to see us; did you think you'd be the only ones interested in such an event?"

Nareen spoke up. "I have been waiting here for most of a year," he said, "living off roots and leaves, watching the changes below, waiting to learn more." He gestured toward the flickering city. "When I arrived, it was still only in the center. Fewer of the—"

"There," Vair said, pointing. "Another one."

I followed the pointing finger, but didn't see anything.

Neither did Andy. "Another what?"

Vair shrugged. "Who knows? Something released from the shadows, to shamble off into the night. Dark and hulking it was, at the edge of visibility, now off in the darkness."

Nareen's eyes were following something I couldn't see for

244

a long while, but then he shrugged. "It could be anything. A fairy taking a shape, a shape taking identity, a myth taking reality." His eyes sought and caught Andrea's. "I've seen two dragons spurt forth and fly away, a dozen deodands stagger off into the night, and scores of large, hairy things, like humans but uglier even than humans." He watched the city flickering in for the longest time. "There. A glimpse, a flicker, a taste of the Place Where The Trees Scream."

The Hand woman stroked the air in front of her. "Possibly. I know I saw a flash of meadow earlier, somewhere outside of Aershtyn."

I was going to ask how she was sure where the meadow was, but I didn't. Magic, after all.

She shook her head. "No, Walter Slovotsky, it was not that. The meadow was ringing by tiny firs, the sort that grow only high on the slopes of Aershtyn."

"What *is* going on down there?" Trust Jason to ask the obvious question.

Vair shrugged, again. "It could be any of a number of things. It's possible that this is but the first tentative feeler in a long time, an attempt to see if the powers of magic and the will of the gods still balance the faerie and the fey.

"Or it's possible that an immature one of them has been . . . Mmm. I don't think I have the words." He looked at me, then spoke a few low syllables, while distant fingers touched my mind. It was only then that I realized that he had been talking in English, not Erendra. "It is possible that an immature one of *them* is loose, creating magical creatures and spinning them off into the solid regions like a child blowing soap bubbles off into the breeze." He smiled, sadly. "Or it could be that I have been quite deliberately misled, and that this is just another part of the duel between the two long-mad ones."

Nareen smiled. "Don't ask an elf for answers; they always have too many."

"How about you?"

The dwarf shrugged. "I don't pretend to have any. Oh, anyone can see the obvious, that magic and the magical spurt out from Ehvenor like molten glass from a holed crucible, solidifying in the coolth of hard reality. But the cause? I'll not talk on causes, or you'll think me to be Vair the Uncertain."

Vair folded his arms in front of him, then brought up one hand and felt at his chin. "I don't know. It is unknown, and perhaps unknowable. Of a certainty, I can see no way of knowing without getting close enough, without getting to the Hall. Perhaps there is a breach between Faerie and reality; perhaps some of the Good Folk simply toy with Ehvenor; perhaps it is the end of the world."

The Hand cleric laid a hand on Vair's arm. "The unknown can be investigated. A breach can be healed, perhaps; the Good Folk may be persuaded to cease their play, if it is just play; the unknowable and the end of all that is can be met with serenity. It is the not knowing that is the problem, almost as much as the knowing too much."

Knowing too much can be a problem?

She gave me a look. Okay. It can fuck up your sense of proportion to all hell. I'd worked that one out years ago, even before Professor Alperson's class. Too much of a sense of proportion is a disability. See, the answer to the railroad problem is that it doesn't matter what you know or what you think you know—Karl was right. The answer is that you don't, for the lack of willingness to make a hard decision, let two people die when you can save one, even if it's only for a moment.

One side of Andy's lip curled up into a skeptical half-smile. "What are the chances of this being the end of the world?"

Nareen scowled. "There is no chance of that. Vair exaggerates. It may be important, but it is not of that importance. The feel is wrong. Lives hang in the balance, yes; but not the reality of reality, not the existence of existence."

Big fucking relief.

The Hand cleric chose her words with special care. "It is necessary that someone go down into the city, to the Hall. What you call the Faerie Embassy."

"And you think you've found your suckers, eh?" I asked.

Vair's thin lips twisted in derision. "Sucker, no. Someone who is . . . unusually expert at finding her way about, beyond her abilities in more traditional areas of expertise. Someone who was called, perhaps." He gave Andrea another one of his penetrating looks. "Though I cannot see who could call you against your will."

I turned to Andrea. "I don't like the sound of it."

"You don't have to." She dismissed me with a wave as she turned back to the Three. "Your problem isn't a lack of power, is it? It's a lack of knowledge. Vair alone has enough power to . . . cut a magical flow, given the right tools. You've made the tools, Nareen, but you can't heal over the cut, stitch space and time back together. The Hand has the power to cauterize the cut, if there should there be need, but not if none of you can see through the indeterminacy."

Her lips were tight as she nodded once, tightly. "The three of you need someone who has been preoccupied with location and direction spells, someone who has skill in that area beyond what she should, someone who can plot her way through with some hope of getting out, and reporting to you what is happening in there, the shape of reality inside."

Nareen sighed. "That is almost the case," he said, sadly, his hand reaching down to a pouch at his waist and pulling a small leather bag from his purse. With exquisite delicacy, his large blunt fingers worked the knot open and slipped a glass eye onto the palm of his hand. "This is the second Eye I have made here."

"I have the first." The Hand cleric reached up and touched her dead, staring eye with a fingernail. *Tick. Tick.* "What one Eye sees, the other Eye sees. So. There are three of us: Me, to see. Nareen, to make the tools. Vair to use them. You are the fourth: one to place the Eye."

I held up a hand. "Now wait a fucking minute. Why can't you do this yourselves. Why Andy? Why us?" *Why me?*

"Why not us?" Vair nodded, conceding the validity of the question, if not the accusation. "Not me, because I would soon be lost within Ehvenor; my abilities are in a different area. Not she of the Hand or Nareen, because I need her sight with me, and I need the tools he will make ready." Vair the Uncertain looked uncertainly at me. "Andrea, because she can expand her powers to navigate through indeterminacy. Jason, because he will go in willy-nilly, as his father would have. Ahira, because there is danger in Ehvenor, and his strength may well be required; Tennetty, because where strength may not be enough, viciousness may serve; you, because where strength and viciousness may be insufficient, sneakiness, pragmatism, and pigheadedness may suffice."

I cocked my head to one side. "And all we have to do is get this Eye to the Faerie Embassy, or outpost, or whatever it is, and then get out?"

"All that is needed," Nareen said, slowly, sadly, "is that it be brought all the way *in*."

CHAPTER TWENTY-THREE

In Which We Foolishly Don't Take Our Time to Think This All Over

Though boys throw stones at frogs in sport, the frogs do not die in sport, but in earnest.

—PLUTARCH

Sense of proportion, pfui.

—WALTER SLOVOTSKY

A FRIEND OF MINE ONCE explained why she did her breast self-exam only once a month. You'd think, given the Other Side importance of spotting a lump early—there are only a few really solid cures for the wasting disease on the Other Side, and all of them work better if you catch it when it's young—she'd spend a few minutes every morning checking. And, hell, if she didn't want to do it for herself, I could think of a few dozen men, myself included, who would be happy to do it for her.

But she explained that those sorts of changes happen so slowly that if you feel for them all the time, you'll get used to the growth of the small lump, and it'll become part of the background—you'll miss the changes, until much later than you would if they surprise you.

Sometimes important changes happen right in front of your eyes and you can't see them.

*　　*　　*

I didn't like it. Any of it.

"What I don't see," I said, "is why her. Why us?"

"Because we're here?" Ahira shrugged unnecessarily hard as he settled the straps of his rucksack over his mail overshirt. He had put the strap buckles in their outermost holes; it now barely kept the rucksack on his back.

"Bullshit," I said.

"There have been things Andrea let drop. I think she's been pulled here, maybe. Think about it."

I remembered the time in her new workshop, and the momentary look of obsession, compulsion that had crossed her face. And then there was the time outside of Fenevar, when the idea of heading away from Ehvenor had scared her.

Ahira slipped a piece of rope under the straps of his rucksack, put a single knot in it, then tied a bow that held the two front straps together.

"By whom?"

He shrugged. "I don't know." He shook his head. "I could be wrong. It doesn't make sense—she's stubborn, and if somebody's trying to bend her will, she wouldn't go along without a fight. Who is there who might try to influence her that she wouldn't resist?" He threw up his hands. "So forget it. Not all my ideas are winners."

I couldn't think of anybody, either. "So why aren't we turning around and running away?"

His mouth twisted into a frown. "Because it doesn't much matter what anybody or anything else wants. The same principle still applies, only moreso: strange things have been coming out of Faerie, and that's started to affect us and the people we care about." He looked at the three around the campfire for a moment. "And because Andrea is going in, no matter what you and I want her to do, and you'd no more let her go in alone than I would."

Well, one of us had to say it, and it was his turn.

"Turn around," I said. When he did, I gave a good, hard tug on the rucksack. Solid. Neither elegant nor comfortable, but wearing it this way meant that his rucksack would stay on his back, yet he'd be able to release it with one quick tug if need be. "It'll do."

"Good." He bit his thumbnail, and considered the ragged

250

edge. "How many individuals or things have you run into that you don't understand?"

"Well . . ." I couldn't help smiling. "Everybody except me and thee, and sometimes I'm not sure about thee."

His frown was sour. "Magical individuals or things."

I shrugged. "Including Deighton? A lot." I started to tick them off on my fingers. "The Wizards Guild, for starts. Does that count as one, or as one per wizard? The Matriarch. The Bright Riders. Boioardo. Those guys in the black robes we ran into outside of Endell a couple of years ago. Thelleren, although maybe I'm just being suspicious by reflex. I've never been sure about Henrad, and . . ." I shook my head. "No. She's stubborn, like the rest of us. I don't know of anybody who could make her do anything, not really."

"Nobody alive," he said.

I didn't envy Wolkennen his job; he was trying to make a case he wanted to lose.

"I still believe," he said, "that you should take the three of us with you. We're pretty good when it comes to blades."

Tennetty didn't quite sneer. "I'm sure you are." She pumped her bowie in its sheath a few times, hard. "Want to—"

"No," Jason said. "Not here and now," he said. "You'd kill him, but he might damage you in the doing of it, and we only have a few sips of healing draughts left."

"I don't understand why you're turning down help." Andrea shook her head in frustration. "We could run into trouble in there." This wasn't her part of the business, and she didn't like the way things were shaping up. But, bless her, she was willing to hear me out.

"It's a matter of practice and trust," I said. "I can trust Tennetty to watch my back when that's her job, and that'll leave me free to worry about what's in front." I looked down the slope. "I don't trust Wolkennen, and I don't know how good he is. I don't need to worry about my back."

Ahira slapped his hands together. "Enough. Case closed. Let's get ready. Tennetty, you've got the Eye?"

"True enough." She displayed Nareen's Eye on her palm. Turning away, Tennetty removed her eyepatch, and brought her palm to her face. When she turned back, the Eye glared from the socket. A good place to keep it, although as she blinked, the blank back side of it rolled forward, and it stared out blackly into the night.

She worked her shoulders under her leather tunic. "Simple job: just bring this—" she tapped at the Eye "—to the Faerie Embassy, or outpost, or whateverthefuck it is." She dropped her hand and looked over at me, looking cross-eyed for the moment. She patted at her various and sundry weapons, then shouldered her pack. "I'm ready to go. Is there any reason why we're standing around?"

Yeah, there was. Maybe the horse would learn how to sing.

"No," Andy said. "Best done quickly."

"Okay, everyone," Ahira said. "Let's do it."

"Wait a moment." Jason turned to Wolkennen. "We know what you are," he said. "You trade in people's flesh. Here and now is not the time and place to settle with you for that, but there will be another time, another place—"

Wolkennen sneered. "Who are you to say what time and place there will be?"

Jason smiled. "Hey, Wolkennen, haven't you heard? The Warrior lives." He turned back to the rest of us. "*Now* it's time to go."

Tennetty and I took rear guard as we walked away. "I don't like it," she said. "They could cut across the top and swing down the east side, then ambush us ahead. Two in front of us, one in back. Nail us with bows before we could get at them."

I shook my head. "Nah." Then who would they get to go into Ehvenor?

But I kept my eyes open anyway, and Tennetty and I both had our swords drawn.

Stone steps down the other side of the plateua dumped us down on a narrow road that twisted down the side of the hills toward the city, alternately revealing and hiding it as we walked on.

I couldn't figure it, not as first. The city was pulsating, and flickering, streets shifting position and constitution. At one moment, one would be a narrow lane, surrounded by low windowless buildings in the night, and without warning or apparent rearrangement, it was suddenly a broad avenue between crisscrossed by walkways in the day, and I couldn't spot the moment where one had become the other.

But, then, as we got closer, the pace of change slowed. Streets stayed themselves longer, the changes coming farther apart, but nonetheless both sudden and unseen. I know: it's not possible for something to change instantly, right in front of your eyes, and for you to not see that it's happened.

Understand why I don't like magic?

The trouble is, of course, that my mind wanted to spot the changes, to catch the flicker or shuffling or shift or transformation, and it wasn't equipped to. Looking for it was like, say, trying to spot bands of color in the infrared: something I wasn't equipped for.

I guess I was paying too much attention to the way the city was peeking out around the next curve when the pack jumped us. It's something you've always got to watch out for around Ehvenor; there's too much magic around there, and hanging around magic drives some humans crazy. I guess it must make them want to leave each other alone, because if it didn't, they would quickly kill each other off. I dunno; not my department.

What was my department, what I did see, and barely shouted a warning about, was the three dark shapes that dropped out of the trees, one claw-fingered hand gripping Tennetty's shoulder, dragging her down.

CHAPTER TWENTY-FOUR

In Which We Learn a Possible Origin of a Previously Familiar Term

Nonviolence is not a garment to be put on and off at will. Its seat is in the heart, and it must be an inseparable part of our very being.

—MOHANDAS K. GANDHI

Just once, I'd like to have an enemy against whom nonviolence would be a workable alternative—workable in the sense of me not ending up dancing on the end of a spear, or cut into tiny, bite-sized pieces.

—WALTER SLOVOTSKY

I SHOUTED A WARNING to the others as I cut down at its broad, hairy back, only hacking once before I had to bring up the sword to skewer the one charging me, its hands outstretched.

The standard drill on that is straightforward: you parry his weapons, thrust, then withdraw with a twist—turning a narrow wound that might not slow him down into a broad one that will definitely sting him a bit—as you pull out your sword and get it ready to parry or cut something else. What you *don't* want is for him to be able to pull either a distraction, where one opponent monopolizes your attention while another one gets to you, or a sacrifice, where he forces you to spend too much time killing him, setting you up for the next one.

Either way, it's parry, thrust, and out-with-a-twist-*fast*.

Trouble was, this thing wasn't only larger and stronger than a human, it was also faster—it rushed up my sword, burying the hilt in its hair-matted belly, and seized me in a bearhug as it lifted me up and off the ground. Or, not quite a bearhug—while it pinned my right arm to my side, I managed to get my left hand free, and smash a bottom-fist down on its leathery face once, then again, and again.

Wrong, wrong, wrong—that had less effect than the sword did. It was like slugging a leather-covered rock.

The two massive arms squeezed the breath out of me, and kept squeezing so hard that the hilt of my sword was pressed hard against my gut. Warm blood—its warm blood—was running down my belly and leg, but *I* was the one losing strength; it seemed unaffected by the sword that had run it through.

Darkness started to close in, but I was able to get my free arm over and around its hairy arm, and liberate one of my flintlocks from my its holster on my left thigh. I cocked the hammer as I brought the pistol up to its head, and then closed my eyes as I set the barrel against its snout.

I pulled the trigger. Fire and wetness splashed my face; with a liquid gurgle, it slumped to the ground, releasing me as it did.

My next breath tasted of sulfur and fire blood and foul sweat and my own fear: it tasted wonderful. I drew another pistol and cocked it, but the others had already dealt with the other two of them.

Tennetty's, the one I had wounded, lay dying on the ground, its chest heaving slowly up and down, bleeding from a dozen wounds, some light, some cuts to white bone; the third had been split almost from collarbone to waist, spilling dark blood and yellowy viscera onto the cold dirt with callous indifference.

Ahira stood over the last one, panting heavily, his axe and mail slick with blood, glossy in the starlight. "Everybody okay?"

"Jason and I are fine." Andrea was behind him, Jason

255

beyond her, his sword in one hand, a flintlock in another. The two Cullinanes were unmarked, as far as I could see.

"I'll live," I said.

"Unh." Tennetty was on all fours on the dirt. She knelt back for a moment, then slowly, painfully got to her feet. "Been worse." Her hair was a bird's-nest, and she had scraped her face badly just above the right cheekbone, but she looked not much the worse for wear.

The three things lay on the ground in front of us.

Take a human, blow it up to one and a half times its size, stretch its face and then cover it all with a thick mat of stinking fur, and that's what you have. Something big and too strong, if not overly bright—if the three of those things had been a bit faster, or a bit smarter, all of us would have been dead.

Ahira knelt over a severed arm and poked at the hand with the hilt of his axe. "Partially retractable claws, and the thumb's just barely opposable. It may be intelligent."

I felt at my side. It hurt like hell, but maybe that was all. I breathed deeply, and didn't feel the broken edges of ribs grate against each other, so maybe I was okay, too.

That's where age and experience had saved our asses. Most of the precautions you take are wasted ones; ninety-nine plus percent of the time that you post a guard, nobody's going to even bother him; the rear guard of the party is usually a waste. Young people learn that too quickly, and not only do their minds tend to wander—so does mine—they also tend not to be able to pay attention to what's going on.

You live through this sort of thing for a while, and your chances of surviving the next time go up.

Nothing to it, really. Nothing but effort and patience and concentration and luck. Nothing to worry about.

I wiped my trembling hands on my thighs.

"What the fuck *are* you?" Tennetty asked the dying creature.

The last of them rolled its head slowly toward her, its eyes wide with pain, certainly, or anger perhaps.

"Urrkk," it said, slowly, painfully reaching out claw-tipped fingers toward her.

And then it shuddered and died.

"Time's wasting," Ahira said. "Let's go."

CHAPTER TWENTY-FIVE

In Which We Enter Ehvenor and I Get Lost

Nothing endures but change.

—HERACLITUS

When you get to my age, you like a little stability. At least int he fucking ground under your feet.

—WALTER SLOVOTSKY

THE MOUNTAIN ROAD bled off onto the flat land at the shoreline, as we walked on while the morning fog crept in and the city insisted on changing in front of us. The road narrowed, became little more than shoulder-width, surrounded on each side by dense brush; we had to walk single file.

We walked for what felt like hours and hours; Ehvenor drew closer, and then dawn threatened to break over the horizon, while a light fog blew in off the Cirric, chilling me thoroughly to the bone.

Tennetty and I had switched off with Ahira and Jason, taking the lead behind Andy while they watched our backtrail. So far, so good.

The only trouble was Andy: she was too calm, her steps too light and easy as we stopped at a fork in the road. I shook my head. That fork hadn't been there before; the road had twisted at that spot, but it hadn't forked.

It did now.

She smiled, and muttered a few quick syllables under her breath. "Right fork," she said, then relaxed.

Her eyes met mine for a moment. "It's okay to talk now; there shouldn't be any decisions for the next half mile."

"It would be nice if it didn't change for awhile."

"Don't count on it." I tried to smile confidently. "How are you holding up?"

She shrugged. "I'm okay. I can handle this."

"Fine," I said. "But we can turn around any time you want."

Her eyes had stopped blinking. I didn't know what that means, I still don't know what that means, but her eyes had stopped blinking.

"I don't think so," she said. Then she corrected herself. "No, we don't turn around here. We keep going."

"We just lost the fork behind us." Ahira's voice was too calm.

I gurned to see the road twisting behind us, vanishing off in the fog well beyond where the fork was. Had been. Should have been. Whatever.

"Good," I said. "I never liked it anyway."

Ahead, the fog thickened.

"Hey, Ahira? What say you and Tennetty switch?" Infrared can pierce fog a bit deeper than visible light, and dwarves can see farther into the infrared than humans can.

They did, and we walked on, the fog thickened further, until I could barely see six feet in front of me.

"Let's close up, people," Tennetty said, beckoning Jason in tighter. "One for all and all for one, eh?"

I would have been tempted to protest, but Ahira nodded. "Makes sense. Andrea?"

She shook her head. "I can't think. The fog is too thick, on the ground, in my eyes, in my mind." Her shoulders hunched, as though waiting to receive a blow, then slackened as she breathed a spell, her fingertips working in front of her, drawing invisible letters in the air.

The fog drew in further, until I could barely see my feet, and Ahira off in front of it.

My heart started thumping.

Look—I'm not normally claustrophobic. A dwarf friend

258

of mine (not Ahira; he doesn't like spelunking) and I once waited out a cave-in for three full days until rescue reached us. I didn't have any trouble; I taught him how to play Ghost in dwarvish. But there's something reassuring about the solidity of cave walls. Nobody can reach claw-tipped fingers out of a cave wall and pluck your heart out; the closeness of a dwarf passage doesn't hide pitfalls and tripwires, or strange creatures waiting to leap out of nowhere and . . .

Easy, Walter.

Andy was guiding us toward Ehvenor by magic; Ahira was looking into the fog, at least a little way further than I could, protecting us from sudden attack. Tennetty, Jason, and I were useless, and a third of that really bothered the hell out of me.

"Just a little further," Andy said, off in the mist, just a shape, nothing more.

The fog rolled up to my knees, and then to my belly, and it was all I could do to see my hand in front of my face.

"Here," Andy said, "take a sharp right, and step forward. No, not the rest of you. Just Ahira. Okay, Walter, you're next."

I turned right and took a step forward, out of the fog and found myself standing next to Ahira in the morning light and thick mud of a narrow Ehvenor street.

I wanted to run, I started to run, but the mud sucked at my boot. It would be like trying to run, well, through mud.

Besides, there was no reason to run. I had just been in dense fog, and now Ahira and I stood in clear light on a narrow street, surrounded by two-story wattle-and-daub buildings, up to our ankles in soft, brown mud. It could have been any street on any city, except for the way that faerie lights, bright even in the daylight, hovered motionless overhead, seemingly frozen in place.

Andy's voice was far away, but I couldn't tell in what direction. "Jason goes next," she said. "Right here. Yes, go right, right here."

And suddenly Jason, and then Tennetty and finally Andrea herself were beside us.

I forced a smile. "Nicely done. I didn't know you could teleport."

Andy smiled; then reached over and gave me a peck on the cheek. "Thank you for the compliment, but true teleportation takes power and control that's only theoretically possible. For anything mortal," she added.

If that wasn't teleportation, I'd like to know what it is.

I guess the question showed on my face, because she shrugged and answered. "It's not teleportation. Teleportation is when you go from point A to noncontiguous point B, skipping the points between. This just happened to be right next to where we were, if you knew where to look."

The air was warmer than it should have been for this time of the morning; I'd expected it to warm up some, but not this much. Cold mornings are better. Give a hot sun awhile to work on the typical city street, and it'll smell like it's been paved in well-aged horseshit. Which it has, come to think of it.

"Waddling Way," Andy said, nodding to herself, beckoning us to follow her. A twisty street, lined by two-story wattle-and-daub buildings, it curved off sharply maybe a hundred feet behind us, and less in front. The buildings were too tall and we were too close to see much over them, except for the distant glow of the Faerie dome to the north.

It was all quiet, and empty, except for the mud, and the buildings, and the faerie lights.

"Is quiet," I said. "Too quiet, kemo sabe."

Ahira chuckled. "Shut up," he said, not meaning it, as we walked after Andy. "Take it while you can get it."

Tennetty turned about slowly, like a camera panning in a full three-sixty, which I guess she was, at least in a sense. I didn't blame her for wanting to take it all in—it was so ordinary, not at all what I'd expected Ehvenor to be. Where was the flickering? The street we were standing on was as ordinary and solid as any street I'd ever seen.

I was going to be the straight man, but Jason beat me to it.

"Where's all the flickers? Why is it all so stable?" he asked.

Andrea didn't turn around. "The flickering was from

indeterminacy. Ehvenor is never really sure what it is, and the uncertainty has been growing. But whatever it is, we're here, and that's determinate. We're in only one time and place."

I had my usual reaction to explanations about magic: "Oh."

There's three theories about how to make your way down a street in hostile territory. My favorite theory is to avoid it in the first place; you very rarely can get killed in places you aren't. Second best is to split the party in two, each group staying on one side, covering the other. It limits the field of fire of anybody hiding in buildings on either side.

Another theory is that you walk square down the middle of the street; the idea is that gives you time to react before anybody or anything can reach you.

I don't much like that one, so I moved away, toward the raised wooden sideway that skirted the alley.

"No," Andrea said, without turning around. "Don't. You might get lost. Can't afford that."

Lost? Look—I'm not the kind who gets lost. I don't have a perfect sense of direction, but nobody's going to lose me on the streets of a ctiy, not wihtout a whole lot of trying.

Right, Walter, so where's the fog bank that was up to your nose?

I stayed close.

Waddling Way twisted and turned for maybe a quarter of a mile until it forked around a vest-pocket park, the left road leading up a cobbled street, the right one down into more muck.

I bent my head toward Ahira's. "Want to bet which way we go here?"

"Right up here," Andy said, clopping down into the deeper muck, sinking in almost to her calves.

"It rained hard here, and recently," Ahira said, his eyes never stopping moving.

"No shit, Sherlock."

We followed her down into the muck, our boots making horrible sucking sounds every time we lifted our feet and stepped—

*   *   *

—up onto the hot, dry dirt of the street, under the heat of an oppressive noon sun and the whistle of music in the crowded marketplace.

"People," Ahira said. "It's good to see people."

That was the moment I expected them all to turn from their buying and selling, sprout long fangs, and leap to me, but sometimes I'm lucky enough not to get what I expect.

High overhead, a dozen wood flutes swirled and swooped and dived through the moist air, moving fast as they piped their tunes, the high-pitched whistling dopplering up and down in counterpoint to the magic melody. Not great music; they played an eight-bar theme, repeated without variation.

We had to step aside, quickly, to avoid two horses—huge things, about the size of Clydesdales, although dappled, not solid—pullling a heavily-laden wagon.

We pressed tight around Andrea, like a bunch of school-kids staying with teacher. Which wasn't so bad an idea.

Okay, okay. I'm slow, but eventually I get it: Ehvenor wasn't just unsure what it was, it didn't know *when* it was. Normally, it's easy to get from mid-morning to noon, but you don't do it without skipping over late morning. Unless everything, time included, has broken loose. Hell, it was possible we'd stepped from today into yesterday.

It was a market day, and the trading was brisk under the whistling of the overhead flutes.

Over by a pyramid of reed bushel baskets, an apple-cheeked appelseller haggled endlessly with a tall, raw-boned man in a traveler's cloak and floppy hat. Beyond them, one of the hulking beasts—shit, I'll call them urks or orcs until you've got a better name for them, thank you very much—gestured clumsily that the butcher was asking too much for one of his hanging haunches of mutton. Well, I hoped it was mutton; it could have been shepherd.

Beyond the street, the dome of the Faerie Embassy waited, separated from us by maybe two or three cross-streets.

"This way, and try not to bump anything," Andy said, working her way through the crowd as a heavily laden wagon clomped by, pulled by two enormous horses. The trouble with a crowd is that you have to suppress combat reflexes. I don't like strangers pressing up against me—I'd rather do the pressing. That's how you work a crowd, and I'm a pretty good pickpocket, actually. Not that this was the time to see if my pickpocketry was up to snuff.

We made our way down the street, past the filled stalls where an overweight appleseller haggled endlessly with a tall man in hat and cloak, past the orc arguing with the butcher, past the shops where the candlemakers wielded their frames and dipped their wicks, where a fat old basketweaver took another turn on the base of the frame she was building.

Something about it bothered me, and I gave Ahira a quick touch on the shoulder, then slipped back to the rear of our group, and looked behind. Yes, yes, you can leave trouble behind you, but monkey curiosity is a survival factor, if you don't overdo it.

They were still at it. All of them. The orc was still haggling over the cost of meat, and the tall buyer was still arguing with the short appleseller, and the basketweaver still hadn't—

A heavily-laden wagon clomped by, pulled by two enormous dappled horses, each about the size of a Clydesdale.

And the flutes were still swooping and swirling overhead through the same eight-bar theme.

I pushed my way up to Andrea's side. "Andy—"

She raised a peremptory finger as she muttered another spell. "We got this way." She elbowed her way through the crowd, between two stalls, and into the cool of the day and the—

—dark of the night near the middle of the square. Well, triangle—three streets dumped on it; the buildings at their ends wedge-shaped, triangular, like pieces of stone cake. No windows, no doors, nothing.

A pedestal holding a statue stood in the middle of the square, although I couldn't see what it was a statue of.

Ever do that experiment where you find your own blindspot? It's pretty simple. You put two dots on a piece of paper about six inches apart, close one eye, and stare at one of the dots as you move the paper closer, seeing the other one only out of your peripheral vision.

Eventually, you'll pass the dot through the blind spot of

your eye, the place where the optic nerve enters. And it'll disappear, although you'll still know it's there, and if you move the paper or your eye just a little, you'd see it, but don't: stare straight ahead.

That's what the statue looked like. Like I Can't See It.

Above and beyond it, straight up one of the feeder streets, the dome of the Faerie Embassy stood, flickering in the night.

Andy hurried us along. "Quickly, quickly," she said, moving us toward another one of the feeder streets.

Ahira held up a hand. "No. Stop. What are we doing—"

She shook her head, her eyes growing wide. "No. We can't stop. It's all breaking loose." Her lips moved, her breath went ragged.

"It's not just the city anymore. It's falling apart." She gestured at the street that apparently led toward the embassy. "The Hand was right: it's connecting with the rest of the world." She gestured at the street. "Walk down that way, true, now it'll take you to Lost Lane, but Lost Lane won't dump you out on Double Circle—go north at the first corner and it will lead you down to the pits; the east road will bring you to a spot a hundred feet under the Cirric, just off the Pandathaway coast; west will drop you in a tree outside a village on Salket. It all," she wriggled her finger, "touches. But you won't walk down there, will you?"

Greet. Andy had an n-dimensional map of the city so crowding the inside of her head that she couldn't remember that the rest of us barely knew what the hell we were doing.

"Let's get the hell out of here," I said.

"No, it's not all of Faerie. Not in the solid regions. Just a piece of it. We *go*, before he gets here." Dragging Jason by the arm, she ran off toward the street.

What did that mean? He? Who, he? I broke into a sprint after her, Ahira and Tennetty at my heels. There was something behind us, something huge, but I didn't take a look at it. We reached the juncture of square and street only a few paces behind her.

"Boioardo?" I asked, craning my neck to look as we lunged into the night and—

* * *

—skidded to a stop two feet from the edge of the hot, flat roof. I stuck out an arm and stopped Ahira from bumping into Jason. A bright noon sun beat down on us, but the blue sky was covered with black bands, arcing from horizon to horizon.

"Quickly, now," she said, "over this way."

We made our way down a ladder into an alley, and followed Andy down the alley and—

—into a vestpocket park, cool and green and minty against the heat of the late afternoon.

I would have said the trees were oaks, except that their bark was edged in silver, and the broad leaves chimed gently, like silver bells, as they rustled in the breeze.

Tennetty's breath was coming in ragged gasps, and I guess I could have used a few moments of a breather.

Ahira looked around. "Can we take a moment here?" he asked, over the ringing of the leaves. "Or do we have to run on."

"Oh, yes," Andy said. "We rest here for a moment," she said. "I've muddied the trail enough for us to do that, at least."

One branch of the ancient oak hung long, within grabbing-and-hanging-on-while-you-grab-your-breath range, which I did. The bark was rough beneath my hand, its silver trimming cool.

Jason reached up and flicked his a fingernail against a leaf. It rang like a tuning fork.

Ahira squatted to the ground. "Well, just in case we need to know, which way do we go next?"

She closed her eyes and thought about it too long, her lips moving almost silently.

I mean, I wasn't timing it or anything, but easily a minute passed before Tennetty started getting twitchy, only to subside at Jason's light touch on her arm. Jason was getting good at light touches; I would have wanted to punch her. (I wouldn't have *done* it, mind, but I would have wanted to. I get nervous around magic.)

Finally, Andy opened her eyes. "You can't see it from here, but there's steps down to the road about fifty yards that way, past the old oak. For the next while, at least, we'll be able to make it almost all the way down the steps—but do skip the top one; it connects off the roads."

I let go of the branch and sat slumped against a tree, letting myself go limp, which took no great effort.

The rough bark was somehow reassuring against the back of my tunic. Maybe I took some comfort in its solidity. My fingers played in the long grass. Long for a park, that is—about four inches in height, dense and fine and green, like a lawn.

Tennetty tapped a finger against the glass eye. "What is going on?"

Andrea opened her mouth, closed it, opened it again. "You don't have the background to understand it."

I've never liked that sort of explanation. The trouble is, it's true, sometimes. Try explaining Heisenberg's Uncertainty Principle to somebody who doesn't know that the smallest possible piece of matter isn't a dust speck, or the rudiments of atomic theory to somebody who things that if only you have a sharp enough knife you can divide a piece of clay endlessly in half—I've done both.

Andrea's fingers twisted clumsily. "We live under laws of nature. Magic is part of those laws. Gravity attracts matter to matter; magnetism attracts or repels; the weak magical force carries information; the strong force carries power." She waved her hand toward the dome of the Faerie Embassy. "But those are just a . . . a subset of the rules of Faerie. When we're in Faerie, or even just close to it, it's like we're a bunch of Newtonians trying to plot their way through Einsteinian space, and wondering why we can't break the speed of light no matter how much faster we run."

She gestured at the park around us, her movements jerky, like she was wired too tightly. "Ehvenor's always been part of the . . . outskirts of Faerie. The Good Folk don't like it much; it's too restricted there, too flavorless. But that's changing, and I'm starting to see too much of it." She stood, and as she stood, the tension in her body eased. "It's not just space that touches, but time. The here and the now." Her voice was low. "At the core of Faerie, at the singularity at

266

the heart of it, all is chaos, all touches, there are all rules and none."

She shook her head, as though to clear it. "But that doesn't have to be here. The Three can anchor it all in reality, if only they know . . . where. Vair is the most powerful, but he's uncertain where to put his fire; Nareen's tools have the solidity and stolidity of his race, but little more." She reached out a finger and tapped at Tennetty's eyes. "They need *her* sight."

I wouldn't have wanted to poke my finger at Tennetty's eye, even at a glass one, but Tennetty didn't react.

Andrea shrugged into her pack. "So we go."

"Why now?" There was a panicky tone in Ahira's voice.

"Because," she said, "I told you; I've seen the paths. In just a few seconds we hear his footsteps, and we . . ."

Heavy footsteps thudded on the ground; we ran down the steps—skipping the top one—and across the cobbled street, down the alley, and—

—into the dark of a cloudy night, lit only by the dim green glow of the stinking mossses lining the gutter.

Ahira pulled a glowsteel from his pouch, and the actinic blue chased the darkness away.

It was just an alleyway, a slim street between two rows of buildings that towered in the night, vanishing up in the distance. There was no sound behind us, but Andy shook her head. "He's too close here—we have to take a short cut by diving deeper into Faerie."

"This way," she hissed, vanishing in the darkness of a doorway. We followed her, through the darkness—

—and into the hard, cold wind of the Place Where Trees Bleed.

The icy air blew unrelentingly through the scarlet leaves, each one dripping crimson at the slightest movement. The giant limbs creaked in their pain. Pools of blood gathered beneath the trees, darkening, thickening in the air.

"*Nobody move*," Andrea said. "Let me move you. The rules are more . . . general here; there's no safety in solidity, not if you don't know where to step." She stepped quickly around, moving so fast it was as though her feet hydroplaned over the damp grass, gently touching Jason once on the cheek. He disappeared with a loud *pop!*

"You have to move just right." She pulled Ahira's arm forward. He staggered forward and then disappeared, too.

Only Tennetty and I were left, but I could hear the footsteps on the ground behind us. One chance only, and not much of one.

Andy's hand caressed my cheek. "Don't move, Walter," she whispered, her voice low. "He's behind you."

Tennetty spun, her sword raised high, but the grasses turned into snakes, winding themselves about her ankles, their long fangs sinking deep into her calves.

She screamed. I don't know why it surprised me that it was a high-pitched, horrible sound, like anybody else's. But she turned it into a grunt, as she hacked down at the snakes, her blade slashing them, turning the ground around her into a mass of bleeding, writhing pieces of reptilian flesh.

The voice was the same:

"Good day, all," Boioardo said. His face was too regular, too pretty, the cleft in his chin too sharp. He was all in black and crimson, from the cowl of a scarlet cape flung carelessly over one shoulder to the black boots with enough shine for an SS officer. His tunic was a red velour, cut tight at shoulders and belted at the waist to reveal the v-shaped torso of a bodybuilder.

He proceeded to sit down on the empty air, like somebody who had forgotten that there wasn't a chair behind him. But before he could fall, a swarm of tiny winged lizards flew down from the trees, the lot of them barely supporting a jeweled throne that they slipped behind him, just in time. Others pulled off his cape and folded it neatly over the back of the throne.

Tennetty grunted again, still slashing at the snakes.

Boioardo crossed one knee over the other and smoothed at the already-smooth black tights. "Oh, please. Don't make such a fuss." The snakes melted at his gesture, but the blood continued to run down her leg.

He blurred in front of my eyes, and when I could focus on him again, he was a slim man, about my age and height, still sitting easily on his throne. Maybe a touch older, less in shape, gray at the temples only. His jaw firm, his mustache evenly combed, an ever-so-slight hint of epicanthic folds at his eyes. He was dressed all in black, except for a brown cloak held fast by a blackened black clasp.

Okay, okay, I'm slow: "I'm more handsome," I said.

Tennetty gave me a funny look. Funnier than usual, I mean. "Than me?" she said.

Andrea's fingers touched me at the temples, and for a moment, he flickered, becoming Tennetty, then Andy, and then back to me. He wasn't me, here, he was just mirroring me, in his own way.

Andy looked me in the eye for just a moment. She didn't need to say it: she had to get the Eye to the Faerie Embassy, and Boioardo had to be delayed enough for her to do that. She knew the path; Tennetty had the Eye. That made Andy essential, Tennetty next in importance, and me expendable.

But she couldn't. Expend me, that is. Not without my permission. That was the trouble with Andrea: she never was cold-blooded enough.

The dream was always the same. Except this time the Cullinane was asking me to do it by myself, and I didn't know if I could.

I froze, for just a half-second—

CHAPTER TWENTY-SIX

In Which I Find the Place Where Only That Which You Have Loved Can Help You

Involve yourself with the world. Reach out. Touch. Taste. Live. Trust me on this one, if on nothing else.

—WALTER SLOVOTSKY

I WASN'T THERE FOR A lot of the next of it, but it happened, at the same time that I was busy fighting for my life, I think.

Or maybe it didn't. I mean, it *happened*—reports for the rest of it are reliable—but there's that problem of time. We don't know much about Faerie, and probably aren't built to know much about Faerie. But we do know that time acts funny in and around Faerie, and there was no question that we *were* around Faerie. And there's no question that time was already acting strange in Ehvenor. That part is certain—when you turn a corner from afternoon and find yourself in dawn, I mean, you don't have to be Albert Einstein to figure out that time has been thoroughly fucked with.

What I can say for sure is that what happened with Jason and the dwarf happened during the next part of their lifespan, just as my fight with Boioardo happened during the next part of mine.

I guess that'll have to do.

And I can't tell you what finally made it all happen. I've been wondering ever since—was it me, or was it Andy and the Three? Both? Something else?

The trouble with this part of the story is that I don't know who the real hero is.

Well, that's not true, either. I do know.

She bought Andy and me a few seconds, and paid in full measure, without a whimper.

Damn it, Tennetty.

Ahira staggered out of the screaming grasses and into the dark, on to the soft carpet, Jason right in front of him.

They found themselves in a small room, suitable for a bedroom or a study, high above the dark streets below. Lit only by a single lantern mounted high on the wall, the room was empty save for the carpet, a desk of sorts up against one wall, and a pile of blankets and a chamberpot off in one corner, next to several canvas sacks brimming with raw vegetables and dried meat.

The desk, such as it was, was interesting. The desktop was a smooth-sided door—the knob was still attached, but it was on the far side, near the wall—elevated by stone blocks at four corners that raised it to knee-height. Books and scraps of parchment lay scattered on its surface, held down by oddments of stone and scraps of ironwork. He made out some Ehrendra glyphs, and some of the rest was in scratchy runes that Ahira didn't recognize, but most of the writing blurred in front of his eyes. Wizard's work.

"Somebody has been living here," Jason said.

Ahira raised a finger to his lips. He wasn't irritated by the boy's keen attention to the obvious, but by his talking. Until they had a better grip on where they were, it was best to keep mouth closed, eyes and ears open.

A heavy wooden door stood half open, leading out into the dark hall. Ahira listened for a moment, but couldn't hear anything. So far, so good.

Gesturing at Jason to keep an eye on the door, he turned to the window.

Outside, just across the street, the Faerie Embassy stood gleaming in all its unfixed glory.

Was it three or four stories tall? And were there long, rectangular windows, like glass doors leading out to a balcony, or were the only openings in the solid expanse broad slits, too narrow even to be arrow loops?

He didn't like looking at it; he couldn't tell. Better to concentrate on the here and the now. Hanging around a wizard's workshop was a bad idea, it was time to—

Jason was beckoning silently to him; the boy had already flattened himself near the single door leading to the hall.

His lips moved. *I hear something*, he mouthed.

Good boy. This time, he wasn't scared. No, that wasn't true—Ahira could smell the fear on him. Jason was bright enough to be scared, he knew he could be hurt or killed at any moment, but that was just another face of the universe, to be dealt with appropriately.

And he knew it. He couldn't keep a smile off his face. This time Jason Cullinane wasn't running away.

His axe held easily in his hands, the dwarf leaned his head close. Familiar footsteps echoed down the hall.

Ahira lowered his axe. "Hello, Andrea," he said.

Andrea walked through the door, but it was a changed Andrea. Her black leather vest and pants had been replaced by a gleaming white robe, woven of fog and light. Her black hair was shot with silver, and her eyes were red and rimmed from either crying or lack of sleep.

Jason took a step toward her, but Ahira seized his arm. "Wait."

She raised a slim hand. "Yes, it's me. Older, perhaps a year, perhaps more, or less? Time is so . . . different here, and I've been hiding and studying in nooks in time, trying to control the madness while I've learned more. I'm older, yes; somewhat wiser, I would hope; knowingly more ingorant, certainly. But I'm still me." A tear ran down one cheek. "May I hug you? It's been so *long*," she said.

—but Tennetty didn't spend any time thinking it out: she dug her finger into her eyesocket and flipped me the Eye while she launched herself at Boioardo.

The glass Eye tumbled through the air toward me.

No. "Tennetty, *don't*."

272

But thinking or saying it didn't make any difference. Nareen's glass Eye, the one the Three needed in order to see through the veil of uncertainty into the heart of Ehvenor, floated through the air toward me. I snatched the Eye out of the air, slapped it into Andrea's hand, and started my turn, but it was too late.

Boioardo had already risen from his throne, moving so quickly that his sleeves and cape snapped through the air, like the end of a whip. He batted her sword aside as though it was nothing, and had his hands on her.

She grunted once as his fingers tore through her flesh the way a backhoe claws through ground, and then he shook what was left of her once, twice, three times, like a dog shaking a rat, and tossed her aside, bloody, broken, dead.

His arms red with her blood, splashed to the elbows; it seemed to bother him in his fastidiousness. He looked down at them, at the red blood wetting his sleeves, and then he gestured once, idly, and the blood was gone. Tennetty lay on the ground, her dead eyes staring off into nothing.

You don't waste time grieving for friends, not during a fight, you don't.

"Now, Andy," I said. "Do it now. Take him. Like you did before."

She shook her head. "Not here, not on the edge of Faerie. I don't have enough power, not enough strength to do it."

Boioardo smiled. "She knows I can follow the two of you wherever in Ehvenor you try to hide."

I pulled Andrea close. God, why did you make women so warm? "Hide yourself for now," I whispered, "but get the Eye where it needs to be. Do what needs to be done."

She nodded, once, quickly, then touched soft fingers to my lips and pushed me away, hard; as she stepped away and vanished I staggered back—

Jason awkwardly hugged his mother, and Ahira let the blade of his axe drop to the carpet.

"How long?" Ahira asked.

She spread her hands as Jason released her. "I don't know. Possibly a year. Perhaps two. I used to keep count of

273

meals and sleeping periods, but I gave that up when I found that I didn't need to eat and sleep much here. Two years?" She walked to the window. "Long enough to learn what it will be necessary to do to walk across that street. Long enough to learn most of the paths through Ehvenor, long enough to learn some truths about myself, long enough to call myself here." She shook her head as she turned back to them. "I'm sorry to be so maudlin. I know it's been only seconds for you."

Ahira smiled at that. "That answers that question."

That part of it made sense, at last. He had known Andrea Andropolous Cullinane for twenty years now, and had known her to be every bit as stubborn as it was possible for a human to be. Her will wasn't subject to anybody else's command. She decided for herself, and nobody else did. Nobody else.

So: who could call Andrea to Ehvenor? Who could bring her here? Who had been calling her here ever since Castle Cullinane? Who was it who had made her stircrazy enough to go out on the road into God-knows-what?

Andrea.

She returned his smile. "Me. Who else?" Her eyes went vague for a moment. "She'll be along shortly, with the Eye."

"And what happens then?"

She shrugged. "I only know a little. She didn't—I mean *I* didn't have time to talk much with her, with me. After we abandoned you two, she took the Eye, and then pushed me off into a strange part of Ehvenor, and I got lost. I had to learn how to find my way back to here. She said that she was going to, that *I* was going to try to walk across the street and bring the Eye there." She looked out the window. "No matter the cost. The rest is up to the Three." Her eyes widened. "Oh, *no.* It was so good to see the two of you that I forgot what she told me—" She turned to Jason. "Quickly, hand me your knife."

—I staggered back onto an empty street in a deserted part of town. Rows of tenements lined the dirty street beneath the dark sky, while cold white light shone up through the cracked ground.

I was alone, but I wasn't going to be alone long, not if

274

Boioardo was following me. The idea had to be to hope that Boioardo was going to chase me, that I could distract him long enough to give Andy time to do her thing, to get the Eye to the Faerie Embassy, and return to pull me out of trouble and away before Boioardo killed me.

Andy was good at locating people and things; it might work, if I could buy enough time. But I'd have to avoid him for as long as poss—

There was a tap on my shoulder, and there he was. It wasn't like looking in a mirror, not really; surely such a self-satisfied smirk would never be found under my mustache?

"A fine place," he said, reaching slowly for me. The light from beneath cast his eyes into shadow, but his too-white smile almost glowed in the dark. "Shall we end it here?"

I started out in high school as a running back; I ducked under his arm and ran, broken-field style. It didn't do any good. There he was, just a half step behind me. Not running, just gliding effortlessly over the ground, his feet never touching the dirt.

He frowned. "This is too easy," he said, giving me what looked like a gentle shove. It didn't feel that way—I slid six feet on the dirty ground, the grit and dirt scraping away the clothing over my left hip, then grinding a wide swath of skin and flesh from my hip and thigh. I slammed against a wall, hard, knocking the wind out of me.

I lay sprawled on the ground, trying to force some air into my lungs. Muscles just wouldn't work right. None of them.

He loomed over me. "Get up. You must be better sport than this."

I rolled to my hands and knees, then staggered to my feet.

"Wait," I managed to croack out. "Give me . . . time . . . recover."

I wasn't sure that my right knee would support my weight, and I could feel ribs grate against each other in the mass of red agony that I used to call my chest.

His smile broadened. "I don't see the need for that." He waved his hands once, and all my aches and pains were gone. It didn't happen with the wave of comfort and ease that healing draughts always provided; one moment I could barely grunt out words through the pain, and the next, all the aches were gone.

Even the scrape I'd taken on my left hip had healed, and the clothing over it.

Stall, Walter, stall. "Just wait a minute," I said. "This is too easy for you. Give yourself a handicap. Don't just look like me. Reduce your strength and speed to mine. Make it a fair contest." If Boioardo had a weakness, it was his arrogance—although who could call him on it? Incredibly powerful, invulnerable, able to assume any form he chose. I would rather have been in Philadelphia.

He cocked his head to one side. "Fair, no; I do not care to lose. Less unfair, certainly. That will make you better sport."

He eyed me carefully, then closed his eyes and concentrated. His form seemed to flow for a moment, then stop flowing, until he looked like me, again.

Boioardo took one step forward. "I'm only twice as strong as you, and but half again as fast." He blocked my punch and backhanded me back, lights flashing on the edge of my vision. "That ought to do."

If you practice something often enough, it becomes part of your muscle memory. Maybe the basic block-and-strike was like that.

He took a punch at me, and I had blocked it, moved in and brought my knee up quick as all hell.

The only trouble for me was that he was already blocking down, and hard.

The only trouble for him is that I'd finally slipped one of my throwing knives into my left—blocking—hand and slipped that in between his ribs. He staggered back, in pain. Not enough pain, but he'd taken on not just enough of my form, but enough of the reality of being human, to hurt.

I would have finished him off, but I'd been through that before with him when he was playing wolf. The best I could do—the best I hoped to do—was to fight him to a stalemate while the others did their thing.

And the best way to do that was to run.

I ran, down the street, and into—

276

—a forest of huge trees, the canopy of leaves arcing fifty feet above my head. Low brush clawed at my ankles and calves as I ran, my feet crashing through the dry leaves littering the floor. Above, tiny green lizards in the trees sang in easy counterpoint to the rhythm of my steps.

I was tripped, sent sprawling; I rolled to my feet, barely avoiding an immense projecting root, one of the huge trees at my back.

Boioardo moved his cloak aside as he faced off against me.

The only plan that occurred to me was to stall for a moment, just a moment, while I readied a knife. Maybe this one would hit something vital, knock him dead before he could regenerate himself.

"The Place Where One Speaks Only Truth," he said. "Just the outskirts of it. Shall we end it here?"

"No, I'd rather stall as long as I can," I said, truthfully, fingers clawing surreptitiously for a throwing knife. "And I'm going to try to stab you—"

Shit, shit, shit . . .

I ran up the root toward the trunk of the tree and leaped for another root, my next leap carrying me beyond the tree, toward a path. His footsteps crashed behind me as I scampered down the path through a bend, to where it intersected with another path, and leaped through—

Andrea turned to Jason. "Quickly, hand me your knife," she said.

Jason didn't move; Ahira shoved him aside, hard, snatching at his belt for the knife, flipping it easily, hilt-first, to Andrea.

She raised the knife and tossed it toward the open door, just as the other Andrea, dressed in black leather, flicked into being in the doorframe.

Ahira's breath caught in his throat.

—into darkness. I tripped, and fell backward, into water and slime, then forced myself to my feet, all wet and cold. I could barely stand without bumping my head on the roof of the tunnel; I steadied myself with my hands against the side. The

277

walls of the tunnel were warm and soft to the touch, the fleshy feel of it broken every ten feet or so by hard rings of something white and bony beneath the surface.

There was light ahead, further along in the tunnel. I staggered along, as quickly as I could. There was a juncture up ahead, barely visible.

Footsteps thundered behind me as I reached the junction and dashed through—

—into the next passage of the tunnel.

Sometimes, even in Ehvenor, a corner is just a corner.

I ran on, my feet making awful sucking noises in the muck, and into—

Ahira's breath caught in his throat.

"*No.*" It had to have been Andrea, but it couldn't have been Andrea. Andrea wouldn't try to kill her earlier self, but Ahira had just given whoever this was a knife.

The blade twisted through the air, barely passing over the new Andrea's shoulder, only to bury itself in an outstreached hairy arm.

Ahira smiled. By God, he *had* been right. White Andrea *was* his old friend.

White Andrea grabbed Black Andrea's arm and pulled her to one side as the thing staggered inside, all hair and muscle and stink.

It closed with Ahira, hairy hands fastening on his throat as it lifted the dwarf bodily from the floor, ignoring the knife still stuck in its arm. The new Andrea, the younger one, raised her hand, but the one in white battted it aside.

"No. We have to go. *Now.* This is where we abandon them. We don't have much time."

Over her protests, the white Andrea pulled the other one out through the door, and slammed it behind, quite neatly trapping Jason and Ahira inside.

—smoke, clawing at my lungs, tearing at my eyes. Strong fingers grabbed at me, but I kicked out once, twice, then dived away into blindness, his coughs and chokes behind me.

I was just starting to wonder if he'd locked himself into

a human form, stuck with human weaknesses, when the coughing shut off.

Fairy, you cheat. He had taken a moment to change a little, to allow himself to breathe smoke wihtout pain, without coughing.

"Well, certainly."

I staggered forward, from the smoke—

The dwarves call themselves the Moderate People; and there is a saying among the Moderate People that condemns immoderate moderation. Balance is important, equilibrium is necessary, but only in its place. This was not the place for balance; here, moderation would have been recklessly immoderate.

The universe dwindled to Ahira's hands, each one on the wrist of the monster. That was all. There would never be more than that, and each hand would have to close, to pry the strong hands away from Ahira's throat.

His fingers clenched tighter, and tighter. But so did the choking hands. His lungs burned, needing air. Darkness crept into the edges of his mind.

There had been a time when sickness had bound him to a metal chair, but that time was gone, and it must not return. He could tolerate almost anything, but not being confined, not being held immobile.

His arms and legs thrashed, uselessly, helplessly.

I will not be held down against my will. I will never be held against my will.

There was nothing else but his fingers on the wrists, squeezing hard, harder against the creature's bone and muscle. Rage flared blue-white in Ahira's mind, giving strength to his hands, washing away thought and intelligence, as a berserker rage built, needing only one more spark to set it flaring.

Bones cracked beneath his palm, the hands eased, and Ahira dropped to the floor, while steel thunked into flesh—

—*again*, he realized.

He had been hearing the sound of a knife hacking into flesh for some time now. All the while that he had been trying to break free, Jason had been stabbing at the creature.

279

Ahira rose to his knees and sucked in a lungful of fetid air. Despite the unwashed reek of the creature and the smell of his own sweat and fear, the air cooling his aching lungs was as exhilarating as a cold white wine. The cold and comfort flooded his body, pushing his rage back, leaving his mind intact.

He opened his eyes to see Jason hack again at the creature's neck, as blood poured down its chest from a dozen wounds.

It staggered back, then forward again, and reached out for Jason, too stupid to know it was dead. Ahira dived at its knee, shoulder hitting hard against fur-covered muscle and bone, tripping the creature. He fastened his hands on its head, the fingers of his right hand tangling themselves in its stiff, wiry hair, while his left hand closed on the massive body ridge over its eyes.

Ahira twisted once, giving it everything he had, rewarded by a single loud *snap*.

That was all it took. The creature shuddered once and went limp, its dead body voiding itself with an awful flatulence. It was all Ahira could do not to vomit.

Both of them gagging, Jason helped Ahira to the window.

"What's going on?" Jason asked.

"I don't know."

The cold outside air helped to clear his nose and his mind, but it didn't provide any answers.

Andrea had abandoned them, but she had done so knowing that they could handle the creature—orc, or goblin, or whatever it was. He leaned further out the window and breathed in the sweet, fresh air.

Below, White Andrea stood on the sidewalk, facing the Faerie Embassy, the Eye held high in the palm of her right hand, an open, leather-bound book held in her left.

Ahira called out to her, but she either didn't hear him or was ignoring him. Andrea took one step onto the narrow street, but as she did, the air around her darkened, then solidified into three dark bands that looped about her body, and slowly, inexorably contracted, forcing her down and to her knees, trying to force her back.

Her gaze dropped to the book in her hand, and her hips moved.

Ahira's hands tightened on the windowsill. His mouth was painfully dry.

Andrea was a powerful wizard, sure, and as White Andrea she had had plenty of time to prepare for this. But too much use of power could drive her insane, and she was fighting out of her league when she took on Faerie. And she'd known that, dammit. She hadn't impressed the spell she was using into her memory, but was reading it from the open book, not trusting her ability to carry it in her own mind and remain sane.

Curling the rest of her fingers around the Eye, she raised her right index finger and gently touched the outer corner of her right eye. A single teardrop swelled there, fattening, growing until it could hold no longer and ran down her cheek, bursting into fire as it fell from her jaw and onto one of the black bands.

Where the flaming tear touched, the band dissolved, leaving behind a ragged hole.

Andrea shed another fiery teardrop, and yet another, until she was crying a shower of burning rain, dissolving the bands of darkness until all that remained of either tears or darkness was a bit of dust, a little ash and soot that slipped from her white robes as she took another step forward.

—and I staggered into the glowing fog, flagstones hard under my knees, a distant roar in my eyes. I got to my feet, not sure which way to run. I could more feel than see a wall to my right, but the fog was thick around me, and there could have been miles of open space in any other direction, or a waiting open pit.

God, Andy, hurry up with whatever you're doing. It would be nice to be saved in the nick of time.

Maybe I could climb the wall. If Boioardo were to climb after me, I could try to drop down on him. Even with twice my strength, he wasn't invulnerable. Given enough of a start, if I could gain enough height, I might be able to land hard on him, smash him to the ground, and crush him either to death or unconsciousness before he could throw off the limitations of the flesh that he had assumed.

Yeah. Sure. And maybe I'd be elected fucking Queen of the May, too.

The fog thinned in front of me to reveal a series of niches, carved into the wall, each of a different size. There may have only been ten or so; there may have been hundreds, thousands, vanishing off into the fog.

In the first one, in the niche right in front of me, was a pair of sneakers.

"Holy *shit*."

They weren't just sneakers; they were *my* old sneakers, my first pair of sneakers, or at least the first pair I remembered.

Stash had always believed in buying irregulars, and had picked up a pair of some famous brand—PF Flyers, maybe?—that the manufacturer had rejected because of a sloppy seam along the uppers. The sloppy seam was still there—just a little crooked; nothing important—and so was the spot on the sole, just below the heel, where somebody, probably Inspector 7, had neatly sliced off the little brand patch when the sneakers had been rejected.

Same blue stripe along the rubber sole, same flat cotton laces, clean and white like they had been the day they were new.

They reminded me of running fastfastfast on a hot summer day, of leaping over low picket fences and scrambling through back yards not just when that damn St. Bernard was chasing me, but because I was ten and it was summer, and that's what you did when you were ten and it was summer.

In the next niche was a fountain pen, a real chubby-barrelled Shaeffer fountain pen with the white dot on the chip, and I knew that if I took it down, and took off the cap, it would write with the blackest of blue-black ink, because that was the ink that was in it the day that Mom had given it to me, the day that I had brought home my first report card that was just Bs and As. How had she known that I was finally going to bring home a decent report? Had she had the pen waiting through most of my elementary school career?

Four As, and three Bs, the report card said; it was in the next niche, all clean and waiting.

It takes longer to tell it than it did to live it; I don't think I'd stood in front of that wall for more than a second, taking it all in.

My teddy bear was in the next niche: an ugly stuffed panda in black and dirty white, one ear half torn off, glossy brown buttons from an old overcoat for his eyes. He waited, lying patiently, the way he always had at the head of my bed.

Bears are like that.

Boioardo had spoken of the Place Where Only That Which You Have Loved Can Help You.

Now I understood. It was a capital-P Place in Ehvenor, yes, on the edge of Faerie, surely, but it was also a small-p place in my mind.

I've lived some years now, and I've touched some things more than casually. You run through enough summer days in an irregular pair of PF Flyers, and they become part of you, not just for the few days and weeks and maybe months that the shoes last, but for as long as there are hot summer days just after school's let out, and as long as there are the tight, springy steps that you can only take in a new pair of sneakers and as long as there are fences and yards and dogs that surely can't be as big with teeth that can't be as sharp in reality as in memory.

It was mine, forever.

My bear was here. No nightmares here, not with my bear waiting at the head of my bed, ready to dispel a bad dream with its familiar warmth.

It was all mine. This was *my* place.

In the next niche was a jackknife. It didn't look like much, I guess, and it was smaller than I remembered it, but the Scout crest had the same scratch on it that it had always had. *My* knife.

It was my knife, the one that big Mike had given me, so many years ago, and it was here, in my hand, the ripples cut into its plastic sides familiar under my thumb.

Look: I know I had a fighting dagger at my waist, and I know that it gave me more reach. But that was just metal, just a tool.

This was *my* knife.

It had meant something to me, and it was here to help

me. What was it that Ahira had said? Something about how it's not just the people in our lives that matter, about how we had best be careful what we make, what we use, because we invest something of ourself with everything we touch.

And I know that a non-locking jackknife is a silly weapon in a fight, so I thumbed open the awl on the back, and held the knife hidden in my hand, just a sliver of metal showing. One punch with it, and the awl could slice hard, deep, through flesh and into Boioardo's eyes.

My knife.

Okay; bring on the demons.

Off in the distance, something roared, a sound both familiar and strange. Not like the growling of a beast, but the roar of an engine. I hadn't heard the sound of an engine in more years than I cared to think about.

Boioardo walked out of the fog, an immaculate imitation of me, his cape curling swirling about his ankles.

"Nice of you to wait for me, Walter Slovotsky," my face said, in my voice. "You ruined my fun; now I'll ruin yours." He smiled. "I always knew that it would end here, here in this Place."

He took a punch at me, but I blocked it with my left arm; it went numb and fell back at my side, but my right arm still worked, and I punched hard at him.

"Fuck you," I said.

His head moved to one side, but the slim steel edge cut his cheek open to the bone, and staggered him.

It wasn't enough. He backhanded me, lifting me up and off my feet. I fell hard to the flagstones, the knife skittering and bouncing away into the fog. I started to crawl off after it, but he blocked my way.

"You lose," Boioardo said.

The distant roar grew closer.

I knew that sound, by God, I knew that sound. Eight cylinders, generating more power than three hundred horses, hauling around tons of metal and glass, painted all black and yellow, like a bumblebee.

Ahira was right. We had best be careful of what we touch, what we make, what we use, because there is some of us in each bit of it, and we'd best be careful what we are. And in the Place Where Only That Which You Have Loved Can Help You, you'd best have gone out in the world and touched a lot, because you never know what you will need there.

I forced a smile. "Wrong, Boioardo. You lose."

The rain of tears dissolved the black bands, and Andrea took another step across the street, toward the flickering of the Faerie outpost.

"She did it!" Jason sighed in relief.

"No." Ahira shook his head. "She's not there yet. Look."

The flickering below took on substance, shimmering shifting into a wall across the street, reaching down through the dirt and up to the sky.

Glassy hands reached out from the wall to push and pull at Andrea, several fixing on her robes of mist and light, others fastening tiny fingers in her hair. Small fingers twisted tightly as they became more substantial.

She turned to another page of the book, and hesitated for a moment, just a moment before she began reading.

Lips murmuring words that could never be remembered, she tucked the book under her arm, and touched her right index finger gently to her left wrist.

A trickle of blood ran down her arm, fat red drops turning all sparkling and golden as they fell to the ground.

She cupped her left hand in front of her. The trickle of blood ran down her wrist and pooled in the palm, swelling. When the pool began to drop golden sparks, she raised her hand, and shook it once, twice, three times. A cloud of golden sparks shattered the ghostly hands into fog, and then into nothingness.

The Eye held high, the book again open in her free hand, White Andrea took another step forward.

"Wrong, Boioardo," I said. "You lose."

It doesn't cost anything extra to die with brave words on your lips, but I wasn't going to die, not here and not now. It was his own fault; he had chosen the Place. Perhaps, in his alien cruelty, he had thought that it would be amusing to finish me off here in this place, in my Place, but his arrogance had betrayed him.

This was *my* Place.

At first, he didn't believe me. Then his smile vanished, and his eyes widened. He looked from side to side for an avenue of escape, but there wasn't any. The wall was to one side of him, and it was coming out of the fog from the other.

Boioardo tried to cheat, he tried to change, but he was too late, and too slow. He had been faster in his changes; now it was as though he was trying to do too much at once.

Too bad for him. You don't face off against the Big Car when you've got other things on your mind.

It was among the last and absolutely the best of the standard American bigmobiles. A huge car, pulled around by a three-hundred horsepower V8, easily enough for the job—a monster of an eight-cylindered engine, it roared like a lion. Two-toned, black and yellow like a bumblebee, wraparound windshield, curved fenders, and a rear deck large enough to camp out on.

Tires squealing as it swerved to miss me, tons of black and yellow steel roared out of the fog and smashed into Boioardo, knocking him back up against the wall.

He tried to rise, but the Big Car shifted into reverse, tires smoking as it lunged back, then shifted into drive and lunged forward to smash him against the wall, steel squealing as the impack crumpled the grill, starred the windshield.

Boioardo had been caught in transition; he rose once more, battered and bloody, too broken to concentrate and change. His fingers bent at impossible places as he threw up his broken hands to protect himself.

"No, *please*."

Pity wouldn't have stayed my hand, and I had no pity. You don't go around playing with people like they were toys, not if you expect any sympathy from me. You don't rend somebody I love to shreds of bloody flesh and then ask me for compassion.

"Do it," I said.

The air in front of Andrea solidified, warped itself into a black wall that separated Andrea from the flickering of the Faerie Embassy.

She put out her right hand, the hand that held the Eye,

and pushed hard on it, lips never quite stopping their motion. Light flared around her fingertips, cold, silent balls of red and whiteness that vanished as they hit the black wall.

She murmured another spell, and waves of thunder crashed, making Ahira's ears ring. But the thunder beat uselessly, harmlessly against the blackness.

She took a step backward, looking from side to side, as though deciding not whether to run, but where to run. Andrea shook her head, black hair shot with silver settling about her shoulders, eyes closed tightly.

Ahira couldn't hear her over the crash of thunder, but he didn't need to hear the words.

Ahira found that the windowsill was splintering under his grip; he forced his hands to open. Crushing the windowsill would do no good. He had been wrong again, dammit. He had thought that a wizard didn't know how far to push magic, what moment would cost sanity, when that sacrifice would be made.

It was clear that Andrea knew that her next spell would cost her more than tears and blood.

She straightened, her shoulders back, and opened the book to a new page, reading slowly, carefully, as she raised the hand that held the Eye, her index finger straightening as she touched it to her temple, as though to say, *I'll feed you with this.*

Her right hand glowed, and as she pushed it forward the black wall melted in front of her. She pitched the Eye toward the flickering of the Faerie Embassy, and then fell to her knees, her face buried in her hands. Her shoulders shook.

"Far off, a distant voice spoke slowly, thoughtfully, the way elves tend to. "I see it, I think."

"Don't be so tentative," another answered. "Use this, and seal it all off."

The world exploded into brilliance, and then faded.

"Do it," I said.

The Big Car gunned its engine once more. Tires squealed on the stones, and the stink of burning rubber filled my nostrils.

It smashed into him one last time, steam from its shattered radiator vying with the fog as it ground what was left of him against the wall. It backed away, leaving Boioardo broken, bloody, dead. If I hadn't known, I wouldn't have been able to tell what he had been.

Slowly, brokenly, the car circled around to me, one crumpled fender nudging gently up against me, as though to ask if I was okay.

The Place faded out around me.

I barely had time to lay my hand on its cold metal flank. I didn't know the Polish, and it didn't matter anyway. It would understand, no matter what the language.

"Thank you, thou good and faithful servant."

And then the mists swirled up, and around, and washed all traces of consciousness away.

CHAPTER TWENTY-SEVEN

In Which We Part Company, and Two of Us Head Homeward, Well, Holtun-Bieme-ward

Every parting gives a foretaste of death . . .
—ARTHUR SCHOEPENHAUER

When you say goodbye to a friend, assume that one of you is going to die before you ever get to see each other agin. If you want to leave something unsaid, fine . . . but be prepared to leave it unsaid forever.
—WALTER SLOVOTSKY

I DON'T REMEMBER HOW we got there, but the next thing I remember was being back on the plateau above Ehvenor. It was like I had been going on automatic pilot. It could have been a shock reaction, I suppose; my extensive collection of bumps and bruises showed that I had taken more than a few blows to the head.

No, there wasn't the next thing I remember. Ahira and I had been talking about what happened, while I looked off into the distance. Andrea, wrapped in a woolen blanket, had been leaning up against Jason, sobbing.

There were seven of us, some sitting, some standing, the fire to our backs, looking out at the ruined hulk of a city below.

The three slavers had fled, or just plain decided to leave.

Ehvenor had stopped flickering, and the mass of creatures flickering through its changes had been unceremoniously dumped in the here and now. Bands of hairy beasts fought with each other through the narrow streets, the wise ones fleeing outward, while creatures of the night ran for the darkness of the hill, escaping the oncoming day.

Dark shapes moved outward, fleeing the solidity of the city, some shuffling along the ground, others taking to the air or diving into the Cirric. I could almost have sworn I saw a dragon take wing and flap off toward the south, but I could have been wrong.

What I wanted was a drink. No, what I wanted was a drink with Tennetty. Maybe a nod and cold smile that said I'd done okay, although why I ever gave a fuck about that cold-blooded psychopathy's opinion escaped me.

Damn it, Tennetty.

I'd have to settle for the drink; I fumbled through my pack and brought forth the flask of Riccetti's Best. It was heavy enough, there was still some left, enough for maybe half a dozen good-sized drinks. I pulled the cork and drank deeply, letting the fiery corn whiskey burn in my throat and warm my middle before I passed the bottle of Ahira.

"Well," he said, considering, "I think we earned that." He took a swig and then offered the bottle to the Hand woman, surprising me.

She declined the offer with an upraised palm, her eyes, both real and glass, never leaving the pageant below. "Magical beasts loosed into the wild, into the earth and air and water," she said. She cocked her head to one side. "Things haven't been like this since I was a little girl."

It only occurred to me later that most magical creatures had been gone from the Eren regions for centuries.

Shouldering a small canvas bag, she turned and walked away into the darkness.

It took me almost a full minute to realize that she had just left, and wasn't coming back. Ahira passed the bottle to Jason, who passed it along to Nareen.

Vair polished a coin-sized ruby, then fit it into an open wire frame. He threw a handful of powder on the fire, and considered the smoke through the lens.

"It could be worse, perhaps," he said. "All of Faerie could have poured through, possibly. If the breach had not been sealed, if the one who cut the breach had not been stopped." He looked at me through the fire of ruby, then tucked it in his belt pouch and crossed his long arms over his chest. "It all would have failed if we had not seen the breach, with the Eye. You have done well, the lot of you." He rose. "Or so it would seem to me." Without another word, he turned and walked off into the darkness. I was sure—I am sure—that he disappeared while he should still have been visible in the firelight.

Andrea, leaning up against her son, still sobbed. Quietly. Jason glared furiously at all of us, as though we could do something.

Nareen chuckled gently, for that is the way the Moderate People chuckle. "There is nothing to be done, young Cullinane. There is only much to be endured." Nareen walked to the two of them and gently, slowly, pried Andrea away from her son, and took her small, delicate hands in his huge ones.

"You see," he said, as though to Jason, although he really was talking to Andrea, "those of us with the gift know a truth, that there is no pleasure quite like using it, like refining it." His broad hands stroked hers. "Most of us know that we must be careful in its use; that if we use too much of the gift, push it too far, we will have to choose between it and sanity, and who would choose sanity compared to the glory of the power rippling up and down your spine, eh?"

His words were gentle, but each struck Andy like a blow; she sobbed even louder, trying to turn away. But the dwarf wouldn't let her.

"No," he said. "You made your decision. To feed your power not with your sanity, but with your ability." His index finger moved in the air, his rough fingernail tracing a fuzzy red glow that swiftly faded. "Your ability to see this as sharp lines instead of a red blur, and all that that implies."

I thought about how, a long time ago, another friend of mine had sacrificed his ability to do magic, and how that had worked out well for him, and I hoped. Maybe it would be so for Andrea, too. Or perhaps not.

Nareen nodded his head, perhaps admiringly, perhaps

with just a trace of condescension. "My compliments," he said. He lowered her to the ground; she squatted gracelessly, her face in her hands.

Nareen turned away.

"Don't leave yet." Jason held up a hand. "Wait. I—we, that is. We helped you. I'd like some help, from you." He swallowed. "There's a friend of mine, running around, doing some horrible things. I need to find him. Help me."

There was that Cullinane grimness about his face again. No matter that he loved his mother, and no matter that she sat on the ground at his feet, weeping—there was something out there that he had to do, and he was about to do it.

Nareen nodded. "Perhaps just a little."

"Okay."

Shit. That's the trouble with trying to be Hercules. You clean out the Augean stables, and then you have to go chase down Pegasus.

Ahira looked over at me, and he was smiling. "What am I going to say?" he said.

I smiled back. "Ask Jason. It'll be good practice."

Jason thought about it for a moment. "That somebody has to take Mother home, but that I'm still too young and stupid—"

"Inexperienced," the dwarf put in.

"But close enough," I added.

"—to be running around on my own." He swallowed, hard. He wasn't going to say anything about Tennetty. I don't know why that was important to him, but it was. "So," he went on, a catch in his voice, "one of you had better come with me. The one that's better at keeping out of trouble, not the one that's better at getting into it."

Ahira smiled at me. "I wonder—who could that be?"

Jason turned to me, and gave me anotheer shot of that grim Cullinane look. I never much cared for it.

"You'll watch out for Mother?" he asked, although it really wasn't a question, but a command.

That was okay. "Sure," I said. "Andrea needs some rest. The two of us, at least, had better camp here for tonight, head up into the hills tomorrow."

It would take a week at least to get to Buttertop, the hill north of Ollerwell that was the nearest of the regular rendezvous places. We could wait there for Ellegon's next circuit through. Might be a few days, a tenday at worst. I could live off the land for longer than that.

I wouldn't get any rest worth talking about, not tonight. I'd have to leave somebody on guard, and a non-speaking, incessantly weeping woman wasn't my idea of a great guard.

Nareen smiled reassuringly. "That can be taken care of, at least for tonight."

I guess I should have been irritated that the dwarf wizard was reading my mind, but his grin was infectious. He reached into his pouch and brought forth a small glass ball, about the size of a big marble, which he placed in the air, and set spinning with a flick of his thumb and a few muttered syllables. "Sleep easily tonight; this will scream at any danger. For us, the sooner we leave, the sooner we can book passage at Artiven."

I wondered how they were going to make their way through the dark of night, but Ahira tapped at his brow.

Darksight, remember?

Oops.

Ahira nodded. " 'Twere best done quickly, eh?"

"There is that."

I clasped hands briefly with Nareen, and gave Jason a hug—which he tolerated with admirable patience—before turning back to Ahira.

"Watch your six, short one," I said. "And if you need me . . ."

He nodded, once, and gave a half-smile. *We'll be fine,* he was saying. *But if we need you, we'll send word.* His grip on my shoulder was firm.

I fed some more wood to the fire while they walked off into the night.

Below, Ehvenor stood in the dawn light, empty, no sign of life save for the gleaming building in its center.

Just as well Nareen left the marble-or-whatever-the-hell-it-was on guard. While I do recall spreading my bedroll and lying

293

down on it. I don't remember actually settling myself in for sleep. Before I was completely flat, I was out.

And I slept like a dead man, only awakened at dawn by the *tink!* of the marble-or-whatever-the-hell-it-was bouncing off a stone.

PART THREE

NEW WORK

CHAPTER TWENTY-EIGHT

In Which the Living Dead Not Only Speaks, but Eats Both Trout and Chicken

Travel, it seems to me, has always done more for flattening the arches, callusing the feet, and irritating the hemorrhoids than broadening the mind.

—WALTER SLOVOTSKY

I EYED THE SKY OVER Ehvenor as I broke camp.

Blue sky, puffy clouds, no dragon. Damn.

Hmm, I guess that should be "as we broke camp" except that "we" weren't doing it. I had made breakfast—jerky and oatmeal; sticks to the ribs. I had packed the rucksacks—fairly, honest; I was putting out the remnants of the fire—okay, I was biologically better equipped for that job.

Andy was waiting for me down the path. She had taken a battered leather book out of her rucksack, and opened it. The letters swam in front of my eyes; I'm not built to read magic.

They probably swam in front of hers, even forgetting, for the moment, that she had burned out her magical ability. Tears do that.

She wiped her eyes on the back of her hand and put the book away, tying the rucksack tightly shut before she slung it over her shoulder.

"Well," I said, "day's a-wasting." I love it when I talk colorful. "Let's get going."

She set off in a slow walk. At least she wasn't crying now. Her eyes were red, and there were dark baggy circles under them. Her hair looked like a bird's nest, and her mouth was set in a permanent frown.

But at least she wasn't crying.

Big fat, hairy deal.

I scanned the skies, hoping for a pair of leathery wings. This would be a handy time for Ellegon to show up and save some wear and tear on both my bootleather and my tender tootsies. But the sky was just full of blue and clouds and birds, and you can never find a dragon when you need one.

We headed off down the path.

There's any number of things one can do with somebody who is busy withdrawing from the world. You can just be patient and let them retreat into their navel, coming out whenever they please. *If* they please.

Now, I'm not saying that's a bad plan. It's probably a good way to handle it; maybe even the best way to handle things. But it's not a Walter Slovotsky way to handle things. Sorry.

"Now," I said, babbling over the babbling of the stream, "anybody can get lost in the sense of not knowing where you are. No big deal, as long as you know how to get where you're going. Not knowing how to get where you're going is the dangerous kind of lost."

It was a nice-sized stream, maybe three yards across where we were, its broad banks providing a wide path. During rainy season, the stream probably overflowed the banks, but it wasn't rainy season.

"This is one of the easier orienteering tricks," I said. "Avoid heading across unfamiliar territory for a point-destination: a town, an oasis, whatever. Point—okay, okay: areas— are easy to miss.

"Roads and streams, on the other hand, are long skinny things. You tend to trip over them.

"So you aim for a road that you know leads to your destination, even if that means breaking right or left of whatever you're heading for. Now, I know the road from Heliven to Ollerwell—it's a long, wide one, crosses a lot of streams up in the hills, certainly including this one. So, unless there's a good reason not to, we follow this stream until we hit the road. Q.E.D."

She didn't answer.

"I know what you're saying," I said. "You're saying, 'Walter, that's all well and good,' you'r saying, 'but you've walked out of Ehvenor before, and so this isn't unfamiliar territoy to you.'

"You've got a good point, and that's a fact. But there's a difference between having been through this area before and knowing it well. Now, I do know the route that we took the last time I walked out of Ehvenor, but that was more than ten years ago, and I think they may even remember me in one of the towns we passed through, so perhaps we'd be just as well skipping it."

She looked at, me, trying not to glare. That was an improvement. At least she was trying something.

I was tempted to try something; I've been in worse-looking company.

If you ignored the reddened eyes and the slumped shoulders, Andy was still an awfully good-looking woman, in or out of her boots and leathers.

But she still wouldn't talk.

There are things I like less than traveling with somebody who won't start a conversation, who won't answer in other than monosyllables, and who cries herself to sleep each night, honest. But most of those involve things similar to sitting up on the Posts of Punishment.

The stream bent up ahead, and I suspected there'd be some fish feeding under the fallen tree that didn't quite bridge the stream. The morning was getting old, and the food in our pack wasn't getting any more plentiful, so I shrugged out of my rucksack and beckoned to Andy to wait.

She dropped her own rucksack and squatted on the ground, silently obedient.

I would have rather she spoke up and spooked the fish.

I crept out on the log. Sure enough, just under the surface of the rippling water, in a quiet space sheltered by the

299

tree, a trio of largish trout hovered in the shadow, either having a quiet chat about fishy life or eating something.

Not for long.

One of the gifts I got in transition to This Side is my reflexes, and while they've been more important, they've never been a lot more fun than when I lunged, scooping up one of the fish and flinging it high into the air, just like a bear with a salmon, except that I'm much prettier than any bear.

The trout thunked down on the riverbank, flopping madly. *Flibitaflibitaflibita.*

Nice-sized, the way local speckled trout often get. Maybe three, three and a half pounds.

I'd sort of hoped Andy would take over, but she just watched it, so I pulled the utility knife from my rucksack—I don't use my dagger or my throwing knives for this sort of thing—then quickly gutted the fish, rinsing off both the fish and my hands in the stream. Ick.

"Now, the *right* way to cook trout involves poaching it with vinegar and spices," I said. "Blue trout is one of the great meals that ever there was.

"A good second choice is to tie the trout to a green stick and then shove it head deep in nice, hot coals. On the other hand, we don't have nice, hot coals, and I'm not going to spend an hour building up that kind of cookfire."

Keeping up a steady monologue, I gathered some dry wood and built a quick cooking fire on the river bank—if you've got some birch bark handy, which we did, and if you're willing to waste a little gunpowder, which I was, you can start a fire real quick.

I cut the fish down the middle and seared the halves on the ends of a pair of green sticks, using a rough stone to grate just a taste of wild onion onto it. It only took a few minutes; all you really have to do with freshwater fish is cook them enough to kill any parasites.

A bit of salt from the saltwell in my pack, and, voila: fish on a stick. Lunch for two.

"What are you going to have?" I asked.

She didn't rise to the bait, and I wasn't irritated enough

to let her go hungry, so I handed her one of the sticks and then quickly wolfed down my own.

Not bad. Not bad at all. Fresh trout, no more than fifteen minutes from the stream, is a dish fit for a king.

Or even for Walter Slovotsky.

I washed my hands in the stream and then scooped some water onto the fire. "Let's go."

The first days were like that. Andy slept when told to, ate what I put in front of her.

To my surprise, she stood her turn at watch and stayed awake and alert while she did, but that was about all.

The nights were cold, and I wouldn't have minded not sleeping alone. But it didn't seem like the right time to bring up the subject, not even of sleeping. I'm a sensitive guy, eh?

So, instead, I kept up the constant monologue as we walked. I swear, I began to run out of subjects; by the third day, I'd covered damn everything I knew (well, almost everything. Some things Woman Isn't Meant to Know). About how to set up a staff in a castle. About how to keep in practice with a bow. About why you keep flintlocks loaded, and how poor old Tennetty always scared the shit out of me.

We hit the Heliven-Ollerwell road late on the second day, and left the stream and trout dinners behind.

Just we were breaking camp the next morning and I was launching into today's monologue—a reconsideration of the Nickel Defense and its suitability for college football—Andy looked up at me and frowned.

"Walter, shut up," she said.

"Well, well, well. It lives." I hefted my rucksack to my back and we started to work our way back toward the road through the forest.

She should have snorted, but she just looked at me dead-pan. "Your sympathy is underwhelming. You don't know what I had to give up."

"Better than sex, so I'm told."

The corner of her mouth may have turned up a millimeter. "Depends on with whom."

"Was that an offer?"

"No."

Sometimes no doesn't mean no, but when it's accompanied by a weak shake of the head, lips pursed just *so*, that's exactly what it means. Which is okay. I can take no.

On the other hand, I was heading home to my wife, to make things work. It would have been nice to have one last dalliance. On the other hand . . . I've run out of hands.

Just as well.

We walked along, not talking. I can take silence, although you'll never get that in the forest. There's almost always the far-off cry of a bird, the chittering of insects, and if nothing else, a quiet whisper of wind through the trees. Not silent at all. Not even quiet, not really; it's only the tallest trees that are quient.

"What now?" she asked. Or maybe said.

I hadn't taken this route before, but I had passed through Ollerwell once or twice. "Ollerwell's just a few miles ahead, just across the river, and down aways. We can buy some fresh food. I don't think we'll be able to get more trout—they tend to fish it out around Ollerwell—but maybe some eel, or some of that bass you find in the lakes up this way. Not beef—I mean, they might have some, but the locals don't eat a lot of beef, and we'll smell of it for days. We *could* splurge on a chicken, if—"

"Shh." She waved it away, tiredly. "I mean, what do I do now? After we get back."

I shrugged. "Whatever you want, Andy. Except magic, so I'm told."

For the thousandth time, she took the battered leather volume out of her pack and opened it.

The letters blurred in front of my eyes, and apparently in front of hers, too.

They would have, even if she hadn't been crying.

Sometimes I call it right: a farmer at the edge of town had a fire going, and a fat capon turning over a spit, sending delicious flavors wafting off into the breeze. We could probably have made a better deal in town, but the crackling of crisp skin over the coals made me part with a Holtun-Bieme copper half-mark with Karl's face on it, which bought me a huge chunk of breast (no comments, please), and Andy an over-sized thigh, each served on a fist-sized loaf of fresh brown bread hot from the oven.

I didn't wait for it to cool, and ended up burning my tongue. It was worth it.

I'd like to report that Andy wolfed hers down with hunger and gusto, but she just ate as we walked through the village, past a couple dingy rows of wattle-and-daub houses and onto the northern road.

Another couple of days and we'd be at Buttertop.

"How about you?" she asked.

At first I didn't answer. It took me a moment to realize that she'd picked up our conversation of hours ago where we had left it off. I hate it when she does that.

"Me?" I shrugged. "I think I'd better take it easy for awhile. Spend some time with the kids, and with Kirah. You?"

She sighed. "I might go back into teaching. English, basic math, the usual. Even if some of the Home youngsters do it better than I could. I don't know."

Maybe, just maybe, if I gave Kirah enough patience and attention, maybe that would do it. Life's like a fight, sometimes; there's times when you have to commit yourself, to lunge full, all stops out, not worrying about what happens if it doesn't work. See, you don't just put something of yourself in what you touch, but you put if in who you touch. After close to twenty years together, Kirah was part of me, and I wasn't going to cut that out, any more than I'd throw away my left arm.

Ellegon found us that night.

I was a bit nervous about camping on the ground close to a road broad enough to be navigable by stars and faerie lights, so we had moved well off the road, onto a wooded rise, and slung our hammocks high in a giant old oak tree while it was still light enough to see.

Actually, I'd done the slinging, and it had only been one hammock. Climbing was hard enough on Andy, but I picked her branches to make getting in easy for her. It had been some trouble, but we'd gotten her settled in and pretending to be asleep, while I climbed further up the tree and seated myself in a crotch between two old limbs, too lazy, or maybe too tired to mess with it all. I just whipped one end of a piece of rope around the tree, and knotted it in front of my chest, so that if I leaned forward instead of back I wouldn't fall out and break my neck.

I let the day slip away. What was that old dwarven evenchant? Something about—

That was, of course, the moment that flame would have to flare loud and bright over the treetops, accompanied by the rustle of leathery wings.

Wake up, folks. Your ride's here. If you hurry, we can be in Holtun-Bieme in the morning.

CHAPTER TWENTY-NINE

In Which We Decide What Those Who Can Do, and Why

It is better to travel hopefully than to arrive.
—ROBERT LOUIS STEVENSON

Never come home unexpectedly. It's a break-even proposition, at best.
—WALTER SLOVOTSKY

Ellegon SET DOWN QUI-etly outside the walls in the gray light just before dawn. I slid down his scaly side and landed hard on the hard ground, twisting my ankle.

"You're getting old, Walter," Andy said, as she lowered herself more gently down from the dragon's back.

Happens to the best of them, the dragon said, turning its broad head to face the two of us. *So I understand. What are you going to do now?*

"Me, I'm for bed," I said. "I don't sleep well in the air."

So I noticed.

Andy patted at her belly. "I'm going to go eat something, then probably some sleep. You?"

The dragon walked away, toward the main road, his wings curling and uncurling. *There's a sheep in the south pasture with my name on it. I'm hungry.*

It was nice of Ellegon to walk away far enough that we wouldn't be battered by dust and grit when he took off. Although, at this point, that would have been wetting a river.

In that case . . . the dragon leaped into the air, leathery wings sending dust and grit into the air to batter at my eyes and face.

"Me and my big mouth," I said.

Andy didn't answer.

The watcman at the man gate let us in through the small-door; we waved aside his offer to wake a welcoming committee. I just wanted to look in on my kids and wife, and then find an empty bed. Or, better, grab a few blankets and curl up in a corner of Kirah's and my room, and let her find me when she woke. I wouldn't slip into bed with her unexpectedly; that would always set her off.

Andy touched my shoulder for a quick moment. "Look me up when you get up. I've got an idea I want to talk over with you."

I nodded, too tired to bother asking what the idea was.

Dawn had been threatening to break outside, but a castle is always dark until the sun is well up, and well before it's down. Not that the staff believed that. Some wisely frugal servitor or penurious asshole had put out most of the lanterns; I had to get one from the rack just outside the kitchens.

I don't believe in madly tittering darkness, but the mirk kind of giggled at me as I made my way up the stairs toward the bedrooms.

Dorann's room was next to Kirah's and mine. I crept in for a quick moment.

Barely illuminated by the flickering lantern, my baby daughter lay under her blankets, all curled up and tiny. It was all I could do not to sigh out loud, although I couldn't prevent a tear or two from running down my face. Dammit, but she looked like she had grown an inch since I'd been gone. You miss so much when you're on the road, whether your business is sales or steel.

I rested my hand against her warm cheek for a moment, and she stirred just a little, then reached up a pair of chubby hands and pulled my hand closer to her face, never coming close to waking. After a few minutes, I gently detached my hand.

God, little one, I never realized how much I missed you.

I shut her door gently behind me, then went to Kirah's and my room. The knob refused to turn; it was locked. Good; Kirah was still practicing ordinary security. I was willing to bet that the secret passage to the room next door was still properly blocked.

I dug in my pouch for my key. I turned the key in the lock with exquisite slowness, and gently pushed the heavy door open, hoping that the hinges wouldn't squeak and wake her.

The bed had been moved in my absence, and a full-length mirror had been set up next to the window, angled to reflect the first traces of dawn light down onto the pillows, to wake the occupants.

Very clever.

But a hint of predawn light was enough to let me make out the faces of both occupants: my wife, and that asshole Bren Adahan.

I don't know how long I stood there, not thinking. It seems long in retrospect, but it probably wasn't.

I do remember, vaguely, what I thought about, in between the moments of anger, and hate, and jealousy, and shame, and guilt.

I thought something about how I didn't believe in a double standard, really, truly I didn't, no matter how hard and fast my heart was beating, no matter how much anger flared red behind my eyes, in my mind.

I do remember realizing how it wasn't being touched that disgusted Kirah, it was being touched by *me*, that it was the feel of my hand, my body against her that she associated with her old life, with rape and slavery.

What had I ever done to deserve that? Nothing maybe. Fine. Who the fuck says you get what you deserve?

I do remember thinking, just in passing, that I could probably pick the lock to Ben Adahan's room next door, and be waiting for him when he made his way back through the secret passage.

And I do remember thinking that standing in an open doorway, tears running down my face, wasn't going to do any damn good, so I swung the door slowly closed and wiped my face on the back of my hand. I had the key almost completely turned when I heard soft footsteps behind me.

I hadn't been listening. Bad policy.

I finished turning the key, carefully pocketed it, and slowly turned, my weight on the balls of my feet.

Janie and Aeia stood side-by-side in the gray light. Janie in a heavy black sleeping-robe, belted at the waist with a thick velvet rope. The robe was far too large for her; its hem touched the floor, and her hands barely peeked out of the sleeves. It all made her her look younger, far too young to be around for this.

Aeia had thrown on a high-length white silk robe. Slim fingers nervously toyed at the belt at her waist. Her eyes were puffy from sleep, but just a bit wide.

I was trying to figure out who had wakened whom, and decided that Aeia had probably wakened Janie. Aeia knew—hell, everybody knew—that Janie could always handle me.

"Hi, Daddy," Janie whispered.

"Hi, sweetness," I whispered back. "What's new?"

With a sad little smile—damn, I'd never seen Janie smile sadly before; I didn't much like it—she took my arm and brought me down the hall to the top of the stairs.

"Some things have happened while you were gone," she said, "some things we all pretend we don't know about. Aeia's been worried you'd do something stupid, but I've been telling her that my Daddy will handle things in a nice, civilized manner, that nobody's going to get hurt." Her face grew somber. "Tell her I'm right, Daddy."

Look: I am more than a collection of hormones and reactions. I could be livid with rage—and I was—but *I* decide what Walter Slovotsky does, not my anger. *I* decide, and I decided that I wasn't going to blow up. Not here and now; not ever. You don't solve this kind of problem with a knife and gun, you really don't.

So I forced my fists to unclench.

"Sure, sweetness. No problem. Truth to tell, I'd decided that your mother and I were through." Well, that was probably true. Since just a few minutes ago, no matter what I had decided on the *Delenia*. Hell, we might go through the motions for awhile. But every time I saw her, I'd replay the scene of her and Bren in bed, and each time I'd try to touch her, she'd see whatever the private hell she saw.

Fuck it.

Aeia smiled. "It's going to be awkward," she said. Her golden brown hair was mussed from sleep; I wanted to run my fingers through it. She slipped her hand into mine, and gripped tightly. "But everything will be fine," she said. "Trust me."

"We'll manage," I said, weary past imagining.

She nodded, once.

"In the meantime," I said, "how about somebody finding me a bed?"

Janie led me down a flight to an unoccupied room on the floor below, and gave me a peck on the cheek. "See you this afternoon. Sleep well." She turned back down the hall, almost stumbling over the hem of her too-large robe.

Aeia came into my arms for a brief moment, her arms pulling, not pushing, her body warm and alive against mine. She rested her head against my chest, then raised her face and kissed me quickly, gently on the lips.

"Later," she said, then turned and walked away down the hall.

The room was dark, and smelled vaguely musty. The bed was lumpy, and smelled more than vaguely musty. But there's one great thing about being dog-tired: you can cry yourself to sleep in about two seconds.

The nightmare is always the same:

We're trying to make our escape from Hell, millions of us streaming down the streets of Ehvenor, running from the wolf-things that think of us only as toys and prey. Everybody I've ever loved is there, along with faces familiar and strange.

There's a street corner up ahead, a place where I somehow know that a right angle turn will bring us to safety, and I shout out directions.

It seems to be working. They flicker out as they turn, and I somehow know, as you can only know in a dream, that they've escaped, not found themselves in the Place Where Trees Scream.

But the wolf-things approach, accompanied by the shambling orcs, their fangs dripping blood.

And then I see him: Karl Cullinane, Jason's father, standing tall, face beaming, his hands, chest, and beard streaked with blood and gore.

"We're going to have to stall them," Karl says. "Who's with me?"

He smiles, as though he's been waiting his whole life for this, the fucking idiot.

"I'm with you," somebody says.

Figures push out of the crowd, some bloodied, some bent.

Tennetty's the first. Not the aging, wasted one, more used up than aged, but a younger, vigorous Tennetty, her sneer intact. "Count me in."

Andy's next to her, looking foxy in her leathers, a small leather shield strapped to her left arm, a smoking pistol in her right. She smiles at me. "You don't think I need magic to count, do you?"

Big Mike hefts his baton, tapping it lightly against his thigh. "Never need anything, eh?"

My brother Steve fixes the bayonet to the end of his empty M16. His smile is reassuring. "Sharp edges don't jam, eh, Cricket?"

Karl looks at me—they all look at me—his bloody face puzzled. "Walter? What are you waiting for?"

I was about to say something, to tell them something important, but—

I woke in a cold sweat, in the dark.

Just a dream. No big deal, I tried to persuade myself as I wiped the sweat off my forehead.

It was dark; I'd slept—or nigthmared, if you want to be accurate—all through the day and well into the night.

Somebody had snuck in while I was sleeping and not had only laid out some fresh clothes, but had filled the copper washbasin, then set the lantern underneath it to keep the chill off, if not keep it warm.

I stripped down to skin and scabbards, then splashed a

little on my face and chest before pulling on the trousers and slipping the shirt over my head. A full bath could wait until I had some food, but not much longer. A nice hot soak was just what the cleric ordered.

I swallowed. Okay. Now, what?

There was a knock at the door.

"Come," I said, slipping the handle of a knife into my hand. I mean, I didn't need to fight with Bren, but maybe he wouldn't know that. It does *not* take two to have a fight.

Andy walked in, a lantern in one hand, a tray of food balanced on the other. "I had one of the guards listening for any sign of movement in here," she said. "I wanted to get to you before things get . . . hectic."

I forced a smile. That was a good word for it. Hectic. I liked that. "And you wanted to talk to me," I said. I bit into a cold drumstick. "You wanted to talk to me about something else, about, say, about how now that you're no longer a wizard, you want to go into what Karl used to call the family business, and about how you need a teacher, and about how I'm not going to be completely comfortable around here for the next while, and about how maybe I ought to be the teacher, eh?"

She nodded. No smile. Just a nod. I wondered if the only place she ever was going to smile again was in my nightmares. "Good," she said, matter-of-factly.

"And what did you think I was going to say?"

"Yes. I thought you'd say yes."

"Okay: yes." I nodded. "I've got to straighten out some things, some family matters, but then we go into training, and we hit the road as soon as we can."

She looked like she had a question.

"Lesson the first: ask it. When you've got time, always ask."

She thought it over for a moment. "Why are you so eager to get back on the road?"

"You want the truth?"

"Sure." She smiled. "Why not."

I shrugged, and looked back to the sweat-soaked rumpled blankets heaped on the bed and floor. "So I can get a good night's sleep."

Author's Note

The heroes in Walter's dream sequences are intended to be Walter's, not mine; there'd be some overlap, but my list wouldn't include many of his selections, and vice versa.

Each of us, after all, does get to—and have to!—pick our own.

—J.R.